W9-BDH-034

Praise for

In Too Deep
AF PAP Bro   157870

Wilton Public Library

DATE DUE

KAR			
SS			

Withdrawn

"As a ... reading, and
Mic ... ly written,
bittersw ... d time again."

"IN T ... it front and
center i ... tee there will
be mon ... is also all too
real, a ... *by Romance*

"I sit h ... rovoke such
intense ... I have never
rea ... oil while
Blog

"I think ... n Too Deep.
It focus ... e it leaves no
physical ... ly, it blew my

"M ... personal
experie ... Jake ... IN
TOO ... nd one that

Wilton Public Library
1215 Cypress Street
P.O. Box 447
Wilton, IA 52778

"In ... rayal on
emoti ... d brave...
This ... reak the

"A he ... d from the
very fi ... aw, happy,
gritty, sad, and oh so very real. Michelle Kemper Brownlow is one author to watch
out for." ~Alba Soloranzo, *Book Pics Blog*

IN

TOO

DEEP

MICHELLE KEMPER BROWNLOW

Wilton Public Library
1215 Cypress Street
P.O. Box 447
Wilton, IA 52778

Copyright © 2013 Michelle Kemper Brownlow
All rights reserved. Except as permitted under the U.S. Copyright Act of 1976, no part of this publication may be reproduced, distributed, or transmitted in any form or by any means, or stored in a database or retrieval system, without prior permission of the publisher.

Sapphire Star Publishing
www.sapphirestarpublishing.com
First Sapphire Star Publishing trade paperback edition, June 2013

The characters and events in this book are fictitious. Names, characters, places, and plots are a product of the author's imagination. Any similarity to real persons, living or dead, is coincidental and not intended by the author.

ISBN-13: 978-1-938404-60-3

Cover Design: Okay Creations

Cover Image: Masson

www.sapphirestarpublishing.com/michellekemperbrownlow

Dedication

To all the silent victims of emotional abuse,

You are not broken. You are not damaged. You are worthy. You are beautiful. You are a survivor. There is a beautiful heart out there with your name written on it. Someone exists who will wrap you in a kind of love you never knew existed. You must free yourself from what holds you down so your heart can accept the unconditional love you deserve.

You ARE worthy of that kind of *Love*.

ONE

September, Fall Semester, Junior Year

The strong force of the wave pulled me under. I gasped for air just before my face disappeared below the surface. My body rolled over and over, my arms flailed, and my head pounded into the sea bed which felt like a concrete floor. The salty water stung my eyes. I forced myself to keep them open, fearing I would slip into unconsciousness from the blow I took to the head. I knew I had to hold it together long enough for the swell to pull me back up when the wave rolled. But something was pulling me deeper. I fought with all my might, kicking against the thick water swallowing me whole. I used my arms like underwater oars and sliced through the depths trying to reach what I needed most, but I was in too deep.

"Get out!" I could barely get the words out before I had to run to the bathroom and void my gut of its contents. Noah didn't move.

I wiped my mouth with the back of my hand and screamed, "I said, *Get! Out!*" I stumbled back into the room, grabbed the box of mementos I'd collected from the last year of our relationship, and dumped everything into the trashcan in the corner. Like a communal grave, there lay movie tickets, dried rose petals, a strip of photos from the boardwalk, all the beautiful letters he wrote last fall semester, an empty beer bottle, and all the rest of what was now just a reminder of the guy I thought I knew.

"Gracie, don't..." His face fell, but he didn't move from the edge of my bed.

"Don't? Don't what, Noah? Don't break up with you? Are you kidding?" My ears burned from his admission of guilt. It hit me broadside. I wasn't prepared for the words he had spoken just moments before.

The rush of water covering me grew cold. Icy. My body quaked. My lungs burned and begged for air. I could see light above. It glimmered and danced on the small waves my panic created. I reached for the surface. Even if I couldn't pull myself up, maybe just feeling the sun's warmth would stop the shivering that threatened to unravel me.

My legs gave out beneath me and I crumbled into a heap on my apartment floor. I sobbed so uncontrollably I gasped for air. I was livid. Repulsed. Crushed and torn. Noah was the love of my life, and things were just getting back to the way I longed for them to be. Back to what used to be our "normal." Before he pledged Sigma Chi. Our relationship hadn't been easy since I transferred to Knoxville. But our story wasn't ready to end.

It went something like this:

Bad boy meets good girl.

First kiss.

Bad boy turns sensitive.

Love.

Good girl gives sensitive boy all of her.

Long distance.

Flowers. Love letters.

Long, sweet phone calls.

Good girl transfers to sensitive boy's school.

Sensitive boy becomes fraternity boy.

Drunken social events.

Secrets revealed.

Fraternity boy pulls good girl under.

Good girl finds herself in too deep.

No matter how hard I tried, I couldn't pull myself to the surface. The harder I flailed, the further I sank... down, down, down. The murky depths laughed as I floated helplessly toward the bottom. Lifeless.

I struggled to breathe through the sobs. My dark bobbed hair clung to my wet cheeks. My heart stung as I felt it tear right down the middle. I wanted to act like I didn't care, like Noah hadn't just plucked my heart out and ground it into the dirty carpet. But I did care. I was nothing without him. I wasn't ready to give up, but at that moment, I couldn't even look at him.

This former bad boy had opened up to me and showed me a side of him no one else knew. No one. It was like our own little miracle. Our oasis. He truly loved me. We were bound by the one-time gift I had given him just months into our relationship. My soul was married to his. Our relationship defined me.

I gasped for breath.

Earlier that evening, I attended my first fraternity formal. My love was now a member of the newly initiated Sigma Chi brotherhood. I was on cloud nine. I wasn't sure I knew what all the hype was, but there was a status level I had reached because I was dating a Sigma Chi brother. It was similar to being celebrity arm candy. Girls were jealous. My whole life, I was the token quiet, innocent girl, so I'd never experienced anything like it. It was a feeling that just gave me a buzz...all the time.

I heard a knock on the door and knew it was Noah.

"You ready, Gracie? You've hit the big times now. Sigma Chi formal. Wow!" Stacy had helped me make sure everything was perfect; my make-up, my hair, the shoes. We based all the decisions off the gorgeous Vera Wang dress she let me borrow. Yesterday she helped me pick out sexy thigh highs so my evening would be perfect.

"Stacy, I am so nervous I could barf. What if I fall in these shoes? What if his brothers think I'm a dork?" My hands started to shake.

"Relax. Please relax. If you puke on this dress I will kill you." She walked to the door and turned the knob in what seemed like slow motion.

The door slowly opened to one fine specimen of fraternity boy. As though paparazzi cameras were flashing, a tux-decked Noah developed frame by frame right before my eyes. And I watched his bottom jaw drop like a stop action film as the door slowly opened and presented me to him. He walked toward me with his hands out in front of him and I instinctively held out mine for him to take. He squeezed my hands and looked me up and down. The smile on his face was wider than I'd ever seen. I was floating on his obvious delight in what he saw. His mouth moved a couple times as though he was trying to form words but no sound left his lips. He was literally speechless. He broke the silence with a declaration I would never forget.

"Gracie," he said my name so slowly. "Oh, Gracie…you take my breath away. Turn around. Let me see you."

He dropped one of my hands and spun me like the ballerina inside the jewelry box I had as a little girl. When we were face to face again he dropped my other hand and both of his came to my face. His lips touched mine so gently it tickled and sent a shiver throughout my body. Three light pecks and a sigh later, he shook his head and whispered, "Wow. Just wow."

"Well, you look mighty fine, yourself." I was just as awestruck but too unsure of myself to go on and on the way he did. He smiled and his big brown eyes drew me in. The gold flecks in them sparkled in response to the strapless, ice blue gown I wore. Noah was one of those guys you see that you wish would just stand still long enough for you to take him all in. His short sandy blond hair framed a face that appeared reckless and boyish at the same time. His skin was still tan from summer, which made the gold in his eyes striking. His eyes were the first thing I noticed the night we met. His eyes and those lips. Strong, full lips that did things to me I couldn't describe. I stood on my toes, grabbed his face and kissed him deeply.

"You two make me sick. Go on, Mr. and Mrs. Perfect, get out of here before I go into a sappy-love-story seizure. Go!"

As we walked in the warm fall air to Sigma Chi, Noah continued to fill my heart with his stolen glances. I felt treasured and cherished. This would be a night to remember.

The inside of the Sigma Chi house had been transformed into a ballroom. It was unbelievable. We still drank from red party cups but the overall ambience was like a fairy tale. Throughout the night, I caught a couple brothers eyeing me. So did Noah and he was sure to send a look to let them know I was taken.

When the energy of the formal waned and party guests became few and far between, Noah and I walked to my apartment hand-in-hand. In my mind, I did the beauty queen wave to all of the drunken people stumbling past us. Cocky? Yeah, it was, but I had endured weeks of distress because my beautiful blond boyfriend went through pledging hell behind the closed doors of his fraternity house.

I changed out of my gown and we both threw on jeans. I grabbed a bright red, low-cut top from a hanger. He threw on his Crazy Eddie's Bar t-shirt from the stack on the shelf. I loved that he kept clothes in my closet. To me it solidified our status as a serious relationship. We headed toward the pounding music blasting from the floor above. Noah would have liked to keep me out of my gown a little longer, but I was looking forward to some quality drinking time with a few *other* guys first.

Jake and Sam were Noah's dorm and apartment roommates until this year. At the beginning of the semester, Stacy, me and two of our closest guy friends moved into the same building off campus.

At the same time Noah moved into the Sigma Chi house. I'll never forget the quizzical smiles on Jake and Sam's faces when we first met. It was like I could see their brains working to piece together a puzzle that, according to them, didn't visibly fit. *"Don't know what you did to him, Gracie, but he's a new man!"*

Jake and Sam quickly became two of my dearest friends. I loved them like brothers. I was in their apartment whenever I wasn't with Noah. And while he was pledging Sigma Chi, that was a lot of time spent with the two other men in my life. Noah never got jealous. It was a decent set-up. Jake and Sam sometimes even joked that they were Noah's stand-ins, and it didn't hurt that they were both adorable.

Jake was, for lack of a better word, *hot*. He was taller than me and slender, but had broad athletic shoulders and amazingly defined arms. His eyes were crystal blue, and his shiny chocolate brown hair was just a little curly when it got too long. He had a gorgeous smile and a quiet sexiness about him that was only amplified by the rugged stubble he usually sported. Sometimes he'd shave it off or sculpt it into a goatee, but either way he was so nice to look at. I don't think he had any idea how gorgeous he was, but I'm not sure how he didn't pick up on the gawking co-eds wherever he went. Sometimes, when no one was looking, I just watched him. I was so in love with Noah, but I wasn't dead. His girlfriend Jessica was a lucky girl. But then again, so was I.

Sam was similar in build to Jake but not quite as tall. The two of them worked out together almost every day so he was cut, and I had no doubt he could hold his own if fists ever flew in his vicinity. He had thick blond surfer hair and beautiful hazel eyes that were quite flirty when he was being ornery, which was almost always. He was a great guy. Super smart, great sense of humor and a big ole tender heart. I wasn't sure how someone hadn't snagged him up yet. He said it was because no one girl could handle all he had to offer. I always giggled when he said that because I wasn't exactly sure what he was referring to when he said *all*, and I was embarrassed by what I assumed he meant.

Jake and Sam's parties were infamous. They'd yet to throw a bad one. I knew their party would the perfect follow-up to our evening at Sigma Chi. When we got to their apartment, Noah and I were welcomed by music so loud it could melt speakers, cold beer, and tons of people crammed into the small living room. Noah spent time drinking and partying with Jake and Sam, and reconnecting with other people he hadn't seen for a while. I hung out with Stacy and a couple girls from down the hall. Every now and then I would get a kiss on the top of my head along with a freshly tapped beer. It was one of my three guys each time. We all laughed and sang and danced together. I loved when they all lived together and was a little bummed that Noah moved away from them, but with this one party we had created "the good ole days." When I yawned for the fifth time in ten minutes, I decided it was time to go downstairs. Stacy had left with her boyfriend, Greg, and wouldn't be home all night. After a semester of barely seeing Noah, I would have paid her a hefty sum of money if she needed convincing to stay at Greg's.

I weaved in and out through drunk dancers looking for Noah to tell him I wanted to leave. But I couldn't find him. An unexplainable and irrational fear shot through me. *He left. Who did he leave with? Where did he go?* Sam interrupted my panic when he handed me something blue in a shot glass. The fruity taste and the beautiful after burn only took five seconds to calm my nerves. I rationalized that Noah was probably in the bathroom.

Sam and I were known for our on-the-spot improvisational dances. I hopped right next to him when our favorite song pounded and jolted the poster frames on the walls. He instantly was the rock star and I was his back-up dancer as we sang at the top of our lungs. We were quite a sight, as usual. We danced and laughed until the song ended.

Sam gave me a big bear hug and lifted me off the floor. "Where's Noah?" I knew Sam missed him, too, and I was sure he wanted to hear more about the perks of pledging. Perks being spelled as g-i-r-l-s.

Again, panic seized my chest. Noah had never given me any reason to distrust him, but that night, something wicked picked at the threads of my heart, threatening to yank the string. You know, the one that never stops unraveling.

"I don't know." My eyes darted around the room as I tried to keep the fear off my face, "Sam, where's Ivy?" Ivy was a very pretty girl who had been obsessed with Noah for more than two years. She would let him say and do anything to her just as long as he was giving her some sort of attention. It was pathetic. I once found old pictures of the two of them in a box of textbooks at Noah's house. The pictures looked like a sexual encounter, but they were fully clothed. It was obvious he was man-handling her into the multiple positions she was in. His face fit the part of a porn star while she consented. Her face was bright red and she was laughing, but visibly embarrassed. The pictures really bothered me. I threw them back in the box and never spoke of them. That was the old Noah. It was the new Noah who loved me.

"Ivy? What does she have to do with anything?" Sam looked confused.

"I don't know. I just realized I haven't seen her either, I—"

"Why do the two of you look so damn serious? This is a party!" Jake walked over and put his hand around my shoulder and squeezed me into his chest as he shouted over the music. Jake's voice always calmed me down. There was something inside him that I'd never experienced in anyone else I'd ever met. I couldn't put my finger on what it was but I liked it. He was so genuine and oh so very nice to look at. I often watched his tenderness with his girlfriend, Jessica, in awe of how he cherished her. He was who I would call if I were ever in trouble. Not that Noah wouldn't come running, but there was something about Jake's friendship that made me think he would run faster.

"Noah. Ivy. Have you seen them?" I started to breathe hard and slapped my hands up to my chest.

Jake shook his head just when someone called Sam away to replace the kicked keg.

"You got her?" Sam looked up at Jake, passing on their drunk best friend. Jake nodded and squeezed me into his chest once more.

"What's wrong?" Jake asked, calming me a little with his voice.

I shook my head and closed my eyes.

"Gracie, you don't really think they are together? Do you?"

"Jake, she really, really likes him. She would do anything to be with him. I don't *know* how far she'd go..." I took a big swig of his beer to soothe my throat that was raw from yelling over the music.

Jake moved so he was standing directly in front of me. He put his hands gently on my shoulders and ducked his head down a little to catch my gaze. I lifted my face and followed his eyes as he straightened. He was so good at getting in my head.

"Gracie. Listen to me. You've had a lot to drink. You're not being rational. He's not the guy he used to be. Hasn't been since you came into the picture."

"I know, but—" He cut me off with his fingers across my lips. Jessica walked over when she spied the two of us almost nose-to-nose.

"Gracie, think about it. Ivy? Really? He has never, nor would he ever, give you up for her. She's a ditz. She has tried for years. He's not interested."

"But..."

"*Shhh. Not* interested," he repeated. "Now let's go find him."

Jessica smiled at me and grabbed Jake's hand.

The three of us walked back the dark hallway just as Noah came out of the bathroom zipping his jeans.

Right then, my sweet, sweet friend had an opening to make me look foolish. But, instead, in perfect Jake character, he turned, smiled, kissed me on the forehead, and followed Jessica into his bedroom. He was so good at being rational. That's what made him the perfect best friend.

Before I could tell Noah I wanted to go, he grabbed my hand, nodded toward the door, and led me downstairs.

I was Cinderella and we had just left the Ball. Of course, we had a detour that got us even more drunk, but soon we were in the castle and my Prince Charming was going to make mad, passionate love to me. Pledging was over. This would be the new beginning we needed.

Spring semester of last year, I transferred from University of Tennessee Martin to U of T Knoxville so Noah and I could be together. Unfortunately, Noah started pledging Sigma Chi at the same time, so I hardly ever saw him. When I did, he was looking over his shoulder, making sure his sadistic fraternity brothers weren't watching while he took a detour to walk me to class. We fought when we were together. The stress he was under paired with how needy I had become was not a good mix. Once I begged him to quit, but he said he was "too far in" to survive quitting. Whatever that meant. So, there was no time for intimacy. And many nights he partied with sorority girls who were special guests at Sigma Chi functions. The brothers at Sigma Chi planned the pledges' every move. There was no time for anyone or anything else. He had been theirs, but tonight he was mine. I couldn't wait to feel his skin on mine. Making love to him tonight would be like pressing the reset button for us.

We barely got in the door and he was tearing at my clothes. We stumbled into the bathroom and into the shower. I wasn't very experienced, but to me, there was almost nothing hotter than naked bodies slick with water. It's sublime. Before I knew it, I was on my knees, giving him something he never dreamed his Good Girl knew how to give.

Two

"I'm leaving!" I couldn't scream loud enough. I imagined it was as loud as I would be screaming if someone was cutting my heart out without anesthesia. I wanted to scream *that* loud. The pain was literally unbearable. I ended a two-year relationship to be with Noah. I left a boyfriend who had never hurt me, in any way. Joel and I didn't argue, and we never fought. Quite honestly, I sometimes longed for a little drama so we would have a reason to make up. But drama wasn't Joel's thing, so Noah's bad-ass demeanor helped to make my relationship with Joel feel boring. Even then, I had a feeling Noah would never be boring. But I had no idea he would drive me to the pits of Hell. I wanted to delete the conversation we just had from this day. The words I asked for tore me to shreds.

"L-L-Leaving?" he stammered, but he remained stoic. He stayed still on the edge of the bed, both hands tucked between his knees.

Fight for me, dammit!

"Yes! I am going to Admissions on Monday and leaving school." I didn't know what I would be doing in thirty seconds let alone on Monday. My threat to leave was just to see him fight for me. After what I just learned, I needed to see him fight. For me.

"No! You can't be serious! You just got here." Finally he moved in my direction. I threw my hands up, telling him to stop where he was. My next sentence came out like a whisper, "Don't come any closer." I was pacing so violently the muscles in my shins started to burn. Then I started to seethe again, "I don't want to be," I gasped for air then choked out the rest between sobs, "Anywhere. Near anything. That reminds me of. *You!*"

Not only was I rendered emotionally unrestrained by his admission, but his delivery was nothing less than horrifying, and it left me stunned.

I replayed the conversation we just had in my mind as I paced around the room. Just ten minutes earlier, we were breathless and panting like animals. He was considerably bigger than me. His body was firm and tough. He wasn't an athlete, but he trained like one. I loved feeling his weight on me as he loved me inside and out. He lifted himself from my body and fell onto the sheets next to me. Between the alcohol and being spent from our love making, I knew I only had a couple minutes to mention his sudden absence upstairs.

"Okay, so, funny story." I flipped onto my side.

His eyes fluttered with exhaustion, but he turned his face toward me and smiled.

"When I couldn't find you upstairs, I was worried you were doing something with Ivy." I was embarrassed I may have insulted him with such a ridiculous concern. I immediately dropped my face into my pillow and giggled. He didn't move.

Thank God! He's asleep! He didn't hear a word I said.

I lifted my head to kiss him before I resigned myself to closing my eyes until morning. His eyes were wide as saucers, as if he was frozen in time. He just stared at me.

"What? What's wrong?"

He was silent, still staring.

"Noah. Stop. You're scaring me!"

"I-I..."

Nothing. He gave me nothing but stuttering.

I gasped.

"Did you? Did you do something with her?" He didn't move. He didn't even blink. "Noah! Answer me!" I pushed his body away from mine. I didn't know whether to laugh because he was making a joke, albeit a mean one, or cry because my world was about to cave in around me.

"I was headed to the bathroom when Ivy came out. She pressed herself against me and said someone once told her she gave head like a porn star. Then she asked if she could show me."

"You said yes?" My stomach turned and I tried to wrap my head around the logic of his response.

"Baby, she was so wasted. She'll never remember."

"Never remember what?" My voice cracked and tears streamed down my face.

"She pulled me into Sam's room and got down on her knees...but before you freak out, let me explain."

I threw my head down and as far into my pillow as I could go. I wasn't sure I could live through hearing this, but I didn't think I could look at him while he explained. Where I thought he was going with this knocked the air right out of me.

"She's so fun to mess with, Gracie. Freshman year I tormented her, making her think she had a chance with me." The photos I had found in a box at Noah's house flashed through my mind. "I followed her into Sam's bedroom because I knew she would chicken out and it would drive her crazy that she had the chance but didn't have the balls to do it."

"She didn't. You didn't let her. Did you?"

"I was just leading her on. I never thought she'd... She's not usually that brazen. I didn't expect..."

Now, he was obviously back pedaling.

"Noah, you're not answering me." I picked up my head. If he was going to tell me he cheated, he was going to have to say it to my face. Even if it killed me.

He was still.

"You cheated on me? With Ivy?" My throat slammed closed, and in a panic he tried to justify what happened and explain how it was *not* cheating.

"I didn't think she'd actually *do* it."

I was still.

"But she did. Before I knew it, she had me in her mouth. But, I only let her do it for a little bit. She didn't make me come. I stopped her right before I finished and zipped my pants." He chuckled like that would convince me further that it technically wasn't cheating.

So stunned, I wasn't sure how my involuntary functions continued. My lungs kept breathing, my heart kept beating, but both were burning with a sadness I wouldn't wish on anyone. More tears rolled. He could have punched me in the stomach, and I was pretty sure it wouldn't have hurt as badly.

In a gravelly whisper, I asked a question. A question with answers that would break me. "Was this the only time you were with someone else?" Then I started to rationalize. I mean, yes, he cheated, but it wasn't because he liked her, right? She was no threat to me. At that moment, I didn't recognize the person in my bed, but at the same time, I hoped a sudden alcohol-induced regression to the Old Noah would be my loophole.

He got out of the bed and started to pace. With the little energy I had left, I sat up and watched him intently, pleading to him silently with my heart for a, "Yes, this was the only time."

"Gracie." He turned and looked me right in the eye, "I love you. Baby, I never knew I could love someone as hard as I love you."

"Just answer the question, Noah." He broke eye contact and rubbed his forehead nervously. I felt lightheaded and caught my head in my hands. Before I knew it he was on his knees in front of me, rubbing the outside of my thighs as some form of comfort.

"Please don't touch me." I slid back on the bed until my back was against the wall and pulled my knees up to my chest.

"Steph was the first." My mind was racing. I didn't want names. Names make them real people. And if this one was first, I was praying Ivy was second because that would only be two scars on my heart. I knew it couldn't handle more than that. He continued. "You and I were only dating a month. You were back home at Martin campus and I had just started pledging." He stopped pacing and sat across the tiny room in the chair at my desk wringing his hands between his knees.

"Well, don't stop now, I'm all ears." My sadness was now bordering on disgust and rage.

"Remember when I called to talk about the study partner I'd been assigned in my Trig class? I asked if you minded that it was a girl."

"I told you it didn't bother me."

"So, I kind of asked permission. That's got to mean something to you."

"You asked permission to *study with* her, not to *have sex with* her." My voice was quiet and deep.

"I didn't have sex with her, we just messed around!"

"Define *messed around*." It didn't matter at this point what his definition was, it would still qualify as cheating.

"I never told her I had a girlfriend. I didn't want her to feel uncomfortable."

"If you had no intentions with her, why would she feel uncomfortable?"

"I don't know. We studied in her dorm. One night, after we quit studying, we drank a little and before I could stop myself, we were naked. Things just got out of hand."

"Damn you, Noah! Would you just own up to it. Tell me what happened with her!"

"One thing led to another and just before I...just before I... you know...went in," I cringed and tried to clear the visual from my mind. I was sure I felt my heart stutter. "I stopped before we did it. I didn't go inside her."

I held my stomach and squeezed my eyes.

"Madison was the second time." He spun my world with those five words. There were three. He wounded me three times. "It was after the Kappa Delta social."

"That was just last week," I yelled. Then my voice quieted and the next words slowly left my mouth. "You came over after." I remembered that night clearly. He showed up at my apartment unexpectedly after the social was over. He was still a pledge but he left unnoticed, risking painful consequences, just to spend the night with me. He was adorably drunk. He was soft-spoken and doting when he was drunk, and it was just the two of us. He became almost little-boyish with his flirty grins and playful glances. I loved it.

"Well, I—"

"Wait," I whispered, "that was the night I asked you if the stain on your shirt was lipstick."

He didn't answer me, just continued with a story that hurt to hear but didn't seem nearly painful enough for him to tell. "I walked some girl back to her dorm because her roommate left early and I didn't want her to have to walk back alone. I knew that was the gentlemanly thing to do. She passed out as soon as we walked into her room. Her roommate, Madison, helped me get her into bed and then we sat and talked for a little. I was so drunk I just wanted to sit before I had to walk back to the house. She started kissing me and I was too drunk to want to stop her."

A sob escaped my mouth because I knew what was coming. I couldn't speak, my sobs were heaving with such fervor my body was convulsing. *Why the hell did you go in? You could have walked her to the door of the building and she would have been safe. Completely gentlemanly to leave from the doorstep.*

"We ended up naked under her covers and we were touching each other and stuff. She started giving me a hand job. But I stopped her when I thought of you."

Oh, mighty nice of you.

"So, I got up and got dressed and told her I couldn't do that to you. Well, she followed me to the door trying to convince me not to go. When she realized I wasn't staying, she tried to get her lipstick off my shirt so you wouldn't see it. But you did."

My brain must have shut off to protect my heart because I didn't fully digest what he had done with the other two girls. I didn't let myself picture it as vividly as I did when he told me about Ivy. I knew I couldn't handle it all at once. So, I focused on his expressions as he explained his deceit. It was the curl of his lips that was the most unsettling. If I didn't know any better, I would think he was only confessing to obnoxiously claim his bragging rights. I wasn't ready for this. We had just hit the reset button. I wasn't ready for it to be over but maybe it had been for a while. It was at the end of his confession that I literally lost it. I started yelling and screaming for him to leave. He sat down on the bed and didn't budge.

I don't know how many times I told him to leave but he wouldn't. Between my violent outburst and my broken heart, I was exhausted. I just needed to lay down. He refused to leave, so I crawled into my bed alone, lifeless. My chest muscles ached from the battering my lungs had taken from the heaving sobs. I couldn't imagine I would ever stop crying. He eventually crawled onto the bed with me, atop the covers, never touching me. He just laid stone still beside me. Just before I passed out, it dawned on me that remnants of Ivy were still *there* when I knelt before him in the shower.

My body landed softly, somewhere. I was finally in so deep that I reached the bottom. There's no air on the bottom. People suffer here.

Three

When I woke up, only a few hours after drowning in heartache, Noah was gone. I wasn't sure if a person could die from a broken heart, but as I floated between conscious and dream state, scenes from the last year with Noah flashed across the insides of my eyelids. I chose the scenes I would relive. I started from the beginning when things were good.

June, Summer before Sophomore Year

"Oh no. You close with Noah tomorrow night." Marie almost dropped her tray of glasses when she passed the schedule. It was almost two in the morning, and my hands were nearly raw from washing dishes for the last hour. My eyes were blurry and all I could think about was sleep.

"Who's Noah?"

"He's this pig-headed, womanizing ass who only talks about the girls he 'bags' and the drunken brawls he's in on a regular basis."

Great. I had only been working at Murphy's for a little over a month. There weren't many seasonal jobs for college kids in McKenzie, Tennessee. But Murphy's, a quaint little café on Main Street, was hiring closing shift. I took the job at the last minute when nothing else panned out. But that meant I would be there…alone…with "Noah" tomorrow night until two or three in the morning. That didn't sound creepy. Holy shit. I was scared to death.

Marie could see my sheer terror. It was a small town, and it was no secret why I had earned the title of Most Innocent in my senior yearbook.

"Whoa, Gracie, breathe," she said. "Just let him know you are madly in love with your boyfriend and he probably won't bother you."

Probably?

I called Joel on my way home. I knew he'd be awake. Both of us working closing shifts at different restaurants sounded like Hell, but it made for similar time off for both of us. Joel and I didn't see each other during the school year. He stayed in McKenzie and went to Tennessee Tech, so chatting in the wee hours of the morning was just one more way to have a couple more minutes with him even if it couldn't be in person.

"And you work with him, when? Tomorrow night? Babe, I work tomorrow night!" He knew my panic because he felt it, too. His virgin girlfriend of two years would be working alone with a womanizing drunk until all hours of the morning. I knew it would be something Joel wouldn't take lightly.

"But what can I do? Leaving Marie without a second closer tomorrow night could get me fired, and I just got this job!"

Joel sighed. "I just wish we *didn't* work the same shifts so I could be there when you worked with him. I would just sit and eat pizza all night so I could keep my eye on this…Noah."

"I know you would." I giggled.

My stomach churned just imagining how nauseating Noah must be. I could only imagine how foul he was by the way Marie grimaced when she described him.

The next night at work, I was a mess. It was like everything I did was in slow motion, as if that would lengthen the time before Noah showed up for work. I was getting ready to take a pizza to a table of regulars when I heard the back door open and Mr. Murphy call out, "Well, look who it is. Welcome back!"

I turned slowly, bracing myself for the sight of a guy that could be cast in a creepy indie film—greasy black hair, stubble, skanky teeth, rancid smell.

"Thanks, man," said Noah as he walked toward me. Everything stopped. He apparently had just showered because his short blond hair was finger-tousled and still a little damp. He wore Aviator glasses and had beautiful white teeth behind a very intriguing cocky grin. He gave me a "hey" and a nod as he sauntered by me to clock in. I was stunned. This couldn't be "Noah." He didn't have greasy black hair, stubble, skanky teeth or a rancid smell. He smelled…delicious.

I actually just described this stranger's scent as delicious. What the hell?

"Hey, how was spring semester?" asked one of the night cooks whose name I didn't even know yet.

"You know, beer, girls, beer, throw a punch, study…same old, same old."

Yep, it was Noah.

"Yeah, I feel ya," said No-Name cook.

I must have looked like a complete idiot when he walked past me for the third time and I still hadn't moved from the center of the kitchen floor holding a now slanted pizza tray on my shoulder.

"Uh, darlin', that pizza's going to get cold if you don't take it somewhere." He slid his Aviators down his nose to reveal a fist-sized, black and blue eye socket. Marie's description of him rang in my brain. But there was something about those big, brown eyes that kept me captivated one second too long. He raised an eyebrow and something in me clenched. I cleared my throat and turned to serve my table their near-cold dinner.

A nervous energy bounced through my body all night. I mindlessly took orders and served tables until the cash registers were closed out and Mr. Murphy said good bye.

I gasped when I heard the door lock behind him and realized I was now alone with Noah. Of course, that gasp caused me to choke on my own spit. It wasn't an easy-to-clear kind of choke. It was an all-out *I-can't-breathe-someone-call-911* kind of choke. I was pretty sure I was going to die. Well, at least then I wouldn't be awake to see what a womanizing ass does to the town's virgin by the light of a full moon.

Noah jumped around the corner. "Hey…hey! What's going on?" He put an open hand across my chest by my collarbone, and he used the other hand to thump my back in an attempt to dislodge what he *thought* was something stuck in my throat. My body hummed with an indistinct undercurrent. My skin warmed right beneath the hand on my chest that kept me still. I was sure these overwhelming sensations were a result of what felt like near-death panic.

I shook my head and wiped my eyes. He took his hands off my body and took a step back. The undercurrent dissipated, and I breathed in slowly and calmly, trying to clear my throat. It seemed to work a little.

I looked up just as Noah handed me a cup he'd grabbed from the counter. I took a huge gulp, to clear my throat before I embarrassed myself further by dying at Murphy's. A sharp sting offended my taste buds followed by an unfamiliar heat that made its way down to my toes, and once again, I was gasping for air.

"What is that?" I said as I wiped my mouth with a grease-stained sleeve and shoved the cup back at him.

"This? Ha..." He kind of scoffed arrogantly like I should just know. "It's my man, Jim Beam...Jimmy will fix what ails ya! You want more?"

He drinks at work.

"No!" That sounded harsh. "Thank you for helping me, but I am not much of a drinker, and right now, nothing *ails* me."

I walked away to pour myself some water from the soda fountain around the corner. It was a small little nook that I could use to gather myself before finishing up in the kitchen. I leaned back against the counter, trying to calm my nerves. I cleared my throat a couple times and started to feel like I may survive the evening. Noah rounded the corner and leaned against the opposite counter, which only put about eighteen inches between us. He crossed his legs at his ankles and smiled. And there he was...Noah...just looking at me, and he radiated a subtle warning that could no longer go unnoticed. The same bad boy current that had an unexpected effect on me a couple minutes ago. He needed to knock it off.

"Not much of a drinker?"

"Nope."

He nodded with a grin stuck at one corner of his mouth. That's when I realized all the inner vibrations weren't Noah's fault. It was my body's reaction to him. I smiled, turned quickly, and walked toward the mess waiting for me by the sink. The sooner I got the dishes done, the sooner I could escape this unsettled feeling I had. Initially, I thought all the humming through my body was a reaction to the fear of almost choking to death. But I don't remember fear being so positively exhilarating. When my little sister jumped out from behind the coat rack, I didn't feel positive or exhilarated, I felt like I could mortally wound her.

"You mind if we listen to some tunes?" he called, making me jump when he yelled from the other side of the kitchen, "or are you not much of a music-listener either?"

"Music's fine." Was he trying to be funny? It made him sound like a jerk.

"Good, because I was going to play it no matter what you said."

What the hell was that?

He blasted AC/DC's "Shook Me All Night Long" so loud, I forgot I was annoyed. There was something in the guitar riffs that shot images of Joel throwing back a beer and watching me dance. I wondered if I could rattle anyone as much as Noah was rattling me. I pushed that thought away when I realized it was no longer Joel, but Noah watching me dance in my mind. I got back to the dirty dishes and pizza pans. The thought of Noah's hands on me was still making my knees weak. Or maybe I was just exhausted.

Four

Saturday, Morning After the Formal

There was a noise in my room that brought me out of the state I wanted to stay in forever; my own little reality. It was a gentler place to live. I liked it there.

"Hey, I don't know what's going on, but this just came for you." My roommate, Stacy, had been one of my closest girl friends since 10th grade, and we transferred from Martin to Knoxville together. I opened my eyes and her concerned look warmed my heart. She touched my back so lightly it sent shivers under my skin.

When I saw the long white box with the red ribbon, I knew what it was—a beautiful bouquet of *I'm a shithead, please forgive me* roses. No thank you. All of last night's pain came barreling back. I burst into tears and turned my face away from hers.

"You wanna tell me what's going on?"

I shook my head and laid still.

"Call me if you need anything." Her voice was uneasy.

I simply nodded face down into my pillow.

I heard her walk out, grab her keys, and leave the apartment. The dozen or so beers I had throughout the last evening's events were clawing at my bladder. I rolled out of bed and stumbled to the bathroom. I couldn't even look at the shower. Flashes of last night's activities in there threatened my sanity. I wasn't sure how I would ever shower there again. I stood up to flush and ended up dry heaving. I knew it wasn't a hangover. I could count on one hand the number of those I'd ever had. This was a sickness brought on by Noah. Stupid Noah. When I threw myself under Stacy's bunk and into my bed, I heard a crinkling sound.

My pillow had rustled a hand written note taped to the headboard of my bed.

Beautiful Girl,

Words cannot describe how badly I feel for what I've done. I hate myself for hurting you. Please accept these flowers as my heartfelt apology. I promise I will never hurt you again. Please give me another chance. I can't bear to think of my life without you.

I love you, Noah

P.S. I will be back at noon to get you for lunch with my mom.

His mom.

Last Day of Summer Before Sophomore Year

"Pretzels and hot mustard, just the way you like it, Gracie."

"Thank you, Mrs. Foster." I grabbed a pretzel stick and dunked it deep in the mustard.

"When will you drop the *Mrs.* and just call me Karen?"

"Thank you, Karen. It was sweet of you to remember my addiction to hot mustard."

She set the tray on Noah's desk and walked over to me. She put her hands on my upper arms and squeezed a little as she looked me square in the face. "Would it be strange for us to have lunch during the semester while you are still close by?"

"Yes," Noah called from inside his closet.

"Noah! Shut up. No, Mrs.—I mean, Karen. It wouldn't be weird at all. I would love to have lunch with you."

She dove in for a hug like she was surprised I said yes. Noah rolled his eyes and walked over to his bed with an armful of jeans. I adored this woman. She and I hit it off right from the beginning. Noah didn't seem all that close to either of his parents. He was the youngest of five boys and by the time the older four were out of the house, Mr. and Mrs. Foster had missed their chance to really bond with Noah. So I guess she enjoyed my reaction to her because she was just craving some teenager love. Whatever it was, I was happy I could be it for her.

"Well then, we will have to schedule some lunch dates. All right, I will let the two of you pack. Noah, we are leaving in three hours so you need to speed it up a bit."

"Yep." Noah nodded but didn't look up.

Three hours. I had fallen for Noah so quickly. It didn't seem like we'd been together long enough to withstand a five-hour distance.

"Can you hand me the stack of shirts, babe?"

I scooped up his t-shirts and buried my nose in them as I walked over to where he was filling a huge duffle bag.

"They smell like you."

"Who else would they smell like?" He turned and kissed me on the forehead. I closed my eyes, and when I opened them, he was holding a shirt out in front of me.

"What? You don't want to take this one? It's your favorite." I draped the shirt over my arm and traced the letters with my finger. *Parker Hill High School Senior.*

"Yeah. But so are you. You can wear it when you miss me."

We had only been officially dating for a couple weeks but it seemed like much longer. Each day we were together we got closer and closer, and he was leaving. I was trying to syphon sanity from the fact that I would be transferring from UT Martin to UT

Knoxville in January. We only had to go one semester as a long-distance couple.

"What's wrong?" Noah zipped his bag and threw it on the floor.

"I just—"

He threw a couple blankets, a fan and some socks into a box on the floor.

"Hand me the packing tape?" He looked up just as a tear rolled down my cheek. "Whoa, whoa. Gracie-girl, why the tears? You're coming to visit in a month, right?"

I nodded, embarrassed I was crying in front of him. I kept my head down and wrung my hands trying to focus on swallowing the lump in my throat so I could speak.

"Listen. I'm not going to get to Knoxville and forget you. Is that what you're worried about?"

"I guess, a little." I whispered just as a sob slipped out.

"Gracie," He tripped over the box in his urgency to get to me. "Gracie, look at me." He held my head so all I could see was his face. "I've never felt this way about anyone. You've got nothing to worry about. I will be counting down the days until you get there. I love you."

I completely inhaled the next sob when he said those three words.

"I do, Gracie. I love you hard. I am yours. You've got nothing to worry about."

I thrust myself to my toes and threw my arms around his neck. "I love you, too, Noah."

I laid my head on his chest and he rocked me from side to side for I don't know how long.

I crumpled the note I found on my headboard into a tiny ball and threw it across the room. What was he thinking? As much as I'd love to see her, I couldn't do lunch with his mom. I ran to the bathroom, dry heaved then ran upstairs to Jake and Sam's apartment.

Five

"Wait, what did you just say?" Jake rubbed the sleep from his eyes. I looked at his alarm clock. It was only 9:30.

"I'm sorry. It's early. I will just come back later." I started to climb out of his bed when he sat straight up and grabbed my left arm.

"What did you say?"

I climbed back on, sat closer to him than before so I didn't have to say it too loud. It felt less embarrassing if I whispered. "Noah...Ivy...he cheated?"

"Wait, what do you mean *cheated*? He slept with her?" He twisted toward me. The covers fell and I was momentarily distracted. He was shirtless, and even with more stubble that usual and serious bed head, the guy was gorgeous.

"No, he let her blow him! In Sam's bedroom. During the party! While I was right in the next room!" I fell into his bare chest and fell apart. I was so thankful Jessica had either left the night before or really early that morning. I was sure she would have had a fit seeing me covering her almost naked boyfriend in tears. I sobbed and sobbed, and Jake wrapped his bare arms around me. He held on and rubbed my back as he rocked me a little. He knew there was nothing he could say to make it right. *I* knew there was nothing he could say.

Before too long, Sam came into Jake's room and listened to me relive the last nine hours of my life in between sobbing, blowing my nose, and throwing myself down on Jake's pillow.

Jake and Sam had known Noah longer than I had, and they had seen his shenanigans with Ivy. Neither of them ever expected it to go beyond playful joking. Sam stood there stunned. "Oh, Gracie," was all he could muster.

"So, now I have…" —I looked at Jake's clock— "an hour to get ready to go to lunch with him and his mom." I sighed and wiped my nose with my t-shirt.

"You're not really going, are you?" Jake and I were lying on top of his covers, staring at the ceiling. Feeling awkward with nothing to add that Jake hadn't already said, Sam left to go clean up the mess that was their living room but not without reaching for my hand and squeezing it. His sweet heart warmed mine.

"How can I not? I adore her. She will know something's up."

"So, what if she knows something's up? He's a stupid ass and you broke up with him. Let him do the explaining." He turned his face toward me.

"I don't ever want her to know."

"Why?" Jake turned on his side and lifted himself up onto his elbow. He rested his head on his hand and yawned. Poor guy. He probably got no sleep. He and Jessica were crazy good lovers. I'd heard stories, and a few times I actually heard how earth shattering the love they made was. They weren't big on PDA, but Jessica wasn't known for being quiet when they disappeared into Jake's room. There were more than a couple nights Stacy and I fell asleep talking about what we thought Jake looked like naked and how amazing he had to be in bed. Jake ran every day, and almost every day, he and Sam would go to the gym and lift. It was no secret his body was in amazing shape.

As he lay on his side across from me, his defined abs were within reach. Again, I was distracted. How good would it feel to be physically loved the way I knew Jake loved Jessica? I was so sad and ached for someone to love me the way I longed to be loved. To forget how much pain Noah had caused me. It wasn't often that I allowed myself to think about Jake that way. I was usually the one stopping Stacy's perfectly choreographed fantasies she shared with me. Jake was my best friend, and it felt like I was cheating on Noah when she would put those images in my head. But on the morning after finding out all the places Noah's dick had been, I decided to let my mind go there.

But then I thought of poor Jessica. This was crossing the line. I needed to stop fantasizing about the things Jake could do to my body. She may have just left before I got there, for all I knew. I had another fleeting thought about lying on the sheets they had rumpled together. I brushed that thought away as soon as it came.

"I don't want to be that girl, the victim."

"So, don't let him make you the victim. He made his bed. Be the survivor and leave the shithead. Cut him off from everything connected to you. Say goodbye and mean it." He stared at me with those blue eyes. His words were harsh, his voice stern, his jaw was clenched, but his eyes held my pain like he was trying to take it from me.

"I'm going downstairs. Thanks for talking." I hugged him then climbed from his bed to go home. Sam caught me at Jake's door and hugged me so tight it pushed out one of the sobs I had been holding back. He kissed me on the forehead.

"Gracie..." Jake's voice wrapped around me like another hug. I turned, knowing his voice would calm me just a little more. "You will be okay without him, I promise. I'll help you get through this."

I smiled and started walking toward the hallway.

"Um, hey..." His voice was a little pained. I turned quicker to see what was wrong. "You might wanna..." With those words, he slowly pointed to his neck, and then to me.

I immediately headed toward his bathroom mirror. "That peckerhead," I whispered. My neck was covered in fresh purple-blue bruises—evidence that he really had sucked the life out of me last night. The tears started again.

Red, puffy eyes, and a turtleneck on a warm September day. That was the only way to go. I had to go to lunch with his mom...and him.

Six

I flopped into my bunk, exhausted from pretending everything was fine at lunch. I guess everything was fine, if imagining I was scraping Noah's face off with his fork seems fine to anyone other than me. Noah didn't do the PDA thing anywhere, but especially not in front of his parents. So, I didn't think Karen noticed anything was different. I spent the entire lunch fighting back tears and waves of nausea. I worked really hard to keep Noah out of my line of sight, I never could have held it together if I had to look at his face. But I felt his eyes on me the entire time, and it made me sick. My chest ached from the heaving and sobbing I had done up until that point, and I just wanted lunch to be over. I was relieved when he said he had some stuff to do at the house to get ready for an event they were having. At the same time, I thought it was a dick move because he should be spending the day trying to make up for what he'd done. Karen dropped me at my apartment, and Noah went his own way. And I did the only thing I had the energy for.

I stared at the underside of Stacy's bunk. Stuck between the rails, under her mattress, were the only mementos that weren't in the trashcan. A crispy dead daffodil Noah picked for me out of one of the many flower beds on campus and a couple *Good Morning, sorry I had to go so early* notes that I'd found on my pillow the few times he slept over while pledging. The tears slid past my temples, and I longed for the guy I thought he was. The guy no one else knew until he fell in love with me. I closed my eyes, my body aching from exhaustion. Before I knew it, I was back in the kitchen at Murphy's making plans with a new friend.

July, Summer Before Sophomore Year

"What are you doing tomorrow night?" Noah passed me with a large stack of pizza pans headed to the sinks.

Noah and I had been working together for a couple weeks. We got along and he made me laugh. He certainly wasn't scary. I'd even started to look forward to working with him. Even Joel realized Marie had obviously been exaggerating and was more comfortable with us working together. Noah wasn't the monster she had made him out to be.

"Nothing really. Joel works, so…"

"Well, it's the Fourth of July. You want to go see the fireworks?"

Somehow, both Noah and I had it off, and he just asked me out. I rationalized, friends do stuff together, right? So, it wouldn't be a big deal. Joel wouldn't care. Noah was just a work friend. The fireworks were out in the middle of nowhere and people from McKenzie rarely headed that way. The major shopping and recreational things to do were in every other direction so I knew I'd be safe from any gossip.

"Sure! Sounds like fun!"

The rest of the night we were slammed with hungry patrons of the McKenzie Street Fair, and quite honestly, by the time we walked out to our cars that night, I had forgotten all about the

Wilton Public Library
1215 Cypress Street
P.O. Box 447
Wilton, IA 52778

fireworks. "Hey, give me your phone." Noah's car was parked next to mine behind Murphy's.

"What?"

"Your phone. I want to trade numbers so I can text you tomorrow about times and stuff."

"Oh, right. Fireworks. Got it."

Noah was so laid back about it that I left the parking lot that night not at all stressed to tell Joel about my plans with him.

Although Joel seemed a bit uneasy about my plans with Noah, he didn't get mad. He was so calm and reserved as I explained Noah's invitation. He agreed that it shouldn't be an issue, but I thought I heard a tinge of sadness in his voice that night.

The next night, Noah picked me up *after* dinner, which made it less like a date, and we drove to a big, wide-open field off the beaten path. When we got out of the car, Noah continued talking about some prank he and his roommate, Jake, pulled on their RA freshman year. I laughed at the thought of trying to fill a dorm hallway with popcorn and followed him around to the back of the car where he was digging in the trunk for something.

A blanket. Aww, he brought a blanket. Or was it always in his trunk? Maybe it's what he uses when he womanizes all the women. Stop.

Growing up, my very conservative mom made my sister and I well aware that if you stayed away from all things "bedroom," you would find it easier to save yourself for marriage. When boyfriends came over, the rules were strict—no blankets on the couch, no lying on laps, and definitely no snuggling in a horizontal position. So, my "bed linen" alarm went into freak mode.

Stop it. It's to sit on, not hump on. We will be watching fireworks, not porn! A couple deep breaths and I had regained my composure.

"This okay?" Noah stopped on a part of the field with a large patch of thick grass and weeds. It wasn't secluded, but we weren't right on top of any families, either.

"Perfect."

We chatted about this and that as we waited for it to get dark. *Dark. Blanket.* I couldn't stop my reaction. My stomach filled with butterflies, and without a second thought, I looked around to make sure my parents were nowhere in sight. Of course they weren't.

There were a few times we hit that uncomfortable silence that has you hoping the ground will swallow you. But overall, it was nice being there with Noah.

"So, where do you go to school?" I asked. I didn't really care, but he was always telling stories about parties and I didn't really know any specifics about him. I doubted he knew much about me either.

"UT Knoxville!" He lifted the bottom of his hoodie and pointed to the bright orange letters on the t-shirt underneath. *Tennessee Vols.*

"No, way!"

He took a huge sip of lemonade then nodded and crooked his neck to question my response.

"I'm transferring there in the spring," I said.

"What? I thought you went to school in Memphis."

"I did, last year. But my parents watch too much news and made a list of all the murders from the day they dropped me off until the last day in May when they handed me a UT Martin application."

"They made a list?"

"Not really, a mental one. I'll live at home and go to UT Martin for the fall. Then head to Knoxville in the spring." Martin was within forty minutes from my house. I really didn't want to go to the University of Tennessee at all. Growing up in this area, it's all I heard about. I feared it would be like 13th grade, and I would just have an extended high school experience. But I didn't want to make waves with my parents who were footing the bill so when I got my acceptance letter, I decided to register and make the best of it.

"My buddies and I just signed the lease for an apartment next semester. Movin' out of the dorms!" He flicked his thumb out of his fist and pumped it over his shoulder. "So, why Martin first? Why not just start Knoxville in the fall?"

"Martin was my only option. When my parents decided to take over my life, they were a little late in the 'get your application in by this date' department so Martin was my only choice."

"Bummer." He held my gaze a little longer than I expected. It was like he was watching a scene that was playing out in his mind. Feeling awkward, I had to look away.

A thunderous boom took me by surprise and I swear my teeth chattered from the vibration. I jumped and gasped a little as the sky lit up in a flurry of vibrant red sparkles. I didn't see Noah's reaction, but when I shyly looked to see if he saw mine, he was smirking. *Shit. He thinks I'm an idiot. Wait. Why do I care?*

The next boom I was ready for. It was a blast so loud I could feel the sound waves ricocheting inside my chest. For a second, I thought my heart stopped beating. It was followed by a blinding flash of white light, and little swirling balls of light fell toward the ground and whistled on their way.

"Ha. Look. Spermies!"

Did he just call those "spermies?" As in sperm?

He leaned back on his elbows.

"Hey, I can't see," he complained, and he swiped at the inside of my elbow joint which bent my arm and made me fall backwards. .

I laughed and propped myself up on my elbows.

Lying. Blanket. Lying. Blanket. Stop.

"Here," he said in almost a whisper, which made his voice raspy. I liked how it sounded. He bent both arms under his head and he motioned for me to use one as a make-shift pillow.

I eyed him suspiciously. "I am not snuggling with you. I have a—"

"I know. You have a boyfriend. That nerd, Joel. I'm not going to rape you. I'm just giving you a soft place to put your head."

Rape me? Idiot.

"He's not a nerd! You've never even met him. He's older than you..." I lay back so he didn't think *I* was a nerd. I glanced over at him to see his reaction.

"*Re. Lax.* I...was...kidding..." He said the last part like I was a deaf person who needed him to speak slowly so I could read his lips.

Nice lips. Very, very nice lips.

Instantly, upon making contact with his arm, I got that familiar jittery feeling as if I had butterflies in my bones. Not all of my bones, just my extremities. I decided the butterflying going on inside my bones was a direct result of my reckless behavior. I had a boyfriend and I was almost snuggling with a co-worker. But it was as though the feeling was a drug. I just wanted to feel it a little longer before I sat back up.

I was trying hard to not flirt so I wasn't giving Noah the wrong idea about this "friend date." But something inside me was stirring. Something I couldn't ignore.

Noah spoke but I couldn't hear him over the crackle of the red, white and blue explosion overhead.

"What?"

He pulled my head close to his using the bent arm pillow, which I was thankful for once I realized how hard the ground was. His warm breath on my face was intoxicating. As he spoke about some fireworks accident he saw on the news, I could smell the soap he used, his deodorant, his toothpaste, his laundry detergent. All those smells combined were an olfactory definition for how alluring he was right at that moment. I sat up for the rest of the fireworks, claiming my back hurt but I just really needed to clear my head and wash the *whatever it was* out of me. Noah and I couldn't be more different. He was rugged and risky, and I was fearful and anxious.

He wasn't afraid to fight, and I was always trying to steer clear of confrontation. I just needed to focus on Joel and stop. But stop what? Seeing and breathing? Because at that moment that's all it seemed it would take for me to melt into him.

"You ready?" When the grand finale was over, we were both sitting with our arms wrapped around our knees. Not touching, which was working much better for me.

"Sure."

He stood up and reached for my hand to help me up. Dammit. Touching. When I took his hand, a jolt of electricity shot from my palm and into my chest. He held my hand the whole way to the car, which made it hard for me to breathe. I knew there was no part of Noah that was interested in me. So, it *was* safe. I may be frazzled around him, but it was not like something was going to happen between us. Ever.

The ride home was actually relaxed and fun. With the windows down, we blared the Classic Alternative Rock station on XM and realized we had the same taste in music.

I had forgotten all my angst about the "spermies" and the "rape" by the time we pulled up to my house, and all the electricity I was feeling throughout the night had dissipated.

"Well, thanks. This was fun. See you tomorrow night," I said as I got out of his car.

He got out too.

Weird. Dammit.

The vibrations came back when I realized he was walking me to the door. I was really looking forward to running in, plopping down on my bed, and calling Joel to reassure him I was fine. I started to get nervous about Noah's intention when we actually arrived at the door.

This is stupid. He's just being polite. I imagined him saying, *Re. Lax!*

"Well, thanks again." I turned to reach for the knob when he spoke.

"Um. I...I had a really nice time. A *really* nice time."

It was weird, now *he* seemed nervous. This guy who I assumed was impervious to any insecurities seemed nervous. I had this effect on him? The thought of that made my toes curl.

"Me too. Thanks." I tried once again to make it to the knob.

"You think maybe I could have a goodnight kiss?" He looked like a little boy asking for another book at bedtime with those big brown eyes and full pouty lips.

"Um...no!" I said without missing a beat. "Boyfriend!"

He rolled his eyes. "I don't want tongue. Just a peck. No strings."

Where in the world did this guy come from? Why would he think I would even want to kiss...those lips...those full pouty lips? Stop looking at his lips!

I shook the thought from my head and suddenly saw this scenario from another point of view. I was the shy girl. The good, not-too-forward girl, who never made the first move. Joel and I fooled around, but I always followed his lead, and the only time I spoke up was when we were getting a little too close to the real thing. I never had the upper hand with a guy. And especially, not a guy like Noah. Some of the stories I'd heard him tell the other guys about his conquests at work made the hair on my neck stand up. But right at that moment, he seemed to be into me. And as much as I didn't want to admit it, I was hopeful.

He was definitely a bad boy, the kind of guy that usually didn't give a "nice girl" like me the time of day. And *he* was asking *me* for a kiss. This could be my one and only chance to have secret bragging rights to something not-so-innocent, but safe at the same time. It was just a peck, right?

I convinced myself this was the innocent side of living on the edge. It was just one more safe way to be reckless. I knew I would never have another opportunity like this again. A thunderstorm was rumbling in the distance and a downpour would soon be upon us. Something about Noah coaxed me out of my comfort zone. I took a step toward him—and went for it.

Our lips met and there was a shock. Literally, a shock. I flinched and pulled back. He was grinning, eyes wide.

"Wow," he said, "I've never had that happen before."

It could have ended there, but I leaned in again. He closed his eyes. I pressed harder this time, hoping the electricity from the pending storm wouldn't zap us again. No zap, but those familiar vibrations came alive in me. Alive in places other than my extremities this time. There was no tongue as promised, but it was a little more than a peck. He was tasting me. I was tasting him. He tasted so good. Surprisingly, he was gentle. Not at all what I had imagined. He didn't even reach out to touch me. He just leaned in.

Okay. Done. Reckless abandon over.

I stepped back slowly and opened my eyes, my lips still parted. It was so much more than I expected. He looked at me with a smirk, put two fingers to his brow, and gave me a little salute. "Night," he said as he turned and walked down the deck.

His lips.

The skies opened, the rain came down, and lightning struck with a loud crack followed by a low rumble. I started to regret the kiss before my head hit the pillow.

Seven

Late Saturday Afternoon, September, Junior Year

I shook myself awake and quickly but carefully sat up, making sure I didn't hit my head on the underside of Stacy's bunk as I'd done one too many times. My heart pounded from being woken by what I assumed was the thunder in my dream. But then I heard a noise in the other room. I rubbed my eyes, and as I stood and turned toward the door, he walked in. I slapped my hand across my mouth and held my stomach all at once. The sight of Noah in my bedroom once again brought all the pain and revulsion back to real time. I couldn't do this again. I sat back down on my bed and buried my face in my hands.

"You need to leave. Now." I didn't look up. I tried to keep my voice as calm as I could so I would appear in control, but I was shaking violently.

"I wanted to thank you for going to lunch today."

"Okay, you thanked me. Now leave."

"I…I just need…"

And with that I stood and charged over to him. Toe to toe.

"*You* need? You need what, Noah? Pity? You think I will feel sorry for you for making a mistake? What about me, you asshole? What about the way my heart feels right now? How about how disgusted I am that you let me do what I did to you last night knowing her mouth had just been there, too? I don't even want to look at you. Get out!"

"Gracie. Just hear me out. Please."

"Noah, there is honestly nothing you could say to me right now that would make me want to be with you again. I broke up with you last night. We are done! Please leave."

"I'm not leaving until you just let me talk to you."

"You talked plenty last night. Hmmm. Let's see, you talked about Ivy... and Steph... and Madison. Are there more sluts you need to share with me? Because, if that's the case, I'm not interested in knowing any more. You do what you want from now on, but I swear to you it won't be with me."

"Gracie, sit down."

"Don't you *fucking* tell me what to do, Noah. You have no right." I wanted to fight. I wanted to reach in and pull his heart out through his face. There was no way he was going to soften any part of my heart with anything he had to say.

"You are right. You *shouldn't* want to talk about it. You *should* insist I leave. But, Gracie, I know your heart. I know it is searching for a reason why I did what I did. I know you are trying to figure out what would have kept it from happening. You're thinking it had something to do with you. And Gracie, I don't ever want you to feel how I know you're feeling right now."

"Oh, now you read minds. So, tell me Noah, what else am I feeling?" He was right. I couldn't get rid of the nagging voice in my head that kept saying, *You were never enough for him, certain things about you just came up short. Maybe if you were a little sexier or more adventurous in bed he wouldn't have strayed. But good girls don't make good lovers, so he moved on when he saw something better.*

"You're telling yourself that I needed more, that you weren't pretty enough or skinny enough. You're deciding that these mistakes I made are because I needed more than you could give me. Gracie, you couldn't be further from the truth. I can't leave this apartment until you hear me out. It would kill me to think you believed any of those things you're telling yourself."

I sat on the edge of my bed and he knelt before me. He wasn't pacing like he was last night. He was steady. He was serious.

"Gracie Jordan, the night I met you I knew I never wanted to go a day without seeing you. There is a quiet sexiness in you that drives me insane. It's nothing I have ever felt for anyone, ever. When you touch me, electricity shoots through my veins. When we make love... Well, there are no words to begin to describe how much I crave that connection with you.

"These other girls. They meant nothing. They were like a 'fall off the wagon' kind of thing. I quit my other lifestyle cold turkey the night I walked into Murphy's and saw you standing in the middle of the kitchen floor holding a pizza. Before you, Gracie, I was out every night messing with girls, seeing how many I could lead on, fist-fighting their boyfriends when I went too far and pissed them off. You've heard the stories. But that all changed because you stole my heart and it hit me broadside."

"Noah. That's how you *used* to feel."

"No, Gracie, that's how I *still* feel."

"Shut up. I'm not an idiot. You don't get naked with other girls if you love your girlfriend the way you just described."

"I need you to see this in a different way."

"There's only one way to see it. You cheated. We are done."

"A recovering alcoholic walks into a bar —"

"Now we're telling jokes? Unbelievable."

"Let me start again. There's this man who drinks way too much and to everyone else that's all he is, a drunk. So, he doesn't have much to live up to. But one day, he sees the opportunity for a career. A great career. So, he decides he's going to quit and he does it on his own. Just wakes up and decides he's never touching a drink again. That was me, the day I met you. But it wasn't drinking that was my problem. I wanted to be with you so badly, I knew I had to give up the raunchy life I was living before you would even give me the time of day.

"So, this guy, he does so well. He stays away from bars and cleans up every part of his life. He is happy. Really, really happy because he got the job of his dreams. A little while after he starts the new job, there's an office party…at a local bar. He knows he needs to go, his connection with his co-workers is really important for his position. So he goes. The minute he walks in, he knows it's going to be a struggle. That was me, pledging Sigma Chi. I walked into something, into a scenario and a lifestyle that was familiar. I knew I needed to focus on you…on us…but I slipped just like the guy in the bar slipped when someone handed him a beer."

By now I was sitting straight up, following his story like the world had stopped around us and it was just Noah and me on the entire planet.

"He knew he shouldn't drink that beer and everything within him fights it but he caves and takes a sip. It crushes him that he had just undone what he was so proud to have accomplished. So he puts the beer down and walks away. Gracie, each time I fell, each time I slipped back into the son-of-a-bitch I used to be, I stopped. I stopped mid-act because I didn't want that life anymore."

"Why couldn't you have stopped before any of it played out? Noah, why couldn't you have stopped when she leaned in to kiss you or when she reached for the button on your jeans?"

"For the same reason that guy in the bar couldn't casually hold that beer bottle in his hand without taking a sip. But you know what? You know what, Gracie? He put that beer down each time before he took a second sip. All three times he caved, but just to one sip. He never got drunk. And each time he walked out of that bar, he promised himself he would never do it again. Then one day, he walks out of that bar desperate for a do-over. He realizes he is stronger than he is giving himself credit for. He tells himself he is worthy of that job he loves so much and that would have to be the last time he caves.

"Gracie, I walked out of that bar for the last time last night. I swear to you. I will never hurt you again."

He leaned in so close I could feel his breath, "I love you, Gracie. I am so, so sorry for hurting you. I promise I will make it up to you if you just give me the chance. Please. I can't bear to lose you."

My heart ached with unrequited love, and my mind was tormented as it searched for what to say.

"Please leave." Two words were all I could handle and they spilled out just above a whisper.

His breath caught. He stood and he turned to walk out. My heart broke all over again. His head hung and his shoulders slumped. I loved him so hard it hurt. I didn't want him to walk away. I wanted him to take it all back, like nothing had ever happened. I wanted to go back in time and re-write everything he told me happened over the last year. But just then, the flashbacks of all the other times he cheated came rolling back like punches. As he closed the door to the hallway behind him, I ran to the toilet and heaved.

I sat on the couch alone all day. I didn't move for hours. I had no idea what time it was when my cell phone chirped with a text from Stacy.

I'm at Greg's. You need me to come home tonight?

I texted back, *No. Thanks. I really just want to be alone.*

When the only light in the living room was the street light shining through the window, I crawled back into bed and looked at the clock. 8:30. I resigned myself to the fact that this is where I would stay for the rest of the weekend. Maybe then, I'd have enough strength to get out of the apartment. Maybe not. I pulled my journal out from under my mattress and turned to something I'd written a week, maybe two, after the fireworks and first kiss entry.

47

At work tonight, Noah melted my heart...he wants me. And he wants me to break up with Joel for him. I have never felt so alive. I have never felt so craved.

I closed my journal, tucked it under my pillow and closed my eyes. I needed to sleep some more. Maybe it would take the edge off the pain. Once again, I fell asleep to memories of the Noah I may have just seen, again...

Night after Fireworks, Summer before Sophomore year

Serving customers with a nervous stomach was never a good idea. I felt like I was on the verge of puking at any second, and Noah hadn't even come into work yet. I felt guilty and curious at the same time. I kissed him. Now I knew what those lips could do to me, and I would have to stay away from being tempted by them again. It was just a friendly kiss and that was it.

Maybe he was sick. Maybe he went out partying after dropping me off last night and was in an alcohol-induced coma and wouldn't be in. Maybe he...

I felt his presence just before he spoke. "Hey there, hotness." He ran his hand along my lower back as he headed toward the time clock. He smirked, I assumed because of the secret he was dying to tell someone. I knew what that secret was, and he needed to just forget about kissing me. He needed to move on to his next conquest because nothing was going to happen between us.

He went right to the back to get more ingredients to fill the toppings area of the cook's table. He didn't give me another look for what seemed like hours.

Jerk.

He coaxed me to cheat on my boyfriend, and now he was done? Well, good. That difficult conversation wouldn't have to happen then.

"Hey, hand me that stack of trays." His voice was low and void of any of the connection we had last night. He didn't even look at me when he asked for them. I would have liked to *hit him* with those trays at that moment.

"Um, can you say please?" I wondered what the gruff tone was all about.

"Yeah. Sure. Please." He waved his hand signaling his impatience. He was such an ass.

I huffed and went to wait on a whole section of little leaguers. I had to ask three boys to repeat their orders because I was so angry I couldn't hear them over the sound of the blood pumping in my ears.

The rest of the night I stomped around, talked about what a jerk he was in my head, and ignored those stupid lips. Stupid, stupid lips.

"Marie, I need to run to the bathroom, I'll be right back," I took my apron off and practically ran to the privacy of my very own two-stall hiding place. I looked at myself in the mirror. What was wrong with me? Why did this bother me so badly? This was what I wanted, just a kiss and nothing more. I couldn't figure out why I was getting so pissed about the "nothing more."

He gave me the out by being an ass, and still, I felt unsettled and twisted on the inside. I couldn't seem to make sense of my own thoughts and feelings. I just needed to see Joel and all of this confusion would end. I wished his work schedule was different. If I saw him, it would erase whatever it was confusing me about Noah.

By the time Marie cashed out and locked the door behind her, I was in a daze, exhausted and confused. Noah hadn't said two words to me in hours. I couldn't take it anymore.

"What is your problem?" I yelled, a little louder than I intended, but it got his attention. I had him cornered against the door of the walk-in freezer. He would have to answer me.

He chuckled, shook his head and licked the corner of his mouth.

"What's so funny? Why are you smiling?" He was infuriating. He waited a second to answer while he held my gaze with the very tip of his tongue resting just behind his lips.

"Darlin', I am just respecting your wishes of not making our little 'moment' a big deal. Did you want it to be a big deal?"

"Well, no. No I didn't. Good," I stammered. "I'm glad that's what you were thinking. Because that was the last time that will happen."

"Sure it is." He pushed his way past me and walked out to cover the topping bins and take them back to the fridge.

"It was the last time! The only time!"

"Okay, if you say so," he called as he walked away.

I just stood there. I felt like an idiot. I had justified our kiss as a simple "thank you" to a friend...who just happened to be a gorgeous guy. He acted like I wouldn't be able to resist him much longer. Is this what he thought of himself? What a jerk. I could resist him. Joel was my boyfriend and that's the number one reason I could resist him.

It was almost two in the morning when we finally had everything cleaned up and were ready to walk out the door. I was determined to get out of the building and into my car without having to talk to him. I headed for the employee exit and yanked on the cold steel door. It didn't move. I tugged again. Nothing. I spun around toward the hook on the opposite wall to grab the keys. Noah silently stood behind me with his hand above my head, holding the door shut. The fact that he was using his physical strength to his advantage was more than a little unsettling. I didn't know him all that well, and it was as if he was trying to prove something. My stomach lurched.

With my back against the door, I could feel the chill of the steel through my shirt. I tried to force my body as far away from his as I could, but he was leaning in, his head tilted toward mine. His breathing was deep and regular. My breath soon synced with his. I don't know how that happened, but it did.

I looked down at the floor so I wouldn't have to look at him in the eye, but his eyes were boring a hole through the top of my head. His body was warm and he smelled so good. He was sweaty from the grunt work it took to clean up after a crazy Little League night, but he still smelled good.

Sexy.

Stop it!

I never should have looked up, but I did, just as he lowered his mouth to mine. His lips were soft and warm and wet. He gently tasted me again.

Stop. Stop. Stop.

Small pecks, one right after the other, over and over, until the butterflies in my bones morphed into an ache between my legs which reminded me I had to stop. Just then, he put his left hand on the back of my neck but kept his right hand above us on the door. His chest pressed into mine and he slowed down the wet pecks I was trying *not* to enjoy. Then he claimed my mouth as his. His tongue slowly circled mine. I suddenly realized there was a thumping beneath my palms. Somehow, instinctively, my hands had moved to his chest. Why was I letting him do this to me? He was intoxicating. He was dangerous and bad. He tested boundaries and lived a little recklessly. He wanted me. He obviously didn't care that I had a boyfriend. He wanted me, and that was all that mattered to him. I didn't know whether to let that win me over or use that to make the decision that he was so far out of my league.

Our breathing increased and our kiss got deeper. There was something so sensual about the way he kissed. I wanted it to last for hours. Although the ache I felt earlier was now throbbing, *I* wouldn't last hours. *I* needed him to stop. *I* needed to stop. This wasn't the kind of girl I was. What he did to me made me lose all rational thinking. All I wanted at that moment was for his mouth to leave mine and travel down to my neck and my...

That's when he stopped. My chest heaved, and his warm breath blew the wisps of hair that had fallen from my short, stubby ponytail. He dropped his hand from my neck and let it fall to his side.

"I need to be with you." His voice was almost a growl as he tried to slow his breathing. The way he said those six little words made my knees weak.

"No." Everything in me screamed, *Take me!*

"Wow."

He shook his head, took a step back, and opened the door. He waved his hand, directing me to go ahead of him to the parking lot. I pushed past him and was thankful for the air that I needed to help me cool off. I hurried to my car, hoping this would be an easy break from his questioning.

"Gracie. Wait." He jogged over to me as I opened my car door and threw my purse onto the seat.

"Noah, there's nothing to...you shouldn't...we shouldn't have...that can't happen again!"

"God, shut up! Hear me out."

He saw the disgust on my face at his blunt directive so he added, "Please."

I nodded and with my hand, I mimicked his sarcastic gesture, coaxing him to continue.

"These last few weeks, I can't explain it. I have never been so close to a girl and had so much fun without banging her..."

I winced.

"Sorry, that was rude. What I am trying to say is I think about you all the time. I look forward to spending my nights in this greasy hole just so I can be with you. I can't explain it. You're a good girl. You make me try to act appropriately without even realizing you're doing it. I am more guarded because I respect you. That's never happened before. This feeling is all new to me, but I think I like it. Shit, I sound like a pussy, but..."

I winced again.

"Sorry." He looked at the ground and turned to walk away, but stopped and looked right into my soul. "Could you just do me a favor?"

"Sure." Why was my heart all of a sudden hurting for him?

"Can you just think about giving me a chance? I just want a chance. I know I can make you happy."

I nodded. I couldn't resist him.

Eight

Sunday, Morning after Noah's Romantic Plea

Sunday was a complete blur. I didn't look at the clock once. I ate a Pop Tart and drank some soda. I slept a lot and cried even more. Monday would bring a new day. Another new chance to be strong and get my shit together.

Sleep.

Monday morning I realized putting makeup on while crying was a nearly impossible feat. I gave up after applying some waterproof mascara and blush. I threw my hair into a stubby ponytail and grabbed my backpack. Today was my easy day, only one class, Childhood Development. As I hurried out and locked the door behind me, I heard the ding of the elevator hitting our floor. I squeezed my eyes, hoping it wasn't Noah again. I took a deep breath and turned around just as Stacy rounded the corner at the end of the hall.

"Hey." Her eyebrows raised and her gait slowed. Was she looking at my bloodshot, puffy eyes or the permanent frown carved into my face? Neither could I hide from her, so I just walked toward her.

"Hey..." She said it slower this time as she dropped her backpack and opened her arms, motioning me into her gaping hug. I couldn't resist the comfort she was willing to provide, even if it was only for a mere moment before I had to run to class. I never needed her hug as much as I did at that moment.

"Oh, Stacy." I crumbled emotionally...again. "He cheated. Noah cheated on me three times in the last year!" Again, my body heaved with sobs. Stacy just held on and rubbed my back. I could almost feel the shockwave run through her. She was in the position poor Jake was in Saturday morning. There was nothing she could say, and she knew it. So she just hugged.

I stood back, wiped my face with the sleeve of my sweatshirt, and tried to force a smile to thank her for her hug.

"Gracie, I will kill him. You know this, right?" She stomped her foot and clenched her fists.

"Stacy, I don't know how to do this."

She rubbed my shoulder and tilted her head. "Me neither. But I'm here however you need me to be. And Jake and Sam are right upstairs. You won't do this alone."

Her devotion to me made me tear up all over again so I could only nod and try to wave away the unshed tears threatening to spill over .

"I'm gonna be late. Will you be home after your chem lab?"

"Yep. Running to class as soon as I get the lab reports I forgot to take to Greg's. But I'll be back."

"'Kay. I will see you then."

Stacy was brilliant. She came to U of T for their amazing science program. We often talked about moving away together after graduation. We would go somewhere that had a well-known university hospital with a competitive research program for her and an opening for a social worker on the pediatric floor for me. But, now all I had to look forward to was the rubber room I would probably be assigned to by graduation.

She tilted her head again and smiled. I turned and walked to the elevator. When the doors closed behind me and the elevator headed down, it hit me that this was as close to Hell as I had ever been before. I just hoped the doors opened at the ground floor and not the real place. Although, I wasn't sure how different those two places would feel at that moment. No matter where I went, the hole in my heart was still gaping. I couldn't outrun it. I couldn't forget it. I couldn't sleep it off. I would have to face this head on, but I knew I wasn't strong enough to do it. Dammit. Why did he fight so hard for me that summer at Murphy's if he was just going to turn around and cheat? He hadn't changed. He was still a man-whore, and I was still confused.

Once I broke up with Joel, and Noah and I were exclusive, I never imagined my life changing again. I just figured you find your future husband in college. They call it the MRS. degree. I thought I'd found him.

Now what?

I sat in my Child Development class in a daze. I could have still been on my bed in Noah's torn UT t-shirt and a pair of ripped sweats for all my thumping heart and racing mind knew. My stomach churned. He cheated. I didn't know how to digest it, how to make sense of what I was supposed to do now. Two full days had come and gone since Friday night, and the pain was still so raw.

It was a dangerous thing to do, but I let my mind travel into the depths of what Noah told me Saturday night. I couldn't hold it back any longer. I suppose I had to focus on it to process and get over it. Dr. Charles' class probably wasn't the best place to do it, but I couldn't stop. It came like a huge wave out of nowhere.

Rolling through my mind were all the situations that should have been red flags for me but somehow I'd missed them.

Last fall he went back to school while I was stuck at home commuting to UT Martin and counting down the days until I moved into my dorm on the Knoxville campus. One night he called to ask me if it would bother me if he had a girl as a study partner for his Trigonometry class. Her name was Steph. He explained that the professor assigned the partners and he didn't want to make waves. My red flag should have been the fact that he could have cared less about making waves. Noah thrived on riding the waves he made. He just wanted her as his partner. But I was too naive and trusting. I never had to have my guard up with Joel, and now I may never let it down.

The next red flag should have been the night he showed up drunk at our apartment after a Sigma Chi/Kappa Delta social. The second he walked in I saw a deep red smudge near the collar of his shirt. Lipstick. He assured me it wasn't. "Some drunk bitch ran into me with her face," he slurred. I used my fingernails to scrape the color from his white shirt but it was a futile attempt. Why did it not hit me at that moment? It was Madison's lips I went to bed with that night. I actually believed the story about the run in with a drunk girl.

I guess I could give myself some credit for the Ivy revelation. I did see a red flag even though no one else did. Friday night, I trusted my gut enough to call him out and I did. And he didn't lie. He told me straight up…every ugly detail. In doing so, he laid the groundwork for me to have significant trust issues.

That's when it hit me…I *knew* of Steph, *saw traces of* Madison, and *tasted* Ivy. Things got worse as our story unfolded. I laid my head on my desk so no one would see the tears pouring from my eyes. Things couldn't get worse. I was broken. They had to start getting better or I may just dissolve in my own sadness.

The sand wafted into clouds of pale as my body surrendered to the slow pull of the deep. My heart and lungs fought to do their jobs in my chest as the water pressure threatened to squeeze me into oblivion. My lungs ached, but water didn't enter them. It was like limbo between life and death and someone was taking their time making up their mind as to whether I would survive this or not. But as of now, it was a slow, painful struggle, and I felt every sensation with a magnitude that threatened to wreck me.

After class, I walked home alone, thinking that is how I was meant to be. Wrecked.

Nine

When I opened the door to our apartment, I breathed some semblance of joy. I didn't think anything could make me happy, but something did. Jake, Sam, Stacy, and Becki were sitting at the kitchen table having what looked like their own private sandwich buffet. Becki was a friend Stacy and I knew from Martin Campus. She transferred when we did, but still lived in the dorms. There was a place set for me, complete with an open Rolling Rock. These four were my lifeline. They were the only reason I was upright.

Before I had a chance to drop my backpack, they were up, standing in a line, waiting their turn to hug me. One by one, their hope for healing filled me temporarily by osmosis.

"We can't have a party without some tunes," Sam yelled as he ran to his iPod already plugged into our speaker dock. "There's nothing a little Pearl Jam can't fix." He winked at me when he hit play. Sam and I shared an obsession with Pearl Jam. We knew every lyric to every song. We had long conversations about our thoughts on the underlying meanings behind songs like "Deep," "Corduroy" and "State of Love and Trust." A calm resonated through me when the first notes of "Amongst the Waves" poured out of the speakers. Music was my drug. It was as close to a high as I imagined I could get at that moment. I smiled at Sam and blew him a kiss for knowing exactly what I needed to drown out the ache in my heart. Funny how music connected the dots between me and the men in my life.

As I walked over to the table, Jake looked up and patted the seat next to him. "Right here, beautiful."

Sometimes his words melted me.

All four of them skipped their afternoon classes and we just hung out. We danced and sang like idiots and laughed until our sides were splitting. Jake and Sam were trying to outdo each other telling Stacy, Becki, and I about all the shenanigans that went on in their dorm freshman year. Every now and then, a story would include Noah, and their voices would get quiet. I could see their brains backpedaling to change to a story that didn't include him.

The day turned to night, and we finished our lunch leftovers for dinner. Soon Stacy was locked in the bedroom studying and Becki left for work.

"You sure you'll be okay?" Jake rubbed my arm as we stood by the door.

Sam walked over pointing to his iPod. "You want Eddie here with you?"

"Thanks, Sam, but I've got tons of Pearl Jam on my iPod."

"No, I meant the real Eddie Vedder...I know people..." Sam's biggest shtick was his claim he had unbelievable connections with celebrities. He could fit it into most conversations, and he always got the reaction he was going for—all of us in stitches.

"Even though Eddie Vedder is probably the only person who could take my mind off the last couple days, I need to turn off all my distractions and get some work done."

"Okay, but don't say I didn't offer." He winked

One more big hug and a peck on the cheek from both Jake and Sam was just what I needed to get me through to bedtime.

Jake turned before he shut the door behind him. "We are right upstairs. You need *anything*, you come get one of us. Okay?" Sam nodded in agreement and they both gave me another quick peck on the cheek.

I smiled.

"Okay?"

"Yes. Yes. Okay. Now go study!" The last thing I needed on my plate was worrying about their grades as they tried to nurse me back to whole. They couldn't fail out. I would never make it without them.

Stacy and I laid in our beds in the dark and talked until the wee hours of the morning. She played a great Devil's advocate. Sometimes it pissed me off, but sometimes it helped me to see things from someone else's point of view; a view that wasn't skewed by my own weaknesses.

"So, what now?" she asked as though there was no question in my mind that I was done with Noah.

"I guess I wait and see if I can trust him again."

"What?!" I heard her sheets rustle so I knew she sat up to yell that at me.

"He came by Saturday afternoon and really opened up to me. He's devastated, Stacy. He still loves me and says he wants me to give him another chance. I have already started trying to let go. But if he wants to try to work it out, I can't say no."

"You can't or you won't?"

"Both."

She sighed and flopped back down. Then silence. Nothing. I hated disappointing people. I just wanted people to be happy with me. Maybe that's why this hurt so much. Noah was right, I felt it was something *I* was missing that made him stray. If he had been happy with me, he wouldn't have gone elsewhere for sex. And I hadn't heard from him since Saturday afternoon, maybe he *wasn't* as devastated as he seemed. Maybe he *would* be okay without me.

"Gracie." Stacy's voice startled me.

"What?"

"I wasn't going to tell you this because I am so effing pissed at him..."

"What?" My heart raced. Did I want to know what she was going to say? I didn't know whether to hold my ears or jump up onto her bed to get a better listen.

"He called me today."

The whole world fell away from me at that moment. My ears got hot, I started to quiver, and I sat up so fast I cracked my head on the bottom of her bunk.

"Ow. Shit. Well...well? What did he say? You better tell me every word he said and in the exact way he said them!" I wrestled with the sheets and blankets until I was standing, staring straight at her.

I could see her face in the strips of moonlight coming through our blinds. I was breathless. Every sweet, romantic thing he had ever said to me came rolling back into my mind. My heart puffed up with anticipation. He loved me. He really loved me. He called.

"He called to check on you. He wanted to make sure you were all right. And..."

"And?" Tears streamed down my hot cheeks, and my chest heaved. My body hummed. This was my Noah. This was the romantic side no one ever expected. That's when I realized I still had hope.

"And he asked if I thought you would forgive him and take him back."

I froze. Images of him smiling and us walking on campus laughing and holding hands flooded my brain. I was Alice falling down the rabbit hole of beautiful, happy memories of what we once were. I remembered the shock of our first kiss, the day in his room when he told me he loved me the first time, his tearful goodbye when he left for school, and the night I gave a piece of myself to him that no one else could ever have. And the reason why his cheating hurt so much. The night we made love for the first time, my soul married his. How do you undo that simply and without pain? You can't. You just can't. The pain was there as a means to hold us together. I was only a partial person without him. I knew I couldn't live like that.

"And you said..."

"I told him you'd be a fucking idiot to take a piece of shit like him back. That's what I told him. Then I slammed down the phone and ran up to Jake and Sam's. That's when we decided to order out. Don't *tell* me you are even considering this! Please. You are so much smarter than that."

All of my emotions intertwined, and I couldn't stand still. I was still in so much pain from his betrayal, but at the same time, I was elated that he was proving he really wanted me back. He really did love me. I didn't have to say a word, Stacy knew what I was thinking. She grumbled something about spending the semester feeling like she was living a repeat episode of some awful soap opera. But it wouldn't be like that. Yes, he had to prove himself, and his trustworthiness had to be flawless for it to work. He needed to understand that he was the one responsible for rebuilding my trust and that wasn't going to be an easy task. I was even more insecure about myself than I ever was before. There was the potential for him to translate "insecure" as "clingy," but he was going to have to bite that bullet and help me through. It was all on him. He had a lot to prove. He had to prove to me that I could trust him. He had to prove he would never make that mistake again. He wouldn't.

He couldn't.

I fell asleep with a smile on my face, still listening to Pearl Jam, "Oceans." My gentle lullaby that night was Eddie's voice telling me it was okay to think about Noah's touch and to hold on even when the currents shift because he will be there.

Ten

Like clockwork, over the next week and a half, Noah texted me three times every day. He had a copy of my schedule from when he was pledging so he basically knew my every move. I could count on a *Good Morning* text before I even left the apartment, some sort of *Hope your day is going well* text on my way home for lunch and a *Sweet Dreams* text in the evening, sometimes just as I laid my head on my pillow. I didn't see him at all, and I never once texted him back the first week. He remained focused on me regardless. The second week I started texting him back.

It was Friday, exactly two weeks since the night of the formal and just a day short of two weeks since Noah had come to the apartment pleading his case. We hadn't laid eyes on each other since. He wasn't being pushy, he was giving me space. Stacy and I did absolutely nothing the weekend in between but watch movies and eat ice cream. Jake and Sam popped in a couple times but said they felt out of place in, what they dubbed, "the estrogen fest."

I was on my way home from class wondering if Stacy made good on her promise to surprise me with awesome plans for the evening when my phone buzzed. I answered it right away and said, "You have amazing plans for us, don't you?"

"Uh…I hope you think they're amazing."

Not for a second did I suspect the call to be from anyone other than Stacy. I certainly wasn't expecting to hear Noah's voice. I stopped dead in my tracks on the sidewalk and steadied myself against the fence woven between the Science buildings.

"Noah."

"Hey."

I silently tried to talk myself out of a full-blown panic attack. There was no way I could speak more than one word at a time.

"Gracie?"

"Yeah."

"God, it's so good to hear your voice. Baby, I miss you so much."

I nodded. I knew full well he couldn't see me, but I needed to focus on not hyperventilating.

"I need to see you. Can you come out to the party tonight? No pressure. I just want you to be near me."

I looked around nervously for someone to hand the phone to so I could outrun the panic that was filling my chest. I hadn't expected it to be this hard to accept Noah back into my heart, but it was like my heart was warning me to run as fast as I could.

"I'm expecting too much. I get it. I'll let you go. Thank you for answering." There was a long silence. I could hear him breathing. "Bye, Gracie."

"Bye."

I spent the next three hours trying to talk Stacy into going to the party with me. I knew I would never be able to walk in alone. I wasn't sure how my body would react when I saw him. She finally agreed then called Jake to see if he would come, too.

Stacy begrudgingly helped me pick something out to wear that was understated and simple. A concert tee, olive drab cargo capris and my Doc Martens. The three of us walked to the Sigma Chi house just as the sun was going down.

"Would you look at this line? Gracie, we will never get in."

"I'll text Noah that we are here and we'll see what happens." Part of me wanted him to ignore the text so Stacy would insist we leave and I wouldn't have to deal with whatever was coming my way on the other side of that door. I thought I'd be excited when I was finally this close to him. I wasn't. I was scared to hurt again.

Hey. Stacy, Jake and I are in line. Outside.

Noah must have been standing at the door because he was at the back of the line in seconds.

"I'm so glad you came." His whole face lit up and he was smiling from ear to ear. He shook Jake's hand and hugged Stacy. I could tell he was relieved that I was there but he was guarded in how to greet me. He took my hand and nodded in the direction of the door. He was nervous. I was nervous. Stacy was still pissed off and poor Jake was along for the ride. We passed to the front of the long line and went right inside.

When I realized skipping the line was a privilege saved for the brothers' guests, I gloated with an ear-to-ear grin. In my mind, I was beauty queen waving all the way.

Apparently, we also didn't have to wait for beer. I had no doubt that was a staple that never stopped flowing at Sigma Chi, no matter the day. Stacy got over her anger at him after they walked away from me and chatted in an out-of-the-way spot. I was almost close enough to read their lips. But with the pounding music and the roaring conversation and laughter that filled the lobby, I couldn't begin to *hear* anything they said. Although, Stacy's "if you hurt her again I will kill you" was loud and clear on her mouth as she poked him in the chest and walked back over to me. Then things were mostly back to normal. Mostly.

I spent the first twenty minutes casually talking and laughing with Noah, Jake and Stacy while I tried to nurse the nagging ache in my gut that made me feel everything I did that night needed to be perfect.

Noah walked away from us a couple times to help with party-goers at the door. Each time I watched him like a hawk remembering what it felt like to lose track of him at Jake and Sam's party.

Something about having both Jake and Stacy there eased my nerves a bit. Noah couldn't do something stupid. They would surely kill him. There was no doubt he knew that.

When Stacy's favorite song came on, she grabbed Jake and I and pushed us toward the dance floor.

"I really don't feel like dancing," I yelled over the music straining so hard I made myself cough.

"Come on, Gracie. It'll feel good to let loose a little." Jake smiled, his eyes pleading.

"I got her." Noah called to them from behind me. "You guys go have some fun and I will stick with Gracie. Won't let her out of my sight." He draped his arm over my shoulder and I melted when his warm skin touched the back of my neck.

Stacy looked torn. She really loved parties for the chance to show off what a good dancer she was, but at the same time she waited for the okay from me. I nodded and smiled. She seemed hesitant, but made a sign with her hand for me to call her if I needed her. I nodded again. She locked arms with Jake and they were off.

"Can we go to my room for a little bit?" His voice was hopeful, and I wanted to be alone with him. I wanted to see what it felt like now.

It was nice to walk into a quiet room, away from the chaos. Noah flipped on some music and we cut through the discomfort with small talk. The stories he told of what went on inside that house were unbelievable.

We ran out of things to say and an awkward silence seeped in. He poured me a beer from the pitcher on the coffee table. He handed me my cup and leaned in to kiss me. My stomach lurched. I kissed back, but that sickness in my stomach was something I had been trying to swallow since I got there. I was mad at myself for kissing back. I was essentially giving in to something I didn't want to do, but I ached for his lips on mine. It made me feel dirty because he wasn't all mine anymore. I'd unwillingly shared him with Steph, Madison, and Ivy. A part of me wondered if I really knew this person I loved. I would never have given up my virginity if I had a doubt that he would revert back to his old self. He was going to have to work for this. Just as Stacy and Jake showed up at Noah's door, his phone rang with an obnoxious ring tone. I went over to pour them some beer from our pitcher when I realized Noah was whispering. I glanced up at him and held my breath, hoping I could make out what he was saying. All I heard was "Okay, bye." Pretty innocuous. But it was the look on his face that almost knocked the wind out of me.

"Who was that?"

"Uh, no one."

"Seriously, who was it?" I giggled a nervous laugh out of sheer discomfort. This wasn't funny. I gave him the "we are doing this different this time, no lies" look.

"Uh...it...it was Madison... It was a number I didn't recognize. I didn't know it was her."

"What?!" I was a very gentle person. I supported PETA, wished I could be in the Peace Corp, and was a member of Greenpeace. But when he said her name, I was ready to change all that and beat the pulp out of her.

"Sorry." He seemed sincere.

"So, what did she want?"

"Actually, she didn't want to upset you, so she was calling to see if you were here tonight because she wouldn't come if you were."

"Oh, that's mighty nice of her. So she knows I know...about her...and you."

I turned and looked at Jake and Stacy who were sheepishly turning to leave Noah's room to head toward the pounding music but stopped when they heard the conversation.

"Yeah, she really feels terrible."

"It's in the past, Noah. Maybe you should tell her I am over it and she should just come out."

"Yeah, right." He chuckled nervously. And Jake and Stacy looked stunned.

I didn't budge. My fists clenched behind my back and my pulse rose.

"Really? Are you serious?"

"Sure. Better yet, let me call her." He looked really nervous, but slowly handed me his phone. I clicked over to recent calls and hit the callback button next to the last incoming call.

"Hey Noah." I could hear her smiling when she answered. Sickening.

"Hey, Madison, it's Gracie, I'm calling you from Noah's phone."

"Uh, okay."

"Hey, listen, I just wanted you to know that Noah and I are fine. I am not mad about what happened. We got through it and I don't want you to think you have to avoid me or check with him before coming out to parties with your sisters."

"Oh…oh…are you serious? That is so cool of you."

"Yeah, well that's how much I trust him. It's all good. I would love to hang with you. Why don't you just head over, the band's about to start."

"Oh, wow. Char get your jeans back on, we are going to Sigma Chi!" she yelled. "Hey, thanks…thanks for being so cool about this."

"No thanks necessary. See you soon?"

"Yeah, see you soon."

I hit end and turned with a nasty grin on my face. Stacy and Jake were still frozen at the door when my head exploded.

"I'm going to bust her fucking head in. I can't wait until she gets here! She won't know what hit her." The words slithered from my lips like venom.

Stacy poured me another beer as I paced around the room. Noah gawked at me, stunned. He picked up his phone and turned his back to me.

"I will kill her." My words came out all breathy because my heart and lungs were trying desperately to keep up with my adrenaline. I was convinced I could shred her.

"Oh, no, no, no. This isn't good. *Noah!*" Stacy spun around toward Noah.

He held up his finger as I heard him say, "Tonight's not going to be a good night to come. Just stay. Just please don't come tonight."

And with that, I pounded the freshly poured beer, and Stacy, Jake and I headed out to see the band. Head banging music was exactly what I needed at that moment. Noah soon found us and we let loose with the band. Danced our asses off.

Noah told us he had to head upstairs, but I missed where he said he was going when the speaker let out some nasty feedback that caused everyone to simultaneously hold their ears. Stacy and Jake said they were ready to leave and they begged me to come with them. But I wanted to stay. I needed to be close to Noah that night after finding out he may still be talking to Madison. I found him upstairs sitting at a big table playing poker with some of the brothers. No girls around him. Party going on downstairs without him. Not a bad sign. Maybe I didn't have anything to worry about anymore.

I breathed in a sigh of relief and walked over to sit on his lap. He laid his left arm across my lap and rubbed my leg with his thumb. My whole body warmed at the feel of his familiar gentle touch. He pressed me into him and held me there for a couple of seconds and I had to catch my breath. My body was craving his. A couple brothers looked up and winked at me, a couple said, "hey," and the ones I didn't know just kept playing. I could do this. I could be this girl...for him. I would try harder to be who he needed me to be so this could work. My heart fluttered when his hand slowly made its way toward the space between my thighs. I knew what this meant. I reached down and squeezed his leg and turned to look at him. He smirked. "I fold." He craved me, too. We excused ourselves to his room.

We made love for the first time since the truth came out. And I pretended it didn't feel different.

Eleven

Noah fell asleep with his body as close to me as it could get, but I wasn't thinking about him touching me, my brain was on overdrive. A flash of Joel and I laying on the hood of his car looking for shooting stars sped through my mind. Breaking up with Joel was the hardest thing I ever had to do. He was so sad, and all I could say was, "I just need to see what this is I am feeling for Noah." I couldn't ignore the feelings I had for him any longer. The gentle vibrations he inflicted on me when we were together began to surge through my veins even when I was alone and just thinking of him.

That feeling of pure electricity became my drug. My skin hummed when he touched me. Palpable energy ran in waves under my skin when he kissed me. My breath quickened when he'd just show up and surprise me on nights we weren't scheduled together. Sometimes I couldn't speak when he drove me home from work—I would just smile. My body almost burst with anticipation when I would wait for him to pick me up for a date. Now I lay next to Noah wondering where that electricity was and what my future held. And if I was honest, I had to admit a small part of me was starting to wonder if breaking up with Joel for Noah was a mistake.

Part of me felt hopeless, like everything around me was crumbling, and I could do nothing to stop it. The other part of me was hopeful that maybe I could rebuild what was broken to ensure that Noah and I would be stronger than ever. As I lay under his body, I felt as though the fire we once had between us was only burning embers. They were still lit but dim. This broke my heart even further.

I rolled to my side and pushed my back into Noah's chest. He sighed, nuzzled his face into my neck and squeezed my naked body even closer. I closed my eyes but knew I was nowhere near sleep. I floated between the past and the present with sweet memories of the Noah who wanted me so badly he would change who he was to get me. I got a glimpse of that Noah the day after the formal when he pulled open his heart for me and let all his feelings pour out. I tucked that memory away for the times when I doubted I was enough to breathe life back into the embers that were not far from being cold dust.

Mid-August, Summer before Sophomore year

It had been two weeks since I broke up with Joel. Noah and I were on our way home from the movies when he pulled onto a wide shoulder of the windy back road and put his car in park. He turned and took my face in his hands. Without a word, he kissed me like only he could.

"I have something for you."

"What is it? A surprise?" I had no idea what to expect. Our relationship was still in the early infancy stages when everything feels new and exciting.

"A song. I want you to listen to a song."

"All right." My stomach started to churn. I was so glad I didn't have popcorn at the movies. I could control my nerves since I didn't have to worry about puking.

"I have a hard time saying what I feel, so I thought he could say it for me."

With that, he scanned the songs on his iPod and hit play. I listened as the song began. I knew this song but couldn't place it. Then it hit me, it was Jack Johnson's "Better Together." I giggled softly. I never thought I'd see this romantic side to Noah. I sat and watched him fidget. He was so nervous, and I couldn't figure out why. I was the unlikely match for him. He could have anyone he wanted. Yet *he* was nervous to tell me he wanted us to be together.

After the first verse, I didn't know what to say. Was it stupid to say, "I think it's better when we're together, too?" Would he burst out laughing and I would wish I burst into flames? I looked down at my hands as I listened to the chorus. I didn't know where Noah was looking. I was too nervous to look up to find out.

After the second verse, Noah reached over and took my face in his hands. He lifted my chin and aligned our eyes.

He smiled the boyish grin that made my stomach fill with butterflies, and he leaned in and kissed me again. Slow and gentle as Jack played on. Where did the bad boy go? I couldn't believe he was being so thoughtful and had planned this whole thing to tell me he was falling for me. What happened to being a pussy? Marie would die if I told her how beautiful his heart really was. But I would keep that little secret all to myself. Holding it deep in my heart, all for me, seemed to make it even more precious. I was in awe of him at that moment.

His kiss became stronger and deeper as a wave of warmth and dizziness came over me. This had to be love. Real love. I had never had my body react to someone like it did when he kissed me. He pulled away and looked into my eyes, his hands still holding my face. He leaned back in and started the sultry dance with his tongue. Without missing a beat, he reached for my hand.

Jack Johnson swooned about his love sleeping next to him. Noah took my hand and pressed it onto the top of his thigh with his. My hand was dangerously close to a part of him I had never touched. What did he expect me to do? Or did he expect anything? My heart raced. I wasn't ready for our touching to go beyond the innocent touching we were already doing.

Jack Johnson must've said the word *together* a hundred times in the song. Noah and I together. I didn't even know what that would look like. My hand shook a little on his thigh, and I worried about having to tell him I wasn't ready. The good-girl guilt set in. I pulled away and looked around, very aware that at any moment we could be caught "parking" and my parents would kill me. Then I remembered they were gone for two weeks. I looked at the clock on the dashboard. I had an hour before my grandfather would be at our house. He was supposed to be staying with Hannah and I while they were out of town. I had just had my nineteenth birthday and Hannah was sixteen, and we were still babysat when our parents had to go out of town. Suddenly, a thought crossed my mind, but it wasn't like any thought I'd ever had before. It was deceitful and risky. I could lie and tell my grandfather I was staying at a friend's. He knew Hannah had overnight plans so this way he didn't need to come over at all. Noah could spend the night with me.

Where the hell did that come from?

Noah must've subliminally sent that message to me. I wouldn't have thought of that on my own. I had only slept overnight with a boy once. Joel. I had gone to his house once when his parents were away. It was safe, though. He knew I wasn't ready for sex so there was no pressure. Some roaming hands, but nothing threatening my virginity.

If I asked Noah to spend the night, it could give him the wrong idea. What if he thought I was ready? What if he didn't take "no" as easily as Joel did? My mind quickly rewound to the night he forcefully held the steel door of Murphy's closed. A shiver ran through me.

Twelve

Finally it was light, the house was coming to life. I hadn't slept all night. Noah was still sleeping. I could hear the brothers on the other side of Noah's door. They were all talking about the party the night before. I looked at the clock, 9:30. I watched Noah sleep as I strained to hear what they were saying.

"Dude, I bagged that hot chick in the short black skirt."

"No way. I think Jonesy tapped that last weekend at the social."

"Shut up, asshole."

"You might wanna wash your pecker, man, she's been around half this house."

Their laughter faded away soon after I heard the side door slam shut. Noah was right, this *was* a tough scene for him to be immersed in. He used to be one of those kind of guys. I remembered Marie describing Noah to me, and those kinds of comments were what she was referring to. I was sure he used to talk that way and brag with his friends but he didn't anymore. He had a tender side no one saw but me. Sure, it made my close friends question what my attraction was to him, besides his obvious physical flawlessness. They didn't need to know all of our details of how we were together. Those details were like our own little secret, and I loved having that secret with him.

Noah rolled over to his stomach and let out a big sigh. I lifted the covers and got a clear view of his beautiful backside. Another one of my beautiful secrets.

But apparently that secret was also shared with a few other women on this campus.

I was startled by the side door slamming again. I couldn't tell who, but someone was in a hurry to leave, that much I knew. There was something sinister about the Sigma Chi house that I couldn't put my finger on. It was like everyone had a secret they wouldn't tell. And I had no desire to hear about them. Regardless, I enjoyed being at the Sigma Chi house. I thought I was pretty lucky to have access to the brothers all the time and not just during parties. Some of them accepted me quickly and some wouldn't give me the time of day. I got the feeling some felt I was a threat to the tough, emotionless façade they protected so dearly. The brothers of Sigma Chi had the reputation of being beautiful, and most of them came from family money, but not more than a handful of them had girlfriends. I almost felt like they looked at steady relationships as a weakness they needed to make sure they didn't cave to.

Noah lifted half his body onto mine and draped his arm over my chest. His breath was still deep and steady so I knew he was still sleeping.

I always did my best thinking while Noah slept. I lay next to him, and ran my fingers across his back as I ran through the events of the night before in my mind. I picked apart Noah's every move and all the things I shouldn't have said or done. I needed to be careful because I almost lost him once. I knew making the wrong move could push him a little further away, and the last thing I wanted was for him to start looking at the single brothers and wanting that freedom.

I wrapped an arm and a leg around him and pressed our naked bodies together. He didn't budge.

I kissed his pouty stale beer scented lips. That got his attention. His eyes popped open at the same time I felt the attention of something else growing against me.

"Morning," I whispered.

"And a good one it will be," he answered.

He kissed me deeply. I wrapped my arms around his neck and held him as close as I could get him. Soon his whole body pressed me into the mattress, and he made a move that definitely made us as close as we could get to each other. He felt good. Powerful and in charge. Somehow surrendering to him made him even sexier. I enjoyed still being deemed the "innocent" one. I wanted him to teach me, show me how to love him.

Noah and I had a chemistry I couldn't explain. Stacy said it was the Dom/Sub relationship because I just followed his lead. I did follow his lead but mainly because I was so inexperienced. Sure, sometimes it felt a little like sex was what he did *to* me and not what we did *together*. This was one of those times. He finished with a low groan and a shiver. Just one time it would be nice if he'd wait for me to be *finished*, too.

"What are you thinking about?" His voice was hoarse and quiet as he rolled off of my body.

"You."

"What about me?"

"How much I love the way you make love to me." I lied. I knew he hadn't just made love to me. He fucked me. But, I guess there was a part of me that thought dropping those kinds of hints would be less confrontational and therefore more tolerated by Noah. It made me sad that we had lost some of our connection. Our connection was so much less than what it used to be and what I craved the most.

"Oh. Hey, do you want to go get breakfast?"

Way to change the subject.

"You don't want to just hang here a little bit?" I hoped we could try to connect again.

He sat up, threw the covers off, uncovering my very naked body, and grabbed some sweats off the back of the door and slipped them on.

"I gotta piss." He headed out into the hallway, leaving the door partially open. I frantically gathered all of the covers and piled them on top of me, feeling very vulnerable. Nice of him to leave the door open. He knew I was lying naked in a house filled with horny guys. I wished he still made me feel protected, like he valued what I was only offering *him*. He used to...I think. Didn't he?

I wrapped myself in all the covers and moved to the edge of the bed just as he walked back in.

"Noah!"

He froze and looked at me like I slapped him.

"The door? Can you please shut it? Someone could walk..."

"Oh good Lord, *Re. Lax!*" he snapped as he reached over and pushed the door shut with a slam. "You think these guys have never seen a naked girl before?"

"They've never seen *this* naked girl. I thought you'd want to keep it that way." My voice trailed off, disappointment evident in my whisper.

That beer I drank the night before was begging its way out. I stood and tried to find all my clothes so I could quickly dress and run down the hall to pee. He was being so insensitive. This Noah scared me.

I usually felt lucky for all the behind-the-scenes stuff I was privy to as a Sigma Chi girlfriend. However, "lucky" was not the word I would use to describe a post-party girls' bathroom. It was horrible. I chose the stall with the least amount of mess after turning down three clogged toilets and one filled with puke.

When I walked back down the hall to Noah's room, I heard his music. I loved that he liked music as much as I did. We'd been to quite a few concerts over the last year. Music was my lifeline. It spoke the things I couldn't find the words for. I remembered Noah's collaboration with Jack Johnson and was sure Noah felt the same way.

I slowed when I got to Noah's door. *Breathe. Happy Gracie.* I bopped into his room singing along with the Violent Femmes, ready to start our day.

He flipped off the music, which was okay because the next verse of that song made me cringe. He was dressed in jeans and a faded concert T-shirt of a band even I had never heard of. Blazing Buttholes. Weird.

"Ya know, they ruin that song with that verse." He tucked his wallet into his back pocket and grabbed his backpack, which was odd, but I was more curious about his comment than I was about the backpack so I started with that as we walked out the door and into the morning sunshine.

"Which verse? The next one that says the f-word?" I agreed. I hated that line.

"Nah, the ML-thing."

What the freak was he talking about? The Violent Femmes were known for songs with shock value. Their lyrics were quick and to the point. Why was he being so cryptic? "Add it Up" was definitely not cryptic. I ran through the verses in my head. I tilted my head and looked up at him when it hit me.

"ML-thing? Make love?" The sun was so bright, I had to squint to look up at him.

His body jolted like something shocked him, and his face curled into a strange expression as we reached the sidewalk. I wanted so badly to believe he was making love to me before we got out of bed. Was this a roundabout way of making sure I knew how he felt about the sensitivity of that act? I felt a different kind of distance between us. One I didn't recognize. My heart called out to his. *Please answer.*

"Hey, I have to study for my Business Admin exam tomorrow, so I gotta go."

Ah, the reason for the backpack.

"What about breakfast?"

And why are you freaking out about the words "make love"?

"Yeah, I don't have the time I thought I did."

My heart called to him again. I stood at the end of the driveway of Sigma Chi. He leaned in and kissed me quickly on the cheek, then saluted and walked away. I spun on my heel and headed toward my apartment in the opposite direction which seemed illustrative of how I felt about us at the moment. Going different directions.

Thirteen

The two-block walk to my apartment felt different. I woke up a proud Sigma Chi girlfriend, but each sentence between us that morning chased away the pride, and I was left with shame. I no longer felt like that girl doing the "beauty queen wave" to all the passersby who saw me leave the Sigma Chi house in the morning. Instead, I hung my head and quickly shuffled past everyone, hoping they didn't see my smeared makeup and bedhead. This was less of the celebratory parade of a few months ago and more like the infamous college euphemism, "walk of shame."

As I walked, Joel came to mind. I hated the feeling that I may be losing Noah just a little more than a year after ending the stale boredom that was my relationship with Joel. Poor guy, he held on for dear life.

I had never cheated on anyone in my life, but what I had done to Joel was unfair. I knew I had to tell him about the kiss. I thought maybe we would fight and he would ask me point blank, "Do you want to be with him?" I did. I knew I did. But I didn't know how I was going to live through breaking someone's heart. My breath hitched as I remembered that phone call.

Early August, Summer before Sophomore Year

The morning after the Jack Johnson serenade I sat on my bed trying to calm my nerves. I took a deep breath and dialed. I kept my hand on my chest as if holding my heart together would protect Joel's as well. I hated that it was by phone, but he had taken a second job, so by mid-summer, we didn't see each other at all.

"Hello?"

"Hi."

"Hey, beautiful!" His voice was so cheery. He said it with a delighted sigh.

Oh good grief. This guy was never in a bad mood. *Please be in a bad mood so this doesn't hurt so much.*

"How was work?" *Please say the most beautiful girl in the world walked into your restaurant and swept you off your feet. Please, Joel.*

"Doesn't matter, I'm here with you now."

"Yeah."

"Sweetheart, what's wrong?"

"Listen, there's something I have to tell you." My stomach was already in knots and I hadn't even told him I wanted to see other people yet.

"Um, okay." I heard the clunk of the footrest go down on his favorite chair. "What?" There was fear in his voice. We hadn't talked about Noah since the night of the fireworks when I called to let him know I was home. But I had a feeling he had started to suspect something.

"This isn't something you are going to want to hear. I want you to know that I do love you, but..."

"There's the *but* I knew was coming. What did that creep do to you?!"

"No, it's not like that. Joel..."

"Just tell me already." He remained calm, but there was more urgency in his voice than I was used to hearing.

I would just have to spit it all out in one long confession. If I stopped, I'd never get it all out. "Joel, the night of the fireworks, I kissed him. I kissed Noah. It was just a small kiss, nothing romantic. Just a peck. And..."

"You kissed him?"

No. No. No. Don't interrupt me.

I was running solely on momentum, and he stopped me dead in my tracks. I needed to get the last part out, the part where I broke up with him.

"Yeah." The line went quiet. I actually thought he hung up.

"Hello?

"Say it again."

"What?" I heard what he said, but I needed a moment to prepare to say those words, and before I stopped this time, I needed to break right into the *I think we need to see other people* part. My heart pounded, and my legs shook so badly the pompoms that hung from my bed post fell to the floor.

"Say it again." His voice was sad and low.

Here goes. I sucked in the deepest breath I'd ever taken, and I held it for a second, hoping I would faint before I had to do this again. "We kissed, Joel. Noah and I kissed the night of the fireworks. And, that's why I think we should..."

"Wow," he interrupted again.

"Wow?"

"I was just hoping it would hurt less the second time you said it. It didn't."

"Please don't hate me."

"Hate you? Babe, I love you with all my heart. We will get through this. We just have to set up some boundaries so he can't pressure you ever again."

Pressure me? Shit. He didn't pressure me. As much as I fought with my mind over it, I wanted that kiss with every ounce of my being. I had hoped Joel would just hate me and break up with me. It seemed desperate of him to hang on so tightly when I was halfway gone already.

As guilty as I still felt for cheating on Joel, replaying that conversation in my mind served a purpose, making the walk of shame go by faster. I walked up to my apartment building and repeated that last thought in my mind, "It seemed desperate of him to hang on so tightly when I was halfway gone already." Maybe I should take my own advice.

I looked up when I walked into the lobby and heard the elevator doors open. Sam and Jake were both laughing as they walked out. But when they saw me, their faces fell. They sped up to get to me.

"Gracie?" Jake said it but Sam's eyes showed the same concern I heard in Jake's voice. .

"Hey guys."

"You okay?" Sam spoke and Jake hugged me. I melted.

"I don't know, actually. Noah is just acting a little weird, that's all."

"You have plans today?" Sam smiled as he spoke.

"Want to hang with us?" Jake's voice was hopeful.

"You need anything at the grocery store?" Sam pointed at me like I needed to know I was the one he was talking to.

I looked around the lobby. "Oh, oh, you're talking to me? Thanks for clearing that up."

"Smart ass," Sam chuckled and pushed my shoulder back.

"So, you didn't answer any of our questions." Jake pretended he was annoyed but I knew he really wasn't. He had more patience than anyone I knew. I giggled at the way they were taking turns firing those questions at me like they had rehearsed it on the way down. I felt the stress leave my body. These two guys were such a gift to me. They were like my Heaven. My safe place in the midst of confusion and hurt. They came as a set. Both would run any direction to catch me when I fell.

"So, what are we doing today?" I asked. I didn't even have to say "yes," they knew my answer.

"We're just headed to grab a speaker wire, fix a speaker" — Jake pointed over his shoulder toward *Noise Boys*, the stereo store on the corner—"then we're getting the car and heading for groceries."

"Oooo fun!" I said sarcastically with a big grin.

They both cocked their heads and gave me the "because you've got better plans?" look.

"Okay. I'll run upstairs and shower. Come down to my apartment after you fix the speaker. I need a few things at the store." I hopped into the elevator, and they headed out onto the sidewalk. Opposite directions. *Deja vu.* I just did the same thing with Noah. But, somehow this time the familiar directional separation felt comfortable, and I wondered why there was a difference.

The doors closed and I pushed the button for my floor. Why did Noah walking in the opposite direction cause me anxiety when Jake and Sam doing the same thing didn't?

Ding.

The elevator reached my floor at the same time I reached my conclusion.

Because I knew Jake and Sam would come back for me.

Fourteen

November, Fall Semester, Junior Year

Stacy shook me awake. I was so disoriented because it was dark. I forgot it was a Saturday night. I kept blinking to make it brighter in our room.

"Party. Sigma Chi. Get up!"

One of the things I loved most about college was the freedom and the ability to nap at *any* time of the day without anyone nagging you about all the chores you could be doing. Another thing I loved was the freedom to take a nap at 8 pm so we could start partying at 11 and go long into the wee hours of the morning.

Right. Tonight was another party. Going from a life of having never been drunk to drinking three or four times a week was exhausting. Maybe God was punishing me for being a party girl by making things unsettled between Noah and I. No. The God I knew wouldn't do that, but I am pretty sure He wouldn't be too happy with me these days either.

I didn't see the romantic side of Noah often anymore. I wasn't sure why it was so hard to find. I felt like it was just behind his heart, but somehow not penetrating the muscle around it. Something tough was keeping that gentle side out. But I'd be damned if I wasn't going to try my hardest to find it again.

"Should I wear these?"

Stacy turned and nodded with a mouthful of toothpaste.

I had just gotten the coolest navy blue, low-rise, wide-legged linen pants. Very vintage hippie which made them so "me." I usually just wore jeans and cute top out to parties, but I looked forward to dropping Noah's jaw with my new outfit. He'd been increasingly distant since the Sunday he ditched me for breakfast a couple weeks ago. I wanted him to see me walk into Sig Chi and decide he didn't want to let me out of his sight. Then, maybe any doubts he might be having would fade away.

I completed my outfit with a navy bandeau top that matched the pants and a gauzy sheer shirt. I knew my bare stomach would peek out under the cropped cut while I was dancing and Noah loved that I had my belly button pierced. I looked on the outside like I used to feel on the inside, confident, fun, and funky. Because that's who he fell in love with. At the last minute I slid a wide headband on to help hold back my new bangs and Stacy said it was the perfect accessory.

"You look absolutely 'Gracie' tonight! Adorable." Jake winked when he spoke. He and Jessica were headed out for the night and met us on the elevator. Jake's eyes didn't leave me or my body. The corner of his mouth curved up just enough that it made me wonder what he was thinking. When his eyes reached mine, he winked again. My stomach flipped. It was obvious I was craving the attention of a beautiful guy because I may have exaggerated what just happened in my mind.

Jessica never sincerely smiled when Jake gave me compliments. She always threw a pained grimace on, feigning comfortable agreement. I usually felt bad. But tonight Jake knew exactly what I needed before seeing Noah, so Jessica would have to deal.

"And I look absolutely...what?" Stacy teased.

"Gorgeous!" Jake smiled and winked.

"Yeah, yeah. Too little, too late, Jake." She pretended she was disappointed, but she was beaming at his choice of adjective.

Stacy and I walked with Jake and Jessica to the end of the block. They turned and headed who knows where. We only had one more block to get to Sigma Chi where Noah would come out and rescue us from the long line, and I could do my mental "beauty queen wave" again. I think Stacy had her own wave, too, which made me smile.

We waited in line for a good twenty minutes when Noah finally answered his cell phone.

"Yo."

"Noah. Stacy and I are waiting at the end of the line. The line that's not moving."

"Well, I'm a little tied up at the moment, Gracie." My name came through the phone with a sarcastic sting.

"Come on, you always come get us. It will only take you a second, please?"

"You're starting to whine. I'm hanging up now."

"Noah!"

"I'm just kidding. God, Gracie. Relax!"

Stacy and I stood and watched at least five other brothers come out and get their girlfriends before we saw Noah walking our way, smiling at a couple giggly freshmen on his way past. I was ready to explode. If I had remembered it was "Casino Night" I would have made sure Stacy and I were there even earlier and then I wouldn't have had to call him.

Calm down. Calm down. This is going to be the night he starts to remember how lucky he is to have you. Being a nag won't secure that for you.

My little pep talk lifted my spirits. It was a silly thing to be so upset over, especially when you compared it to cheating. I imagined I was waving at all the girls gawking at my hot boyfriend, wondering why we got to cut the line.

Because I sleep with him, honey. I'm the lucky one. Enjoy the line.

His sexy smirk came back as we entered the house. I beamed.

"What are you wearing?" Noah asked with a loud chuckle, announcing to the entire lobby of party-goers that his girlfriend was a dork. I wanted to die. I opened my mouth to respond, with what, I don't know, when he turned to one of the pledges and said, "Can you get "Janis Joplin" and her friend some beers?"

He threw an "I'll be right back," over his shoulder and disappeared into the crowd.

I felt like an idiot. I looked stupid. My newly cut bangs came with issues of not knowing what to do with them, so I thought the wide headband would solve the issue and suit my outfit, too. Apparently not.

I turned to Stacy who had not heard a thing because she was ogling the brothers like she was at a fraternity-boy buffet. She had detailed daydreams of getting her hands on any one of the beautiful boys in front of her. I felt bad for Greg. She'd never cheat, but the way she gawked and what I knew went through her mind was borderline infidelity.

She winked at me and mouthed, "Go find Noah" as she skipped off with Hank, the senior who held the "drive-thru" record in the house. I would have to text her *not* to leave the dance floor with him. I only knew about Hank's "accomplishment" because, along with the perks of being a brother's girlfriend, comes knowledge of things about the brothers that make you want to clean out your ears with bleach. At Sigma Chi, "drive thru" basically meant his room was like a fast-food place and, unbeknownst to the girls who went in, they were just holding a spot in the drive-thru lane. I think his record was twelve. Some of them were "happy meal" orders, meaning more than one girl at a time. Disgusting.

Thinking about Hank's room was only a temporary reprieve from my embarrassment about the "Janis Joplin" comment. Sometimes when Noah was drunk, he would get flustered at house parties like he was the mayor and had to make sure everyone was having a good time. This didn't bother me until he got out of my line of vision, which he was at that moment. When three of the brothers strolled by looking me up and down and nodding with approval, I decided to swallow my insecurity about my outfit and make the best of the night. Doing that meant having Noah by my side.

I found him downstairs doing shots at the bar. It was a lot cooler in the basement so I was glad to find him there. I walked up behind him and slipped my arms around his waist and laid my head against his back. He was sweaty, but he smelled so good. He twisted his body so I had to drop my arms. He stepped away a little as he chuckled and turned to me revealing who he was doing shots with.

"Gracie, this is Lily. Lily, this is Gracie."

Your GIRLfriend?!

"Hi, Lily." I smiled politely. Who knows, maybe I just stole Jessica's pained look. "How do you guys know each other?"

"Noah and I have the same Business Admin class."

My world shook just enough to knock me off balance. He walked away from me that one morning headed to study for his Business Admin exam. Had she met him somewhere? Did he break our breakfast plans to be with her? Oh, God, I hated this feeling. I felt like I was teetering between sanity and insanity. I felt so weak, and I couldn't seem to catch a break.

When the band got there, the party got a little better. Lily was nowhere in sight and Noah stood right behind me on the dance floor. With his hands on my hips, we bounced and thumped our bodies to the beat of the music. I didn't know what it was about the reverberation of a drum beat and your guy's hands on you, but mix that with five or six beers, and you have a good girl that wants to be a bad girl. I pressed my backside into him a little harder just for fun.

The last song ended with a group of girls squealing their heads off and pawing at the lead singer. I turned within the loop of Noah's arms and kissed him on the chin. I tilted my head back and he looked down. I smiled and he smiled back. Wow. Those big dark eyes and pouty lips could almost make me forget all my insecurities. He ran his hands through my hair on either side of my head, knocking my hippie headband to the dance floor. Holding my head still, he leaned down and kissed me deep and passionately.

There you are.

He took my hand and we headed toward the lobby which was between the dance floor and his room. That's when I remembered Stacy. I couldn't disappear while she was with Mr. Drive-Thru, and I didn't see them on the dance floor anymore. I stopped and pulled on Noah's hand, gripping it tighter.

"I have to go find Stacy to tell her where we will be in case she needs me."

"She will be fine. What do you think will happen?"

"It just wouldn't be cool to desert her."

"Whatever." He threw the hand that was holding mine into the air as he let go.

I yelled across the crowd that I would meet him in his room, but my voice was raspy from yelling over the music all night. He wasn't stupid, he knew what we were going there for. He would be there when I got there.

I found Stacy refilling her beer sans Hank. She had bumped into one of the girls that lived next door to us. Amy assured me she and Stacy would leave together, and Stacy promised me she had no plans to do anything with Hank. With that, I was off.

Noah's lights were off. My stomach flipped. Was he in there with someone? I hit the switch and was relieved it was empty. I leaned my forehead against the doorway and tried to settle my mind and my stomach which was too full of beer to do any more flipping.

"Hey, you looking for Noah?" Brad's voice startled me then made me smile. He seemed to be the nicest of the brothers. I liked him.

"Yeah. Have you seen him?" It was hard to not let your mouth fall open when you looked at Brad. His coal black curls sat loosely around his face in almost a bob style. He had crisp green eyes that pierced your mind, as if he were sending you messages and didn't need your permission to do so. I assumed to the girls who wanted him, those messages started with the words, "I would like to…"

I broke his gaze when my pocket buzzed. It was Stacy. She was leaving with Amy.

"Yeah. I just saw him by the dance floor. Looked like he was looking for someone. Pretty sure he's waiting for you," Brad said.

Brad and I walked down the hall until some drunken slut carrying an open bottle squealed, threw herself at him, and they both fell to the floor. I don't think he even needed to send her any messages. Quite honestly, I didn't think she even cared. She would do anything he wanted after she kicked the bottle of vodka she just spilled all over him. I shook my head and went to find Noah.

How lucky was I that I didn't have to look like an idiot to get my guy's attention? Noah was leaning against the wall waiting for me…um…talking to Lily. The closer I got, the clearer I could see how close they were actually standing to each other. It was obvious I was struggling to even hold my guy's attention for longer than four minutes. She giggled and never dropped her gaze from his eyes. He leaned in as he laughed, and it looked like he was moving in for a kiss. I froze.

Lily saw me out of the corner of her eye, and when she looked, Noah looked. They both stayed really calm. No one flinched. I deduced from that, I was overreacting. If they were trying to get away with anything, they would have done the "uncomfortable dance," trying to rearrange their positions and look less shady. *Whew.* When I walked up, I flashed Noah my "are you ready" smile and slid my arm around his waist. He just looked at me like he had no memory of our plans to go to his room together.

"What?"

I didn't know one innocuous word shot at the right velocity could pierce your heart and steal your breath. With that one word he made *me* feel like *I* was interrupting *their* plan when in reality she was *really* interrupting mine. I just stared at him.

"Do. You. Need. Something?"

Are. YOU. Kidding. Me?

"Um."

How can he make me feel so stupid? I am such an idiot, right, Lily?

"Stacy is heading home," I lied. She already left.

His look intimidated me. I had to finish what I wanted to say before he shoved me further into the idiot hole.

"I wanted to make sure I was staying over tonight before she left."

I knew I was staying over. But I wanted Lily to know. I wanted her to know I would be naked soon with the guy she was flirting with. My guy. I puffed up at that thought.

Yeah, bitch, he's mine. Step back and leave... Please. No, erase that "Please." Why was it so hard to be justifiably firm? I can call you a bitch, I have every right. You are making him sway in the wrong direction. Leave. Bitch.

Wow. Even though all of that was in my head, it sure felt good to stand up for myself.

"No. You can go."

I almost forgot that I asked him a question at this point.

"What?"

Please, please, catch me before I fall. Don't crush me in front of her.

"I said no. Go home with Stacy. I will see you tomorrow."

My feet felt like someone had filled my shoes with concrete. I flashed a fake smile, nodded and headed toward the front door. My goal was to get out onto the stoop without falling apart.

The thick wooden door slammed closed behind me with a deep growl. The guttural sound may have been the next nail in my coffin. I'm not sure I had breathed since the last words he spoke. I could see him and Lily through a window still standing in the same spot, same position. They say when you have an insurmountable task, you should take everything one day at a time, one minute at a time. I didn't know how I would get home without falling flat on my face, dissolving onto the street, and sliding down the storm drain where I could be with my own kind. The ugly and the thrown away.

I walked home — one sidewalk square at a time.

Drowning is an awful way to die. Breathing is an involuntary process that keeps your body alive. Keeping your body from breathing when everything in your brain is telling it to breathe is a violent struggle. I was drowning. Holding my breath. My body was convulsing and flailing at the bottom as I begged my body not to breathe. I wanted to beat death, but every ounce of my being knew that holding my breath was only staving off death. I started to succumb to the defeat…

I sat on the curb outside our building and texted Noah two words.

im done

I felt empowered and lost at the same time. I needed to stand up for myself and let Noah know I was worth more than what he was offering, but I wasn't sure he would fight for me. I walked into our place and locked the door behind me. There was a note from Stacy in the spot on the back of the steel door that we reserved for letting each other know of our whereabouts. She found Greg on the walk home and was staying for the night. I was to call her if I needed anything.

I undressed and threw on Noah's Parker Hill High School t-shirt. I dug through the clean laundry pile which was shrinking at the same speed the dirty pile was growing. I found one pair of boy short style panties at the very bottom of the pile. That meant my to-do list the next day consisted of one thing—laundry.

I climbed between the covers and hit play on my iPod, praying for a deep sleep. A loud and demanding knock at the door stopped my heart. By the time I got to the peephole, I had run through all the horror movie murder scenes I'd ever seen that included the "mysterious knock at the door." I was shocked to see Noah through the fisheye lens.

"Hey." I think I spoke before I even opened the door but he didn't need me to say anything.

He stepped in, closed the door behind him and turned the lock. His hands landed on my hips at the same time his eyes rolled. "You're so fucking hot right this minute."

"Am I?" I spoke through clenched teeth. I was so mad at him.

"I need to slide these panties off you right now."

"What about Lily?" He obviously hadn't gotten my text.

"Gracie, she followed me everywhere. I couldn't shake her. I actually hoped you'd get mad so I could have the excuse to come after you and get away from her."

"Noah. That doesn't make any sense. We could have just walked back to your room together." His excuse sounded completely bogus. Maybe he had gotten my text and he was withdrawing his jackass move.

"But maybe I like your place better. It's quieter here and there are more places than a bed to fuck."

"Is that what you like to do to me, Noah? Just fuck me? Why don't you *make love* to me anymore?" I tried to remove his hands that were now inside my panties and tightly grasping each of my ass cheeks, but he was too strong.

"I can make love to you, Gracie." His mouth was on mine before he finished saying my name, and he was walking me backwards to the couch.

"Show me, Noah," I whispered in desperation against his wet lips.

He growled. When the backs of my thighs hit the armrest, he broke our kiss and pushed me backwards onto the cushions. My hips stayed propped up on the arm, and he stood between my knees. There was a fire in his eyes, and I could see there was something smoldering in his jeans when he unzipped and stepped out of them. He peeled my little black boy shorts from my hips and slid them down my legs. He dropped his boxers, took off his shirt and stood there in front of me in all his naked glory.

"Make love, you said?"

I nodded.

"Let me show you."

And that's when he proved to me once again that he no longer remembered how to make love, he only knew how to fuck. I wiped away the tears that streamed down past my hairline, the ones he didn't even notice. To get through the next five minutes, I pretended I liked it that way. I didn't. Inside I was screaming.

Fifteen

Mid-November, Fall Semester, Junior Year

"Want to try?"

I looked at Brad with obvious offense. I couldn't believe what was happening.

"No. Thank you, Brad. I need to go." I pushed his hand out of my face and scanned the room of stoned Sigma Chi brothers, who probably thought I was such a baby. But I didn't care. Noah knew my stance on drugs, yet invited the guys in when they came to his door prepared with small baggies of marijuana and what I soon learned was a water bong.

I watched Brad suck a huge amount of smoke from the top of a transparent red tube. The bubbling sound the water made took my attention off the other guys who were smirking at my tantrum as I stormed toward the door.

"Stop it, Gracie. I told them you were cool. Now, look how you're acting." My back was against the door and he leaned into me with his hand resting above my head. He was talking just above a whisper so no one could hear but me.

"Noah, why did you even let them in? Can't they smoke that somewhere else?"

"It's no big deal, Gracie. It's just pot."

"Do you smoke it with them? Have you been doing drugs, Noah?" I glanced over his shoulder when I realized my voice was significantly louder than a whisper at that point. But the stoners passing the bong were so totally out of it, they heard nothing.

"Settle down. It's not a big deal. You're not going to pull the 'innocent' card are you? Because that card has been void for quite some time, Gracie."

My heart sunk, "What the hell is that supposed to mean?" I knew exactly what it meant.

"Come on, Gracie. You're not that pristine little girl anymore. The one who knew nothing about anything faded away a long time ago. Now you can be fun and a little reckless and stop pretending."

My heart was clenched so tight, I thought I might pass out. What was he saying? Instead of him seeing me for who I really was, for how my heart spoke, he was gauging my worth on the things I'd done up until that point. Things I'd done solely because of him. Some that I regretted. Maybe he was right. I let him pull me away from everything I believed in.

"You think I'd be more fun if I smoked pot with you? Noah, what about that is attractive to you?"

"If you did this for me, that would be hot."

"What?" I looked at him like he was speaking another language.

"Gracie, if you would put your halo away for just one second, you'd see it's really not that big of a deal."

"That's not what you said, Noah. You said it would be hot if I did this *for you*. For you?"

"Yeah, if you sacrificed your 'good girl' thing, just because you were doing it for me, that would be so incredibly hot."

He nailed it. That's what I had been doing for most of our relationship. I looked into his eyes hoping to see a glimmer of hope for us. Maybe he was right. Maybe trying to hold on to my goody-two-shoes attitude was what was driving the rift between us. Was I kidding myself to believe I was still the same Gracie? If I had become a different Gracie, she would have different standards and maybe she would think smoking pot with her boyfriend was just another way to share something together.

"Dude. Noah. You want any?" Brad held up the bong that had made its way around the room and nodded his head in its direction.

"Yeah." Noah started to turn to walk back over to where we had been sitting. He turned back to me and held out his hand. He really wanted me to do this. The smile on his face was one I hadn't seen in a while. It was right between sweet pleading and naughty flirting.

"Noah." I tilted my head a little and bit my bottom lip.

"Fine." He dropped his hand and shook his head as he walked over and took the bong from Brad. I watched him flick the lighter into the valve at the bottom and then he sucked in a deep breath, pulling sadistic smoke fingers up through the water and into his lungs. He closed his eyes and let his head fall back as he held it in as long as he could.

When he opened his eyes and looked back to where I had been standing, I was gone. But when he passed the bong to the right, I took it in my hands and snapped for him to give me the lighter. A smile spread across his face as he exhaled what was left of the smoke through the left corner of his mouth.

"Here, let me light it for you." As bizarre as it seemed, I felt a connection with Noah at that moment that was different, new.

I placed my mouth over the top of the tube and watched the flame singe the crushed leaves in the valve. I looked up at Noah and he nodded, gently coaxing me through the process, teaching me, guiding me. I exhaled through my nose to make room in my lungs for one more thing that threatened to pull me apart at the seams. I sucked as much in as I could. I closed my eyes to concentrate on not choking the smoke right back out. A few staggered chokes busted their way through my pursed lips but I kept most of it in. I passed the bong to my right, and Noah took one of my hands in his. I looked into my lap at our clasped hands and slowly exhaled the last of my resolve.

"I have to go." I stood and choked out a little more smoke. I had to grab the arm of the couch to keep from falling on my way to the door.

"Gracie."

I kept a steady gait down the long hallway to the front door. If Noah really wanted to stop me he would have been able to catch up before I walked outside. I walked a block before looking back, hoping he was walking out the front door of the house. No one. No one was coming. And I had no clue as to the direction my life was going.

By the time I knocked on Jake's door, my brain was floating. Not like being drunk. It was really like floating. I didn't like it. A long talk with Jake was what I needed.

I jumped into Jake's arms as soon as he opened the door. But as soon as the top of my head was nestled into the side of his neck, he must've smelled it. He took hold of my arms and pushed me back. Still holding my arms he tried to hold my gaze but I couldn't. I was stoned. The way I felt standing before him at that moment was my gauge for what I had just sacrificed.

"Gracie."

He knew. The tears rolled from my bloodshot eyes. I kept my head down but lifted my eyes to see his face. He closed his eyes and slowly shook his head.

"Jake. I need your arms around me again." Jake had helped me through so much since the semester started. Jake and I had a long talk the day after Noah tried to make love to me as an apology for the whole "Lily" episode. Our conversation started via text because I was too embarrassed to go into those kinds of details face-to-face. But Jake soon came down to the apartment and I fell asleep in his arms after spilling my heart to him. There were no words for the unexpected comfort Jake's arms gave me. I needed that again.

"Gracie, you didn't..."

I looked back down at the floor.

"Gracie, you're better than this. What are you doing?"

"Jake! Can I just come in? I just need you..."

"No." His sharp words were out before I finished telling him what I needed.

"Jake?"

"Gracie. I just can't...I don't...I'm disappointed, Gracie. This isn't who you are. I think you need to go down to your place and sleep this off. Call me when you wake up."

"Jake."

"Go, Gracie. Sleep."

I turned and walked toward the stairs. Jake was my best friend, he had never turned me away. I walked down the stairwell and realized I may have just sacrificed the only thing holding me together.

Sixteen

December, Fall Semester, Junior Year

Turning me away that day was the best thing Jake could have done for me. Sure it felt like a slap in the face at that moment but that's exactly what I needed. I had a long talk with Noah that night and told him I wasn't caving on this. Drugs of any kind were never going to be okay with me. I told him I had no interest being around him if he was going to smoke pot.

Instead of having Noah take me home and bring me back for Thanksgiving break, which was just a couple days after the pot pow-wow in his room, Stacy and I rode home together. Technically, I guess, we didn't break up the night he chose Lily over me, and things seemed strained after I basically gave him the "it's pot or me" ultimatum. So, I purposely made tons of plans with Stacy. Noah and I texted, but we didn't see each other at all over break.

It was actually nice reconnecting with Stacy over the weekend. After my fill of turkey and stuffing, I went to her house for dessert and stayed over. We got up in the wee hours of the morning to head out for Black Friday shopping. Thanksgiving break was just a long weekend so there was barely any time to miss Noah.

Noah called the night before we left to head back to school and begged me to ride with him. Stacy and I had been having so much fun, and it felt amazing to laugh as much as we were. I was really looking forward to our long ride back to school. He pouted when I said no, and I almost changed my mind and bailed on Stacy, but then I remembered the disappointment on Jake's face and I decided to continue making my own decision regardless of what Noah wanted.

The ride proved worth it to ditch Noah. Stacy and I dumped our stuff in the apartment and ran right upstairs to share our leftovers with Sam and Jake. We barged right in hoping to surprise them, but that backfired as soon as the door swung open. Instead of finding Sam and Jake hanging out, we found Jake and Jessica in quite the naked tangle. They were on the couch and there was a pile of clothing next to it on the floor. Jessica quickly grabbed something from the pile to shield her naked torso and Jake jumped up, quickly pulling on and buttoning the jeans that were at his feet. He and I entertained a tacit glance until I turned when Stacy pulled me back out into the hallway.

We laughed it off the whole way down the stairwell, but my laugh wasn't real. The unsettled feeling in the pit of my stomach was unnerving.

"Hey. You okay?" Stacy ushered me into our apartment while she held the door with her foot. We walked into the kitchen and put the desserts in the fridge. I didn't know how to answer her so I just shrugged and changed the subject.

"You want to see a movie tonight?"

"It's no big deal walking in on them, you know. Greg's roommate has walked in on us more than once. This is college, it happens."

"Yeah. You're right." What she didn't realize is that I wasn't embarrassed that we walked in on them. The nagging sting in my chest was a result of seeing Jake with her...*with* her. They weren't big on PDA so, except for the times she was *Oh God*-ing from the bedroom, their love life was pretty private. I had never seen them make out or do much more than a little kissing here and there. But seeing them like that did something to me that I couldn't translate.

I plugged my cell phone into its dock in our room while we unpacked. I finished refolding some of the clothes I threw in my bag last minute and then grabbed a take-out menu from the kitchen and turned on Netflix to see what Stacy and I could get into for the evening.

"Hey, someone is blowing up your phone." Stacy had been in our room meticulously unpacking for at least twenty minutes while I clicked through channels and tried to decide what I was hungry for.

"Throw it to me?"

"She peeked out from around the open door and tossed my phone across the living room.

There was a whole string of texts from Noah. Some must've come in after my phone died in the car.

You back yet?
Wanna come up for pizza later?
Are you ignoring me?
Gracie.
Please call me when you get back.
Are you getting any of these texts?
Gracie. I miss you.

The last one had only come in two minutes prior to Stacy throwing my phone at me. My head was swimming. That was the most Noah had ever texted me in one day, let alone in one afternoon. My thumbs hovered over my keyboard while I tried to execute the perfect response to his pitiful plea for attention.

"Gracie! Help!" Stacy's cry was half laugh and half desperation. I ran to her instead of texting Noah back. She stood in our closet balancing a stack of sweaters over her head that she wasn't tall enough to push all the way back on the shelf.

"You know, if you just held them like that, they wouldn't get the 'fluff' smashed out of them from the weight of that insane pile." I smiled and watched her panic.

"Gracie!"

"I got you. Here." I stood behind her and reached the top of the stack and pushed. My phone vibrated noisily over and over on the coffee table as other texts came in from Noah. I couldn't wait to see them so I ran to the living room. Stacy squealed again, and I heard the soft thump of twenty-some sweaters hitting the floor. I heard her mumbling, but knew I didn't want to know what she'd just called me for choosing Noah over her.

I plopped down on the couch and unlocked my screen.

Helloooooo?

What does a guy have to do to get your attention these days?

Why aren't you answering your texts?

I giggled and gave in.

Me: *Sorry. Phone was dead.*

Noah: *There you are. You are one hard girl to get ahold of*

Me: *Good things come to those who wait*

Noah: *OK. I waited. Now come up here.*

Noah: *Please.*

Me: *K. Miss you too. Be there in 10*

Before I had my phone in my back pocket it buzzed again.

Jake: *Gracie. I am so sorry for earlier.*

Me: *No, I'm sorry. We should've knocked.*

Jake: *Ha. Yeah*

Me: *Next time*

Jake: *Have a good break?*

Me: *Too much food. Fun w Stacy.*

Jake: *Wanna come up and talk?*

I knew what he was referring to. I'd never forget the look on his face the day I showed up high. I hated that I disappointed him.

Me: *Can't. Headed to Noah's.*
Jake: *Soon? I miss you.*
Me: *Soon. Miss you too*
I ditched Stacy and Jake to go spend time with Noah.

Seventeen

I walked to Noah's anticipating a sweet welcome considering he was so intense about getting ahold of me.

"Hey Gracie," Brad waved as he headed to the kitchen with a stack of dishes curled up in his other arm and balanced against his chest.

I waved and headed to Noah's room. I hoped I wasn't going to walk into something reminiscent of a Bob Marley poster like last time. I didn't want another confrontation. I wanted him to take my stance on pot seriously. And I really missed him.

Before I had a chance to knock, he threw the door open and lunged into me. He wrapped his arms around me, pushed me across the hall and up against the wall.

"Noah, what in the world..."

"Gracie, it's been too long since I've seen you. That makes me crazy."

"It does?" I wasn't sure what this heart-felt reunion was all about.

"Yes." He ushered me into his room and closed the door behind us. "Here." He walked over and sat on the couch and patted the cushion next to him.

"Hmm, no funky smell. You just smoking in someone else's room?" I laughed when I said it but part of me knew he was always one step ahead of me and that could have been his plan. I wanted him to know I was on to him if that's how he planned to get away with it.

"No, after you walked out and said you didn't want to be around me if I was smoking, I spent the whole next week smoking."

"Nice." I rolled my eyes and sat with that cushion he patted between us.

"No, hear me out. I smoked so much pot that week I think I baked my brain. But getting high was only replacing what I was missing. You."

"So, you can replace me with drugs. That's real romantic, Noah." I rolled my eyes.

"Gracie, listen. What I am trying to say is I thought I could but I can't. I really like the feeling of being stoned, but I like the feeling of you better." He moved to the cushion between us and put his hand on my knee. "If you are in my life, I don't need drugs. Don't walk away from me. I'm giving it up to show you how much I love you. I don't need it. I need you."

I was speechless. Noah hadn't been this sensitive in quite some time. When he was trying to get me to break up with Joel he was, but I hadn't seen this side of Noah for a long time.

"I really don't like it, Noah."

"I'm done. I didn't know I could miss you as much as I did."

"Do you love me, Noah?"

"Of course I do, Gracie."

"Then tell me."

"I love you, Gracie Jordan."

I took his face in my hands and slowly pulled him to me. I brushed my lips across his then gave him a peck on each cheek. His eyes were closed like he was savoring every second. It made me smile. I pulled him in for a hug, and he nearly crawled inside me. He was pulling us together in a way that spoke volumes. I just wasn't sure I could translate what he was saying.

"It scares me, Gracie." He didn't move when he spoke, just continued hugging me close.

"What scares you?"

"The emotions I feel for you. Sometimes I don't know what to do with them. I get scared and I do something stupid to push you away then no sooner do you walk out and I'm dying to touch you."

I pushed back and put my hands on his shoulders. "Why is loving me so scary? Doesn't that just confirm that you want to be with me?"

"I guess it does, but I don't always think I am ready for that. It's like subconsciously I'm hurting you so you can move on and find someone who can love you the way you deserve to be loved. I don't know if I can always give you that kind of love."

His words held a weight that *I* wasn't ready for. I felt like the room tilted. I closed my eyes not wanting to display any emotion that would cause him to change the way he was opening up to me. Before I could speak, tears slipped out from between my eyelids. I tilted my head forward and onto his shoulder hoping he didn't see them trailing down my cheeks. I couldn't take this kind of yo-yo love for much longer. It would crush me. Something had to change, and at that moment, I knew I was ready to fight. Stories like ours—bad boy meets good girl—don't usually end up in the happily-ever-after category, but I'd be damned if I would let that stereotypical statistic doom us to Hell. I just needed to help him through his uncertainty. I needed to *love* him through it. I simply could not envision my life on campus without Noah. When I thought about it, my body would respond with panic. Instantly my palms would sweat and my teeth would start to chatter. That was one reason, but the biggest reason hit me like a ton of bricks. I couldn't walk away. Our relationship defined me. I didn't know who I was without him.

"I'm not ready to give up on us." I lifted my head as I spoke and Noah wiped my tears.

"Let's get through these next couple weeks and then it's Christmas break. We have a month at home together without any of the pressures we have here."

"Okay. Please don't give up on me." A sob slipped from my mouth.

"If I ever gave up on someone, Gracie, it would be me, not you."

Eighteen

The night before we all headed our separate ways for Christmas break, I was lying in bed trying to sleep, wondering if Noah was pulling one over on me with the whole pot thing. I hated struggling with trusting him, but ever since he cheated I picked apart every little thing he said so I wasn't ever blindsided again.

Living my life like that was wearing me down. Stacy didn't get it. I knew Becki respected me enough to not give me her opinion. "Figure it out on your own and you'll be stronger for it," was her mantra. The only person I knew I could trust to give it to me straight was one floor up and probably sound asleep.

Me: *Jake*

Jake: *Gracie*

Me: *You up?*

Jake: *No, I often text while I'm sleeping*

Me: *Smart ass*

Jake: *You ok?*

Me: *I need to talk but if you're in bed, it can wait*

Jake: *I'm unlocking the door now*

Me: *Be right up*
Jake: *Lock the door behind you and be quiet, Sam's got a girl here*
Me: *Ew*
Jake: :)

I quietly got out of the bunk so Stacy didn't wake up, grabbed my keys and looked in the mirror to wipe away any stray make-up left from the day. I was always too tired to wash my face before I slept, but I was graced with my mother's complexion, and luckily there were no ill effects from my lax in hygiene. I put a hair tie around my wrist and looked down at what I had on—black cami and red shiny soccer shorts. I was one classy girl.

The hallway and stairwell were eerily quiet. I looked at my phone and realized it was two in the morning. I had no idea I had been lying awake that long. I never would have texted Jake had I known it was the wee hours of the morning.

I slipped into their apartment, bolted the door and assumed I'd find Jake on the couch studying but the living room was dark. I walked down the hall, tried not to hear whatever was going on in Sam's room and carefully pushed open Jake's door. He was lying on his side, covers tucked under his one arm and his other arm tucked under his head. He was a beautiful sight. Yes, we were just friends, but there was no denying how flawless he was. And those eyes. I shook my head and quietly walked over to his bed. I worried about what Jessica and Noah would think, but it's not like I was planning on getting under the covers with him.

Before I knew what was going on, Jake grabbed me at the knees and threw me over his body and onto the empty side of his bed. I squealed at the surprise and then giggled so hard I got the hiccups. He always tried to outdo himself in ways to make me scream. I was an easy target. My imagination ran on overdrive, and he could always pick up on when I was zoning out, which is exactly what I was doing when I was standing next to his bed just then.

"Jake! Sam probably heard me scream."

"No, worries, he's heard—"

I smacked him in the chest, "TMI. Jake. TMI!"

He smiled and fluffed his other pillow for me. I laid down facing him in the same position he was in. We just looked at each other smiling and still giggling from my near death experience.

"So, where's Jessica? I figured she'd be here tonight, with break starting tomorrow."

"Nope. She is doing that semester exchange program. She's headed south to Louisiana for most of Spring Semester. She leaves really early tomorrow so we already said our goodbyes."

"Ew. In *this* bed?"

"Relax, you're safe." He pushed my shoulder back and laughed.

"So, Jake. I need your help."

"How 'bout you tell me what made you get stoned with Noah, first?"

"Weak moment?" I winced a bit, hoping he would fall for it.

"It was more than that. Talk to me." He scooted closer and tucked my hair behind my ear. I rolled over onto my back and crossed my arms over my stomach.

"Jake. I hate that I am even going to say this out loud, but...he makes me feel like an idiot sometimes. I mean, part of why he was so taken by me in the beginning was because of how innocent I was. He liked that I was so naïve and didn't know about a lot of things. And now, it seems like he isn't happy unless I sacrifice that for him."

"Hm. That's messed up."

"Do you think less of me for smoking pot, Jake?"

"Gracie, our mistakes don't define us, they help us make the choices that will one day be woven into who we become."

"Wow."

"What?"

"You're deep at two a.m."

"Gracie, you can't let him steal who you are. You need to make choices based on who you are...right here." He poked his finger into my chest. "Don't make decisions because Noah is standing behind them convincing you they are the right choices *for* you."

"See, it makes so much sense when *you* say it. If I am thinking of someone else in the same situation, I would give them that exact advice, although not as scholarly as you just did." I giggled and poked him in the bare chest that was peeking out above his comforter.

"So, take your own advice, Gracie."

"It's not that easy. It's like he's got strings tied to my emotions and my common sense. I can't seem to think for myself when he wants me to do something I've never done before."

"Does he make you feel guilty if you don't want to?"

"Sometimes, but mostly he just makes me feel stupid. Like I'm too immature to make a sound decision. So, he makes it for me."

"Gracie! Only *you* should be controlling the things you are doing with your mind...and...your body. Gracie, please don't let him take things from you that you aren't ready to give. Promise me."

"It's not like that, Jake. It's not like he knows he's making me feel that way. I just do. I guess maybe I am just reading into his expressions and assuming what he's thinking. Maybe I am just too insecure around him to think straight sometimes."

"I wouldn't doubt that he knows exactly what he's doing. I've seen him in action."

I had never been conscious of the things we spoke about in Jake's bed. It was like pieces came together when Jake and I spoke. My thoughts flowed freely and they made sense. I never felt like I had to be anyone but me when I talked to Jake. He was so comfortable. I rolled over on my side again so I could see him as he spoke.

"You shouldn't be with someone who makes you feel that way, Gracie. Look, Noah is my friend but I have seen what he can do. He's crushed more than a few girls on this campus. I know we've all seen him make a big change, but you still have to be careful."

"I know, Jake. He wouldn't hurt me on purpose. I know he loves me. I think he just wants me to be a little more adventurous. I think he gets sick of the goody-two-shoes-Gracie."

"The Gracie I know," he laid his hand on my cheek and kissed me on the tip of my nose, "is one of the most incredible people I have ever met. Her smile lights up a room and everyone feels her joy because, take it or leave it, she comes with no pretenses. You get all of her. The second you meet her, you've got her heart. And her security in her convictions is what makes her shine."

Tears flowed in a stream across my face and onto the pillow under my head. Jake gently placed his hand on the side of my face and wiped the tears away with his thumb.

"Oh, Jake." I sobbed out his name and crumbled in his bed. I didn't know how he could still see me as the girl he just described. I wasn't sure I even remembered her.

"Come here, Gracie. Let me hold you." He lifted the covers so I could climb under. He enveloped me in all that was Jake—his strength, his honesty and an indescribable level of friendship I never knew existed. I didn't know what was to come with Noah, but I knew Jake would never walk away from me. I didn't know how to do life without him.

I slept soundly in Jake's arms all night and woke up to a sweet kiss on the forehead, still wrapped up in him. There was something almost magical about the emotions and revelations I had when I talked to Jake. Sometimes it was as simple as deciding whether or not to change my major, and sometimes it was as complex as navigating a relationship that was dissolving beneath me. The platonic love he showed me was stunning.

Nineteen

Christmas Break

After a week of grueling finals, Noah and I were ready to run away together. I was excited to spend the long drive planning out exactly what we would do for the month we would be home. I felt a slight pang of guilt that I spent the night with Jake but was still floating from the connection we had. And the crying I did while he held me proved to be quite cathartic. I jumped out of his bed determined to never sacrifice who I was for a relationship, even the one that currently felt like it was hanging in the balance.

"Okay, so we can do the zoo, shopping and a long hike the first week, then—"

"Hang on." Noah reached into the inside pocket of his jacket and took out his phone.

After "This is Noah," I listened to all of his responses, which were mostly *yes* and *no, sure* and *thank you,* but I couldn't figure out who he was talking to. So, when he hung up I was eager to hear who interrupted our Christmas break planning session.

"Gracie, I got it. I got the internship!"

"That's great, Noah. What internship?" My stomach rolled and my hands started to shake. He decided on an internship without telling me about it, first. I was hurt.

"The one in Jackson. I'll be working with an internal auditor at one of the big pharmaceutical companies there." I panicked at the thought of him being that far away from me.

"That's great, Noah. When is it?" I was happy for him but was unsure what this opportunity meant for us. Based on where we were in our relationship, I knew it couldn't survive long distance.

"Monday. It starts this Monday!" He pounded on the steering wheel and bobbed his head all around. He was visibly excited for this internship that was cutting into our month home together. But I needed to stop being selfish. An internship was a big deal. We'd be out of school and getting jobs in less than two years.

"That's great news. So, you have to move there?" I braced myself for the answer so I didn't fall apart when he said *yes*. He let out a roaring laugh which made me wish I had braced myself so I didn't feel stupid. I sunk into my seat like a little girl who just got laughed at by the class.

"Gracie, no. Jackson is only an hour away from McKenzie, and the internship is just for Christmas break. I'll commute. But we will have to cut down our plans to just a few things we can do on the weekends before we go back to school."

"Oh, I thought I wasn't going to see you for all of break."

"Gracie, you're going to have to realize that being juniors means we will soon start applying for jobs. There's a good chance we'll be separated at some point. I don't want that, but we have to be realistic."

I didn't want to think about that. Noah and I were just starting to understand the issues in our relationship and why he kept pushing me away. I needed to focus on that, then we could consider how we would survive a long-distance relationship.

"First things first." I needed a change in venue.

"Yeah?"

"I have to pee." I pleaded with my head tilted and my bottom lip pushed out.

"Of course you do." Noah laughed.

We pulled off at a rest stop, and while I went to the restrooms, Noah stocked up on snacks for the rest of our ride.

"So, what are you and Noah planning for over break?" My mom was giddy with excitement that I was home for a whole month. Her voice was squeaky, and she didn't stop bouncing from task to task for at least the first two hours after I walked in the door. Noah and I decided we would give my family time to dote on me and just go out the next night. His family didn't dote.

"Well, we are going to the movies tomorrow night and maybe shopping on Sunday, but Monday he starts an internship at a pharmaceutical company in Jackson."

"Wow. That's an hour away. So, whatever will you do with your time all those long days while he is working?" She was being sarcastic in the way she said it.

"Hang with you, Mom." I couldn't help but smile. As much as I wished I had Noah all day every day for the next month, I was thrilled to have some girl time with my mom.

"And me!" My little sister popped out of nowhere.

"Hey! And, yes, you, too, Hannah." My sister was a junior in high school, and although we weren't close as little kids, I'd always hoped when she got older we would bond in a new way. Maybe Christmas break would be a good time to focus on that. She ran over and for a second I thought she was going to throw her arms around me. But she stopped short and gave me a one-armed half hug. She and I were so different. I craved physical touch, and she wasn't a big fan. I realized then that I should practice loving Noah the way I loved Hannah — on his terms.

My dad came home for dinner and swallowed me in a big "Daddy" hug. I melted. It was said when you grew up you would find a mate that resembled the kind of dad you had. I only hoped I could be that lucky. The way my dad loved my mom was a beautiful example of how it should be. Sure, they fought and got pissed at each other, but there was no betrayal or trust issues, and certainly no drugs. Noah and I had a long way to go to resemble my parents, but I thought we could do it.

I lay in bed that night staring at the numerous posters on my ceiling. It was a montage of everything I loved—Pearl Jam, little babies dressed like punk rockers, Red Hot Chili Peppers and a small poster of Alternate Tragedy, a band Stacy, Becki and I stalked in Knoxville. But in the center of it all was the one image I couldn't take my eyes off of. It was the infamous VJ Day photograph, the black and white photograph of a sailor bending a nurse backwards over his arm and going in for her lips. The photo was taken by Alfred Eisenstaedt in Times Square in 1945, and well over sixty years later, it was still a symbol of the ultimate romantic encounter. I wondered how much longer Noah could stand me being the one trying to hold us together. I was a hopeless romantic. But without the romance, we were hopeless.

Twenty

First Week of Christmas Break

"I'm starving, want to go get something to eat?" I had a blast taking Hannah shopping. We dressed each other up in goofball outfits and took dozens of pictures. We would laugh in the dressing room until we almost peed ourselves or were asked to leave by management. I thoroughly enjoyed this trip home because our relationship seemed to evolve quickly from big sister/little sister to just sisters.

We headed to the food court and settled down into a comfortable booth near the fountain we used to throw pennies in when we shopped with my mom.

"So, what's new? I feel like we haven't really connected since summer."

"Maybe if you would have been home for more than ten minutes over Thanksgiving we could have." She was obviously being sarcastic, but something in her tone made me think something *was* new and there was something she needed to talk about.

"You need to talk." It was a statement, not a question. Sometimes Hannah was hard to read, but sometimes she couldn't hide her emotions from me. This was one of those times.

"Gracie, there's this boy..." She put her burger down and hung her head between the palms of her hands. "I love him so much and we...well, we *were* getting pretty serious."

"Does this boy have a name?"

"Let's just talk, okay? Please don't be mom right now." There were tears already welling up in her eyes. She didn't need prodding, she needed her sister.

"It's me, Hannah. Please tell me what's going on."

Hannah proceeded to tell me about this boy she was head over heels with. She explained in detail all the romantic things he did when they first started dating. He sounded too good to be true. And what she told me next made me hate myself for not having the time for her over Thanksgiving.

"So, wait. He said what?" I couldn't believe what I was hearing.

"He said if I didn't do certain things with him, he would dump me."

"Certain things as in sex." I knew exactly what she was talking about.

"Well..."

"Hannah, I won't tell mom."

"Yeah. He said he'd love me more if I did."

"That's a big step, Hannah. And if anything happens that causes you two to break up, it will tear your heart out of your chest." My mind somersaulted back to the confusing emotions I had the summer before Noah left for Knoxville, right after we started dating.

"He loves me, Gracie. He really does. He just wants to take our relationship to the next level." The air quotes she made with her fingers clued me in that the words she spoke were *his* words.

"Love doesn't push, Hannah."

"What does that mean?" She shoved a couple more fries in her mouth waiting for an answer, but where this conversation was going was taking me to someplace deep in my soul that acted as a mirror and my own relationship stared back at me. It was surreal. Tears waited just under the surface, threatening to spill out.

"Love is patient—"

"Sunday School? Seriously…Mom! I know that verse, it's hanging next to Mom and Dad's wedding picture over the fireplace. Love is patient, love is kind. It does not envy and does not boast…blah, blah, blah."

"Look, I know it sounds sappy and too good to be true. But I think there is merit to its advice." We grew up going to church and saying our prayers. We went to vacation bible school every summer as kids, but since I left for college, I guess I left that part of who I was behind. Or maybe I walked away from it the night I lost a part of myself I could never get back from Noah.

"So, what are you saying, Oh Wise One?" She was trying to lighten the mood. I could tell she didn't want this to be a cry fest and neither did I. The mall was not the place to have this conversation.

"If he truly loves you, he will be willing to wait. Don't let him push you to do anything you're not ready for. It's a big commitment. A gift you won't get back. Make sure you save it for the *right one,* not just the *one right now.*"

She filled her cheeks with her milkshake and nodded, "Thanks, sis. Guess you know what you're talking about." She lifted one eyebrow when she finished her sentence.

"I do, Hannah. You just have to trust me on this one."

"Got it. Now, can you please eat so we can go try on those geeky prom dresses?"

"Absolutely!"

We dumped our trays and headed to The Prom Shop. It was one of those seasonal spaces at the mall. As soon as the Halloween costumes moved out, prom gowns moved in. As if anyone was thinking about prom while they did their Christmas shopping.

I sat on a bench inside the dressing room while Hannah tried on the fifteenth gaudy gown. The store had wifi so I looked up the "Love is patient" verse on my phone. It had been a long time since I actually looked at the frame over the fireplace.

The words written so long ago somewhere in the desert, spoke volumes to me as I read them sitting on a bench at the mall.

Love is patient, love is kind. It does not envy, it does not boast, it is not proud. It does not dishonor others, it is not self-seeking, it is not easily angered, it keeps no record of wrongs. Love does not delight in evil but rejoices with the truth. It always protects, always trusts, always hopes, always perseveres.

I worried about the advice I'd just given to Hannah. I didn't believe there was a love like that. I didn't know anyone who could love like that, no one was that selfless.

"You ready?" Hannah came out carrying a pile of dresses she never intended to buy.

"Yep. We just have to get Mom something. My feet are killing me, let's get this done."

My phone buzzed and I flipped over to my texts.

How are you, beautiful? Ready for Christmas?

My heart stuttered when I looked at the sender…Jake.

Jake was that selfless. Maybe there was hope for Hannah finding someone like that. I wondered what Jessica did to deserve him. I was sure the rest of us just weren't that lucky.

"Noah?" Hannah elbowed me in the side as we headed to mom's favorite store.

"Huh?

"You guys must be doing okay because that goofy grin is ridiculous." She pointed to whatever she thought she saw on my face.

"Yeah. It was Noah." I lied but I didn't know why.

Me: *Shopping with Hannah. Miss you.*

Jake: *Miss you, too.*

Me: *Merry Christmas, Jake*

Jake: *Right back atcha Gracie*

Twenty-One

I called Noah as I climbed into bed. We'd just spent the second weekend of break at his house watching our favorite movies and eating his mom out of house and home. His internship and the two-hour-round-trip commute were wearing him out. Christmas was next week, and that meant our month together was half over.

"Hey." His voice was low and sharp when he answered.

"What's wrong?" God, I hated when the conversations started off this way.

"I'm just tired, Gracie," he snapped.

"I'll let you go."

"Don't go all drama-queen on me. I'm not pissed at you, I'm just beat. This internship is killing me." He yawned and I heard his covers brush over his phone.

"I wish I was there with you."

"Well, you'd get to watch me sleep. That's all I have enough energy to do."

That was not the response I hoped for. I wanted him to say that having me in his arms would make his day and that he wished he could fall asleep with me against his chest.

"I'll let you go. You should sleep."

"Okay. I'll call you tomorrow."

"Goodnight, Noah. I love—"

And that was the end of that.

My olfactory system woke up before I did on Christmas morning. The smell of eggs and bacon, toast and coffee tormented me until I swung my legs over the side of my bed and forced myself upright. Noah was the first person I thought of. I couldn't wait to give him the vintage concert t-shirt I found. Right after Christmas, Noah and his family always headed to New England to see his mom's family and to ski at some resort in Vermont. He got special permission from the company he was interning with to do a research paper in place of the last week of his internship. He'd be gone for New Years so Christmas day was the only day I would see him before we headed back to UT. I grabbed my phone and started to text him but decided to wait for him to text me first.

"Wow, Mom. You went all out!" I couldn't believe the spread that was before me. In addition to the smell of eggs and bacon that lured me to the kitchen before my eyes were open, there were, muffins, fruit salad, bagels and flavored cream cheese and three different kinds of fruit juices.

"I love when our house is full again."

"Well, by the looks of it, you have invited half of McKenzie to share it with us."

She laughed. She knew she always made way too much food, but it was her way of loving us. Food was the answer for everything. Sad? Cry into a carton of some ice cream. Happy? Celebrate with some chocolate cake. A rough week called for

Mexican food. And apparently Christmas morning was a celebration of breakfast foods. All of them.

The four of us ate, opened presents and laughed for most of the day. It was different being an almost-adult on Christmas morning. There were no toys for my dad to put together, and we weren't in a mad rush to unwrap everything all at once. Our family festivities lasted hours. It was slow and very sweet.

When everyone headed to the kitchen for seconds, I walked back to my room to get my phone. I laughed out loud when I saw there were four messages.

Stacy: *Merry Christmas!*

Sam: *Ho! Ho! Ho!*

Becki: *Wait til you see what I got!*

Jake: *Hope Santa was good to you*

I texted them all back and then gave in and texted Noah.

Me: *Merry Christmas. I love you.*

He texted right back.

Noah: *ILY2*

Me: *When will I see you?*

Noah: *My parents are going to a party at the neighbor's tonight. Want to come hang here? We'll be alone for a couple hours.*

Me: *Sounds perfect*

Noah: *Cool. Call you later*

Me: *<3*

I helped my mom clean up after the left-overs-for-lunch buffet while my dad and Hannah took naps. I was sure they were both in food comas.

She asked all kinds of questions about school and Jake and Sam. She asked about Noah and could probably tell I didn't want to delve into that topic too deep.

"You two okay?"

"Yeah. He's just stressing because of this internship."

"I notice something different in you lately. You seem...I don't know what the word is."

She put the hand towel over her shoulder and turned around toward me to finish, "Gracie, you have always been the bright and bubbly spot in our lives. Your spirit sings when you enter a room, and lately it's like someone has turned your volume down. It just worries me."

I grabbed the towel off her shoulder and walked behind her to dry the stack of dishes on the counter. I needed to break eye contact because I was on the verge of breaking down. She described the same girl Jake did just before we left on break. As I heard it leave her lips I tried to picture the girl she saw. I couldn't.

"Gracie, just don't let him steal away your joy. Please. No boy is worth that." She stood behind me, put her hands on my shoulders, kissed me on the cheek and left me at the sink. I got the feeling she knew I was choking back tears. I buried my face in the cool, damp hand towel and cried until there were no more tears.

Twenty-Two

When I got to Noah's, his parents had already left for their party. I thought about all the things we said we were going to do over break, but it all just got away from us. But the times we did have together were sweet.

"I can't wait for you to see what I got you," I squealed as I plopped down on the couch.

"Can I give you mine first?" He seems boyishly excited.

"No. Mine first."

I handed him the gift bag and bounced up and down while I waited for him to open it, "Open it, open it!"

"All right. You're so cute right now." He took my chin in his hand and pulled it to him. He kissed me deeply and then sighed. A big smile spread across his face when I started bouncing again.

He opened it slowly, I assumed just to drive me crazy. When he saw what it was, he beamed.

"You like it?"

His eyes lifted to mine and he pulled me in for a deep hug. He held on longer than usual which took me by surprise.

"Where in the world did you find a real Melvins concert shirt?

"I have my sources." I felt like Sam bragging about his connections. I waited for my comment to click with Noah but it didn't. It made me sad that there was a distance between Noah and the two guys he used to do everything with.

I tried really hard to get Noah something meaningful that couldn't be translated into *sappy*. The Melvins certainly weren't sappy. They were one of the original grunge bands but were a little more hardcore than I typically enjoyed. But Noah loved them.

"My turn," he reached down beside the couch and handed me a box. We shared a smile and a sweet kiss before he got a little giddy, too. "Open it."

What was inside took my breath away. It was a ring. But not "the" ring. It was a delicate silver band with five letters etched deeply into the surface. G-R-A-C-E

"My name."

"Sort of."

I looked at him a bit confused.

"Gracie, I suck at being the guy I promised you I would be, but you have shown me so much grace and given me second, third, fourth…more than enough chances to get it right. Beautiful grace is what you give me. There are five letters on the inside, too.

"Trust."

"I want you to be able to trust me. There are no secrets between us. Everything is out in the open. I know I have screwed up, but I don't want you to worry one more day that I could ever love anyone more than I love you right this minute."

"This is the best gift anyone has ever given me, Noah. It's beautiful. Thank you."

The rest of our evening was spent in each other's arms. We didn't make love that night, but what we did share seemed so much deeper. Noah being able to promise me that he had no more secrets was huge. It meant a lot to me. My heart felt renewed. This could be the new start we needed.

"Noah."

"Yeah."

"I'm sorry all I got you was a t-shirt." I giggled shyly and looked up at his face.

"I love my t-shirt, Gracie. And I love you." He squeezed me tight, and I thought I felt something different between us. Or was it just hope?

Twenty-Three

January, Spring Semester, Junior Year

It was dark as I walked home from meeting with my advisor after deciding I needed to lighten my load. Eighteen credits were way more than I was ready for. I thought about Noah and the ring he gave me. It made me smile. Two weeks in and things were still wonderful between us. I was convinced we had been through the worst of our relationship. I hated walking home in the dark so it was good my mind was busy on something other than the possible rapist that could jump out from behind every bush, which was usually what I thought about. I must have the strongest heart ever. It had been through a lot over the course of my relationship with Noah, and my irrational anxiety didn't give it any time to rest.

I was almost at the edge of campus when I saw the silhouette of a man sitting on the park bench that bordered the edge of campus and the sidewalk of College Avenue. My heart started pounding. I was headed toward the lighted street, so turning around and running away from the bench would doom me into darkness. I stood up straight, held my breath, feigned fearlessness, and kept walking.

Go ahead, jump out and get me, asshole, you can't hurt me any more than I've been hurt. So, come at me.

When I got within three feet of the bench, I glanced over so I would know which way to run when the mad rapist lunged for me.

It was Noah.

He sat there with a smile on his face and a big basket of some sort next to him.

"Come and sit with me, beautiful."

"Good Lord, Noah, you scared the crap out of me. What are you doing?"

He smiled and tucked some of my hair behind my ears as I sat down. I could still hear blood pumping in my ears with each beat of my heart. I concentrated on calming my heart rate while I waited for him to answer.

"I was waiting for you."

"How did you know where I was?"

"I ran into Stacy earlier and told her I wanted to surprise you. She got all pissy and told me you wouldn't be home because you had a meeting with your advisor. I guess she's still pissed about last semester." He rolled his eyes. "I know you only walk this pathway when it's dark. It wasn't rocket science."

I couldn't stop looking at his face. It was so gentle at that moment. He was smiling and his voice was calm and soft. I soaked up every detail and could almost feel my heart grow a little bit.

"What is that smell? Is there food in there?"

He nodded. "Mexican from Southern Solstice."

I was starving and he had food from our favorite Mexican restaurant at the other end of town. This was all premeditated. He had to plan this...this wasn't just serendipity. He was courting me, winning back my heart. It had been so long since I had such a peaceful feeling with him on this campus. I was almost dizzy with delight.

"Look, I know how shady much of what I did last semester looked. I cheated then I was distant. I pissed you off and stayed at the party with Lily that night. I smoked weed. I fucked up." I just stared at him. My brain was reeling and my heart was stuck on pause.

"Can you forgive me?"

"Noah...I..." I didn't even know what to say. I wasn't sure if I ever forgave him for any of the shit he pulled. I pretended I did. He had never actually asked and I wasn't sure I could be convincing with a "yes." I was willing to put it out of my mind, but I wasn't at the "forgive and forget" point yet.

"Listen, I fuck up a lot. I know I do. But I love you, Gracie. I know I don't say it enough and I don't show you enough. But this— the picnic, the ring—this is me making an effort. I want to make you happy, and I know I've been failing miserably lately."

I sat and took in everything he said, fully expecting a camera crew to pop out of the bushes because the whole surprise picnic thing had to be a prank. It was too good to be true.

I just had to figure out how to hold on to the place we were at that moment, that mood he was in right then and there. I would have done anything to ensure he wouldn't turn away from me again. I didn't know what to say. I was frozen. Petrified to be the one to wreck that perfect moment. But my journey toward healing had to start with forgiveness. And this was my starting point.

"Of course I forgive you, Noah. As long as we agree that I had every right to see all those things for what they were. Deceitful and wrong."

The words poured out of my mouth before I could stop them. I couldn't believe what I had said. I had never stood up to Noah that way. I had never made him admit what he did was shitty. A shock of panic ran from my toes to the top of my head. I wasn't sure which Noah would answer that question. But before I could process the situation enough to turn my question into something less accusatory, he answered me.

"You had every right to be pissed and every right to break up with me." He pressed his full lips to mine. "Now, you need to start eating these tacos or we will be here all night."

Picturing us sitting on that bench and talking for the whole night was the most beautiful scenario I could imagine. I threw out one ballsy question, and it didn't piss him off. I so badly wished I could predict his reactions. They were never the same twice. I was always walking on eggshells. But right now, I was sitting and Noah was making an effort. I kicked the eggshells under the bench, smiled, and grabbed for a taco. Noah reached for my hand and pulled it to his mouth. He gently kissed across my knuckles. I watched him press one last kiss onto the back of my hand. He closed his eyes and breathed deeply, as if he was trying to pull me so far into him that I would never run the other way.

"Look at them. Why can't you be romantic like that?" Her voice startled me. I pulled my hand from Noah's lips and turned to see a couple walking down the path past us. The girl smacked her boyfriend on his chest. He looked over at us and rolled his eyes.

"Thanks, dude. You make the rest of us look like idiots."

Noah smiled and nodded. I smiled at the girl. If she had any idea what we had been through since fall semester, she may not have swatted at her boyfriend.

When our picnic was over, Noah walked me back to my apartment building. We couldn't stay together on Thursday nights now because we both had eight o'clock classes on Friday, and we learned last semester that it was harder to get up after a night of sex and/or fighting. I actually didn't want to stay together that night because it could very well ruin the previous two-hour park bench date. I hated that I felt our relationship was as unpredictable as a roll of the dice. But I had nothing to compare it to but Joel. I just assumed some relationships were rocky and some ran smoothly.

"I'll see you tomorrow." Noah pulled me into him with the belt loops on my jeans. It was a little cool that night, and I wasn't sure if the shiver that ran through me was from the cool breeze or if it was from sheer excitement.

"I'll call you after class and maybe we can plan something?" I wasn't intending it to be a question, but that's the way it came out—like I needed his permission to call him. Noah didn't always treat me the way the girl who smacked her boyfriend assumed. I let things go that I should have addressed because I was scared of losing him. I was trying so hard to heed Jake's advice about not sacrificing who I was to keep the peace between Noah and me. But I had a hard time shaking that self-conscious little girl who was so afraid to look stupid. I may just have to pick and choose what to call him on as I worked up to being sure of myself. Stupid? Maybe. But I had to start somewhere.

"Sure. Sounds good." He leaned in and tilted his head so our foreheads touched. He stared into my eyes, but didn't say a word. If there was any time I wanted to read someone's mind, it was at that moment. I smiled up at him and tried to harness the power I needed to see into his heart. And with that, the skies opened and it started to pour rain.

"Shit! I have to get this basket back without it getting ruined. It's a Sigma Chi antique. See you tomorrow."

Noah turned and quickly ran away, trying to shove as much of the basket under his oversized sweatshirt as he could. I didn't have time to say anything. I just watched as he ran in and out of the portions of the sidewalk illuminated by street lights. I watched until I could see him no more. I stood in the rain for I don't know how long, hoping it would wash away all the pain he had caused me. I closed my eyes and leaned against the cold bricks of the building. If you truly forgive someone, does that mean the things they did to you shouldn't hurt anymore? If that was the case, I was lying to Noah and myself by saying I forgave him.

As the rain from the wall soaked into the back of my sweater, the tears dripping off my lowered chin soaked the flowered scarf Noah bought me last summer right before he came back to campus to finish pledging. I lifted it to my face, it smelled like him. I took it off and tucked it under my shirt so the rain didn't wash away that part of Noah or the memory of that night. Sometimes I saw glimpses of our relationship like the scent of the scarf. Its existence wasn't a given, it would only survive if I protected it.

I thought what I felt the night he gave me the ring would stay with me and give me strength for this next chapter of our relationship. But, at that moment, I felt so in over my head with emotions. I was rattled. I was elated and terrified all at the same time. I felt solely responsible for keeping our love alive but I really wasn't sure how to do that. I was treading water, just hoping to stay afloat.

Twenty-Four

Becki was one of those friends that would hear you out, say nothing while you cried and complained, never offering any advice. She was just there to listen. She and I talked a lot. She still lived in the dorm we moved into when we transferred which was only a couple blocks from Sigma Chi. It came in handy because if I left Sigma Chi, I could get to her dorm quicker than I could get to my own apartment. I could rehash everything, gather myself, and go home and no one had to know anything had happened. Especially Stacy. She couldn't tolerate one more of Noah's fuck ups.

Becki's boyfriend wasn't much of a partier so she and I rarely got to hang out and drink together. So, the weekend Shawn was in Philadelphia for a job interview, she came out to Sigma Chi with me. We were excited to just have a chance to drink and have a good time together.

For much of the night, we danced, goofed around and hung out with some of the brothers that usually didn't give me the time of day. Becki had that effect on guys. She was an artist, and most guys found her obvious sensuality quite intriguing.

"Things seem good between you and Noah." Becki leaned forward so I could hear her over the music blaring across the dance floor.

"Really good actually. I almost feel like I'm holding my breath, waiting for something to come out of nowhere and knock the wind out of me."

"Beers for my pretty ladies," Noah bounded up to us spilling beer out of the cups as he got closer. He handed a cup to each of us and then was called away by one of the pledges trying to break up a fight. He stole a quick kiss and ran off to do the opposite of what most people expected him to do.

"So, you really think he's going to fuck it all up again?"

"I don't know. I feel so guilty for even saying that. But I was naïve before and look where it got me. To some extent, shouldn't we always be conscious of the things that threaten our relationships?"

"Conscious, yes. Waiting for it to happen? That's messed up, Gracie."

"God, Becki, I don't know how to forget all that's happened. I wish I could just wipe it clean and start over. I feel like we will never get back to where we were."

"You may not. This may be when you decide if you're going to sacrifice what you deserve for something you settle for. Ya know?"

"You sound like Jake. That's almost exactly what he said right before Christmas break."

"And what did you say when he said that?"

"I didn't say anything, I cried into his pillow."

"Whoa. You were in bed with Jake? How did I miss that?"

"It wasn't like that. I needed to talk and it was two in the morning. I climbed in bed, cried and stayed the night."

"Does Noah know?"

I shook my head. I knew Jake and I may have crossed the line. How would I feel if Noah did the same thing with a girl? But what Jake and I had wasn't sexual, it was honest and easy.

"It's loud. Let's go upstairs. I want to show you Noah's new room."

"Whoa, he's got digs upstairs. Awesome."

"Yeah. It's a lot bigger and we get to go up the big windy stairs to get to it."

"Well, let's go!" We giggled. The huge staircase was the centerpiece of the house but during parties the upstairs was off limits.

Becki and I slammed a beer and headed up to Noah's room. He didn't lock his room during parties because not just anyone was allowed upstairs.

"Hey Pete!"

"Hey, girl! Havin' fun?"

"You bet!"

"Dude, why are you sitting here?" Becki never held back when something didn't seem right.

"Pledges sit on the landing making sure no one comes up who isn't supposed to. I'm Pete, the man on duty tonight."

"Well, rock on, Pete!"

Noah talked about Pete like he was an idiot. I had overheard some of the hazing Pete had to endure because he was a little more sensitive than the other pledges. I still didn't get the hazing thing. Maybe the hazing and the fact that the Sigma Chi house held some secrets that could get people in trouble was why I found it eerily intriguing.

Becki and I got to Noah's room. We could hear music coming from inside. My stomach lurched. Fear immediately gripped me that there might be a girl in there with him. Becki picked up on my alarm. "Right there's the keyhole. Take a peek if you're so worried."

Becki would never have taken any of Noah's shit. She would have kicked him to the curb the night he admitted to cheating, and she never would have looked back. Sometimes I wished I could see where I would be if I had done just that. But, I didn't like to think about being without Noah, it made me nauseous. It made me panic.

The fraternity house was ancient, so the keyholes were just that. Key holes. I bent down and looked in, but held my breath. I summoned strength from Becki. I saw Noah right away. He sat on his couch just staring at his hanging tapestry while Jane's Addiction threatened to shake the plaster off the old stone walls. He had a dazed drunk look on his face, and I started to laugh. He turned and I darted away from the hole.

"What? What's so funny?"

"Wait a second and then look. It's like he's waiting for a show to play out on that wall hanging."

Becki and I both bent down at the door and took turns peeking in and giggling quietly. We tried to decide if we should knock or scare the piss out of him by barging in.

It was the most fun I'd had at the house in a very long time. I started to associate this place with all the bad things that I tucked away in the back of my mind. All the uncomfortable things—the secrets, the misconceptions, the humiliation. It was hard to find innocent fun here. It scared me but I was determined to beat the odds. And at that moment, we were doing just that, having some innocent fun.

I lost my balance and toppled backward and landed on someone's shoe. Becki laughed and we both stood and tried to place who the two obviously annoyed girls were.

"Um. Excuse me." She motioned toward the door, whipped her hair off her shoulders, and rolled her eyes at her friend. I was not thrilled with her tone, especially since I didn't have the balls to get nasty with her, so I just turned on a smile and decided to be helpful. Becki was just waiting for a long enough silence so she could flatten the bitch.

"Sorry. Whose room are you looking for? I can tell you where it is." I smiled sweetly.

And then I can kick you down the stairs.

"This one." She pointed to Noah's door and cracked her gum.

Fuck you.

"Well, this is my boyfriend's room, but I know all the brothers so I would be happy to help you find whoever you—"

With that, the door flew open and Noah stood in front of me with fire in his eyes. His lips twisted as though they were holding back a flood of obscenities. He motioned for the girls to come in without taking his eyes off me and shut the door in my face.

I was stunned. I twisted my grace/trust ring around my finger as I tried to decipher what had just happened. I had pretty much let the Lily thing slide, giving him the benefit of the doubt. But the way he humiliated me in front of those two girls was the straw that broke the camel's back. I'd had enough and I wasn't leaving until I told him to go fuck himself!

I'm not giving in this time.

He was going to have to realize he couldn't be so selfish. He couldn't have the best of both worlds. He needed to understand my feelings mattered. He needed to treat me with respect. The hurt and disappointment I felt was valid, whether he thought I was overreacting or not. My feelings were valid. And "I'm sorry" wasn't a tool to simply wash the slate clean just so he could dirty it up again.

I waited at the top of the stairs and tried not to let Pete know I was crying. I told Becki she didn't have to stay with me because the less he felt ganged up on, maybe the better he would listen to me. I tried to collect myself before I banged heads with him.

I heard his door shut so I wiped my face and turned to cut him off. I rounded the corner and almost ran into the two girls. They veered around either side of me which left me toe to toe with Noah who had been following them pretty closely. I teetered a bit.

The combination of adrenaline and alcohol was getting to me. I glared up at him and stood my ground. He glanced up at the girls, who must've stopped after they passed me, and nodded for them to go ahead.

"What's your deal?" He ran his hands through his hair. Instantly, I was wondering why. Was he trying to cover up something by fixing his hair? What had they been doing in there for the last fifteen minutes? It couldn't be healthy to be so twisted up inside as to whether the person you loved was faithful or not. I twisted my grace/trust ring again.

"Not here." I pushed him backwards and pointed to his door. I was completely riding on the drunkenness but it was giving me the balls I needed to be firm with Noah.

We walked in and he threw himself down on the couch with his arms crossed. He slammed his feet up on the coffee table one at a time, crossed at his ankles.

"So, talk. What have I done now to piss you off?"

Was I really that much of a nag that all I did was remind him of what a shithead he was? Was I over reacting? I didn't know what to think anymore. "Noah, you are acting like letting two girls into your room and slamming the door in my face isn't a dick move. In what reality is that not supremely rude?"

"I heard you."

"Heard me what?"

"I heard you get all bitchy with them, 'this is *my* boyfriend's room...' and I didn't think it was fair to them that you were being like that. The way guests are treated at this house reflects on Sigma Chi. I'm protecting the brotherhood."

"What about the way girlfriends are treated?"

He stayed silent.

This hurt. First of all, I had swallowed every ounce of rip-your-eyes-out aggression, put on a sweet face and took on, what I thought was, a helpful tone for the sheer purpose of *not* coming across as a bitch. It was really important to me what people thought of me. Maybe too important. Maybe that was part of my problem. How could he twist the scenario around on me and make me second guess my own tone? I was going crazy. There was no doubt about it. I was losing myself.

Secondly, he chose to stick up for them and "the brotherhood," which made me look like the idiot. He was protecting them from his bitchy girlfriend instead of putting me first.

"Noah! I was not bitchy at all! I was trying to be helpful. How should I know that girls are roaming the house looking for my boyfriend? I truly thought they were just in the wrong wing of the house at the wrong room."

"Sure you did." He stood up and walked toward me. "Are we done?"

I swallowed the knot in my throat, stifled a sob, and said, "You need to sober the hell up. Call me when you realize what an asshole you just were."

I turned and walked out, even slammed the door for effect. The last image of him in my mind was a forlorn panicked look. I wasn't expecting that reaction from him at all. And I am sure the look on his face was because he was not expecting mine. I was going to have to keep these balls to deal with this side of our relationship.

I wasn't to the front door before all the emotions from the night poured out of my face. I held my face in my hands and ran to the sidewalk, hoping no one saw me. I ran the whole way home. There was a small part of me that hoped I would die from a collapsed lung. I was so not an athlete. That would show him, wouldn't it? He would have to live with that guilt for the rest of his life. I couldn't seem to make him feel guilty about anything else, maybe if I died while running from him he would.

I knocked on Jake's door. Nothing. I assumed he and Sam were out sans ladies. I could text him, but I knew he needed some guy-time. I slid down the wall next to their door and sobbed. My lungs hurt from running the whole way home, and my heart hurt from the pommeling it just took in Noah's room. The hallway started to spin. I reached for the floor to hold on.

"Gracie?" Jake was out the door and on his knees in front of me in less than a second.

"Jake." It's all I could muster. I didn't even have the words for how confused and hurt I was.

"Come here, baby girl." He helped me up and took me by the hand. I was crying so hard I could barely see where I was going. He slipped his arm around my shoulders to guide me back to his room.

"Sit down, Gracie. Let me take off your boots." I couldn't see his face because my face was covered with my hands, but his voice was so soft and gentle. His room was warm and there was soft music playing from his iPod. He stood and lifted my sweater over my head which left me in a jean skirt and an old Ramones concert tank.

"I'm going to go get you some water. Get under the covers, I'll be right back."

I slid out of my skirt and threw myself between his sheets. My inhibitions were gone after all I had to drink so the fact that I was in Jake's bed in next to nothing wasn't even an issue for me.

"Sit up. Have some water so you're not hung over in the morning."

"Thanks."

"Whoa. Gracie." He pointed down at my bare legs that stuck out below my shirt when I struggled to sit up. "Let me get you something." He turned and rifled through some folded laundry and handed me a pair of sweats.

"I can't." I tried kicking my legs out from under the sheets and I just got more tangled.

Jake carefully took me by the ankles and slid me to the edge of the bed. He put my feet through the leg holes and stood me up. When he pulled the sweats up to my waist he kissed me on the forehead. "Gracie-girl, what am I going to do with you?"

"You're a good friend, Jake." I fell back, patted the bed next to me and he climbed in without hesitation. I crawled as close to him as I could get. His strong arms were around me in no time, my face was buried in his neck and his chin rested on the top of my head.

"Get some sleep, beautiful. No one's going to hurt you tonight."

Twenty-Five

Three days later, Noah still hadn't called, so after dinner when Stacy left for Greg's, I caved. I left a message that we needed to talk. Within ten minutes, he called me back. He said he was busy helping the pledges with something, but I could come up in twenty minutes if I wanted to.

"I'm not sure that's a good idea. I just wanted to talk on the phone."

"Come on. I don't bite. I'd like to see you anyway."

What? For the three days I heard nothing. Now he acted like he missed me. My heart fluttered, but I kept my wits about me and tried to squelch my hopes of walking into his room to a bevy of lit candles and soft music and a very sorry, very turned around Noah.

Actually, I didn't even know if I would like that at this point.

I was proud of myself for leaving the way I did Saturday night. So, I thought I could give in to his request to go to the house because I was still a couple points ahead...if we were keeping score...which I assumed gave me the upper hand. I was really only concerned with my own score because little by little, I was growing some balls and standing up for myself, and we all knew if a score was in place, he would be in negative digits. Although, I wasn't convinced he thought so.

When I walked into the house, Pete was carrying a tray of dirty dishes through the lobby. He slowed down and his lips parted like he was going to ask me something, but then his eyes apologized as he tipped his head in what looked like pity and headed to the kitchen. That's when I realized he would never make it to Hell Week. He was too soft for this house. I shook the thought from my mind and took the stairs to Noah's room.

As always, music was pumping through the thick wooden door. I stood in the hall and slowed my breathing, but my body started to shake as it filled with fear, with dread of the conversation I had to have with him. I needed to, in no uncertain terms, let him know that I was better than the way he treated me at this house. I had no interest in dating Jekyll or Hyde. Regardless of the conversation, I didn't think I could be in his room without trembling. Inside his room, Michael Hutchens belted words to "Don't Change." Words I hoped to hear from Noah. Words that would assure me I wouldn't need to change for him.

When I walked in, he turned around. I saw his breath hitch. He smiled and sat on the couch. I couldn't have been more confused than at that moment. His smile worked me over each time, like his very own restart button and he used it to his benefit. I walked over and sat on the edge of the coffee table facing him.

I wasn't going to let him hit that magic button this time. But I could have used a fast forward button to get through the nightmare of a conversation that followed.

"So, the other night..." I couldn't believe *I* had to start the conversation. We'd been sitting down long enough for him to say the two words I was waiting for—*I'm sorry*.

"Yeah. What the hell was that?"

"Sometimes I just don't get you, Noah." My hands shook so I clasped them in my lap so it would go unnoticed. I was not going to back down like I usually did.

"You don't get *me*? How about you and your jealous rage? Huh? What was that?"

I was so frustrated before he even finished that sentence that I could have spit nails. "I wasn't jealous. I was pissed."

"Pissed at nothing." His expression was turning, I was losing the Noah I walked in to.

"Nothing? Nothing?" I took a deep breath. Noah's face twisted into something that scared me, and I was trying to stave off whatever depravity was lurking under the surface.

"Gracie, you went all psycho! Do you know how stupid you looked to them?"

His words punctured me and shards of my spirit spilled out. He had been angry with me before but name-calling was a new low, even for Noah.

"I wasn't psycho and I'm not stupid. I was trying to help—"

"Help? You helped, all right. You helped yourself right into the role of jealous girlfriend."

"How many times do I have to say it, I. wasn't. jealous! I was—"

"Oh, right, you were being helpful. Explain how flipping out was helpful in that situation."

I stopped talking and replayed the events of that night in my mind. In my mind, I was being a bitch to those girls, but I thought I had control of my tongue when I actually spoke to them. Shit. Was this *my* fault?

"Noah," I could feel my throat closing, tears were imminent, "I didn't mean to flip out. They came at me with attitude and I tried my hardest to stay calm so I didn't come across bitchy. But that's not even the issue—"

"Really? Because that was my issue with the whole shitty night."

What bothered me the most about this conversation was not even the direction he kept trying to take it. It was the stagnant way he spoke the words and how effortlessly they came to him. He was on autopilot. It scared me that this quiet viciousness came so easily and seemingly at the flip of a switch.

I thought back to the conversation we had about him pushing me away when he felt overwhelmed by the love he felt for me. Was this situation a result of what he felt that made his breath hitch when I walked in? I was at a loss. I told myself I would stand up to him, but I also said I would love him through this struggle. But what he was struggling with now was an anger that had me frozen.

"My issue was that you invited them in and slammed the—"

"So, now you have a say in who I have in my room? You're my warden, now?"

"Dammit, Noah! You are pissing me off!

"Welcome to my world, Gracie. Welcome to my world."

Nothing made any sense. I tried to get my thoughts straight but as soon as I started saying them, he interrupted me and twisted things around to make it look like I was just a psycho who fed off of innocuous situations turning them into something they weren't for attention. I was so frustrated within fifteen minutes that I dropped my head into my hands and sobbed. I felt abused by the up and down control he had over my emotions. I couldn't take it anymore. I wept.

"And there they are. The tears."

I looked up and his face was cold, his eyes were hollow. It was like I was spilling my heart out to someone I didn't know, like someone else inhabited his mind and body. I was so scared at that moment that my chest started to tighten.

"Look..." He remained stoic, almost rehearsed. "I don't like when you make me feel married. I don't want that."

I didn't think my chest could get any tighter, but at that moment, I was sure I would suffocate. I knew he'd been struggling with his feelings for a while. But I had no idea he was headed down a road of uncertainty. We had just spent a beautiful Christmas together. He gave me the grace/trust ring. But now it was as if when we came back to campus, the curse of the Sigma Chi house rolled back into the picture, our picture. I had built up a wall since September so that the things he did hurt less. I tried to protect myself from all he dished out. I rationalized it as "getting through the tough spots." If we could get through *this*, then we could head back in the right direction. If I didn't make a big deal about *that*, then he would be more tolerant when I opened up about bigger issues.

I got through his void of emotion by pretending he was smiling on the other side of the phone as we talked on nights I couldn't see him. I pretended he was making love to me when that's not at all what he was doing in his own mind. I even belted out whimpers of ecstasy so his brothers would think we had unbelievable chemistry. The distorted truth was, I was hoping if I could make everyone around us see our relationship working, maybe it would. But maybe this was the end. Maybe I had to come to terms with him being too much of a coward to just end it. That's when I realized, every time we had broken up, it was because *I* broke up with *him*. He *was* a coward. I swallowed the bile that rose in my throat, took a deep breath and gave him the out he obviously needed.

"So, we are done for good."

"No." He looked at me like I completely missed his point.

I have no fucking idea which way is up right now.

"Then what?" I was so sick from this roller coaster ride, I wasn't sure I could take another up or down.

He shrugged.

"Fine, Noah. You just think about it and I will let you alone." I got up and walked toward the door. I had to will my legs to support the weight of this insanity or I would be in the fetal position on his floor.

"I have to study anyway." His expression had changed. His eyes weren't fiery anymore, they were empty.

"Can you at least hug me before I go?"

Let me show you how it's supposed to feel. He walked over to me. Without looking at me, he rolled his eyes and threw his arms up over my shoulders and let them just hang there. I hugged for the both of us, trying to hold on to every last shred of sanity while convincing myself I could feel something from him. I couldn't, but I had gotten really good at pretending I could.

I walked to Becki's dorm and replayed everything to her. She got out some shot glasses and we did a couple vodka shots. I told her I made the decision to walk away before he broke me completely. She was supportive and agreed it needed to be done. I knew if she was voicing her opinion, it was something that needed to happen.

I wasn't there for twenty minutes when Stacy texted me that Noah had just called and asked where I was because I wasn't answering my phone. I checked my missed calls. Yep. He had called. I flipped my phone off silent and did another shot. And with that, his face showed up on my screen. Incoming call.

"Hi, what are you doing?" His voice was slow, almost sweet. Almost.

"I'm at Becki's."

"Why?"

"Because I needed to talk to someone."

"Why?"

"Because I obviously can't talk to you."

"Why?"

Oh my word, I was going to throw the phone across the room. What was he, five?

"Because you have to study."

"Do you want to come over?"

"For what?"

He was sucking me back in. I reached for Becki in my mind as I saw myself caught in a whirlpool somewhere in the middle of an expanse of dark water with no solid ground in sight.

Drowning.

"To watch a movie?"

Are you kidding me? How does this make sense to you?

"I thought you had to study." I was livid.

"I'm done, I can't anymore." His voice was barely above a whisper.

"Why?" *Because you're Jekyll now and it was Hyde who wanted to study?*

"I'm just not in the mood."

"You were anxious to get to work when I left."

"But now I can smell your perfume and I miss you. You can stay."

"What?"

"You can stay over."

"Are you kidding?" My voice spewed disgust and was louder than usual. I got a thumbs up from Becki. She was pulling me up.

"Please?" His voice became more desperate with each word he spoke.

I was silent. I wanted my Noah back so badly that I endured each blow then took the apology too easily. I knew I did. But the love and affection I craved from Noah was being dangled in front of me. It gave me hope that the Noah I fell in love with was clawing to get out. I couldn't give up on him now.

"I promise I'll be affectionate." He knew exactly what I was craving and he dangled it a little closer to my heart.

Just thinking about him voluntarily wrapping his arms around me made my stomach lurch.

"I have to go." I hung up before I even waited for a response.

I looked at Becki with an I-am-an-idiot expression.

She patted my leg and handed me another shot. I fell back on her bed just as my phone rang again. It was Noah.

"Hello?"

"Can you bring me food?"

And that's where his second biggest hold on me was secured — my willingness to take care of him. He knew if he gave me the impression he was in need of something, I was there.

So, we compromised. I was caving to him again but I wasn't about to be his go-fer. We met at the corner pizza place and walked back to the house together. Pizza, what I was holding on a tray the day he took my breath away for the very first time. And now I was barely holding on to my own dignity.

"I think I have a conclusion. What do you think about this?" I could hear hope in his voice.

I closed the door behind me and sat back down on the coffee table.

Déjà vu.

He continued, "How about I be more affectionate and we see how it goes?"

"So, you want to stay together?"

"Yeah."

"Noah, all this up and down between us is making me feel like I am insane. Maybe we just need to be done." I felt the tingling start in my toes.

"Gracie, hear me out. I was sitting here trying to study and all I could smell was your perfume, and I missed you. I missed you with everything I have in me."

"Noah, I had to *ask* for a hug and you barely gave me that. And a half an hour later you miss me?"

"I can't explain it."

"I wish one of us could explain it. I feel like I'm losing my freaking mind, Noah."

He walked over to the couch and sat facing me with his legs on the outside of mine. He grabbed my hands and tilted his head.

His big brown eyes softened and my favorite pouty lips pouted on purpose. I smiled and looked away. I just couldn't resist him. I loved him so much it hurt. He took my face in his hands and lifted my lips to meet his. It was a kiss that could have stopped time. Not deep or overtly sexy. But tender, soft and loving. "I'm trying," he whispered and breathed hope into my parted lips.

We finished our pizza and climbed into his bed. He snuggled in real close, hugging me from behind, and rested his face right by my ear.

"Thanks," I whispered. I wasn't even really sure if that was the right word.

"For what?"

"Making an effort." I turned my head so his lips met my face.

"*This* isn't an effort." He spoke against my cheek and squeezed me a little tighter.

"I thought you hated this."

"I don't hate it. I convinced myself I did because I love you so much sometimes it scares me."

For the first time in ages, I fell asleep in his arms with a dry pillow, a smile on my face and hope in my heart. Maybe his heart had come around.

Twenty-Six

I woke up in Noah's arms. My heart was still hopeful. The fact that we fought because I stood up to him and he initiated the make-up and didn't even try to get me naked was huge.

He stirred and peeked at me out of one eye. "You're still here."

"You didn't want me to be?"

"I absolutely want you to be. I hated last night."

"Me, too." At that moment, I wondered if his heart felt as tortured as mine. I wondered if he was capable of feeling the kind of pain he inflicted.

"You wanna talk?" In two years, he had never started a conversation with those words. I jumped right on it.

"Noah, last night was hell. I felt like I was in an episode of the Twilight Zone. It was like you were talking out of both sides of your mouth. One minute, you don't even want to hug me and less than an hour later we are in your bed, fully clothed, and you can't let go. What the hell?"

"The longer we are together the more pressure I feel for the whole 'forever' thing. That scares the piss out of me. I have never, ever pictured myself married, but when you say 'I love you' more than a couple times or say you want to 'make love' I get a flash in my mind of two old married people. I don't want that. But I want *you.*"

"I am going to be honest with you. I need you to tell me you love me and I need you to stop fucking me and start making love to me. I can't be with you if you can't give me those things." The words were out of my mouth before I could think. I just set myself up for a manic roll of the dice. I didn't know *who* I would get when he responded to that.

"I do love you, Gracie. For some reason it is just hard for me to say. I can't explain it. Maybe we should take a break from sex for a while. I think it confuses things even more."

"Really?"

"Yeah."

I really didn't know what to do with that suggestion. I wanted to believe that he was exercising restraint as a means to help us connect more deeply on other levels. But I couldn't help worrying that this was the beginning of him letting me go.

I left Noah's when he realized he was late for a brothers' meeting. I needed do some laundry and I needed to get my mind off everything. I threw a load in at the corner laundry place and ran home for more quarters. I ran into Jake about a block from our apartment, so he tagged along.

"So, how's the semester going with Jessica away? You miss her?"

"Sure I do. But she's having a great time already, so I'm happy she's getting the chance to do this." He smiled and pulled some of my laundry from the dryer.

"Does it make you sad that she's gone?"

"Sad? No. Why would it make me sad?"

"I don't know. Just wondered." I did know. If Noah left for some kind of semester abroad thing, I would be a basket case. I would have myself so worked up and so scared of what he was doing, I think I would die. It would be nice to be so secure in a relationship that you didn't have to worry the person you loved the most was loving someone else while you were apart.

"How are things with Noah?"

I looked up at him as I fed more quarters into the washer and rolled my eyes.

"That good, huh?"

"Let me give you a taste of the last week."

Jake sat down on one of the plastic chairs bolted to the floor. He propped his feet up on a stepstool and crossed his arms over his chest, "Ready."

"You sure?" He was nowhere near ready but he nodded. "Just before I climbed in your bed last weekend, Becki and I were at Sigma Chi. Noah ended up getting pissed at me and invited two girls into his room just before he slammed the door in my face. Yesterday was the first we spoke since then and it was because *I* called *him*." I stopped to give Jake a chance to respond.

Jake had this way about lending an ear that fascinated me. He didn't always say much, but I knew for sure he was taking it all in. I also knew when he was biting his tongue, holding back when the truth could hurt. He nodded for me to continue.

"I went up yesterday to tell him what he did was unacceptable but every time I tried to get a whole thought out he would interrupt and twist my words around. I felt like I was losing my mind, so after I forced him to hug me, I left and went to Becki's."

"Forced him to hug you?" He repeated the words like he was repeating something I spoke in a foreign language he had no idea how to translate.

"He's just in this weird place, Jake. He's scared of what we feel for each other. He feels married. So, anyway, I'm at Becki's and he calls and says he couldn't stop thinking about me, he missed me, blah, blah, blah. I went back over—"

"Tell me you really didn't go back over? Gracie—"

"Wait. He said he will try to love me the way I need him to. I just feel like he needs me to walk him through this. He loves me."

"He will try to love you the way you need to be loved? Be careful, Gracie. Don't let him control you." He stood up and walked over to where I was. I stopped folding when he leaned against the washer and pulled me so I was standing in front of him, his feet on either side of mine. As soon as I looked up and into those crystal blue eyes, the tears began to flow. He pulled me in for a long hug. I gave into the sadness and soaked his shirt with my tears.

Jake typically let me finish a thought before talking me through the difference between what I *thought* was happening and what was *really* happening with Noah and me. He was such a gentle soul with a mature and loving heart. And lately I couldn't get enough of his hugs.

I had been filling the emotional gaps between Noah and I with time spent with Jake. We were either watching TV, doing laundry together, or going out for ice cream. Sam was usually studying or out tutoring the less brilliant, so if he wasn't with me, poor Jake was left all alone. I was happy to take a turn at being his stand-in as he had done it so many times for me—snuggle stand-in only. It was easy to talk to him. He didn't judge or push. He just listened…and sometimes got emotional in his responses. I was sad for him that Jessica was away but glad for me that he had more time on his hands because he was a great sounding board. He'd known Noah longer than I had, so often his insight was something no one else could give. And he was oh so lovely to look at. When we walked on campus or around town, I would secretly count the number of heads he turned.

Jake insisted on carrying both my laundry baskets and gave me the empty laundry bag. I hoped his arms wouldn't fall off before we reached the apartment building. But as I eyed their obvious definition, I was sure my two baskets were nothing he couldn't handle. Maybe it was because Jessica was gone, but I was noticing more about Jake's physique. I couldn't help myself. I seemed to pick up on every nuance. More than once, I'd been distracted by his abs peeking out between the bottom of his shirt and his low-slung jeans when he would reach for something. Today I noticed his arms, a couple days ago it was his hands. I thought of Jessica. I wondered what it felt like to hold on to someone you knew wouldn't let you go.

I enjoyed his company while I put my laundry away. I opened my closet door and threw my laundry bag to the bottom. When I turned around, Jake was within inches of me. After dealing with Noah's multiple moods, I was startled by Jake's close proximity. Without warning, he took me into his arms and hugged me so tight I teared up again. He squeezed a little tighter and whispered in my ear, "Gracie, you are an amazing girl. You are beautiful and kind and you have the biggest heart of anyone I know." He pulled back and looked me straight in the eyes. "But you have to see that Noah doesn't respect you, he is controlling you."

"Jake!"

"Listen, if no one is going to be brutally honest with you, I will, because I can't stand watching you break."

"Stop." I shook my head and put my face in my hands.

"Gracie, listen to me. This is like a train wreck. Everyone is watching and everyone is seeing the same thing. But for some reason, you aren't seeing the damage he is causing. This is eating you alive. He is stealing away the Gracie we all love and leaving an empty shell. It hurts me to watch. Honey, he doesn't love you!"

His voice got louder and his grip on my arms got a little tighter when he repeated himself. "He doesn't love you!" his voice trailed off.

I wiggled free and ran into the other room. "*Stop it*, Jake!"

He followed. "How does he show it? If he loves you, tell me what he does to prove it to you."

"He...well..."

"See, you should be able to come up with something immediately. You can't."

"How can you..."

"He treats you like shit." His face softened and he started to tear up. "I see you crumble more each time we talk about what he's done to you. He's changed back into the old Noah, and he doesn't deserve you. You are way too good for him. When are you going to see that?"

"Jake, you are my best friend! My very, very best friend! How can you say these things to me? How can you stand here and hurt me like this?" The last question came out as a whisper.

He walked over to me and wiped my tears. He took my face in his hands. "Because sometimes being the best friend means telling the truth even when it hurts."

I crumbled in his arms and he helped me to the couch. I don't know how long we sat there, but I eventually cried myself to sleep. When I woke up, I was covered up with a blanket and there was a note jotted on the receipt from our last take out order lying on the coffee table.

Remember to not settle. You are worth so much more than you give yourself credit for.

Love you to pieces, Jake

Twenty-Seven

End of January, Spring Semester, Junior Year

Jake and I started talking a little more regularly about the things that troubled me. Our talks went much deeper now. It was like we broke the seal with that one painful conversation in my apartment, and now I could open up to him even more than I had been able to before. I really had never trusted anyone as much as I trusted Jake.

Thank you, Jessica, for going away this semester.

Noah made good on his new attempt at being affectionate. He snuggled in close and held my hand while we watched TV or lay in my lap while we talked about random things from our day. We had stayed true to our "no sex" decision, but I couldn't tell if that was helping to focus more on the emotional side of our relationship. I still worried it was making the shift to "just friends" easier for him.

It was a little more than two weeks before Valentine's Day, and I still couldn't get the conversation with Jake out of my mind. It had been on a continual loop inside my head for the last two weeks.

Over and over I heard him say Noah didn't respect me or love me. I didn't want Jake to be right. Noah did love me. He just had a hard time saying it.

I was working on not over-thinking things. Instead of having a twenty-minute internal struggle as to whether I should stop by on my way home from class or wait for him to call me, I decided that I would turn over another new leaf and I was just going to follow my heart and stop in when I missed him or call when I needed to hear his voice.

As I carried my new excitement for being boldly spontaneous toward the Sigma Chi house, I threw that little voice in my head to the curb. That's when I saw Noah walking toward me.

"Hey." He flashed his bright white smile. His eyes were gentle and that smile…it was genuine.

"Hey. I was just going to surprise you." I waited to see his reaction to my spontaneity.

"Well, I was just going to take you for ice cream." He reached for my hand.

My stomach did a flip flop.

"Don't look so shocked. It makes me look bad." He smiled when he said it so I knew that was his way of telling me he realized what an ass he had been over the past… I lost count of our timeline, but I didn't want to keep score anymore. We were still working to clean that slate. We were starting over, again, and it felt wonderful. My heart swelled, and without second-guessing, I grinned and reached up and kissed him on his cheek. I smiled the whole way to iScream.

His twenty-first birthday was on Valentine's Day. But I was sure he was way more excited to turn twenty-one than he was to celebrate with hearts and flowers. While we were in line, we talked about his fears of what a twenty-first bar tour means to his brothers.

"They will try to kill me!"

"Noah, I have seen you drink, you'll be fine. You could come over after your bar tour and I can nurse you back to health."

He paid for both of us and we headed back outside. The sun was brighter when we left arm in arm and my heart was warmer.

"You'd be the cutest nurse I've ever seen. I'd like that." He leaned over and kissed me on the nose. In his sweet proclamation of "I'm really trying," he hit his chin on the top scoop of my ice cream cone and knocked the whole thing out of my hands. I stopped walking, looked down, and frowned. It was no secret how much I loved ice cream.

"Oh no, babe!" He made a funny frown and threw his arm over my shoulder as we stepped over the melting mess on the sidewalk. Three steps later, he was spooning his ice cream from his dish into my mouth as we giggled about my dessert's early demise.

We acted silly all the way back to the house, and I was floating on cloud nine because it finally felt easy and natural. I couldn't stop smiling as we climbed the stairs hand in hand. We walked into his room, giggling about a funny story he was telling me about poor Pete. That poor guy, he was either sadistic or stupid. I laughed along, but in my gut, I felt so badly for him. I didn't want to risk ruining the mood by turning all humanitarian on Noah.

When I walked over to hang my coat on the back of his door, I saw it. My stomach lurched. I blinked a couple times to hold back the tears stinging my eyes, took a deep breath, and decided to ignore what was in the trashcan so I didn't ruin the surprise.

I walked over toward Noah just as he flipped the radio on. "Be right back. Gotta pee."

I walked back over to the trashcan and took a longer look. Sure enough, there had been a bouquet of flowers inside the cellophane wrapping still held together with a pretty pink ribbon. He bought me flowers? He didn't even know I was going to surprise him. I quickly looked around, hoping to see a bouquet. Nothing. No sign of a romantic gift anywhere. I wasn't breathing and time stood still when reality set in. The sadness in the song on the radio was breaking me. I didn't know why until I focused on the lyrics.

That's all I needed to ruin the last two hours. Stupid Don Henley convincing me I was a fool because I'd never see the truth that sometimes love just isn't enough. Tears poured down my cheeks.

"Oh my word. What is wrong now?" His annoyed tone paired with his empty eyes shredded me.

"Who did you buy flowers for?"

"What are you talking about?"

I wiped my eyes on the backs of my hands and stood up directly in front of him. He pushed the door shut behind him which revealed the trashcan in the corner that held the remnants of a romantic gesture...one obviously not meant for me. I pointed to the trashcan and looked him dead in the face. I was livid. He was two different guys in one body. One I liked and one I despised.

"It's nothing. God!" Now his voice was sharp and loud.

"Nothing? Did you buy flowers for *yourself?*"

"No! Let it go!" He said it like he was warning me.

"Let it go? Do you think I'm an idiot?" *I am an idiot. Who else but me would put up with this shit for so long? I have hope? Hope for what? There's nothing left to hope for.*

We rarely got loud when we fought, but we were getting loud. I could have strangled him at that moment.

Like a smartass, he looked around aimlessly like he had to think about whether I was an idiot or not before he answered, "No, it's just none of your business!"

"Are you kidding me? How is it none of my business? I am your girlfriend!"

He grimaced and made a guttural sound as soon as the word "girlfriend" was out of my mouth.

"See. This is the kind of stuff I hate about being 'married!' What if I just wanted to buy some flowers for a friend?"

"We are so far from being married, Noah! And it would be a sweet gesture if it was something you also did for me every now and then."

"I've bought you flowers before! Don't make me the bad guy here!"

"Yes, you are right." I calmed my voice so I wasn't yelling anymore. "You have given me flowers...when you fucked the virginity right out of me and when you admitted to sleeping with half of campus." I took a deep breath and used all the strength I could muster to yell, "Who. Were. They. For?! I have every right to know."

He spun around and looked me right in the eyes. He had walked away from me but now he slowly stalked back. With each step he took, a sinister smile spread across his face. His eyes were brazen. I was petrified.

"You want to know? You really want to know." His smile was so sour. "I bought the flowers for Lily. Lily from my Business Admin class."

Someone could have sliced my throat at that moment and I wouldn't have known. I was numb. Waiting for him to decide he wanted her had been a slow and painful death for my heart.

"Why did you buy her flowers?" My words came out sounding like my last breath. Everything in my body threatened to stop working. My breathing was shallow, I didn't blink, the tears continued to stream down my cheeks, but the muscles that were controlling my face had given up I couldn't hide the effects of his crushing blow. I felt fifty pounds heavier, and I realized my knees could give out at any minute. I reached for the door knob to steady myself as I awaited his final swing. He took two steps closer so he was right in my face and smiled from ear to ear. I braced myself.

He spoke slowly. I could feel his hot breath on my wet cheeks. "I invited her to a function the other night, and I thought it would be a sweet gesture to get her some flowers for when she got here."

I stopped breathing.

He scoffed and walked away.

"What function?" My words were barely a whisper.

He spun around, bent a little at the waist and in a deep revolting shout said, "I don't want. To. Be. Married!" And with that he turned back around, walked over to his radio, pushed a button and his iPod came to life. He spun the volume to max. He looked over his shoulder and smirked.

There was no way he could hear me so I mouthed the words, "*You* are the idiot. We are done."

His face was stone.

I left. But I stood against the cold plaster wall to catch my breath.

The Toadies were still blaring. I could feel the bass vibrate against my back and was sure it was the only thing beating in my chest.

Twenty-Eight

His arms around me were strong and they kept me warm. Being wrapped in his body made me feel protected. His chest moved in and out against my back, and his breath was warm on my neck. His lips were right near my ear and he made quiet noises while he slept. I wondered what he was dreaming. I squeezed his arms tighter to me, closed my eyes, and went back to sleep.

I woke with a jolt that broke his hold on me. I sat straight up and searched the room for the clock. The blankets fell to my waist, and the chill from the room made me shiver. When I realized it was only dinner time and I wasn't late for class, I pulled the covers up over my head and fell backwards onto the pillows. My head still pounded from all the crying I had done before I climbed into bed.

Jake pulled the covers back, revealing my face, brushed the loose strands of hair from my face, and kissed my forehead.

"You okay?"

"Oh, Jake, I just want this to be a bad dream. I am losing my mind."

He snuggled in closer and wrapped me in his signature bear hug. He had no words and once again I found my mind playing "what if?" What if I had fallen for someone like Jake instead of Noah? We'd probably be rolling in the sheets instead of him trying to hold me together.

Jake and I had a lot in common lately. We both missed someone, and having someone you trust physically close to you seemed somewhat healing. The fact that there were no expectations was a bonus. All of our friends started to think it was more than what it truly was. "What friends nap together?" they questioned sarcastically. It didn't matter what they thought. Jake and I needed each other. It was really just that simple.

"Love you, Gracie."

"Love you, Jake. It was a nice nap."

I left his apartment, and before I got to the stairwell, I heard Sam badgering him about his new bed partner. I smiled to myself. Jessica wouldn't love this set up, but Jake wasn't cheating on her. He was just being there for me. Under no circumstances would I lure a loyal boyfriend into a cheating situation. I knew all too well what that felt like from the girlfriend's side. I would never cross that line with a guy who was in a committed relationship.

When I reached my apartment, Stacy was on the phone. I was thrilled. I could sneak in, grab some clothes, and hop in the shower without having to explain my smeared make up and bed head. She was hard to deal with lately. She was sick of me being with Noah, and her grades were slipping. Not a good combo.

She looked up. "Oh, wait, she just walked in."

This time, I didn't even hope it was Noah. I knew it wasn't. Nor would it be again.

Stacy handed me my cell phone.

I looked at the screen. Mom.

"Hi, Mom."

"Hi, honey. Where were you? Stacy had no idea how to get a hold of you. I was worried."

"I was taking a nap with Jake. Upstairs. I plugged my phone in before I went up there." I knew as soon as it was out of my mouth that it was a mistake. Even Stacy winced.

"A nap with Jake? Could you explain that, please?"

My mother thought I was Daughter Theresa, and I had just stumbled into the "bed linens equal sex" conversation. I was in no mood to justify my actions, and I just wanted to spill my guts to her and tell her about all of the sex acts Noah introduced me to so she could stop making me feel guilty for not being a virgin anymore, which she thought I was. But even if I was brave enough to do that, I didn't have the energy.

"Honest, Mom. It was just a nap. Jessica is away and Jake and I were talking and fell asleep."

"Well, don't you think Noah would have something to say about that?"

"No." That whispered word was all I could muster.

We talked about my classes and how all my projects were going. She told me how work was and how Dad had been traveling a lot more lately so she was enjoying the one-on-one time with Hannah, but couldn't wait until I came home again.

"Spring Break is only six weeks away, can you believe it?" I could see her grinning through the phone.

No, I couldn't believe it. I wondered what my heart would be doing in six week. I had no idea. This horrible rollercoaster I climbed onto the night of the Sigma Chi formal was not the ride I signed up for almost two years ago in the kitchen of Murphy's, and it was barreling at a speed I couldn't keep up with. If I had known what the risks were, I may never have climbed aboard.

Noah and I hadn't even talked about Spring Break plans. Noah lived ten minutes outside of McKenzie, and Jake was staying at school for the break instead of heading back again to his hometown in Wyoming. He would be almost five hours away. Who would be my rock? Could I really go all break without seeing Noah or would I cave? I couldn't even think of telling the girls any of this.

They would hunt him down and kill him. So, I would swallow all that happened, put on a happy face, and stay numb. We broke up. That's all. It was the safest way to exist right now. I hung up with my mom and got in the shower.

I was walking from the bathroom to our bedroom wrapped in a towel and in a complete daze from my scalding hot shower. "Um, mixed company, Gracie. Put some clothes on." Stacy's voice brought me around. Jake and Sam were both eyeing me and grinning from ear to ear. I squealed and ran into our room and shut the door.

When I came out dressed, I found out they came down to see if Stacy and I wanted to go out for a little while. They couldn't have had better timing. She was stressed over one of her classes and I just wanted to get out of the place where this whole nightmare started. I was starting to hate being in my own apartment.

My spirit lifted and my sides ached. We laughed hard as we sat in the front window of Café Best, a little artsy place we sort of made our second home. We had just completed our very own impromptu "Food Tour." Translation—we ate our way down College Avenue. All of our friends were turning twenty-one or counting down the days to their own Bar Tour. We were still twenty. I only had to wait until Spring Break to be the big two-one and Stacy, Sam and Jake's birthdays were all in the summer, but we wanted some kind of "tour" tonight. People went all out for their celebratory drunk fest. Some coined a name for the event and some even had shirts made. It was fun walking down the sidewalk and seeing groups of people all dressed alike with a creative slogan on their brightly colored t-shirts. My big birthday would happen in McKenzie. Fun.

I thought about Noah's twenty-first birthday that was in a couple days. I wondered how many Valentine-less girls he would sleep with that night. Twenty-one? Yuck. I couldn't believe we were over. Really over.

"Hey. No sad faces at this table." Jake reached across the table and squeezed my hand.

"Wait? Why are you sad?" Stacy looked hurt that she was finding this out from Jake and not me.

Sam looked up from his coffee.

"Noah and I broke up. He took that Lily girl to a function I didn't even know about. But I'm okay," I lied.

"You guys always work things out, maybe this is just a bump in the road." Sam didn't know much of what had really been going on. He just knew we had broken up a couple times this year.

"These last few weeks have been more like a rumble strip than a bump in the road. But I've had it. We are done."

Stacy had no reaction. She just kept eating. She was obviously sick of my drama.

"I'm proud of you," Jake whispered and winked then squeezed my hand again.

I breathed in a sharp breath and realized three little words had been the first step in breaking the pattern.

We. Are. Done.

Everything in me screamed for surrender. I was confused. Why did my body think I had a choice in this slow drowning? I didn't have a choice. If I did, I would have swum to the surface long ago. "Just let go," it begged. Let go of what? I got a burst of energy and frantically looked around. My eyes stung. I could barely hold them open in the salty water, but I strained to see what my mind insisted was holding me under. My lungs screamed for air. I was close to death and this was my last chance to save myself. The rolling of the waves above sent shards of light to the bottom in flashes. One of those flashes revealed something I couldn't believe. A white-knuckled hand wrapped around an old corroded anchor that had obviously plunged into the ocean floor many decades before. The urge to gasp was strong when panic set in. Whose hand was that? Had someone else come to the depths with me? I waited for the clouds of sand to settle from my body's movements. That's when my view became even clearer. On the next flash of light, I set my eyes on that hand and followed it back to a wrist and then to an arm. My eyes traveled up the pale lifeless arm…to my own shoulder. I was the reason I was drowning. My aching fingers sprung open and my body lifted off the ocean floor and slowly started floating up. Up. I was headed up.

Twenty-Nine

Early February, Spring Semester, Junior Year

Jake said he was proud of me yesterday at Café Best. I wasn't very proud of myself. I was faking strength. I wasn't strong at all. Flashes of all the things I had let Noah do to my body came flooding back and made me sick, proving my weakness. Maybe Jake wouldn't hold me so tightly during our naps if he knew all of that. I wished I could take it all back. Noah said we were just trying new things, but some of those things left me feeling like a blowup doll with a beating heart. We were never getting back together, so the sick feeling in the pit of my stomach would never go away. He was now my ex-boyfriend. I no longer shared those intimate memories with someone who loved me. I walked away from him and all the pain he caused, but I couldn't take back those firsts. I had experiences with him that would no longer be "new" to me. I'd done them. That made me feel cheap. Along with my heart, he stole my good-girl status. That made me feel used. All that was left was damaged goods. And that made me feel dirty.

The best distraction for a healing soul was one of Jake and Sam's kick-ass parties. It was Friday night and there was no question we'd be spending the evening with the two hotties upstairs. Stacy and I drank while we got ready. It was awesome that we didn't have to brave the chilled winter air to get to a party.

"So, what now?"

"Um, I'm going to shave my legs," I answered from the shower.

"No, jerk, I mean what's your plan for being a free woman on a college campus of thousands of boys?" She giggled knowing I knew exactly what she was asking the first time.

I had no idea what I was going to do. Could I move on to another boyfriend? I was uncomfortable being alone. I stood under the hot water and tried to imagine what it would feel like to be single. It had been a long time since I wasn't someone's girlfriend. I didn't remember what that felt like or how I was supposed to act. I worried I was addicted to the feeling of being with someone. My psychology professor mentioned "love addiction" in class not too long ago. He didn't say much about it, just coined the phrase to make a point. I doubted there really was such a thing, but curiosity got the best of me, and after I was dressed, I looked up the term while I waited for Stacy to get out of the shower.

"*Like other addictions (drugs, alcohol, gambling, sex, work, and the list goes on), the dependency to a person (their object – drug of choice) allows love addicts to feel alive – a sense of purpose – and to gain a sense of meaning and self-worth in the world: they are driven by a fantasy hope that the drug of choice – a person – will complete them.*" – *Schaeffer, p. 61*

The definition hit me like a freight train.

"You never answered my question," Stacy called from the bathroom and knocked me from my daze.

"I am just going to focus on school and my friends, that's my plan."

"You mean school and Jake." She walked out of the bathroom with a sly grin.

"Stacy! Not you, too. Jake and I are just friends."

"Okay, if you say so."

I walked around the corner, grabbed her towel and ran. She squealed, pissed that I made her run naked around our apartment, but it changed the subject, and I would laugh over that moment for years to come.

We could hear the bass pumping as soon as we opened the door to the stairwell. That nervous party energy started at my toes and reached my buzzed brain cells just as we opened Jake and Sam's door. The heat that poured out of the room could have supplied ample warmth to every apartment on their whole floor. When you packed a hundred and fifty people in a small living room, it got hot. And that was exactly why I wore shorts and a light button-up top.

Jake and Sam rounded the corner from the kitchen with big smiles and cold beer.

"Your libation, my ladies." Sam spoke like he was a jester and we were royalty. Jester, yes. Royalty, not quite. He handed a beer to Stacy and Jake handed a beer to me still smiling at Sam's drunken humor.

"So, loser has to accompany Sam for refills." Jake elbowed me knowing I was no stranger to pounding a beer. And, truthfully Stacy sucked at it. I looked at Stacy, winked and Jake yelled, "Chug!"

Stacy gave it a good effort but she was still gulping when I slammed my red cup onto the table. "It would help if you guys challenged me when you were drinking something I actually liked." She huffed and threw her dark curls over her shoulder then linked arms with Sam and they headed to fill mine and Jake's cups. Jake walked over and wiped the dripping suds from my top lip with his thumb. I glanced over Jake's shoulder at Stacy peeking around some really tall guy. She lifted her eyebrows and mimicked Jake wiping my mouth. I shot her a glare and looked away. Jake was too sweet to be a rebound guy, even if I wanted a rebound guy...which I didn't.

We played a great game of Jack Ass at the kitchen table as the other party-goers drank and danced and drank and danced. I didn't know the rules to Jack Ass so Jake and I were a team. We laughed more than we drank, and we beat the pants off everyone. It was a good thing we hadn't been playing strip poker or it would have turned into a much different kind of party. I giggled at that thought. Then I realized there was no one there I would like to see naked. Ew.

"What was that?" Jake looked at me quite puzzled as the drunken card players left us alone at the table.

"What was what?"

"You just smiled and then made a face like you sucked a lemon."

"Oh." I pulled his head closer so I wouldn't have to scream over the music. "I was thinking it would have been funny if we had been playing strip poker but then I looked around at him and him and her." I shook my head again.

"You've never played strip poker." Jake's voice was hopeful.

"No. Of course not. Really?"

"Yeah, I didn't think that was a 'good girl' game. I'm going to go grab our beers." He winked, stood and headed for the kitchen.

I was surprised the bathroom was not occupied, but I needed to get away from the chaos for a second and think. I didn't know what to do with the "good girl" comment. I was still struggling with how to categorize myself. In my heart, I still felt like a good girl but I guess I really had ruined myself for any other guy that came after Noah. I locked the door, put the toilet seat down, and sat with my head in my hands. Maybe I was "addicted" to our relationship because Noah was the first for everything that was sexual in nature. Part of the beauty of our relationship was being the innocent one that was nervous to try new things and sometimes didn't know how to *do* those things. There was sweetness to him teaching me, guiding me. My mind flashed back to one of our firsts.

Mid-August, Summer before Sophomore Year

We lay on my bed at home. The bed I had since my family moved into this house when I was four. The bed my parents lulled me back to sleep in after a bad dream. That bed. And *we* were lying on it. Noah drove me home to an empty house after the movies. My parents were away again and I actually worked up enough nerve to tell my grandfather I'd be sleeping at a friend's which was what Hannah was doing that night. My house was empty except for me and the hottest, most dangerous guy I'd ever been alone with. I shivered at that thought.

"What's wrong?" We were facing each other.

I shook my head. "I'm just not used to doing things like this."

"We're not *doing* anything."

"Well, my parents would kill me if they knew you were even in our house while they were away." Wow. Just saying the words sent a piercing stab through my chest. It would break their hearts if they knew what I was doing. But, Noah was right, we weren't even doing anything.

For the last four hours, we had just been lying on my bed talking. Sure, we were making out like crazy—he even got to second base—but we weren't doing anything I hadn't done before.

"Do you trust me?"

"Sure, I guess."

"You guess? You asked me to spend the night with you, sweet little virgin girl, and you *guess* you trust me?"

"Okay." I looked down at my body as though I was looking for something. "Yeah, look at that, I'm still a virgin, so, yeah, I trust you."

He chuckled and tucked some of my hair behind my ear. "Could we get undressed and get under the covers?"

Panic shot through my bones. I am sure he saw it on my face, if not felt the jolt of the bed when I reacted.

"I'm not going to pressure you. No sex. I just want to be closer to you."

"I don't want to get completely undressed," I said without hesitation. I knew what it would feel like — well, I imagined what it would feel like to have that kind of sexual charge between us *and* be naked, too. That would be too much for both of us.

"All right. That's fair. How about just T-shirt and panties?"

Wow. That sounded so daring. So sultry. Something I had only done once before. Joel and I got a hotel room after my senior prom. He thought maybe we would have sex, but I had no intention of that happening. He got me down to my bra and underwear when I freaked. I am sure he took the coldest shower in history after he got home that night.

"Okay, but you can't look."

"Whatever." He smiled, but sort of rolled his eyes. He thought I was a dork. *Ugh. I am a dork.*

He turned to face the opposite wall, and I whirled my legs off the side of the bed. I was shaking. There was an ache stronger than anything I had ever felt throbbing between my legs. I wondered if that feeling was the girl equivalent to a boner. At that moment, I was glad I was a girl — I didn't need him knowing how turned on I was. I wondered if he was having that same throbbing. I got a clear visual in my mind of what that would look like on Noah. Wow. That wasn't a very "good girl" thought to have, it was risqué and naughty. And it made the throbbing worse. I felt as if I could explode. I just wished I could release the tension and then I wouldn't have to worry about things going too far.

We both slid back under the covers and turned back onto our sides so we were facing one another again. He was shirtless. I gaped. Heat radiated off of his chest and I just wanted to touch him.

So, I did. His chest was soft and warm. He reached under the covers for the bottom of my shirt, and he lifted it just as I gasped and my hand shot down to stop him.

"Please trust me. I just want to feel the parts of you I can't stop thinking about."

I swallowed the last ounce of moisture in my mouth and slowly let go of his wrist. That was the sexiest thing anyone had ever said to me. I could have melted. His fingers gently walked under my shirt and to my stomach. He had to be able to feel me shaking. Every square inch of me felt rattled. And that ache—I didn't know what to do with that ache. The deep pulsating sensation was more than a little overwhelming. Joel was more into the hand jobs I gave him than he was into helping a girl out with her own frustration. Not that I would have let him. By the time Joel finished, I was so panicked my parents were going to catch us that my ache was long gone. It had never built up to anywhere near the intensity I was feeling and Noah's hand had only reached my stomach.

Noah began to kiss me so gently. I could barely feel his lips as they brushed across mine. I peeked and his eyes were closed. There was such a peaceful look on his face. This was the boy I was petrified to work with? The womanizer, the brawler, the drunk? And he was in my bed? Touching me? This was so hot.

As our kiss deepened, and his hand slowly slid up my body and he cupped my right breast, this time my bra wasn't between me and his hand. *I should make him stop. This is going too far.* But I didn't want to. I wanted to feel him. I wanted to know what it would feel like to have his hands all over me. Where was that "good girl" now? Was she sleeping? Her alter ego was wide awake and taking in every sensation he was creating with her nipple between his fingers. He had done this before, there was no doubt in my mind. But right then, I didn't care. It felt so good to be touched by him. So good.

As our breathing increased and became audible, I reached low for him. I only touched him through his boxers, but he obviously felt the same things I did. He groaned a bit as I rubbed him through the thin layer of fabric.

He stopped kissing me for a second and he pulled back and looked into my eyes. His gaze had changed. It was no longer sweet and gentle, it was hot and needy. Oh, but I couldn't give him what he wanted. I knew what he wanted, and although I was on the verge of something explosive, I couldn't give it all up. I wasn't ready.

He blinked once and as his lips grabbed mine. His hand swiftly moved from my breast, down my shivering stomach and into the front of my panties. The way he claimed that part of my body threatened to shatter me into pieces. He found that one spot in a way that told me, I'd never have enough will power to make him stop.

Heat started at my feet and bloomed up my body. Goose bumps rose to the surface everywhere. I realized I was starting to moan. I stopped. *Good girls don't moan.* I had to break my lips away from his so I could get enough air into my lungs. My head began to spin. I was screaming on the inside. The intensity of what he was doing to me below the sheets was astounding. I pulled him close so he couldn't see my face because I didn't know what it was doing. My eyes were pressed shut, my mouth open and gasping quietly for breath. There was a build-up coming. Something started within the bones of my pelvis that was so far beyond an "ache." I couldn't think. I couldn't control my body, although I kept it perfectly still out of sheer shock of the sensations it was absorbing. A few more strokes and I inadvertently pulled my hips away from him out of fear. I don't know why. Maybe I was afraid of what would happen. I had never had a boy bring me that far. Never.

He looked concerned. "Are you okay?"

My chest heaved and my breath billowed from my mouth. "Yeah."

"What's wr—"

I slid my left hand under his head and pulled his mouth to mine. I broke our lips apart for a second and in a small shaky, breathy voice, uttered, "Don't stop."

I pressed my hips back to where his hand waited. His fingers slid down again. I couldn't stop him now. Not even if I wanted to. If I didn't release this tension, I would surely go mad. I tried so hard not to make a sound, not to move too suggestively. I wanted this, but I didn't want to be too eager. I still wanted to be a "good girl."

My body was way ahead of my brain, and even if I would have stopped his hand again, my brain was not driving this force that was coming over me in waves. There was a rhythm to the sensation, a strength that rolled my eyes back. They squeezed shut so tightly that I saw flashes of color. I broke away from his mouth with a gasp and a whimper. I pushed my chest into his and put my head over his shoulder. He applied just a little more pressure and I exploded. My grip increased around his neck and my breasts flattened against his sweat-beaded chest. I couldn't stop. I made a couple sounds I didn't recognize, held my breath, and forced my body to stay still on the outside. But inside I writhed, screamed, absorbed the waves of pleasure that were so new and so completely fantastic. Noah had given me something that I had no words for.

My breathing slowed. I gasped a couple times then my body went limp. I didn't want to stop hugging him. I was embarrassed. He had been in complete control and I had lost control of everything. I gave myself over to him and gave my control away.

He slowly dragged his hand up my stomach and across to the small of my back. He pulled his head back trying to look at me. I didn't want him to see me. I wanted to dissolve into the mattress. I didn't know what to do now. I hoped he didn't want me to reciprocate in some way. I had no idea how to match the level of intensity he had just created.

"Hey." He tucked my hair behind my ear and lifted my chin. "Are you okay? Did I hurt you?"

"Hurt me?" I giggled and a huge exhale escaped my lungs. "No, you definitely didn't hurt me."

"Then what's wrong?"

"Nothing's wrong. I am just a little embarrassed. Kind of shy about this stuff."

"But, you've done that before," he said it almost like a statement and a question at the same time.

I shook my head and tucked my face into his neck under his chin.

"What?" He tried to push me back so he could see my face, but I held on tight and just kept shaking my head while pressing my embarrassed grin into his neck.

"Wow. Joel is more of a dork than I thought."

I stilled. My smile faded. That was a low blow. If I was going to stick up for Joel, I would need to look at him. Yeah, I wasn't ready to look at him. We soon drifted off to sleep disheveled and wrapped up in each other.

I stood in Jake and Sam's bathroom staring at myself in the mirror. I now knew that feeling all too well. The high of sharing something so intimate with Noah and then the kick to the gut soon after. Sometimes that kick came as a post-sex excuse as to why I couldn't stay over, sometimes it was a hurtful jab that he thought was funny but left a bruise on my heart. I could make a list. But as it was happening, it was hard for me to believe he was trying to be mean. I sat back down, unable to look myself in the face any longer. There was no doubt my "good girl" status had to be retired. So, what did that make me? I had given that innocence to Noah, and he took it and crushed me with that fact. I decided at that moment I would be a born-again virgin. I made the mistake of giving in too soon. But not again. This shop was closed.

The knock at the door made me lift my head so quickly, I lost my balance and slid from the toilet to the floor. Although graceful, I was still embarrassed by my apparent drunkenness. I washed my hands, even though I hadn't done anything in there but think. But I didn't want the person knocking to think I was one of those people who didn't take personal hygiene seriously. I shook my head at myself as I opened the door, realizing I was still being a stupid good girl, worrying what everyone thought of her. This was going to be a hard habit to break.

I went right to the make-shift dance floor and made a Gracie sandwich between my two favorite slices of bread. Jake and Sam giggled and kept dancing. God, I loved these guys.

Thirty

We drank and drank that night. It was like we were worried there would soon be a shortage of beer and we had to suck it all down while we had the chance. Jake and I walked out into the hall to get away from the melting heat in the apartment. A window sat at the end of the hall, so we headed that way to open it and let some cool air in. Jake held my hand as we walked. Such a sweet guy.

He reached into the deep windowsill and pulled the window back, exposing the screen. The early morning chill that had settled into the seal whined as he moved it even further. I leaned and pressed my back against the wall to give my legs a break. They were burning from the show me and my sandwich bread guys had just performed.

"Here. Sit. Give your legs a break." Jake grabbed my hips and slid me in front of the open window then hoisted me up onto the deep sill. It was just wide enough for one person. Part of me felt badly that I couldn't offer him the same rest. He leaned against the wall next to me and just looked at me.

"What?"

"I'm just hoping you are really done with Noah this time. You deserve so much better than that."

"I know everyone thinks that, Jake, but not everyone has seen the side of him that I have. Not everyone knows what's really inside him."

"Gracie, there are things about Noah that I know, too. Things you don't. I am pretty certain those things would cancel out any sweetness you see in him, but it's not my place to share them. I won't. This has to be something you do. I just want you to know I am here to pick up the pieces no matter what. I promise."

"I know, Jake. I am not sure how I could ever repay you for all the support you have given me these last couple years." My eyes filled with tears. It's always easier to cry when you're drunk, but I knew that wasn't why I was crying. My soul was exhausted and craved the gentleness Jake was giving me. I cried because I didn't feel I deserved that from anyone.

"See. You don't even know your worth, do you?"

I wiped at my eyes, trying not to destroy what was left of my make-up, and tilted my head, assuring him I didn't really understand what he was asking.

"The fact that you think you owe me. My friendship and love come unconditionally. You are worth that. Please don't ever feel you need to reciprocate."

I was in awe of the friend I had before me. His sparkling blue eyes, which sparkled a little more with each beer, looked into my soul and lifted me up to a place I hadn't been in a long time. I could almost see myself differently in those few seconds of enlightenment. In my mind, when Jake spoke like this, I was strong and capable. I was a girl who could—no—who *would* walk away from Noah and never look back. Too bad my physiology disagreed. Even the thought of that made my chest get tight.

We were both startled by the apartment door squeaking open.

"Would the two of you just do it already? The suspense is killing everyone!"

One of Sam's friends that partied with us often was leaving the party. He looked back over his shoulder and gave Jake a thumbs up then threw his arm around his girlfriend's shoulders. They stumbled down the hall to the elevator.

"Why does everyone insist we are going to hook up?" I was so annoyed that people felt they had the right to assume and predict things about my life. Especially that guy. I didn't even know his last name.

"It's just because we are together all the time. They don't understand how we could spend so much time together and not hook up." He smiled and stood between my knees with his hands on my thighs. I looked down at his strong hands and without warning saw them exploring my body. *What the – ? Jessica.*

"I know this will come out the wrong way, but I'm really glad Jessica is gone. I know that's selfish, but you have been such an amazing friend. Thank you, Jake."

"Please stop thanking me. I actually enjoy being with you. It's not like spending time with you is torture...well, not *that* much torture."

He ducked as I swung to smack him in the forehead. We laughed hard. It felt so good to laugh. Laughing truly was the exact opposite of crying. Crying sucked the life out of me, but laughing filled me up, sometimes so high it felt like I could float. This was one of those times.

I hugged Jake around his head and pulled him into me and laughed a little more. Just as I released my hold on him, I got him good. Smack—right in the forehead.

He bent over like he was seriously injured, then looked up at me out of the corner of his eye. When he saw I was giving him no sympathy, he stood back up and took his place between my knees. My body had cooled off to the point of almost being cold. I touched his strong arms just under the sleeve of his T-shirt to see if he was still hot. When I grabbed his arms, I felt him flex. It was kind of cute he was trying to impress me. Like he needed to do that. I turned to close the window when I shivered. When I turned back, the look on his face had changed. His expression looked so serene and happy, but there was something else that I couldn't decipher. He squeezed my thighs with his hands.

"Kiss me."

My breath hitched. And I no longer questioned his expression.

"Jake."

"Kiss me." His face was kind and sweet, but there was a need deep in his eyes that was new to me. And that need, framed by his strong cheek bones and jaw and coupled with the stubbled goatee, made me squirm.

"Jake, no. Are you crazy?"

"I just really want to kiss you right now."

"Okay, pretending there aren't 150 people who could potentially walk out here and see us and then kick up the teasing another notch, I couldn't kiss you anyway."

"Noah?"

"No. God, no. I am so pissed at him, I couldn't care less."

"Then why?"

"Jessica."

"What about Jessica?"

Before I realized it, my breathing had become shallow. A sudden swarm of butterflies filled my stomach. I shook my head. It must be the beer. I had never considered anything like this with Jake or Sam. Pictured it? Sure. But considered it really happening? Never. I'd kissed them both on the lips probably a thousand times and there was never anything but friendship in them — for all of us.

"I could never do that to another girl. Help her boyfriend cheat."

"Just one kiss."

Wow. Who knew someone could switch gears like this inside of five minutes. I struggled with what I was feeling. After everything with Noah and how close Jake and I had gotten through it all, a tender kiss would be so comforting. The contact high I was getting from the look on his face made me think maybe I wanted to kiss him as much as he wanted to kiss me. *What the hell? Someone slow this bus the fuck down.*

But there was no sense struggling with whether to kiss him or not. I wouldn't bring the kind of pain to Jessica that Steph, Madison, and Ivy handed me.

"Jake." Tears streamed down my face. I wanted what he was offering so badly. "I can't do the same thing to Jessica that was done to me."

"What if I told you it wouldn't be cheating?" He wiped away a tear from my face.

"How would it not be cheating?" Part of me was hoping he really had a good reason so I could stop the slide show in my mind of what his kiss could be like. But another part of me couldn't imagine what the reason would be so I knew it wasn't going to happen. We would be crossing a line.

"Jessica told me she wanted us to see other people while she was away. We aren't exclusive right now. Haven't been all semester."

I stared at him and tried to process what seemed to be coming to me in slow motion. Something about this admission was so sexy. I couldn't believe what he had just said. We were both unattached. Without another moment's hesitation, I grabbed the back of his head, slid my fingers through his short auburn waves, looked him straight in the eyes and pushed myself to the edge of the windowsill as I wrapped my legs around his torso. We kissed like it was the last kiss we'd ever feel. We were breathless. He reached up and held my face in his hands. He directed my head in the opposite direction of his each time he pulled away and came back in. He was unbelievably adept with his tongue. I didn't want him to stop. My body ignited with a yearning I assumed was the result of too much beer and a broken heart, but I didn't care. What he was doing to me was exactly what I needed, and he knew that.

Jake was not someone who played around with a girl's heart. So the passion in his kiss came completely unexpected. His hands moved down my arms and up my back and down again, stopping just before my hips. My body was hyper aware of every part of his body.

Our kiss slowed and became tender and gentle. His hands moved up to my face in an attempt to keep the pace going. He was firm and intentional. In between light pecks were deep, passionate kisses that felt so much stronger than what I thought was just curiosity for both of us.

"Now, that's the action we've all been looking for! Wow!"

Without even hearing the squeak of the apartment door, we were being observed by Sam and a couple other people. Our kiss came to an abrupt halt, and we tried to compose ourselves. Sam smiled and shook his head. Jake looked up at me, his eyes asking if I had an explanation for them. I didn't. Simultaneously we both shrugged and laughed from nervous energy. I realized my chest was still heaving with deep cleansing breaths. He had literally taken my breath away. My cheeks burned with heat.

Sam walked back into the apartment and the rest of our audience headed for the elevator. Jake and I remained in a similar state of confusion.

"Two thumbs up, baby! Don't stop on our account!" one of the drunks yelled as he fell into the elevator.

Jake slowly turned and looked at me, and I waited for a reaction. I was relieved by his expression. There was no mistake— he was as blown away as I was.

Wow.

I fell into my own bed that night completely sober but more confused than I'd ever been.

My head broke the surface of the water, and I breathed the breath that saved my life. The sun was so warm. I could feel it deep in my bones, a warmth that pervaded my every pore. The small breeze was lifting goose bumps to the surface of my wet skin, but it wasn't making me cold. It reminded me I was still alive. I was above the water. As long as I could keep floating, maybe I would be rescued.

Thirty-One

Contrary to what I feared, the kiss between Jake and I did not adversely affect our relationship at all. Nothing was awkward. We were on a much more intimate level now than the friendship I had with Sam. I felt like we had melted into each other the night of the kiss. We now had a connection that was just ours, it couldn't be shared with anyone else.

Each time he held me while I cried, the night he respectfully helped me into more clothes before he helped me into his bed, the conversation we had while doing laundry all brought us one step closer to that kiss.

In the days that followed, I couldn't help the way my body reacted when Jake's hand brushed over mine, or when he'd press his hand into the small of my back to guide me into the elevator. I wondered if it was simply a *crossing the line* energy because we shared something neither of us had ever expected would happen between us. I kept telling myself it was only a couple weeks until Jessica came home, so this was just what it looked like...*friends with benefits*? No. It was deeper than that, not cheap like that term insinuated.

Jake and I spent even more time together, trying to soak up as much of each other as we could. We stayed up all night and talked when we were supposed to be studying. We kissed every chance we got and our naps were a little more than naps now. Jake was so obviously any girl's dream. He made my soul sing. I didn't let myself daydream enough to be upset knowing ultimately, he and Jessica would get back together. It was almost as if I was just happy to have him for however long I could. His love and gentleness were a blessing, even if it had to go back to being a friend-love. I'd take it.

Having Jake taking up part of my heart made my run-ins with Noah more bearable.

Noah's twenty-first birthday rolled around and I almost forgot. Someone pounded on our door at three in the morning, waking me from sleep. I stumbled from my room and through the living room. At first I was surprised and a little shaken to see Noah standing on the other side of the door when I looked through the peephole. For a split second, I wondered if he wanted to be the first to say, "Happy Valentine's Day." Then I silently smacked myself for even thinking it.

He fell through the door and draped his arms around my neck. "Noah, geez, you are too heavy to do that."

"I'm sorry, beautiful."

"I guess I'll forgive you." I ran my fingers through his tousled blond hair. He really was gorgeous. He was funny and cute and very flirty when he was drunk. My heart pulled in his direction and I flirted back. He missed me, I knew he did. He could have gone home with any girl along his Sigma Chi Bar Tour route but he didn't, he came to me.

That night I realized something had changed in me because I didn't want him to stay.

"So,IhadlikethirteenshotsandIcanrememberallofthemthatsho wgoodIam…" He slurred everything he wanted to say into one big run-on word.

What was I supposed to say? *Good job? Way to go?* I just smiled.

He paused and just stared at me after he stabilized himself on the arm of our couch.

"What?" I was really not a fan of being stared at. It was disconcerting when someone looked you in the eyes, said nothing and just kept staring. I looked away and busied myself picking up papers he knocked off the arm of the couch when he sat.

"You're pretty." He said it slowly and with a frown. He lowered his head and turned his attention to the hands that wrung nervously on his lap.

What the hell was this? It was almost like we had traveled back to the night he played "Better Together" for me in his car. My heart softened.

I smiled and thanked him, but my brain was already working overtime, preparing for the possibility of the advance he may make if he could steadily walk to me. Which was doubtful.

"I'm…I'm…never mind." He got up and tripped his way to the door.

There was a part of me that wasn't ready for him to go. It had been so long since I had seen this side of him. But there was another part that couldn't wait to lock the door behind him.

I walked over toward the door. "You, what, Noah?"

He fumbled with the doorknob and looked up at me for help. I moved his hand from the knob and opened the door for him. I motioned for him to walk out into the hallway while I wondered if he was going to answer my question. As drunk as he was, there was a good chance he didn't even remember I asked a question.

"You were right. I am an idiot. Night."

But he stood there, and I saw the hope in his eyes that I would reach out and hug him or ask him not to go. I may not have fought either of those scenarios if he had made the move first, but he was, in a way, letting this be my move.

"Sometimes you are an idiot, Noah. And right now, you're really drunk. Go sleep it off." I smiled and he tried to return a smile as he turned to walk to the elevator. I watched him step in and lean his head against the cold silver wall then I closed my door and locked it. I should have known his birthday would always trump an excuse to celebrate the most romantic day of the year.

There was something so empowering about turning the deadbolt. I was in control of keeping him out. And I was oddly okay with him leaving. I stood by the door for a few minutes and digested what had just happened. He came to see me, let me know he realized how badly he screwed up, and willingly gave me the decision-making power in whether he stayed or left. I let him go. Jake would be so proud of me.

Jake.

My heart was buzzing. I wasn't sure what was happening to me emotionally, but I did know I didn't feel completely out of control when Noah walked away. It was almost like taking that step with Jake had reminded me of how I was in control of my own destiny. Or maybe I was just high on the power trip of locking the door behind Noah. I imagined him walking home, pulling off his clothes, and climbing into bed. Alone. I did miss him. A small part of my heart wanted to climb into that bed with him.

Instead, I quietly went into our room, grabbed my journal and my big blanket and took up residence on the couch. It had been so long since I used my journal to sort out my thoughts. After the last two years, it ended up just being a very depressing account of all the things Noah did that sliced my heart a little deeper. But I felt like I was on an upswing. Maybe this journal was not doomed to a sad ending. Maybe it would chronicle a girl who rebuilt her spirit by learning to stand on her own two feet. I skipped three pages and started to write what was on my heart at that moment. By the light of the TV, I tried to write down what my heart was whispering.

Mid-February, Junior Year ~ If I could have one super power for the next 30 minutes I would plead for the ability to see into the future. I have no idea what I am doing. Jake and I have gotten way more intimate, kissing and touching on a level I never thought we would reach. Physically, we have moved beyond "friends," but I have no idea what my heart is doing. I have feelings for him that are truly indescribable. I guess this confusion could simply be because I have never blurred the line between friend and lover. I've only had one lover. Things haven't gone that far with Jake, but when we are in the heat of the moment, there are parts of my body that are calling out to him, parts that friends don't touch. He doesn't know that, of course. But he doesn't push, not even a little. That makes me feel so safe and that feels so good.

Then there was tonight when Noah stopped by drunk. I felt strong. But if I was completely honest, there was a small part of me that was sad when he walked out the door. He's still my addiction.

"Hi, my name is Gracie, and I'm an idiot addict."

Jessica will be back over Spring Break, and Noah and I will be in McKenzie, not seeing each other. Will my heart be able to take seeing Jake and Jessica together? Did I just dig my hole a little deeper?

Just in case anyone cares, I am waving the white flag. I surrender. I'm exhausted.

Thirty-Two

I sat in a beanbag on the floor with my notebook open in my lap. I watched Jake at the table as he studied and I studied him. His strong jawline, his intense blue eyes, and long eyelashes brought comfort to me, and I struggled to know why all of a sudden there was this charge between us. It was intense. I wasn't sure how we were formerly oblivious to something so remarkable. It reminded me of that feeling when someone's touch was so new and your body hummed when they reached out for you. But those touches weren't firsts for Jake and me. We had been friends for years. We had hugged and cuddled, held hands, and shared lip-to-lip pecks, so this new energy that ran through me when I caught him looking at me or when his hand brushed over my leg was virtually unexplainable. It was unexplainable, but I liked it.

My eyes drifted to his strong hands. I thought about what it felt like when they touched me. They were always warm. Staring at his fingers made me think of places on my body I wished they had been. Instantaneously, my ears got hot and my stomach rolled nervously.

"Hello…anybody in there?"

"What?" The volume of my response mirrored the level of embarrassment I felt. Thank the Lord Jake did not have mind-reading super powers.

He flinched at my volume, then smirked. "I won't even ask."

"Thanks."

"I was asking you if you wanted to go grab something to eat, I'm starving." He was still grinning.

I looked at the clock. "It's three a.m. Don't you want to sleep? Am I making you feel like you need to stay up because I'm still working?"

"Not at all. Who needs sleep? We are young, we can sleep when we're dead."

"I'm in, let's go." I was up on my feet in no time.

The night was cool, so I held my arms close to me as we shuffled down the sidewalk toward the all-night pizza place.

"Hey. You're freezing. Here." We stopped and Jake took off his sweatshirt—at regular speed, but I saw it in slow motion. His tight stomach muscles flexed when his t-shirt lifted. It was all I could do to not reach out and touch each groove of his six-pack abs.

I grabbed the bottom of his shirt. "Let's keep your clothes on, hot stuff, you're gonna cause an accident."

"You're a freak." He chuckled and threw his sweatshirt at my head. It smelled like him. There was a clenching in the pit of my stomach that could only be one thing, but I wrote it off as a really big shiver. My word, what the hell was going on with me?

We gorged ourselves on pizza then slowly walked back home. We held hands and our arms swung like we were little kids on the playground. It had only been a week since our kiss, but it seemed like much longer; that could be because we used our nights during the week when everyone was asleep as an excuse not to sleep and spend every waking minute together. We would climb into bed just before the sun came up and sleep a couple hours, go to class, come home, and start our sweet pattern all over again. It was like we had shoved a whole month of extra hours into the last couple weeks before break.

The apartment was warm, and after our chilly walk, the need for sleep hung low over our heads.

"Are you almost done?" I asked through a yawn.

"Do you want me to be almost done?" He caught my yawn.

"No, I mean, if you want to be. Or I could just go down to my place to sleep. I just can't keep my eyes open anymore. And I have to make it to my psychology exam tomorrow."

"No, don't go!" His eyes begged me almost as loudly as his voice did. "Just go climb in my bed. I'll be there in a little bit."

"Promise?"

"Yup."

I smiled and reluctantly removed myself from the warm confines of the overstuffed beanbag next to the table where he sat. His papers and books were spread out like a fan as he hurried to finish his own studying.

I stopped at the table and kissed the top of his head. His hand reached out and wrapped around the space between my knee and the pockets of my sweatpants. He squeezed. My whole body jolted. I quickly headed toward the bedroom and climbed into bed still in his huge sweatshirt, trying to keep my mind from imagining what it would be like for him to touch me in a way he hadn't yet. But it was so hard because I now knew what it felt like for his lips to go to unmarked territory. I stripped from the waist up and let Jake's big sweatshirt glide back down over me. There was something so sensual about being bare underneath something that smelled like him.

Just a couple nights before, after Sam went to bed, Jake and I had a couple beers after we called it quits on the studying. Our kissing turned into full on almost-drunk making out. Before I knew it, we were lying next to each other on the couch. A flash of my mom reminding me what happens when you "lay" somewhere with a boy bolted through my mind. While he kissed my neck, his hands fumbled with the buttons on my shirt. He looked up at me as my shirt fell open and asked permission with his eyes to go beyond. I closed my eyes and heaved my breasts toward him. He let out a sigh that may have had a bit of a soft growl to it, but the blood pounded so hard in my ears I couldn't be sure.

When he took me into his mouth, we were floating. There was a sensual connection between Jake and I that surpassed anything I had known before. Joel and I were young and had no idea what we were doing, and Noah always just did what he wanted. But with Jake, even when I was on the receiving end, I felt like an active part of whatever we were doing. And on the couch that night, he made me feel as though my soft moans and quaking body were giving to him what his tongue was giving to me. That was new for me and it was beautiful.

I sat up and fluffed the pillow. My pillow. In Jake's bed. I had to shake the hot thoughts from my head or I would never get to sleep. Poor Jake studied at the table, and I was lying in his bed trying to rein in my hormones so I could get at least a couple hours of rest before throwing myself into the academic part of my life that had taken a very, very backseat this semester.

The bed jostled a bit and startled me. It was too dark to see anything, but as soon as his arms swallowed me whole and he pressed the front of his body against the back of mine, I knew it was him. I could feel his spirit, truly feel what a good man he was and how there was nothing hidden between us. We were almost as close as two people could get. Almost.

Thirty-Three

Jake's lips were on my neck before my eyes had even opened. I wasn't sure if I had ever been that tired. Sometimes what you think will be a power nap dooms you to feeling more tired than you were before you closed your eyes.

I lay still to see what he would do if he thought I was still sleeping. We were still in the same position we were when I passed out from exhaustion, just two hours before. He reached around and took the hair that had fallen over my face and softly tucked it behind my ear. His hand glided down over my neck so lightly. Goose bumps rose on every surface he touched. He must have seen them too because he tucked the blankets tighter around me and snuggled in closer.

I was enjoying the warmth of his body and the quiet of the apartment when his alarm went off. Wow. Seven o'clock was painful this morning. Had I slept downstairs, I could have gotten at least another hour of sleep because my exam wasn't until ten. He, however, had his last architecture lecture at nine. Time with Jake had been ranking above sleep over the past couple weeks.

I rolled to my back which placed our lips within centimeters of each other's. I squinted to see if he was awake. He was. He smiled. "Good morning, pretty."

"Aw. Well, good morning, handsome." My voice was hardly a whisper.

He brushed the rest of my hair from my forehead and laid his hand alongside my neck. Leaning in, he softly kissed my lips. He pulled back, and once again, his eyes asked for permission to take it a little further. I closed my eyes and lifted my lips to his. A fire burned on this February morning that would be hard to extinguish. Our kiss was deep and intentional, gentle but strong. His tongue pushed through my lips and encircled mine with an urgent gentleness. His mouth was warm as he tasted every part of mine. I had no trouble following his lead because I trusted him. My chest heaved with deep breaths, and I had to pull away a couple times to gasp for air before consuming him a little more.

His hand slowly slid from the side of my neck across my collarbone, to my shoulder. He squeezed a little as he slid his hand all the way down to my fingertips and clasped my hand firmly. This was hot. This was so hot. My mind flashed back to that morning after Noah's confession. That morning I was giving myself permission to imagine what it must be like to make love with Jake, and five months later, I wouldn't think twice about giving him permission to make love to me if that's how far things went. Not long ago, I'd claimed to be a born-again virgin, but the way Jake made me feel, I wasn't so sure I could hold out much longer.

Jake reached for the bottom of his sweatshirt I was still wearing and pulled it up over my head. There I was, naked from the waist up, and there he was, holding back the covers so he could see me. His eyes grazed over every inch of my stomach and breasts, and I felt beautiful. I felt clean.

I rolled over to my side so our skin would touch. He gasped as soon as I pressed my breasts against the muscles of his warm chest. I grabbed his head in both my hands and kissed him wildly as his hands roamed across my back and down to the waistband of my sweatpants. I would have let him slide them off of me right then and there, but I knew he was mindful of not rushing us into any situation we shouldn't be in. He paused, then brought his hand to the back of my neck and returned my wild kiss with a very slow, very sultry, very soft kiss that brought a soft moan to the back of my throat. His morning stubble just made the whole scene more sultry.

He gently rolled me to my back and slid his body on top of mine. He framed my head with his hands as he rested on his elbows. His hands were in my hair and his stubble brought the blood to the surface of my skin. He brushed his lips from my neck to my lips and back to my neck again. Slinking my arms up under his, I splayed my hands out across his strong shirtless back. His body started to rock, and that's when I felt his need for me growing between us. Slowly, I spread my legs so he could settle down in between them. I told myself it was so the pressure of my hip bone wasn't hurting his man parts, but if I truly dissected my feelings, I would have to admit it was because there was an ache in my body that wanted him pressed tightly against it.

He found that spot instinctively and began to move. I moved in sync with him and it was like music. We were two different people singing the same song, and it was perfect harmony.

He kissed down my neck and my hands continued to feel every inch of his broad, muscular back. I was reeling. There were no clear thoughts in my head. I couldn't have thought about anything else if I wanted to. All I could focus on was his touch and how the weight of him on top of me made me feel so safe.

He pushed up, straightening his arms and looked me in the eyes. "You okay?"

I kind of giggled and breathed out the word, "Yes."

He stayed raised above me for a little longer. I watched his eyes as they took in every part of me that was exposed. I placed my hands on his chest and gently glided them across him. I watched his face as my hands roamed down his torso and toward his stomach.

His eyes fluttered as if he was trying to keep them from rolling back into his head. The line of hair between his bellybutton and the waistband of his shorts called to me. When my hands touched low on his stomach, he gasped and his body shuddered. I picked up my head and looked at where my hands were touching and our foreheads met. This time, my eyes rose to his, and without words, asked his permission to touch him more intimately than I ever had. His eyes fluttered again and his breath hitched.

That was a yes.

I pushed his shorts down as far as I could reach with my hands and he wiggled the rest of the way out of them.

He was naked.

Incredibly, beautifully naked.

He hovered over me as I took him in both my hands and felt every inch of his need for me. His skin was so hot. He was ready.

He let his body fall to my right side, and his warm hand traced around each of my breasts and down and around my bellybutton. I couldn't take my eyes off him. I had imagined him naked before and I knew it would be quite a sight, but I had no idea how beautiful his sinewy body truly was. His fingers gently tugged my panties down past my hips, and he rested his hand at the top of my thigh. Raising his leg, he hooked his foot around them and pulled them to my ankles. His hand swept from my thigh to the place I ached for him to touch the most. He sucked in a deep breath when he felt how much I truly wanted this.

"Oh, God…" His words came out in a long, hot exhale as he slid two fingers into me. My body clenched around him and he sucked in a quick breath and dropped his head to my shoulder.

The depth of what I was feeling physically was new territory to me. Deep ecstasy saturated me to my bones. Every cell of my body ignited with a fire that roared but was beautifully gentle at the same time. Our bodies heaved and rolled, but without crossing that final line that would seal the deal and make our relationship more intimate than it had ever been. Sweat rose to the surface of my skin as his naked body learned every square inch of mine. His hands were magnificent and his kisses reached a new level of unbridled passion. Some friends move to the next level and call it "benefits," but what we were doing was so much more. So much deeper.

He raised his body over mine once more, his hands firmly planted by my shoulders. A tiny drop of sweat left the tip of his nose and landed in my hair. The trail it made to my scalp made my body shiver.

"Look at me." His voice shook a bit as he spoke.

I lifted my eyes from my gaze at the space between us below the covers. I reached up and held each of his biceps in my hands as I savored every nuance of his beautiful nakedness. Sweat glistened on his chest. Then my eyes reached his.

"I want to make love to you."

I caught myself mid-gasp. I stared into his gentle, beautiful blue eyes.

I breathed in a shaky breath, lifted my hips, and whispered, "Please."

The second our two bodies became one was undoubtedly supernatural. There weren't words for the level of sensation that surged through my body. We shook and writhed, our breathing spastic.

My mind could focus on nothing but what was happening second by second. I didn't know if I made any noise or spoke, and I couldn't say if he did either. But my body didn't know what to do with the intensity of what we were sharing. We were making love — really making love. And that's when I realized the profundity those two words held. This was a new first for me. A first for Jake and I. Jake would be the first to ever make love to me.

Suddenly our unbridled passion took a turn. As his rhythm inside me increased and intensified, I felt myself losing control. I opened my eyes and met his. Our soulful connection at that very moment would stay with me for the rest of my life. I cried out as the tension building began to unravel me from the inside out. His breathing became more rapid and his eyes squeezed shut but then opened again and locked on mine. A couple deep moans rolled from his parted lips, and we spiraled out of control into an earth-shattering climax. Simultaneously. Eye-to-eye. Soul-to-soul.

His movements slowed. My insides pulsed and flexed, reeling in the experience we had just shared. His arms gave out and he pressed me into the bed. He propped himself on his elbows by my head and used both hands to wipe my damp hair from my face. He kissed me deep and gentle, and he ended sweetly with three little pecks. He slid onto the bed next to me, rolled to his back, and threw his arm over his face as he tried to regain control of his breathing. Just as I worried he was afraid we went too far, he jolted up to his elbow, laid his right hand on my neck, and rubbed my jawline with his thumb.

"Wow."

"Yeah, wow," was all I could muster.

"You are so damn beautiful."

I rolled toward him, took his face in my hands and sucked gently on his bottom lip "And so are you."

We sunk into each other's arms and fell back to sleep. I was late for my final, but I could have missed it and the "F" would have been worth the beauty I experienced in Jake's bed that morning.

Thirty-Four

"So, now what?" Becki blurted out. It seemed as though one of them was always asking me that question.

Stacy was speechless, in shock after I told them about my morning. She, Becki, and I met for lunch downtown.

"Was he good? I always got the feeling he would be intense in bed. Maybe it's his eyes, I don't know, but please tell me he is good..." Becki was never too shy to ask anything. I loved that about her.

"Truly? I don't have an answer for 'now what?' I don't know. And I have no words for what he did to my body this morning. Honestly, Becki, trying to describe it would take something away that I'm not willing to give up."

Becki and Stacy both slid their elbows across the table and caught their chins in their hands, sighed and spoke together, "Wow."

"Yeah, wow." I was still in awe.

We left Café Best and walked in the bright sunshine on an unseasonably warm winter day. I heard nothing of the conversation between the two of them. I think they tried to pull me in a couple of times, but after seeing my dazed look, they gave up.

Becki headed toward her dorm, and Stacy and I headed back home. We were quiet the entire way. Clearly, there were questions burning in her mind. If the tables were turned, I would be dying for details. But she was respecting the thought lines between my eyebrows. She knew I couldn't make sense of what my heart was telling me now.

The elevator doors opened and simultaneously she pushed 3 and I pushed 4. She looked up at me kind of sideways. "So, are you going to move in now?" She smiled.

I knew she was kidding and that my answer wasn't necessary, it was just her gentle way of letting me know she missed me without putting more pressure on me.

Outside Jake's apartment door, I looked over at the windowsill where our crossing-the-line behavior started. I walked over and ran my hand along the sill where I had been sitting that night. We were both so drunk, but we both knew what our hearts were feeling. The alcohol had nothing to do with that kiss other than giving Jake enough nerve to ask for it. I remembered his hands on my legs and the tender way he kissed me that night. All of it seemed so surreal but so natural at the same time. It was Jake. It was me. Who knew our friendship would reach another level? I chuckled out loud. Everyone had been saying we were headed in that direction. Everyone except us.

"What's so funny?" Jake's head peered around the door.

"What are you doing?" I laughed when he asked because he looked like he was a dismembered head.

"One question at a time. Mine, what's so funny?" He walked over to where I stood and leaned next to me against the wall. His body faced mine as I looked out the window, trying to clear my head enough to answer his question.

"I was just thinking how everyone predicted we would hook up while we were trying to convince them that we were just friends.

And now look at us." I looked down at my hands. I wasn't sad. I was still reeling over the beautiful thing the two of us had shared that morning. Even still, I was confused.

"Yeah. That's kind of funny. But what happened between us this morning was more than a hook up. You realize that, right? You know I wouldn't..."

"Oh, I know, I know, you don't have to explain. I guess I am just worried about how this blurs the lines. Because now what?" I sounded like Becki and Stacy.

"I don't know." He reached for my hips and turned my body toward him. His hand tilted my chin back and his eyes comforted me mirroring the genuine honesty of his words. He didn't know what would come next but I trusted him to hold my heart gently.

"Me neither." I closed my eyes.

"But I do know it was beautiful." He wrapped his arms around me.

"Beautiful. Really beautiful, Jake." I laid my head on his shoulder.

A tear rolled down my cheek and a small sob slipped out. Jake pulled me even closer. His strong hands rubbed my back and his soft voice calmed my soul. "*Shh*, don't cry baby girl, we will figure this out. But, no matter what, nothing changes the fact that I love you and our friendship comes first. Always."

"Always," I repeated with a quiet sigh of relief because I couldn't bear to lose Jake, too.

This was so different than being confused and crying in Noah's room. The juxtaposition of these two polar-opposite men in my life was unexplainable. One man I couldn't hold on to to save my life, and I knew one would save my life if I held on to him. But I didn't deserve someone like Jake. He deserved so much more than what I could give him. When I looked in the mirror, I no longer saw the girl I used to be. I let Noah pull me this way and that way, then finally let him pull me apart, and he left behind only a fraction of who I once was. The carefree spirit I was once known for had been painfully scraped away. Jake deserved more than the shell of a girl I was. I didn't recognize that girl. I was embarrassed by her.

Thirty-Five

March 15th–Spring Break ~ Headed to McKenzie today, break is until April 1st. April Fool's Day. Interesting. Noah and I broke up. Jake and I made love, and he has been saying "I love you" more often - I THINK he means as friends but not sure if he…

A knock at the door made me drop my journal. I picked it up, slid it back into my backpack, which I chucked onto the pile of stuff I was taking home for Spring Break.

I was expecting Jake. Instead, Noah stood on the other side of the door when I swung it open with a smile. My smile fell and he saw it.

"Well, thanks for the less-than-thrilled reception." He made an ugly face and pushed passed me, knocking me off balance.

"Noah, I didn't…"

"Whatever, I don't care." He looked around at the emptiness that surrounded us. I wondered if he was seeing it as emotionally significant as I was. Then he disappeared into my bedroom. I was thrilled I made plans to ride home with Stacy later that day. You couldn't pay me to ride home with him. Grouch.

"Can I help you with something?" I was a little annoyed that he still felt he was welcome here after he spat hate at me in his room over a month ago. That's when I realized I hadn't seen or spoken to him since the night of his twenty-first birthday. We had never gone that long without any contact after a fight. How was it that I didn't realize that until now? I usually kept track in my mind of how many hours until he called or until I saw him on campus. He was like my fuel—no matter how nasty it tasted, I needed it to keep going. Just seeing him on campus used to fill me up a little. Sometimes I would give in and call him or stop by. My tank would take on more fuel—sweet or nasty. Any of it would keep me going just a little longer. But this time I had made it a whole month without refilling my tank. I was really making the break. That thought both empowered and terrified me.

"I just wanted to see you." He sat down on my bed and looked down at his folded hands.

I was running out of energy. This year had sucked the life out of me. The ups and downs of his attitude toward us wrecked me emotionally.

"Why don't you have your grace/trust ring on?" Noah's question brought me out of my confusion, and I looked over at him. Big brown eyes stared at me with raw sadness in them.

"It's right over there." I pointed with a nod over to my jewelry box on the dresser.

"But it's not on your finger."

"Why do you even care, Noah? You don't seem to like me. Remember? That's why we broke up."

"Of course I like you," he said with shock in his tone.

I stared at those big, sad brown eyes and wondered how they and the angry heart below them could exist within the same person.

"Well, you're really not very good at showing it."

The cocky face came back. "Well, the brothers on my floor say they hear how good I am at showing you. All the moaning and screaming you do when you're there." He lifted his eyebrows in a sick attempt to flirt with me.

Oh man, he opened himself up for this one. This was my chance to show him what it felt like to be on the receiving end of cruel intentions. This was my chance to rip into him and tell him that I had faked every single one of those porn-star moments just because I knew he would thrive on the notoriety. At that time in our relationship, I just wanted him to like something about me. Apparently I put on a good show because he fell for it…every time.

Now was my time to give him a dose of hard reality, a chance to watch him wince with pain I was administering. The tables were turned at that moment.

But…

I couldn't. I couldn't intentionally hurt someone. Not even the person who crushed my spirit to the point of being unrecognizable.

A wave of nausea came over me, and I had to stabilize myself on the desk I stood next to. Hearing him describe those times in his room made me want to puke. He had molded me into something so cheap and hollow. I wondered if I would ever find beauty and peace to fill myself back up. Jake gave me that peace and made me feel beautiful, but I was still so confused about what was happening with us. I couldn't expect him to be my rescue.

"Anyway, I just came here to see if you'd changed your mind about riding home with Stacy. I'm packing the car."

I rolled my eyes. It was just like him to allow himself to get emotional and then stop before he really laid his heart on the line. Coward. He put the wall back up and pretended he had a good reason to come to my apartment. He stood and walked over to me. Eye contact with Noah sent shivers through me. A knock at the door gave me an excuse to walk away without making eye contact as I turned my head to yell, "Come in."

"I brought you something." Jake's voice startled me, but I could tell he was smiling when he said it. I quickly went to go see what he had. His face lit up as I rounded the corner from the bedroom. He stood there with two huge cups of our favorite ice cream from iScream. My mouth dropped open and I squealed. His eyes sparkled, so genuinely happy to make me smile. Then they darted behind me and his face fell. "Hey, man, what's up?"

He was so sweet to surprise me, knowing how much I dreaded leaving him behind. As much as I wanted to get out of the apartment for a couple weeks, it meant I'd soon be separated from the only thing holding me together – Jake. And it also meant Jessica was flying home to spend some of Spring Break with him. I could only imagine where Jake's mind went when he saw Noah following me out of my bedroom. He continued to smile, but it wasn't the same smile. It was forced.

"Just stopping by to see if she needed any help with all the crap she's lugging home. Break *is* only two weeks, Gracie." He rolled his eyes and nodded his head in my direction. "You going home, man?" Why was he getting all puffed up and attitude-y? He had no idea what had been going on with Jake and I so he had no reason to act like an ass.

But Noah never really needed a reason to be an ass.

"No, staying here. Too expensive to head west again."

"Right."

Jake nodded.

Wow. This isn't awkward.

"Before you know it, everyone will be back. Will catch ya then." He threw up a wave to Jake and didn't even look at me when he called out, "I'll see you at home, Gracie. Enjoy your cute little ice cream date," in a sing-song voice as he left the apartment. What an idiot. I was embarrassed to have him act like that in front of Jake. And what made him think we were seeing each other over break?

Thirty-Six

Jake and I sat and ate our ice cream silently for a couple minutes until I got up enough nerve to apologize for Noah being a jerk.

"Sorry."

"Huh? Sorry for what?"

"Sorry he acted like an ass."

"You think I expected more from him?"

I laughed and peeked up at him as he played with his spoon in his now coffee ice cream soup. He was so darn adorable, but right then, he looked pained by something. Was I hurting him? I didn't want to hurt him.

"I don't have any plans to see him over break. I don't know why he said that."

Jake nodded.

We quickly moved to small talk and laughed for a while until he got quiet again. I needed to say something, but I didn't know what. I opened my mouth to play verbal roulette and hoped for the best.

But before I could say anything, he spoke. "Jessica knew this would happen."

I looked at him funny. "That we would eat ice cream together?"

He smiled with his mouth full and shook his head.

"No. When she left, she told me I was going to fall in love with you."

An unforeseen wave of emotion knocked me back into my chair.

Seeing my discomfort and confusion, he smiled apologetically and kept playing with his ice cream.

He said, *in love.*

I still had no words.

"Look, you don't have to say anything. I just wanted you to know."

My heart started to beat faster. If he was hoping I would reciprocate with that same announcement, I couldn't. I loved Jake deeply, but at that moment, my heart was turned inside out about everything. There was no way I could entertain that notion without it exploding. I couldn't.

I remained speechless.

"Honest. Relax. No pressure. I just wanted you to know how I feel. That's all. Now, you need to finish packing."

And with that he stood, took my empty dish, and dumped it in the trash can. He walked back over and reached for my hands. He stood me up and enveloped me in a huge hug, then whispered, "You don't need to love me back. I will take you however I can have you. Just having you in my life is a blessing to me."

He kissed me on the forehead, tilted his head as he smiled, then walked to the door. I hung my head. Tears stung my eyes.

"Hey."

I lifted my head. He stood in the threshold. "Come up before you go, okay?"

I nodded, and as he let the door close behind him, a single tear made its way down my cheek.

The most genuine, selfless, kind, beautiful soul I had ever met just told me he was in love with me. But my heart was so shattered that I didn't know what to do with the love he was offering. If I let Jake in, his love would only seep out through the cracks. His love was worth holding onto but my heart wasn't ready. *I* wasn't ready.

I turned the music up and threw myself into packing. The whirlwind of feelings and self-talk in my mind were hard to keep up with. I had no idea what to expect from Noah, if anything, while we were home. If it was anything like Christmas break, I would have to be really strong and not give in to empty promises. Some sort of calm washed over me as I recalled the tenderness I saw in Noah in December. But that feeling soon evolved into panic as I momentarily relived all the things that tore at my heart over this last year.

My mind drifted to what had just happened at my table. My heart felt peaceful, and I couldn't help the smile that spread across my face. But I struggled with the possibility of hurting Jake if I didn't say I was in love with him, too. I wanted to be with Jake but I feared I was so wrecked that I could never truly love him with a whole heart. I needed to put aside what I wanted and wish he and Jessica the best. The tears came more steadily and the sleeves of my sweatshirt were soon used to wipe away the remnants of a broken heart.

A couple hours and a pile of tissues later, I walked up the steps to the fourth floor. I left Stacy in her car in the parking lot, and it was time to say goodbye to my best guys upstairs. It was time to face Jake, and still not have the words he wanted to hear.

I just walked in. No knock. He sat on the couch reading the paper and listening to music—Pearl Jam, "Black." I walked over and fell into his arms. He just held me quietly. The lyrics of this song were beautifully sad. Eddie Vedder's voice pined for a heart he no longer held. He called out asking why that heart couldn't be his.

I snuggled into Jake's arms as deep as I could go and wondered which of our hearts was singing those lyrics the loudest. Jake had always been the peace and beauty that could fill me back up when my soul was troubled. What I felt in his arms was a gift, a gift Noah never gave me. He couldn't. He wasn't capable of the kind of love Jake could give. Jessica was a lucky girl.

"Are you going to tell Jessica about us?" I cringed at the thought.

"Yeah, it wouldn't be fair not to."

"True. You think you guys will be okay?"

"I don't know what will happen."

I nodded into his shoulder. My chest tightened at the thought of seeing them together.

"What about you and Noah?" There was a small hesitation before he said his name, but it was so small I wasn't sure it wasn't just me not wanting to hear him say it.

"I think we are really over this time. It just hurts so deep."

"I know, baby girl, I know. I am so sorry you are hurting. If I could take it all from you, I would."

I looked up into his eyes. I knew he would. He was just that beautiful of a person. My mind went back to the day he cried as he told me Noah didn't respect me. He had the same look at that moment. I had to look away when I saw tears forming in his eyes. I wasn't sure if he was hurting for my heart or his, or both.

I talked myself through the confusion as we continued to sit in silence. I couldn't say I love you, even though I was feeling a level of love for him that I hadn't known before our kiss. I would love to say it to see his face light up, to see the tears turn from sadness to joy, but my heart was too fucked up. I wouldn't say it for fear I would cave to Noah yet one more time. The very last thing I wanted to do was hurt Jake. I would never forgive myself. I was the kind of broken Jake needed to stay clear of. I needed to protect him from the mess I was. If I hadn't thought it before, I knew now, I had to save Jake's heart from the trouble I would cause it. It broke my heart each time I felt his chest rise, just about to say something, then fall when he held it back. What else did he want to say?

I resigned myself to the fact that Jessica would be in this apartment in a week, and I was going home and would be within ten minutes of Noah for the whole break. Would Jake and Jessica get back together? Would my time with Jake amount to nothing more than just a beautiful memory? That hurt to think about.

Our last kiss that day was perfect. Neither of us held back. The spring sun beat through "our" window in the hall. That kiss was like a whole conversation.

I washed up onto the beach. It was warm. The sand was soft like big pillows. I laid there and listened to the beauty of nature while I soaked up the soul-healing glow of the bright midday sun. This was where I wanted to stay. This was a safe place. Nothing could hurt me here. The darkness was gone.

But I couldn't help feeling the last little pecks were a "goodbye." This transition could be the hardest yet because, as much as we both longed to hold on to that moment forever, we may just have to let go.

...the waves came a little closer and touched my toes, letting me know they were close enough to pull me back in. The last place I wanted to be right now was back in the torrent of the ocean, gasping for breath and fighting for my life.

Thirty-Seven

"So how was your little ice cream date? What the hell? You two in preschool?"

"Noah, stop being such a jackass. You know how much I like ice cream. Jake was being nice. You should try it sometime."

I should have known Noah would call and interrupt the fun I was having with Stacy. Windows down and music blaring was the only way to head home. Especially after the day I had just had.

"Yeah, I know a lot of things you like." He clicked his tongue and I could almost see his sick and twisted grin. That made my stomach churn.

But Jake's talents far surpass yours. My mouth opened, but I lost my nerve. I just needed to hang up. "Noah, I need to go."

He was pissed but he growled out, "Goodbye." I reached into my backpack and grabbed my journal and a pencil. I wasn't sure what I was going to write, I just needed to let something out of my soul before it exploded all over the inside of Stacy's Jetta. Her beige interior would be an easy backdrop for the sort of ugly that would splatter from inside me. I reached forward and turned up the music.

My journal fell open and a purple sealed envelope fell onto my lap. I turned it over and saw my name in Jake's handwriting.

Stacy looked over and smiled. It was a simple card with two big numbers on the front. A two and a one. Inside there was some silly poem about drinking and puking and doing it all over again. In Jake's handwriting at the bottom was a simple note.

Wish I was the one ringing in your big birthday with you.
Love you, Jake

It was hard to hide the huge grin his words evoked. "So, you making the switch?"

"Stacy, I have no idea what I'm doing. Jake told me he was falling in love with me."

"Are you kidding? Damn, you are one lucky girl."

"But I don't think he should."

"Don't think he should what?" Stacy was trying so hard to hold eye contact but the fact that she was driving kept pulling her gaze from boring a hole in the side of my head.

"Love me. Not like that anyway. After the shit with Noah, I've lost myself. I don't even know who I am anymore."

"Do you trust Jake?"

"More than I've ever trusted anyone." I quietly drew in a deep breath while trying to hold back the tears.

"Then trust him that *he* knows who he's falling in love with. Let him help you find yourself again, Gracie. You deserve to be loved the way I know Jake will love you."

I nodded and slid down in my seat. I wasn't sure there was room for Jake in my heart because I wasn't sure I had pushed all of Noah out. I knew they couldn't both exist there. Lyrics from the next few songs dulled the ache in my chest. I sat perfectly still and just absorbed the meanings and innuendos that always seemed to speak to me in times like this. The clash of the symbols, sharp beats of the drum and Ronnie Winter's voice pulled me from my daze. He sang of a girl who was repeatedly slammed face down by her boyfriend but kept insisting it didn't hurt. The Red Jumpsuit Apparatus wrote "Face Down" about abuse. The lyrics hit me hard. I needed Jake's arms but he was now three hours away.

I closed my eyes and took in the lyrics to every song like medicine for my soul. I couldn't text Jake that I needed him. That was only helping him to hang on to something I didn't know I could give him. My phone buzzed.

Jake: Hugging you right this minute.

God, he was incredible.

Me: Hugging you right back. You have no idea how perfect your timing is.

Jake: Well that's good to know.

Me: :) Thank you for the card.

Jake: :) Bday plans?

Me: None.

Jake: Why?

Me: Stacy is headed out of town with her family. Everyone else is flying away somewhere exotic.

Jake: Why didn't WE think of that?

Me: Seriously.

Jake: Call me if you need me.

Me: I always need you, Jake.

Shit. I should never have sent that. My damn fingers got away from me and I hit send.

Jake: Ditto

Oh, Sweet Jesus, help me.

Thirty-Eight

There was a knock at my door but I just barely heard it because Neil Young was "Rockin' in the Free World" through my ear buds.

"It's open," I called out probably louder than I needed to but it was always hard to judge my volume when I had music pumping into my brain.

My mom walked in carrying a load of my clean laundry. She smiled, set the pile on my dresser and came over to sit on my bed with me.

"You didn't have to do my laundry, Mom. I do it myself at school." I smiled letting her know it was appreciated and then plucked the buds from my ears.

"So, tonight's the big night." I should have known she would be dreading the night I could legally drink. Little did she know I dreaded spending my birthday with Noah. He had called a couple days before and convinced me going out was a reasonable request because, after all, it was my big night. I didn't want to spend my birthday at home so I caved.

"Yeah. You're officially old."

"No. *You're* old. Not a kid anymore. An adult. A *responsible* adult."

"Ma, you really think I will be irresponsible tonight?"

"I didn't say that. Did I give you that impression?"

"You always give me that impression, Mom." I looked up at her through guilty eyes.

"Gracie, my intention is not to make you feel irresponsible, I'm sorry if I make you feel that way."

I looked down at my hands, folded and placed in my lap. I sat cross-legged on my bed like a preschooler and thought of Noah's idiot comment about Jake and I sharing ice cream. She would think it was irresponsible to stay with Noah.

"Mom, do you think people can change?" I needed her opinion. I was scared this question would take us into uncharted territory, but I was so lost, so confused. I would take anything she could give me.

"Yes. I think they can," she paused and reached out and touched my knee, "but only if change is part of their own agenda. I don't believe people can change *for* someone else. I think they can try, but I don't think it is ever a long-term change."

I looked down at her hand on my knee and I thought of all the times we sat in these exact spots and talked about boys. She always knew how to help me sort out my feelings. I took her hand in mine and twirled her wedding band around her finger.

"Gracie, if you *need* him to change, you *need* to walk away.

I was so torn up even my mom, who was the eternal optimist, started questioning my decision to continue to have Noah in my life.

"Mom, you know the phrase 'Love conquers all'?"

"Sure I do, Gracie. But how can it be love when it doesn't make you happy? I haven't seen you smile more than twice since you've been home. I'm worried. You're not the girl I sent off to school a couple years ago. Do you remember that girl?"

"I don't, Mom." I bit the inside of my lip so I didn't cry.

"Honey, maybe it's time to say goodbye to Noah. Maybe your story is over."

"Did Daddy ever hurt you?"

"Gracie?" I felt her body jolt to attention.

"No, Mom. Not physically. Has he ever been mean?"

"Mean? Not once."

"Never?"

"True love and a mean spirit cannot coexist in a relationship. They are two opposing forces. Someone who is consistently and/or intentionally mean, in my opinion, is not able to accept or give unconditional love."

The ring of my cell phone startled me, and I let go of my mom's hand to answer it. She smiled at me and brushed some loose strands of hair from my face.

"When will you be ready?" Noah's voice didn't sound all that excited about taking me out for my birthday.

"I can be ready whenever you need me to be." I put my hand over the mouthpiece and whispered, "It's Noah."

She stood and kissed me on the top of my head and whispered, "Don't ever settle, Gracie. You're worth your weight in gold."

I couldn't hold it in anymore. I tried but failed to swallow the sob that tried to escape my throat. Whenever I forced myself to visualize that it was really over with Noah it was like I was standing on the lip of a precipice. There was nothing that came after it. No more steps to take. It just ended. And I saw nothing ahead of me. Nothing. Just empty space.

I watched my mom leave my room and was in awe of the woman she was. As I worked to swallow unshed sobs, I wondered if the love she felt from my dad is what gave her the strength she exuded. She was so sure of herself and so happy. For a minute, I forgot I was on the phone with Noah. I wiped tears from my face and tried to focus on what he had said.

"I'll be there at nine."

"Wait. You're not picking me up until nine for my birthday *dinner?*"

"No dinner. Just appetizers or something, then at midnight we get you loaded."

It was then I realized maybe Noah wasn't going all out for my birthday because I made it very clear that this was not a get-Gracie-drunk-and-have-my-way-with-her kind of night. Noah and I were done. Over. We were going out as friends. Just friends.

"I see. So, no comedy club. Just drinks at the bar?" Jerk. Over the past year, I had dropped at least a hundred hints about wanting to go to a comedy club for my big night. I wanted it to be something memorable enough that I wouldn't miss having a bar tour. Even as just friends, he could have at least given me that.

"We don't have to do *any*thing..." His tone made me shudder.

"No, I didn't mean for it to sound ungrateful. Just making sure I have the plan straight."

Here I am again. Apologetic.

"Look, I have to go. Meet me at Chubby Louie's at nine?"

"Meet you? You're not coming to get me? I have to drive?"

"Jesus! Fine! I will come get you."

"You know what, Noah, don't do me any favors. I don't need you to entertain me on my birthday, I am sure I could find someone else to take me out."

I knew he would get a flash of me and Jake in his mind with that comment. Part of me felt badly for using Jake that way. But I just really wanted to go out for my twenty-first birthday. Technically, I guess I was using Noah for that.

"Would you just calm down. I was joking. Of course, I am picking you up. I'm going to be pouring drinks down your throat. You won't be in any condition to drive."

"Noah, I am not getting shitfaced tonight. I just want to..."

"Oh. My. Lord! Why are you being so overly sensitive? It's getting on my nerves."

"Sorry. See you at nine."

It was all I could do to hold in the next wave of sobs until I hit end on my phone. He talked out of both sides of his mouth, and it had me walking on eggshells when I swore I wasn't going to do that anymore. Nothing I said was right. It was more than just mood swings. Sometimes I thought he was certifiably insane. But most times he convinced me I was the crazy one.

Why would he even offer to take me anywhere if it was such a hassle? It would have been less painful if he just said he had other plans. But as I rehashed the phone conversation I realized he was incapable of being who I needed him to be. He gave it a good shot pretending to be a good guy, but his true self kept peeking through the façade. I was a mess and my stomach was in knots trying to build up my self-confidence before he got there. I wanted to see him hesitate when he saw me. I wanted to see that look in his eyes that I hadn't seen in so long. I wanted him to want me. Because, now, he couldn't have me.

I threw my iPod in the dock, maxed the volume and hit shuffle.

Eve 6, "Inside Out." Something about a heart in a blender. How appropriate. I threw myself down on my bed, buried my face in the pillow I'd had since I was little. And just like a little girl I cried until my body convulsed with each staggered breath.

Beautiful oblivion. That's where I was the night of my big birthday. Sometimes being oblivious could be beautiful. But as I teetered on the edge of insanity I realized there was nothing beautiful about oblivion.

Buzz.

Jake: Have a happy birthday. Be safe baby girl.

Thirty-Nine

Black and white striped, scoop-neck top, threadbare jeans, and my favorite black Converse. I was ready. What better time to start learning how to be "me" and not someone defined by anyone else. I refused to exist to solely be the person that filled a specifically shaped space in Noah's life.

The first ten minutes of the ride to Chubby Louie's were quiet and awkward, but a couple good songs later and it was the exact opposite of what I was expecting. Of course it was. Because *I'm* the crazy one. It was like he had flipped a switch and the Noah on the phone was not the same Noah I was riding with in the car. We sang to classic rock and laughed our asses off when one of us would sing the wrong words. At one point, he reached over and squeezed my leg. I moved my leg away.

"You look hot," he called out over The Allman Brothers as we pulled up to a red light.

I looked down at my hands trying not to look uncomfortable.

"What's wrong?"

Apparently I suck at that.

"Nothing." I shook my head and looked out the window desperately wanting to get to Chubby Louie's.

"I love to hear you laugh. It's sexy when —"

"Noah, we are celebrating my birthday as friends...just friends, okay?"

He pulled ahead when the light turned green and turned into Chubby Louie's parking lot. His face softened and his eyes, those big brown puppy dog eyes, were sad. He looked straight ahead at his steering wheel. I tried not to let his apparent sadness get to me. But my heart flinched just a little.

"Noah, we broke up. I obviously wasn't enough for you. You always seemed irritated with me."

"I just got irritated when it felt like we were married. It freaked me out."

"We've been over this. All the things that define a relationship...those are the things you don't like?" I laughed out of discomfort and because I was terrified this would be the worst birthday of my life if I didn't try to lift the weight of this conversation.

He looked a little confused but laughed along with me then grabbed my hand and kissed me across my knuckles.

"How about I just try to be less of a dick and we see how things go?"

"How about you just try to be my friend."

"Come on, let's go in and get ready to drink together...legally." He covered up his lack of response to the "friend" comment by changing the subject to drinking. I hoped it sunk in so we could have fun.

Chubby Louie's was always a good time. It was this hole in the wall kind of place off the beaten path that people from all walks of life enjoyed. There were people who looked like they came straight from work. There were local community college kids taking advantage of the cheap appetizers and buy one-get one bottles of beer, and people who didn't seem to have any specific demographic-defining characteristics.

We got a table in the back. It was dark and not as loud as the tables by the bar and the dance floor. We had two and a half hours to entertain ourselves until I could have my first legal drink. I was actually excited. Noah's mood stayed steady, and the pressure I was feeling in the car actually lifted a bit. I couldn't remember the last time it was just the two of us and we weren't mad at each other.

We inhaled some orgasmic clam dip and pita bread and an obnoxious plate of nachos while Noah listed all the crazy shots I could pick from for my first drink at midnight.

"Noah, can't I just have a beer? I already know I like it."

"Nope. It's customary to push your limits on your twenty-first birthday. Just be glad you don't have twenty Sigma Chi brothers throwing shots down you hand over fist. I actually thought I might die that night."

"Well, I'm glad you didn't. But, I only know the real easy shots...I've never even heard of a Cement Mixer or a Prairie Fire. What's in those?"

He threw the bar's laminated shot list across the table. I assured him that anything that coagulates in my mouth or has tabasco sauce as the secondary of two ingredients was not passing my lips.

"How about a Buttery Nipple or a Blow Job?"

"Are you propositioning me or naming shots?" As soon as it was out of my mouth, I regretted it.

"Which would you prefer?"

"Calm down, Casanova. Tonight is about two friends *drinking*, not having sex!"

"Damn." He flashed a smirk that instantly made me queasy.

I rolled my eyes and played with a stray tortilla chip drowning in salsa. I really needed to steer away from anything he could twist into a sexual innuendo. It was no secret how our animosity could turn into passion, especially after a couple drinks.

But I wasn't going to let that happen. So for the next two hours, small talk was on our menu. Random benign topics seemed to keep the conversation clear of any R-rated implications."So, think I can get you drunk enough to–" Even if I had doubted that question was headed in the sexual direction, I could see it in his eyes.

"Noah, quit it. It's not funny anymore. We are not having sex."

"So, you're serious about this 'friend' thing."

"Yes. Very."

The waitress stumbled up to our table in a tizzy. "What can I get you two?"

"One Prairie Fire." Noah completely avoided eye contact with me.

He's buying himself a shot. I looked at my phone. 12:07 am. This was his chance to ring in my big day and he bought himself a shot.

"I will need to see I.D." She impatiently looked back and forth between us and her other tables in our section. I hadn't realized how pretty she was until that moment as I watched her fidget with her order pad. She was totally someone Noah would go for. My stomach flipped over. I didn't think I'd ever be able to flush my system of the mental snapshots of him cheating. Friends or not, it still hurt.

I looked up at Noah and he was staring at me through angry hooded eyes. I was that toddler again, waiting to get yelled at for something I didn't even know I did wrong.

"Well, are you going to show her your I.D. or what?" He looked up at her and winked, "She's new at this." Then he rolled his eyes.

"Noah, I don't want…"

"Your I.D. She can't stand here all night, Gracie."

I blindly reached into my purse and pulled out my wallet. I handed her proof that I had been twenty-one for ten minutes. Ten minutes into twenty-one and I was already holding back the tears.

The knot in my throat burned as it threatened to break the dam of tears hiding behind my wasted attempt at sexy eye liner.

"Oh, wow! Happy Birthday! I'll be right back with your drink."

I stared into my lap blinking away the tears. Each time I peeked up to see what Noah was doing, he was staring at the MMA fight on the big screen. I longed for the one chance to throw him into a bloody cage with the monster of a man on the TV.

Just then a ukulele-playing little man was standing next to us, strumming the one-of-a-kind Happy Birthday song you only heard at Chubby Louie's. Our pretty waitress came back with a wink for Noah, a shot for me and an instant camera.

"Smile," she said as she stood to the side to get both Noah and I in the picture.

I tried my hardest to be convincing, but smiling was not working at that moment.

I watched the instant photo slide out of the front of the camera. I didn't even know you could still get those cameras. I guess Chubby Louie's had been there longer than I thought.

"This one's on the house." She said as she laid our check for the food and the photo on the table and smiled at both of us. I noticed she gazed a little longer at Noah than me.

The ukulele guy followed her away from the table still strumming his wacked out tune.

"I don't want this drink, Noah. I'm sorry."

Once again, I'm apologizing for his ass-hat behavior.

I saw the line of his jaw tense up.

"I'll be in the car. Don't come out until that's gone. It's all you're getting for your birthday."

And with that he grabbed the check and walked away. I didn't turn around to see if he was serious. I knew he was. I was frozen. If there was ever a situational slap, that was it. The pain of his "slap" radiated from the inside of my body out to my extremities. A wave of nausea came over me, then the dizziness set in, and soon my arms and hands tingled like there was a team of spiders clawing to get out. I sat still so I didn't alarm anyone around me. I was mortified that I was sitting there alone, on my birthday, which, thanks to Ukulele guy, was no secret to anyone around me. There I sat with one lonely drink in front of me while the guy who once held my heart waited in the car.

I spun the shot glass with my fingers and watched the pathetic image of me as it slowly appeared on the shiny square beside my Prairie Fire. Noah had ducked out of the way of our waitress's aim, so in the photo I appeared to be celebrating alone. Who was I kidding? Look at me—I was alone. I assessed the situation that I had obviously lost control over. I had walked on eggshells all evening and still I pissed him off. How does this happen? I have never annoyed another human as much as I annoyed him. So why does he keep coming back? Why does he flash those puppy dog eyes and want me to give him one more chance? Three hours earlier he offered to try to be "less of a dick." I searched my brain and came to the conclusion that "here's your shot, I'm leaving" may have been the dickiest move he had ever pulled, besides cheating. We'll call it a tie. Lately, all he knew how to do was be a dick.

The only thing I had control over at that moment was the shot of tequila and tabasco in front of me. I tightened my grip, breathed deep to settle my stomach and threw it to the back of my throat. I slammed the empty glass down harder than I intended and every person within a two-table radius was immediately staring at me. I was sure of one thing at that moment. I was on the edge of that cliff staring out into nothing. But I was done.

I walked out of the restaurant leaving the photo on the table. No more mementos, thank you very much. I clenched my jaw so hard I was sure I would break my teeth, but it was the only thing I could do to keep from bursting into tears. As soon as the warm evening air hit my face the tears fell. By the time I got to Noah's car, my face was soaked. I quickly wiped them away and slid onto the front seat silently. Not that he could have heard my sobs anyway with his music blaring. I sunk into the seat and slammed the door. He didn't even look over at me as he threw the car in reverse. If he had done anything right that night it was keeping his music loud for the entire ride home so that my ragged inhalations between silent sobs went unnoticed. He pulled up to my house and just stared straight ahead. I grabbed my purse, lurched my body from the car, and slammed the door as hard as I could. As soon as I got inside, I slapped my hand over my mouth and let out a guttural scream I had never heard before. Thankfully, it was late enough that everyone was sleeping. I quietly walked back to the hallway, slowly closed and locked my door, hit play on my iPod and quickly turned it to a decent volume. Quiet enough not to wake anyone but loud enough that no one could hear me cry from the hallway.

Changing our status to just friends did not take the edge off the pain caused by Noah's twisted behavior. I wasn't crying because I was hoping I could find the old Noah, I was crying because even when the relationship pressure was off and I was just his friend, he still found me so insignificant and easy to hurt. And it frustrated the hell out of me why he continued to try and pull me back in. I wasn't getting back in this time. He'd be lucky if we even saw each other again over the next two weeks.

The water lapped up further onto my legs and the strong undertow pulled me toward the waves. I knew if I gave up now I would be swallowed by something that would roll me more violently than before. I couldn't let the ocean take me. I dug my fingers into the sand and pulled against the current. I wasn't sure if I was strong enough to make it but I wasn't going to die without trying my hardest to pull myself away from the depths that had a hold on me before. I reached out for the one thing I knew could save me at that moment…

Forty

"Gracie. Are you okay? Please, say something!" Jake's voice was sleepy and panicked. I knew he would see my number on his phone just in case I couldn't speak. My mouth was trying to hold in the sobs while my brain formed the words.

"I...I..." I couldn't. I didn't even know where to start. I wasn't even sure I wanted to admit to being so stupid and thinking that ringing in this special birthday with Noah would be anything but painful.

"You're scaring me. Please just say something. Tell me what's wrong."

I spent the next hour vomiting all of the night's hell to Jake. Most of the time he was the quiet listener, but I could hear the vile anger in his voice when he did speak. Jake's anger didn't scare me like Noah's did. I wasn't afraid Jake would leave me, I knew he wouldn't. There was nothing I could do that would cause him to walk away. Having someone like that in my life was the only thing holding me together.

"I am so sorry, baby girl. I wish I was there to hold you so you could get some sleep."

"Me, too." That's when I realized this was what he meant when he said he would take me however he could have me. He told me he was in love with me, and now I was once again detailing the further breaking of my heart by his former roommate. He was putting his own heart second because I was sure it was killing him to hear all the details of my night if he truly did love me. He would be my friend first, even if I couldn't love him back. I had no words for the kind of selflessness I didn't know existed before Jake.

When I realized how my pain over Noah must be hurting him, I decided to stop. I needed to turn it off and make sure he was okay before we hung up. I shouldn't have called him. Now my heart was breaking over the two most significant guys in my life. One because he hurt me and one because I may be hurting him. I closed my eyes and took a deep breath. Sleep. I just needed to sleep.

"Are you sure you're okay? I can stay on the phone with you as long as you need me to."

"No, Jake. You've already done so much. I can't thank you enough for what you do for my heart."

"I love you. You're my best friend. I am always here for you. You know that."

"I know. Thank you."

"No thanks necessary. That's what friends do." He was assuring me that his "I love you" was intended to be friendly and not guilt inducing. I wanted to tell him how much I loved him but I couldn't.

"I love our friendship, Jake. I don't know what I would do without you."

"Well, the feeling is mutual."

I wasn't sure how I landed such a beautiful friend. But his unconditional friendship was stunning. And it went both ways. I wasn't sure if I could ever reciprocate what he gave me, but I would die trying if he ever needed me the way I needed him. But he'd never be as stupid as I had been.

"Go to sleep, sweet girl. You need to get some rest."

"Goodnight, Jake."

"Goodnight."

I don't even remember pressing end or laying my head on the pillow. But when I woke up bright and early Wednesday morning, I knew I hadn't remembered to pee before I went to bed. I sprung out of bed, wrestled with the lock on my door, and ran to the bathroom. I could hear my mom in the kitchen and assumed my dad was still home. As soon as I washed the tear-stripes of mascara from my face and pulled my hair back into my signature short ponytail, I headed toward what smelled like eggs and bacon. My customary birthday breakfast.

I stopped at the end of the hallway when the kitchen table came into view.

Flowers.

Too little, too late, Noah.

"They're from Jake," my mom said with a crooked smile.

Be still my heart.

Forty-One

It was Friday morning, the second weekend of Spring Break and I hadn't heard from Noah since he brought be home from Chubby Louie's after the celebration that would go down in history as The Worst Twenty-First Birthday Ever. I'd been twenty-one for a whole week and still felt like a lost little girl floating on an inflatable raft in the middle of the ocean. Hopeless.

I woke up missing Jake. It could have been the sweet dream of being wrapped in his arms that had him on my mind but lately there was rarely a moment that he wasn't on my mind. Our early morning and late night calls were what kept me on my feet and not in a puddle of self-pity. We'd spoken or texted every day of break, except yesterday. I grabbed my phone from under my pillow and hit re-dial. He was the only one I had called since we'd been on break. I looked at the clock, I had slept away most of the morning. I knew he'd be up. He was probably out of bed and showered after a long run.

"Hey." He obviously had looked at the screen before answering and knew it was me. Just the smooth and sleepy sound of his voice warmed me and made my face feel a little flushed. I smiled into my pillow and rolled to my side. It sounded liked he'd slept in, too. Maybe if I pretended he was in my bed and we were waking up together it would give my heart respite from its chronic ache.

"Morning. I miss you." To anyone else, our conversations would probably sound like he was my boyfriend, but I knew I didn't have to qualify what I meant to Jake.

"Yeah. Me too." I could hear a rustle that I imagined was him rolling to his side as well. I pretended he was behind me with his arms wrapped around me.

"What's on your schedule today?"

"Um. Not much." Something was off. Jake was a man of few words, but I could usually get more than three words out of him at a time.

"Jake, you sound funny. Everything okay?"

"Who's on the phone, baby?" Jessica's voice startled me. My shallow gasp was audible. Her voice was close, she was almost as close to him as his phone. Oh my fuck! They were in bed together. Shit.

"I'll let you go. See you next weekend." And I hung up before he could speak. I knew he would have stayed on the phone and talked with me, but I couldn't bear to hear her voice again. A sour feeling rose in my throat. She was back. They were together.

My phone buzzed.

Jake: Gracie?

I turned off my phone. The doorbell rang before I even had a chance to feel guilty for not answering. I threw the covers over my head and lay there, eyes wide open. It rang again. *Can someone please get the door? I'm too busy feeling sorry for myself to get up.*

Ding dong.

I groaned as I pulled myself from under the covers and flung my legs off the edge of my bed. The UPS man was going to get an eyeful because I didn't even have the energy to pull my sleep pants on. The super huge t-shirt I wore to bed was longer than some skirts I had. I would just have to reach around the opened door, sign something on his little clipboard and throw the package on the hall table before jumping right back into bed. No one was home. I could have slept all day. Stupid delivery guy.

But when I rounded the corner into the foyer, I could see Noah through the side window to the right of the door. My heart slammed its next beat so hard I was sure someone standing in front of me would have seen my ribcage lunge forward.

"What do you want?" I said the words on my side of the window. He didn't need to hear me, he had to be expecting something like that. He knew I wouldn't be happy to see him. I was pissed that he was at my door. Flashes of my birthday night coursed through my mind one by one. I winced and squeezed my eyes closed hoping to wring the images from my head.

"Gracie, I know you don't want to open the door, but I need you to listen to what I have to say." He was talking louder than he needed to for me to hear him. I was instantly annoyed. I shuddered.

"So talk." If I kept a locked door between us, I could walk away whenever I'd had enough.

"Can I please come in?"

"No."

"Okay, I'll talk through a window if that's the only way you'll listen." He waited a couple seconds like he thought I'd have a change of heart and open the door. When he saw that was not in his cards, he started talking. I leaned my forehead against the cool glass and watched his lips form words that proved introspection, self-awareness and a level of thought so deep I could do nothing but hold my breath and wish he wasn't doing this to me.

"Gracie. I haven't had a solid example of how to show love or how to accept it. At least not the depth of love you are willing to give. I don't know how to reciprocate that without feeling terrified. I never expected to fall so hard for you. I never thought I could love someone so hard it hurt. But I can. I do.

"Gracie. When you look at me and I know you can see all the way into my soul, my first instinct is self-preservation. I instinctively push you away so you won't climb deeper into me. Your heart is so big, Gracie, it could swallow me whole, and that scares the shit out of me because I shouldn't be worthy of that kind of love. I don't deserve you. I guess in a twisted sort of way, I push you away to save you."

The window steamed from the warm breath escaping between my lips. I remembered the conversation I had with my mom. She said only if it was of their own volition could someone truly make a change. I couldn't believe what was happening in front of me. A huge part of me didn't want it to be happening because Noah and I proved to be a disaster. I knew I couldn't handle one more blow from him. My sanity was already climbing the walls. But, as if they had minds of their own, one hand turned the deadbolt and the other opened the door. Cool air across my thighs reminded me I was still only in a t-shirt. I motioned for Noah to follow me back to my room. I needed to put more clothes on so he didn't ruin his heart-felt apology by making a move on me. He sat on my bed and I pulled sweats off the hook on the back of my door and slid myself inside them. I sat down next to him. He took my hands in his.

"I am head over heels in love with you, Gracie. I have been since the night you kissed me after the fireworks. I've always thought that shock between our lips was a sign that you were the one. I'm terrified of that. If I let myself truly feel the level of love I know we are capable of, then what happens if you leave me? I don't know how to handle that kind of pain. I am sure I've never felt something that severe."

"Noah, you just described what you have done to me, over and over and over. You have split my heart wide open so many times because, unlike you, I don't know how to guard my heart. I opened it to you almost two years ago, and I've been giving you all I have ever since. I can't turn it off, I don't know how. So, when you pierce me with your hateful words, the pain is palpable. It takes me to my knees." There was no holding back the tears. I didn't even try to. I was done walking on eggshells. Again.

That's when he did something I never thought I'd see. He fell into my lap and cried like a baby. I had taken all the pain he had inflicted on me and threw it straight to his heart before he had the chance to get that wall back up.

"Gracie," he lifted his head and I watched tears stream down his face. "I can't control myself when it comes to protecting you. You've seen me almost waste guys when they flirt with you at parties. And lately I guess I've subconsciously been trying to keep you out of harm's way by pushing you away. So, I act out and as soon as you leave, I'm in a heap on the floor because I hate myself for hurting you. You say you just want us to be friends and sometimes I want that, too. But then I think of you with someone else and it rips me apart. The thought of you sharing with someone else what you've only given to me tortures and wrecks me."

My mind rushed back to the morning Jake and I made love. Noah had no way of knowing that had already happened. Part of me felt bad for this, but the part of me that kept score licked her finger and made a tally mark in the air. He isn't the only one that holds that part of my heart anymore. I had one proverbial foot out the door. I breathed in slow and deep and stuck to my guns.

"Noah. I don't know if I can go back there. We need to be friends, first. Real friends." I knew in my heart there was no way Noah and I would ever come close to the friendship Jake and I had. I wasn't sure I should ever expect that level of connection with anyone else for as long as I lived.

Noah's eyes were red but I saw something click. He nodded. Then he leaned in and hugged me. My body went slack in his arms. He was saying and doing everything right...but it was too late. I didn't think I could ever let him back in. I thought of the ring he gave me for Christmas. My grace and trust was gone. I was trying to step out of his heart but it was proving more difficult than I ever dreamed.

"Will you go somewhere with me tomorrow?"

"Where?" I was almost scared to ask.

"The Cookeville Jazz Festival." He pulled back and looked me in the eyes, our noses almost touching. I could feel his warm, desperate breath like each one could be his last.

He knew of one way he could get me to spend the day with him. Music was my weakness. I would have gone to a concert with Charles Manson if he was my only ride.

"Sure." I tried to convince myself I hadn't just caved. In agreeing to go away with Noah, I was helping him learn how to be "just friends." Wasn't I?

"Perfect. I will grab you in the morning."

I heard the sound of the garage door going up, and I knew my mom was probably freaking out because Noah's car was in the driveway, which meant we were home alone together. If she found us in my bedroom, she'd kill us both. The panic I was feeling was reflected in the look on Noah's face. He knew what her response to the guilt-laden scenario would be. We darted into the foyer. Just as I was trying to figure out how to explain his puffy, bloodshot eyes, he kissed me on the cheek and was out the door in a flash. I brought my hand up to where his lips touched. What was I doing? I stuck my head out the door and called to him.

"Hey!"

He turned but continued walking backwards to his car.

"Friendship means no dick moves."

"Got it." He smiled, saluted and was down the driveway in no time.

"Gracie Ann Jordan!"

Now I had to go deal with the premarital sex police.

Forty-Two

The sun through the windshield warmed my legs as Noah and I left for the Jazz Festival in Cookeville. The drive was a little over three hours, just long enough to have fun, but not long enough for uncomfortable silences to seep in.

"So, how'd you explain your way out of our sketchy situation yesterday?"

"Oh, yeah. I meant to thank you for making it look like you were running from the scene of the crime. It would have been easier on me if you would have just stayed and said hi to her."

"Are you kidding? She may be small but she could kick my ass if she thought I was…well, we both know she could kick my ass."

"I told her we were standing in the foyer talking for just a couple minutes before she got home and you were late for something, and that's why you didn't stick around."

"Gracie Jordan lied? That's one for the history books."

"I wouldn't have had to lie if you wouldn't have pussed out." I grinned, knowing he wasn't expecting that.

"Did you just call me a pussy?"

"I may have."

He shook his head and chuckled. I was sure we were both thinking back to all the times he stopped himself in the middle of that word because he knew it made me cringe. It still did but I forced it out just to see his reaction. Maybe we could be just friends.

An hour into our trip we were still happy. We talked and goofed around all while singing made-up words to songs we thought we knew and calling each other out on our ridiculous lyrical substitutions. He hadn't crossed any of the boundaries I had preset in my mind.

"This is fun, Noah." He nodded to me and the music and smiled as he butchered the song he was trying to sing. I giggled. I was genuinely having fun with Noah.

We were stopped at a red light when he threw something at me I wasn't expecting.

"So, what's up with you and Jake?"

I slowly turned my face toward his and tried to decipher the emotion behind his eyes. It wasn't sad. It teetered between playful and twisted and cocky. I didn't know what to make of that. Did he really want to know? Would Jake want him to know? Noah said his anger was a result of him protecting me. He wasn't afraid of a good fist fight, and it terrified me to think of him and Jake toe-to-toe. I hadn't planned on telling Noah anything about Jake and me because it wasn't any of his business, but I was a horrible liar. We were in a car, less than two feet from each other. I couldn't walk away or pretend to get distracted.

"Are you fucking kidding me?" He yelled so loud. My heart stopped and then beat a couple extra times to catch up with my shallow breaths. He pounded his hands on the steering wheel so hard I truly thought the air bag would deploy. I had seen Noah angry before, but this was a vicious anger. It was something I'd never seen. Ever. Based on our conversation in my room, I could now translate that anger as fear. But it didn't make it any less terrifying. I either had to be ridiculously creative with my answer or just flat out lie. I was so panicked at that moment. I didn't want to be responsible for him taking out this level of anger on Jake when we got back to school. Who knew what he would do. The thought scared me. I actually had to shake my head to rid it of that visual.

"I didn't answer you." Staying calm, I tried to look as innocent as possible. It was getting harder and harder to do. That realization made me nauseous because he could use the truthful answer to his question in ways to hurt me deeply.

"You didn't have to!" He slammed his foot to the floor when the light turned green and made the hairpin turn so quickly, I was sure to the car would flip. His little Mazda wasn't heavy enough for the centrifugal force that came its way. In that split second of sheer consternation, I saw Jake's face. He was smiling at me, and just as he reached out toward me, the car came to a sudden screeching halt. There was no crash. No busting glass. It was then I realized my eyes had been closed.

When I opened them, we were conveniently parked in an empty parking lot across from the intersection we had just bolted through at the speed of light. Noah punched the switch on the radio. An uncomfortable silence filled the air, and he stared me down. Blood pumped in my ears, and for a minute, I actually thought it was the pounding bass from a passing car. I lowered my head, folded my hands in my lap, and slid so I was facing forward. I was overwhelmed with fear. The psychological pain I had endured since September could not compare to being on the receiving end of the back of his hand.

Even though he'd been in tons of them, I'd only seen him fight once, but it scared the hell out of me. It was two semesters ago when he felt it necessary to warn some guy at a party that his particularly rough advances toward me were not okay with Noah. They certainly weren't okay with me, either, but the guy was strong. I struggled to break free from his hold around my body. But he was way too big. He squeezed my ass as tight as he could and ground his groin into me with his jaw clenched. His heavy eyelids hid half of his pupils. He was wasted.

Noah came out of nowhere, pulled the drunken assailant off me and jumped him. This particular goon was bigger than Noah, but the unexpected attack had the guy at an extreme disadvantage. Noah's right fist hit him so hard, I thought his face would slide right off his skull. Two teeth flew into the middle of the dance floor, but that didn't stop Noah. He went ape shit. Four Sigma Chi brothers had to pull him off the guy who, by then, was a bloody mess.

I had seen firsthand what Noah's angry hands could do, so I sat completely still and braced myself. I didn't know if he was going to throw insults or fists, and I wanted to be ready for whatever was coming. The silence in the car was deafening. My hair slipped from behind my ears creating a convenient curtain between us. I couldn't see where he was looking or what he was preparing for, but I wasn't going to move. I squeezed my eyes shut and waited.

In a forced calm but depraved whisper, he spoke. "You fucked him, didn't you?"

I opened my mouth to speak, but nothing would come out. I shook in fear of what he might do if I told him the truth. My heart pounded with the thought of his reaction if I lied. He'd see right through it. I didn't have an answer that would get me out of this without all hell breaking loose.

"Look. At. Me." There was an injured tone in his voice.

I took a deep breath. I had to find a level of strength I'd never summoned before to get through this, so I needed to stay calm. The minute I let myself get emotional, he would swoop in for the kill, belittle me, and win. No matter what. It was what always happened. Knowing it was fear behind his anger didn't make me any less terrified. There was no talking him down once he escalated to this level.

I tucked my hair behind my ears, turned my whole body to face him and looked him straight in the eyes. I clenched my jaw in fear, but hoped he saw it as strength.

"I want to know, now. Did you have sex with Jake?"

"Noah…"

And in that millisecond of a pause, he threw his hands up into his hair and leaned forward, face-first into the steering wheel.

"You didn't even let me answer. You're making assumptions."

"They're not assumptions. I saw the way he looked at you when he brought you ice cream the day we left for break. I have seen you two on campus. I watched the two of you drunk-dancing at *Mitchell's* one night last month. I hated myself for hurting you the way I did that day you were in my room. That day when you said 'we are done,' and I knew you meant it, was the worst day of my life. I wanted to talk it out with you. I couldn't bear the thought of losing you…"

I couldn't believe more raw honesty was tumbling freely from his heart. I didn't dare say a word. He continued, "A couple days later when I got my head out of my ass, I came looking for you. You weren't at your apartment so I ran up to Jake and Sam's. A bunch of people were in the living room, but I didn't see you. When I asked if they knew where you were, Sam got all nervous-like and pointed to the hallway and said you were sleeping. You were probably fucking him right then. And I was standing in the next room! Dammit, Gracie!"

A scenario flashed through my mind. I could almost feel Jake's gentle hands on me and feel his warm breath on my neck. That memory was rudely interrupted by the eerie echo of Jessica's voice on the phone when I called Jake. My heart stuttered at the thought of them in bed together.

Sam had never told me Noah came looking for me. I couldn't believe how full circle this had come. This nightmare all started when he was letting Ivy give him a blow job in Sam's bedroom while I was in the living room. I was stunned at the irony. But I needed to keep my head clear so I could take a firm hold of this conversation and not let it go. I knew the word "slut" was right around the corner if I didn't take the bull by the horns at that very moment.

"Noah, Jake and I got a lot closer after Christmas. Jessica was gone. They agreed to see other people, and you and I were broken up."

He slammed his fists on the steering wheel again and shook his head. He squeezed his eyes shut, took a deep labored breath, and waved me on with his hand. "Continue," he said through clenched teeth.

I couldn't believe how emotional he was getting. This was killing him maybe almost as much as it killed me that night after the formal. Maybe.

"Jake and I were kind of seeing each other. But what went on between us is really none of your business." Those were almost the same words he said to me about Lily when I found the flowers in the trashcan. If I had ever doubted God wanting anything to do with me after all I had caved to this year, He was on my side that morning. I couldn't have choreographed this level of irony myself. I tossed a silent "Thank you" toward Heaven.

"None of my..."

I held up my hand and shook my head. "I'm not finished. Who I was seeing and what we were doing while we were both single is none of your concern...especially, especially when that person is your former roommate."

My heart beat so fast, I was sure I could keep two people's full blood supply pumping through their veins simultaneously. Each time I stood up to Noah, it was a little easier and seemed a little more natural. I used to just cry, that wasn't "standing up."

"I don't know what to think." His voice was quieter.

"What to think about what? I am not your girlfriend, Noah, and I haven't been for a while. You didn't think I would wait for you..."

"Yeah, I think I did. I never thought you would run out and find somebody new."

"I didn't 'run out' and find somebody. Jake and I have been best friends since I transferred, and while you were pledging, we shared a lot with each other. He was missing Jessica while she was away this semester, and you and I were a mess. Jake is who I turned to because he never failed me."

"I failed you." His voice was barely a whisper.

My gut reaction was to make him feel better by saying that wasn't true, but it was true. And today was apparently a new start for me, so I responded gently but honestly. "*We* failed, Noah. Our relationship just wasn't meant to be."

"What? Don't say that. What can I do to make you see I don't want to be without you ever again?" His voice was abrupt and unnerved and his eyes were begging me for another chance.

"Noah…"

"No, I'm serious, I will do anything. Anything. Just name it."

"Noah…"

"Gracie, hear me out. You and I are different, I've always felt that way. Sure, we fight and break up, but I never thought it would be the last time. I may not have reacted the right way to your affection and how much of it you wanted to give me, but that doesn't mean I didn't want you. I think about you all the time."

"Well, it's nice to know I'm still in your head."

"You always will be. I don't know how to be without you."

"You sure didn't have a problem when you were letting girls in your room and slamming doors in my face. Damn it, Noah, you have multiple personalities!" I tried so hard to not get emotional, but this conversation was ripping my heart out. Tears welled up in my eyes.

"Oh, no, no, please don't cry." He reached up to wipe them away, and I pulled back and used the back of my hand. He sunk back into his seat in such a way I knew he couldn't believe I had just pulled away from him. Honestly, I couldn't believe it either.

"Look, Noah, I couldn't take the ups and downs anymore. It was exhausting. It broke my spirit. It broke *me*."

"I am so sorry. I will fix it. I will change, I promise!"

Holy shit, he was panicking. He was ready to fight for me like I wanted him to the night he told me about Ivy and Madison and Steph. I wanted him to say all these things that night. I wanted him to fight for me and he didn't. He just sat on my bed and gave me nothing.

"I don't expect you to change, Noah. We just need to move on." Did I just say *that*? I was quite proud of myself, and honestly, the first thing I thought of was how proud Jake would be. Maybe I should have been jumping up and down with pompoms in my mind but I wasn't. The guy I had given up everything for and given all of myself to finally wanted to love me the way I needed him to. My heart was breaking to see him so desperate.

He closed his eyes, shook his head and pulled out of the parking space.

I thought about all that hung in the balance. Our history together, it was our story, and I still was unsure how to write the ending. I stood up for myself and it felt amazing but I was still teetering on the edge of that precipice. I almost did it. I almost ended it for good. But putting an end to our relationship would probably mean I would never see him again. As desperate as he was, I knew if I called it quits for good, he'd be gone.

The current that threatened to pull me back into the vast expanse of the deep grabbed me tighter than it ever had. One final yank and the strength in my fingers would give way. The dry sand my hands had dug into for dear life wafted through the air but wouldn't hold me if the tide came in. One big wave and my body would be pulled backwards into the very Hell that tried to take my life the first time.

Forty-Three

Once our conversation calmed, we decided to keep driving and follow our original plan to spend the day in Cookeville. But we didn't talk at all. We had the music up pretty loud so it wasn't as uncomfortable as it could have been. Once we got to the festival, we entertained small talk as we darted in and out of crowds and haggled with the vendors. We had been walking around for a while with the sun beating down on us, and with the stress of the first half of the ride there, my head was splitting open.

"So, in the car, you diagnosed me with multiple personalities. You want to explain that to me?"

"No. Not right now. Noah, my head is killing me. I need to sit." I had no interest in getting into it again, especially not with a migraine.

"You go sit. I'll go get us a couple waters."

In the last two hours, Noah had transformed into someone I used to know. Someone I'd been missing for a long time. He was attentive and gentle and kind. He offered to get me water for my headache, for God's sake. I couldn't remember the last time chivalry was part of our relationship.

I thought about what it would be like to keep this Noah as my friend but get rid of the others I'd unfortunately been introduced to. I thought of Jake. Our relationship was so easy and so honest. My heart actually ached thinking of him reconnecting with Jessica. Her hands on him...I gasped out loud just as Noah walked up behind me.

"Okay. Split personalities. You need to explain..." He opened my water and pulled a small packet of ibuprofen from his pocket. "And take these."

"You walk around with drugs in your pocket?"

"Yeah. You may have been able to get me to quit smoking pot, but anti-inflammatories, these babies are my real vice." He laughed genuinely and tore the packet so I could get some relief. "I got them at that little stand over there where I got the water. Now stop changing the subject. Me. Personalities." He sat down across from me at the little rickety picnic table carved full of names in hearts.

"I'm not sure what you want to know, Noah. I was just kidding."

"But there has to be some truth to it for you to even have that thought. What are my personalities?"

I sighed. This conversation could go either way. It could open his eyes to see how he'd been treating me, or it could make him defensive and pissed off. But, I wasn't responsible for his emotions. I jumped in with both feet.

"Well, there's a real Noah, a romantic one, a loner one..."

"Slow down. I know who the real Noah is." He kind of rolled his eyes like it was obvious. But he had no idea who that guy was. "Okay, so the romantic one..."

"Oh, you *really* want to talk about this. All right, the romantic one can predict my every move before I even know it. He pays attention and treats me to surprises. He also says *I love you.*" I watched him closely, there was not even a hint of a flinch when I said those three little words.

"Wow. Okay." He seemed hungry for every detail. "So, there are more?"

"Oh, yeah, let's see, there's the loner one."

"What is he like?"

"Well, he needs no one and isn't afraid to let everyone *know* they aren't needed. He's the one who doesn't want me to call. *He* wants to be the one to decide when reaching out is necessary."

"You really think I'm him?"

"Part of you is, I've become quite familiar with Loner Noah"

"You don't like that one." He took a sip of his water and tipped his bottle so it was pointing at the grimace on my face.

"No, not especially. He makes me sad and self-conscious."

This was actually one of the most sweetly intense conversations Noah and I had ever had, with the exception of the one we had the day before and the ones before and after we made love for the first time. He was so sweet and gentle and very careful to make sure I was ready. And the dozen roses the next day made me feel like he cherished my gift.

The conversation about Noah's personalities was almost as intimate as what I experienced that night. He usually didn't entertain "sappy" and "deep" for this many minutes strung together, and *he* was the one initiating it.

"I'm sorry I make you sad."

I just looked away before the tears came. I was sorry, too. More sorry than he would ever know. He left scars inside me that I would always feel whether we were together forever or not.

"Tell me about another one."

"Noah, we don't have to…"

"I need you to do this for me, please." His voice was strained.

"There's a daring Noah."

"Oh, that sounds…better?"

"Yeah. I like that one. He's brave and a little reckless, but that makes him so sexy. As long as we're being honest here, romantic and daring would be a beautiful combination." I realized when I said it I was giving him all the ingredients that, at one time, may have won me back. I didn't want to give him false hope, but part of me was curious how far this conversation would go before he blew a fuse.

"Really? I will have to remember that. Are there more?"

"There's one more...but we can stop."

"Please don't stop, Gracie."

I took a deep cleansing breath. "There's an angry one." An uncontrollable shiver came across me when I pictured his face within inches of mine the day he spat out his confession that he and Lily had gone to a function together. The evil smile on his face as he watched me cry would stay with me forever.

"Do I want to know about him?"

"I wish I didn't know him. He scares me a lot." I had to look away from him because even though his face was somber and pained, I could almost see the evil smile from that day transposed over his current expression. It was almost like one of those kids' books that have the pages that turn in sections and you can give little spindly legs to a body builder or a vampire's grin to a baby just by the portion of the page you turn. In this case, I had turned the seedy grin page over on top of the Prince Charming face. I bounced my knees under the table to keep myself from reacting.

"And who is he?"

"That's who you were in the car. It scares me, Noah. You scare me when you are that guy." I looked up at him and saw the regret in his eyes.

Tears came out of nowhere. I wiped them with my sleeves quickly so Noah didn't have time to reach for me. I really didn't want him to touch me. My legs shook under the table, my heart was racing and my mouth was dry just from reliving the last two angry Noah moments. I reached for my water and guzzled half of it.

"Gracie, your hands are shaking. Do I do this to you?" He knew the answer before he got the question out. "God, I'm so stupid! I don't like this anymore. Can you tell me about the real one, the real Noah?"

"I can't." I hung my head and the tears fell.

"Why not?" He reached across the table and took my hand. I was too exhausted to object.

"Because I don't remember him."

Forty-Four

The main band shell bellowed a familiar tune. Noah stood and tossed our water bottles in the trash with one hand and reached for my hand with the other. I looked up at him to gauge his mood before I put my hand in his. We both knew there was nothing else to say. He closed his eyes for a bit longer than a blink and sighed. He dropped his hand and turned away. I stood and followed him to the music.

As we listened to the up and coming jazz sensation, Picasso and the Golden Monkeys, play a long list of soulful instrumentals, Noah stood behind me. Something had changed in our short walk to the center of the crowd. When he put his hand gently on my waist, it didn't make me flinch. Soon he slid his other hand around and clasped them both across my stomach. I didn't know if it was exhaustion that kept me from knocking his hands away or if, even though I stuck to my guns, I was still holding out hope for a breakthrough. His heart was closer to mine than it had been in nearly half a year. He turned his head toward mine and used his cheek to push back the hair that had fallen from behind my ear. His soft stubble grazed my skin. His lips brushed my temple and held their position long enough for a swarm of butterflies to fill my stomach. I was still in awe of his silence at the end of our conversation. He didn't get angry. I wasn't afraid of him. I stopped shaking. He took that hard truth and absorbed it. He didn't fight back. He was taking all the blame. I closed my eyes and tried to only remember the sweetness of our relationship. I tried to pretend nothing ugly had ever happened to see what that felt like. I pretended this gentle guy snuggling in behind me had never shattered into many different personalities. I wanted to be able to sift out all of the pain and only have the happy memories left behind. I wanted to remember the real Noah. But I couldn't. Maybe I needed to focus on the "new" Noah and stop trying to make him someone he could no longer be.

He moved his lips down to my ear and breathed words into my soul, "This feels so good."

I closed my eyes and wrapped my arms around his. I wanted to hold on to this moment forever. No matter what happened, I just wanted to remember him like this. But it was a tightrope walk with Noah. One wrong move, and I was free falling.

"Let's go have a picnic." He spun me out of his arms, took my hand, and led me through the bevy of PGM fans. When we made it out of the crowd, he stopped walking and turned so quickly I ran right into him. He reached for my other hand and squeezed them both, coaxing me to look up at him. I lifted my chin and tilted my head back. I was welcomed by my reflection in his big brown eyes. It killed me to imagine Lily's reflection in them. Had he held her this close? Had they been intimate? I doubted I could ever look at him and not see the others that most likely still swam in his mind.

He let go of my left hand and placed his warm, strong hand along the side of my face. When his lips met mine, there was a familiar shock, one I hadn't felt in so long. I let him take me, and the world melted away. I would give anything to be able to bottle that feeling and breathe in its magic each time the spark ran out of

Noah. Something in me ached for him. He was right there holding me close and kissing me with a passion we hadn't shared in way too long, but I was smart enough to know I didn't hold his heart the way he held mine. I let him have the kiss, but everything in me was calling out to Jake.

My breath hitched when my favorite pair of blue eyes popped into my mind. I could see him smiling at me, and that's the moment it was evident, Noah did not really have all of my heart anymore. I loved them both. My heart held two men, one because I wanted him to help me find what we once had, and one because he could help me find the girl I once was.

Jake had a magnetism that didn't give me a choice to ignore what I was feeling, and Noah had a leash on my heart that gave me a choice I never seemed brave enough to make. I could release the leash and walk away. Trouble was, I didn't know how to detach myself from all the memories of what we used to be together. Not yet, anyway. But I did know I couldn't expect Jake to wait until I figured out what I was doing. Maybe he was the one I should let go of. The pit of my stomach fell into my shoes.

Noah pulled back and looked me in the eyes. "You do know that I love you, right? I really do love you. I just suck at knowing how to show it. I get scared about what I feel and I push you away."

My mind spun in a Jake and Noah vortex. I wished I could make time stop long enough for me to have a break from both of them to figure out who I was before I decided who I wanted to be with. Girls dream about having guys fight over them, having more than one to pick from because it makes them feel sought after and wanted. Right then, I didn't want to be wanted. I wanted to be loved for real and forever. I believed they both loved me for real, but I wasn't sure both were capable of loving me forever.

"I love you, too." I whispered the words because I could barely breathe.

Forty-Five

I was happy and shredded at the same time. Things felt familiar but somehow familiar didn't feel right anymore. We headed home after dark so the pressure was off to completely hold it together. It was easier to silently cry and go unnoticed in a dark car than it was to cry in broad daylight. My brain was spinning so I was glad Noah once again appeared to be totally into the music in the car and wasn't paying attention to anything else. How was I going to make sense of any of this? I wish life came with a do-over, but even then, I wouldn't know what to do. If I hadn't fallen for Noah, I never would have met Jake. So, was Noah just the stepping stone to my forever? Or was Jake the one who could build me up so I would be strong enough to stay with Noah forever?

"Listen, I love this new song." Noah's voice startled me. He lifted his hand from where it rested on my thigh and turned up the music. I assumed he was trying the Jack Johnson tactic again.

But when I heard the words, everything in my world came to a screeching halt. The singers took turns singing about being in love with their best friend. The melody was beautiful and the lyrics twisted my heart and made me long for Jake's hands on me. But he and Jessica were probably having a romantic reunion. I needed to let go.

It was hard to hide the tears that came from hearing a song that screamed Jake as I sat in Noah's car considering giving us another shot. The words "in love with my best friend" echoed in my head on a continuous loop. Noah wasn't my best friend. He never had been. Our relationship just wasn't like that. I broke down and bawled uncontrollably. Noah had no idea what to do. He changed the station and kept driving. Surely he thought I was crying because of him. What he didn't know was my heart was breaking into two equal pieces—one was Noah's and one was Jake's. Jake thought he knew what he would get if he and I were to be together, but I didn't think he knew how shattered I really was. My heart would break if I let him go and my heart would break if I let him settle for me.

We pulled into Noah's driveway and just sat. I was numb. I wasn't sure what either of us was waiting for. I could have gotten out, hopped into my own car, and driven home, and he could have gotten out and walked into his family's home. But we just sat.

"Want to come in?"

I knew I should say no, but something in my psyche kept making me feel like if I could make familiar feel right, I wouldn't have to jump off the proverbial cliff into the deep unknown. Sometimes the comfort of familiarity beat out common sense.

"Sure, but just for a little." I felt the ground give way a little, like the universe was trying to remind me this was a jump I shouldn't make.

His parents had probably been asleep for hours. The house was dark and everything was locked up. We walked in and carefully navigated toward the couch. The smell brought back sweet memories of when we first started dating. There was a temporary peace in my soul. I breathed those memories deep into my core and deduced maybe familiar was more comfort than numb.

Noah found the TV remote on the arm of his dad's favorite chair and hit the on button. The ear piercing shriek of a woman being chased in a horror flick poured out like poison. My heart sped, my face got hot, and I instinctively held my own ears, as if that would muffle the sound for his parents.

As soon as the sound was at the lowest setting, we both laughed and shushed each other. When we flopped down on the familiar cushions they let out a hiss that seemed to be a whispered reminder that we had come back. Back to a place we had spent numerous hours doing numerous things. We naturally fell into a familiar position with each other as Noah flipped through channels. We sat side by side, with our legs somewhat intertwined. Familiar felt good. We both let out a sigh and a giggle. I think that's when we realized we had both been holding our breath. The rush of adrenaline still surged through my body from the volume mishap, and the intimacy of our conversation at the festival had followed us home. Unfortunately, there was no remote for that. I would have liked to turn it down because it was shrieking almost as loudly as the woman on the TV. Our breathing increased. His chest rose and fell quickly under my hand. Mine was doing the same. And we were doing nothing more than staring at the television. He turned just enough so we were eye to eye. It looked like he was going to say something and then he just dropped his head to my shoulder.

I'm not sure what came over me, but this time, I reached for his chin and lifted it until our lips were touching. My eyes had adjusted to the dark, and I could see his wide eyes trying to read my intentions behind the kiss. It was deep.

Before I knew it, we were tearing at each other's clothes and reacquainting ourselves with each other's bodies. Soon we were naked and entangled on the couch. The familiarity of his body pressing against mine with nothing between us was something I had craved for so long. I could barely contain myself. I needed to feel him inside me. I needed us to be connected in the most intimate way possible. When he slid his hand between my thighs, there was no question what I ached for. And with the pressure on my hip coming from below his waist, I had no doubt he was headed there.

Our bodies rolled to the edge of the couch and fell to the floor onto small piles of clothing we had just strewn around. There was an explosion of lust like a runaway train. In the waves of passion, I pictured us walking on campus together. I imagined there was no tension and no drama, just two lovers working toward finishing college and starting their new life together. From the sheer emotional marathon I had run that day, I drifted away.

Jake's bed looked empty. There was a panic in my chest that I couldn't ignore. I ran to the next room, he wasn't there either. No one else was home. Music blared, but the apartment was empty. I heard the faint tune of a familiar song about best friends in love and realized it was *our song* that was playing. But where was he? I ran back down the hall and into Jake's bedroom again. I was frantic and trying to focus on any one thing. That's when I saw it—a folded piece of paper on Jake's pillow. I climbed onto his bed. His scent wafted up from the sheets. If I wasn't mistaken, there was a little bit of me in the aroma that wrapped around me. Just that scent covered me in calm. I slowly opened the folded paper. When I saw Jake's handwriting, my body calmed even further.

"I will wait for you."

I stood up, took off all of my clothes, and climbed between the sheets. I grabbed a pen from his night stand, turned the note over, and wrote my own message.

"I'm here."

"Wake up, Sleeping Beauty. Your mom and dad are going to kill you. It's really, really late." Someone's hands shook me awake.

I shot straight up and realized I was naked on Noah's floor. It was two in the morning. That was not the "here" I was dreaming about, and somehow what should have just been a beautiful reunion of two souls in love felt wrong.

So very wrong.

Confused and sick to my stomach, I threw my clothes on and shoved my bra and panties in the front pocket of my shorts, and darted toward the door.

Noah sauntered over, obviously still glowing from the moments before we fell asleep and not realizing my panic had nothing to do with the time or my parents. He reached to pull my face to his, and I instinctively took a step back and into a bigger wave of nausea.

"What's wrong?"

"I can't...we have to...I can't do this, Noah. We shouldn't have done this."

I left him standing naked in the doorway and ran to my car in tears.

The strong force of the wave pulled me under. I gasped for air just before my face disappeared below the surface. My body rolled over and over, my arms flailed, and my head pounded into the sea bed which felt like a concrete floor. The salty water stung my eyes. I forced myself to keep them open, fearing I would slip into unconsciousness from the blow I took to the head. I knew I had to hold it together long enough for the swell to pull me back up when the wave rolled. But something was pulling me deeper. I fought with all my might, kicking against the thick water swallowing me whole. I used my arms like underwater oars and sliced through the depths trying to reach what I needed most, but I was in too deep.

I was right back where I started. Drowning. Slowly.

Forty-Six

As I drove the familiar route home, my heart broke for Noah. The crushed look on his face when I stuttered through the admission of a huge mistake made me so sad. A vision of Noah in the parking lot of Murphy's coming to terms with the fact that I wouldn't break up with Joel for him flashed through my mind.

He had no idea that I was breaking down because I couldn't stop picturing my sweet Jake. I couldn't win. I was going to hurt someone and that alone was going to wreck me. I didn't know how much more damage my heart could take before it stopped for good.

I never understood people who committed suicide and why they would want to end their lives. But, at that moment in my life, I got it. I would never kill myself, but I understood the feelings of confusion, hurt, anger, and sheer panic that could push some people over the edge.

I heard Jake's voice close to my face before I got to my bedroom and slammed the door. That's when I realized he was probably still sleeping when I called. But, oh, his sleepy voice, how I

missed that sleepy voice in my ear every morning. I tried to speak, but I couldn't.

"Gracie, are you crying? What's wrong?"

Anyone on the outside would view this conundrum and think I had been an idiot to be confused over who I wanted to be with. Jake looked like the obvious choice. But that was something that I'd learned over the last year. Noah would beat me down but then come back to rescue me from the pain he'd caused only to beat me down again. It was a vicious circle. But when someone consistently knocks you down only to switch gears and be the sudden hero who also picks you up, you start to believe that you are worthless and weak because you couldn't do it without someone else's help. Then, when the thought of leaving that person enters your mind, you become anxious, worried that if he's not there and he can't pick you up, soon you will just be too pitiful to save. So you let him lift you one more time.

I looked at the opportunity I had to be with someone who was gentle, caring, genuine, trustworthy and beautiful. I would be safe from emotional trauma with Jake, but I worried I was just too much work for him.

"What did he do, baby girl. Did he hurt you? Gracie, say something!"

"Jake, he opened up and showed me a level of affection I haven't seen for a very long time. We kissed and I let it go too far. I was doing so well being strong. And then... Oh, Jake."

There was silence on the line.

"I'm here, Gracie." I so badly wanted to see his face so I could read what he was feeling at that moment.

"Are you mad?"

"Not at all."

But you're disappointed in me. "What are you thinking?" I squeezed my pillow closer to my chest to prepare for the truth.

"I'm sad that you fell back into your old pattern with Noah. Sad for you...and maybe a little sad for me, too. I'm also sad that you think you don't deserve more. I wish you could see yourself through my eyes. I wish you knew your worth. I wish I could protect you from this pain. I wish you knew how truly beautiful you are and how much more you deserve. I think if you could see that, it would be easier to walk away from someone who is sucking the life from your remarkable heart. It would make it easier if you realized you deserved to have the same magnitude of love given to you that you so willingly give away. Gracie, you have a resplendent soul that draws people in. Your vibrancy is addictive. You have so much to offer this world and the people in it, but you can't do that if you're living in hell."

"Jake," I whispered.

"As I see it, you have a big decision to make. Are you going to settle?"

"I don't want to, but I am so scared to walk away."

"I know it's scary to end something that feels like it's all you've known. Trust me, I just did it."

They broke up. It was then I realized I hadn't been there for Jake the way he had been there for me. I was such a mess I never stopped long enough to ask him how Jessica's visit went. I didn't look beyond myself long enough to think about the fact that he could be hurting, too. I knew Jake was unsure of how her visit would go. I realized that when I asked him if he was going to tell her about us. But then I heard her over the phone, from his bed. The assumption I made was very possibly the reason I let Noah back in, metaphorically and literally. "I suck. Jake, I am so sorry for not asking you how your weekend with Jessica went." I winced when I realized it was because I really didn't want him to recount any intimate moments between them. I couldn't handle it. "I've been selfish in our conversations. All we talk about is me and Noah."

"Baby girl, I'm a big boy. She left this morning, and I am just fine. Now, are you going to do what's best for your heart?"

"That's just it. Every time we have been together over break I have told him we were just friends. Then this happens. He sucks me back in and I'm powerless. Do you think less of me, Jake?"

"No. I think sometimes we need to fall a couple times before we can stand on our own."

"Help, Jake. I feel like I'm going crazy."

"Tell me what you want, Gracie."

"Jake, with all of my heart, I want him out of my life. This isn't healthy. I'm not who I want to be when I'm with him."

"Then, it's got to be over. Really over."

All I could give him was silence.

"Gracie, what are you thinking?"

I think I love you, Jake.

For a minute, I imagined Jake and I as a couple. It was a sweet image. In an instant, I saw us holding hands and walking together in the sunshine. He was smiling as he watched me throw my head back in laughter. A swarm of butterflies went crazy in my stomach. I wanted to be that happy. Just to play devil's advocate, I imagined staying with Noah. Immediately, I saw myself crying, slumped into the corner of a couch as he stood across the room with his back to me. I never wanted to be that sad again.

"So, I have to do this in person, right? I can't just call or text him?" I laughed a little, knowing that answer before I asked the question.

"Well, yeah, you are going to have to put on your big girl panties for this one."

"You've seen my panties, Jake. There is nothing big about them."

I heard his breath catch over the phone, and I worried I took it too far. I was just trying to lighten the conversation to take the pressure off.

"You are already broken up. You just have to let him know that no matter what he does, he cannot win you back. You're done. For good."

"I know. But now I realize breaking up was the easy part. In the heat of the moment I wanted it to be over for good, but never once did I consider it really was the last time."

"Oh."

Oh God, with one stupid sentence, I had cheapened the beautiful thing that happened between Jake and me. Now he had to be thinking I let everything happen between us knowing Noah and I would get back together. There was nothing cheap or impulsive about my decision to make love with Jake. It was no secret our souls were drawn to each other.

"Jake, what happened between us was..."

"Hey. Don't change the subject. You need to focus on you and finally ending this relational yo-yo pattern as soon as possible and with as little damage as you can."

"He asked me to ride back to school with him on Friday. If I have this conversation with him before, the ride will be unbearable. If I do it during our ride," I paused, "...that's just not a good idea." I was stuck. There was no way of getting out of this without one last, final stab from Noah. That one could be the one that unraveled me.

"All right, well, how about this...is there any chance you can come back to school a couple days early, like Wednesday instead of Friday? Tell Noah it has something to do with one of your classes and you can't ride back with him. We'll work out a plan while you're here. Then you don't have to do it alone."

"That sounds perfect." The sweet hush of peace fell around my shoulders.

"I think I know someone who could share some living space for a couple of days. Sam is gone until that following Monday. You know how he waits until the very last minute to come back after Spring Break."

My heart skipped a beat. Staying with Jake for five days with no one else around sounded like Heaven. I wanted his full attention, the freedom to let go of all my worries and pain without worrying someone would walk through the door or interrupt our conversation because they needed a ride somewhere.

"I'll drive myself back and my parents can drive my car back home when they come up for Parents Weekend. A Jake stay-cation. It sounds perfect."

"Looking forward to it." I could hear the smile on his face as he breathed out the words.

Forty-Seven

"Gracie, tell me again why you need to go back early?" My Dad's head was under the hood of my car. He always checked my oil and topped off my windshield washer fluid when I was headed somewhere far.

"It's for a class, Dad."

He ducked out from under the lifted hood and turned around slowly, wiping his hands on the rag he pulled from his back pocket. "You going back to be with Noah or Jake?"

My mom was apparently keeping him up to speed on my drama, but I knew the assumption he just made was his own. He was no dummy. I should never have lied.

"Daddy, I'm going back so Jake can help me figure out how to break up with Noah once and for all. I've tried so many times, but I can't seem to get him out of my life for good."

"A swift kick in the ass would do. Let me know if Jake needs any help with that portion of the plan." He walked over and kissed my forehead.

I loved how protective he was of me. It felt good to have men in my life who loved me to the ends of the earth.

"So, Jake will be there. Your mother seems to think you were planning on being there alone."

"Jake will be there. I told him I was coming on Wednesday, but I thought it would be fun to surprise him and show up a day early."

"Guess I'm going to have to meet this Jake." He flashed an all-knowing look my way. It was a *don't ever think you're gonna pull one over on me* look.

I raised my eyebrow and shook my head. Fatherly instincts. He could see Jake written all over my face.

I left for Knoxville with my music blaring. I was so excited to be alone with my thoughts for a couple hours. I wasn't sure if Jake would be at the apartment when I got there, but it didn't matter. Somehow my old apartment building had been calling to me like a mythical siren. I was just hoping the shipwreck that once was my life would all be washed away, and I could walk into the building just excited to see Jake and not reminded of the pain I endured there.

I worked through a lot in my mind as I drove alone. My iPod and I were getting pretty serious, it was the second best support system I had. I blared my music with the windows down and not a care in the world…well, I pretended I didn't have a care for those five hours. Eddie Vedder, Adam Levine, Anthony Kiedis, and Billie Joe Armstrong propelled me forward over hills and into valleys. The air was fresh. I was smiling because Jake was at the finish line. And it was so much fun that he didn't even know it.

I could barely contain my excitement as I parked my car, grabbed my bags, and ran into the building. The smell of newly cleaned carpet welcomed me and awoke my soul. I stepped onto the elevator and pushed the button for the fourth floor. I was smiling so wide my cheeks ached. That's when I realized the memories of my last two weeks of the semester with Jake had risen above the shitty memories that had happened first. The moment I knocked on Jake and Sam's door, I stopped breathing. Nothing. He wasn't home.

A guy I only vaguely recognized was suddenly next to me. My obvious elation had kept me from hearing him come up and out of the stairwell.

"Hey, Gracie."

"Hey…" I couldn't remember his name to save my life.

"Malcolm. From downstairs." He smiled.

"Oh, right. Malcolm. Sorry."

"No worries, just dropping off a speaker I borrowed. You need to get in?"

"Actually, yeah. I'm surprising Jake and just assumed he'd be here." He reached above the door frame for the extra key I completely forgot about and swung the door open.

"I really have to pee," I bent at the waist, my bladder begging me to run. I called back to Malcolm through the door, "Nice seeing you again, Malcolm." My pee dance was soon followed with happy foot tapping in the seated position. I was so excited to be there.

I washed my hands, fixed my hair, and took a minute to breathe as I looked at myself in the mirror. Could other people see what pain I carried on the inside just by looking at me? I could see it. I smiled into the mirror to see how genuine it looked. It could probably fool most people into thinking I was carefree and happy. But I would have to push the envelope to fool Jake. But I didn't have to pretend for him. He wouldn't kick me to the curb. I took my hair band out and let my mini ponytail fall into the now long bob.

In some ways I felt like the "sophomore me" and the "junior me" were two different people. Sophomore Gracie was hopelessly in love and quite intimate with a boy who brought excitement and sometimes reckless abandon into her way too boring life.

Now Junior Gracie stared back from the mirror. She wasn't my favorite person. When I looked into her eyes, I knew the pain she carried. I knew what Noah stole from her. I knew how much of herself she gave up for him and what she put up with that no one else knew. Some of it, not even Jake knew. I saw worry in the fine lines by her eyes. Her future was uncertain, and for a girl who once took everything day by day and lived life flying by the seat of her pants, she felt like she was being held against her will. Even after she ended it with Noah, she worried he would continue to have a grip on her heart.

Could I ever freely give my heart and soul to another man? Would I cheat someone wonderful out of knowing and being loved by my whole self? Shaking my head, I realized I no longer recognized the tired girl staring back at me.

The sound of the apartment door slamming shut broke me out of my little pity party, and I immediately said a prayer it was Jake. I looked back in the mirror and wiped away the shadows of mascara smudged under my eyes. I fluffed my hair, but resigned myself to pulling it back up again. I leaned against the door trying to hear his voice.

Please let him be home.

"Malcom. Shit. I thought you were Gracie." Jake sounded out of breath. He shouldn't have been expecting me. *Malcolm, please remember it's a surprise.*

"Dude, thanks for the compliment, but she's got way nicer legs than me. I was just dropping off your speaker. I would tell you if she was here." I could hear mumbling but couldn't make out what was said.

I slowly opened the door and heard Jake say, "Dammit, the whole way up the elevator I thought I smelled…"

The door squeaked and startled him out of his sentence. His face exploded with joy when he saw me standing in the bathroom doorway. He grinned and walked toward me with open arms as he finished his sentence "…her perfume."

"Surprise," I whispered as I melted into him and turned my face into his neck. His scent was like a nepenthe for my soul. I could stay in this one spot for the rest of my life and be happy.

Forty-Eight

"So, you want to tell me what went down with Jessica?" I couldn't believe they broke up. I wondered who broke up with whom and why he seemed so chill about the whole thing.

We sat at our favorite table at *Mitchell's*, a fun little bar around the corner from our apartment building. I couldn't help taking him all in as he looked around for the waitress and pointed for her to hook us up with another round of Rolling Rock. I reacquainted myself with his strong jaw line, his kind face and honest eyes. He really was beautiful inside and out. My eyes wandered along his short hair that curled a little on the ends. My eyes moved across his strong shoulders, hard muscle peeked out from under his short sleeves. For a few wonderful seconds, I wasn't aware of my surroundings because my eyes were drawn swiftly to his hands. Gentle but strong hands. Hands that had done things to my body....

"We broke up right before she left for Louisiana to finish her program."

"Did you guys fight?"

"Not at all. We were excited to see each other. We celebrated a little, but it fizzled quickly."

The ever so slight exaggerated curve of his eyebrow told me I had no interest in knowing *how* they celebrated. A pang hit my heart. I coughed so Jake didn't see the reaction I was having on the inside. I wasn't the last person to touch him. It felt like the lights dimmed and the room started to spin. I had staked my claim and didn't even know it. But looks like we both had a lapse in judgment. *Does that make us even?* That's when I realized there would be no scorekeeping with Jake. The result of that revelation was my release from the hold Noah had on me. I was ready.

"You still didn't tell me why you broke up." The curiosity was killing me. I didn't know what I wanted him to say, but I needed him to say it.

"Gracie—"

"Jake Rockwell, I tell you everything. I lay my broken heart down and ask you to help me put it back together. Why don't you want to tell me?" I whined a little but held a playful smile.

"It's complicated, Gracie. I don't want to add anything to the pile of shit you've already got going on. Let's just—"

"You have spent most of the time we've known each other putting yourself second and me first. For once, I want to be able to do that for you."

He growled and threw his head back. "Gracie Ann, you don't know—"

"Jake!" I stomped my feet under the table and watched the corner of his mouth turn up,

"You are so freaking adorable." He reached across the table, pushing beer bottles out of the way and wrapped my hands in his.

"*Jake, what* don't I know? I *know* you're my best friend and I *know* you need to hash out what's going on inside your head and your heart. And I *really* know I will kick her in the tits if she broke your heart."

Jake smiled just before his head dropped and hung between his shoulders. I wasn't sure what that reaction was for so I just waited. He lifted his head and positioned his bright blue eyes directly in front of mine so I could see nothing else. He squeezed my hands in his and took a deep breath. I was hanging by a string holding my breath.

"The moment I saw Jessica at the airport" — he squeezed his eyes and shook his head a little — "I fell harder and further and deeper in love than I'd ever been. That's when I knew."

"What? I don't get it." I had no idea what would make him walk away from that kind of love.

"Gracie, I fell harder for *you* the moment I saw her. I knew I had to tell her the truth. And she let me go."

Once again, he had left me speechless. He pulled my hands up to his mouth and kissed my knuckles. He let go of my hands and ran his through his soft curls. He rubbed the thought lines on his forehead and slammed the last of his beer. I wondered how many of those lines were because of me.

"But," he let out a long hot breath, "I'm fine. It's only tough because we've been together for so long. It just seems strange to not 'be' with someone. I really am okay, just trying to get used to remembering what it is like to be single."

He loves me.

He smiled and raised the beer the waitress just dropped off for him. I raised mine. We clinked the bottlenecks.

"Here's to being single." He winked when he said it. Something about that wink made the floor of my stomach clench. I recognized that feeling, but this time it was stronger. I knew I should say something in response to what he just told me happened at the airport, but I was still speechless.

The thought of being single usually made me sad, but in that moment sitting across from a beautiful — single — soul and feeling a couple beers running through my veins, it was actually exhilarating.

Jake and I went back to the apartment to grab a blanket and a cooler with more beer so we could spend the rest of the day in the Allen Street Park, a virtually unknown grassy knoll just outside campus limits that had the best weeping willow I'd ever seen. I thought about my mom's strict judgments on lying down with boys. I smiled and shook my head, thinking about what taking naps with your best friend leads to. I guess she was right.

Forty-Nine

I used Jake's chest as a pillow and we made a giant letter T with our bodies on a soft plaid blanket. I picked apart dandelions as we talked and laughed about everything that didn't have to do with Jessica or Noah. Back when Noah was pledging, Jake and I spent all of our time together talking. We didn't watch TV or movies. We just talked, for hours upon hours. We had the most random conversations. They were fun. It's how we found out most of what we knew about each other. But not long ago our question sessions morphed into a warring game that could happen at any time. There were no limits to what you could ask, you had to answer honestly and you couldn't pass. It was funny how the rules just evolved over time. We recently renamed it Buckshot Questions because the subjects that came up were all over the place.

"When and where was your first kiss?" I initiated the unannounced game. I turned my head enough to see Jake's smile. It made my heart beat faster.

"In fourth grade. On the playground."

"Wow, you slut!"

Jake chuckled and tapped his temple like he was having a hard time thinking of something he had never asked before. "What was your most embarrassing moment?"

I cringed just thinking about it. "Gym class. Sixth grade—"

Jake interrupted my answer with laughing, on the verge of howling. "You. In gym class. I can't even—"

I rolled over and slapped him so hard on the stomach that he grunted and folded at the waist. He sat up and turned onto his side which made my neck bend at a ninety-degree angle and my head fell to the blanket. So, I spun around and mirrored his position with less than twelve inches between us.

"If you would have let me finish... The embarrassing part was that I ripped my pants in gym class. And why did you automatically associate embarrassing with the image of me in gym class?"

"Oh, no reason." He rolled his eyes dramatically. "It's your turn, ask me something."

"What's something you regret?"

He rolled over onto his back and folded his arms behind his head. I scooted over on my stomach and rested my chin on his chest.

"Wow, you jumped right into the big questions. Usually we start off small and work our way up. You sure you want to get heavy already?"

"Who said you had to answer with something heavy?" I winked and touched the crook in his arm where it bent. It was moist in the crease from the warm weather. Touching his sweat jolted my mind back to his sweat-beaded body hovering over mine. It hadn't been that long but seemed like forever since we had made love. Probably because of Jessica's visit and all the shit with Noah piled up. It made it difficult for me to jump that hurdle to get back to my intense memories of that morning in Jake's bed.

Damn Noah.

Not only did he haunt me with the pain he had caused, but now his shit was piling in front of the only beautiful thing left in my life. There was a new vibe between Jake and me that, no doubt, went deeper than friends. Spiritually deeper than I ever thought we'd go. But I wasn't sure either of us was ready for a new relationship. Were we?

I couldn't shake the fluttering butterflies in my stomach from the thoughts about Jake's sweat-laden body sliding across mine. What we shared that day was remarkable. I was in awe of the way he moved while he was inside me, as if he already knew my body well enough to know just what to do. It made every sensation beyond intense. I remember the tension building and the waves crashing over me. I thought about the way his eyes locked on mine when I couldn't hold the tension at bay any longer. I arched my back and let go just as...

"...I exploded!" He chuckled and looked down at me.

My mouth hung open. Had he just read my mind or had I been speaking my indecent thoughts out loud? I was mortified. I buried my face in his belly and covered my ears.

"What are you doing? Why are you hiding?" Jake was giggling so hard my head bounced off his ab muscles.

"You finished my sentence...wait...didn't you?" No doubt I was blushing. I had nowhere to hide.

"Finished *your* sentence? *I* was the one talking. But from this tizzy you are in, I am thinking you were breaking the first rule of Buckshot Questions...the listening part. You can't just fire the questions and then not wait to hear the answers before zoning out." He flicked me on the forehead with his finger.

"Ow. Okay, sorry...what did I ask you?"

"Oh, no, you already had your turn. So I'd like to know what was going on in your mind when I said, 'I exploded'?"

"That's really irrelevant. It had nothing to do with anything."

"But that is my question. It seems you have forgotten another rule of Buckshot Questions—no passing. Maybe I will repeat my answer if you answer my question."

I was intrigued as to what story he told while I was daydreaming about him making love to me, but I really didn't want to tell him what I was thinking.

"Okay, so we are even. One cancels out the other. We can both remain silent for that round." I liked making up my own rules when I felt trapped. He usually didn't let me do that, but I saw something in his eyes that told me he wasn't going to push.

"Fair enough. What's something *you* regret?" He smiled a devilish smile that turned my insides to jelly.

"Wait, isn't that in the rules? You can't repeat my question back to me."

"No, it's *not* in the rules, and yes, I *can* repeat your question back to you. So be careful what you ask for, silly girl!" My chin was resting on my hands on his chest, I could feel each time he sighed or giggled. He tousled my hair and then brushed it out of my face and tucked each side behind my ears. His hands were slow and gentle. He rubbed my jawline with his thumb and then poked me in the nose. "I'm waiting…"

I hated the word "regret" because it reminded me of how many I actually had. I wish I wouldn't have asked him that question. It was not a question I wanted to answer. Ugh. I searched my brain for something that didn't feel offensive. But my mind sloshed with images of all the things I regretted.

"I can't." I looked up at him just as my eyes filled with tears.

"Hey, Gracie, this is supposed to be for fun. We don't have to play if it's going to upset you."

"Jake, I just have so many, and that is so embarrassing."

"Embarrassing? Since when is anything between us embarrassing? There's nothing we have to hide from each other, right?"

"No. You're right."

"That wasn't a ploy to get you to answer, I'm just—"

"No, you're right. There's nothing I can't tell you." I took a deep breath to clear away the nausea. Sometimes when I relived the hurtful things that happened between Noah and me, I would either puke or break out in hives. I figured it meant my heart was trying to purge my soul of something ugly. I knew what that ugly was, but I didn't need to paint a gruesome picture for Jake. I would answer honestly, but I would give him an answer that wouldn't make him cringe.

"One thing I regret is…" I lowered my head so my forehead was resting on his chest, sighed, then lifted my gaze into his sparkling eyes. "…losing my virginity to Noah. I wish I would have waited longer because now he holds something that someone else deserves a lot more. I can't ask for it back. A part of me is his…his forever. He will be a scar on my heart for the rest of my life. On my wedding night, I won't be able to give my husband all of me. That's my biggest regret."

This time the tears didn't just come to my eyes, they burst out of my face. Jake sat straight up and pulled me into his arms, and I situated myself across his lap. He rocked me gently and rubbed both hands over my back. I cried like a baby. I couldn't believe that I had allowed myself to be raked across the coals so many times. Each time I added the weight of new regrets. God, there were so many. Whoever I ended up with would have to be a saint to take on all my fucked-up-ness and still love me for who I was. Somewhere along the way I lost myself. When I looked in the mirror, I didn't know the girl looking back. But that girl was me. Sometimes I didn't like her. I didn't want to be that girl anymore, but I didn't know how to be anyone else, and that broke me in two.

Fifty

We got back to the apartment after dinner and I jumped right in the shower. I was in and out in no time. When Jake headed into the bathroom, I quickly dressed and went right to my favorite playlist on his iPod. I snuggled into Jake's pillow and scrolled through the songs.

Over the last couple months we created a "nap" playlist which I thought was cute. There would be no way for anyone else to look at that list of songs and think it was anything other than a playlist for when he sleeps...alone. I relived a part of every memory as I listened to small snippets of each song. There was a story behind almost every song, and the songs that didn't have a specific story to relate them to had lyrics that spoke for us.

"I Melt With You" by Modern English has a lyric that is all about making love being the best with one specific person. I knew why we both agreed on this one. It referenced that perfect morning that I obviously daydreamed about more often than I realized. Although we hadn't made love since, I knew for both of us, it was a beautiful gift that we would keep forever. Not a regret.

"Beautiful Tonight" by Eric Clapton was the song we sort of slow danced to one night at *Mitchell's* at the end of last semester. We had gone out without our normal entourage. It was just the two of us. We listened to an acoustic band and each drank a pitcher of cheap beer that night. To anyone watching, our "dancing" probably looked a whole lot more like "holding each other up while we swayed." That must have been the night Noah was talking about when he told me he'd been looking for me after our last big fight. There was a selfish satisfaction in knowing he saw us dancing that night. Later, we stumbled home and stopped just about every block to make out. It was sloppy and a little rough, but in a sweet Jake kind of way.

"I Don't Want to Miss a Thing" by Aerosmith was just one of those songs that was sprinkled with unspoken thoughts between us. It was all about savoring a moment with someone, a moment you never want to let go of. Jake had been such a blessing to me over the last couple years. Our friendship and love meant everything to us. I could honestly say he saved my life, and there were times I feared if I closed my eyes for too long, he would disappear. He really was too good to be true. I wanted to hang on to his friendship as long as I could. I didn't want to miss a thing.

"Comfortably Numb" by Pink Floyd was our rock star debut at a friend's party during finals week sophomore year. I thought Sam would wet himself laughing at us singing on a make-shift stage in one of Jake's classmate's kitchen. Neither of us could carry a tune, and we didn't know all the words, but damn it was fun. That song would always be ours in my mind.

"Fuckin' Perfect" by P!nk made time stop. There wasn't just one scenario for that song. I saw the love on Jake's face when this song played. All of the many nights I cried in his arms for hours after being humiliated by Noah, he would brush the hair off my wet cheeks and wipe my eyes with his sleeve and remind me quietly to never think less of myself for what Noah put me through. That I'd always be perfect to Jake.

At the time, I wished it was Noah who could say those things to me. But I knew Jake meant those words even if he meant them in the friend perspective. That in itself was perfect to me.

There were so many songs and so many memories. As the naps became a regular occurrence and our nap list grew, I told him I would need to approve of each song. There were thirty-one songs so far.

I was glad his shower was a long one so I had time to lay on the bed and relish in the sweet moments of knowing Jake while skimming through our playlist. *Wait, thirty-two songs.* The only song I hadn't approved was one called "Lucky" by Jason Mraz and Colbie Caillat. I wasn't sure I knew it so I hit play.

I turned up the volume a little and listened closely to the sweet rhythm of the thrum of the guitar. Then the lyrics came. They took turns singing of the luck they've found because they've found themselves in love with each other…best friends. I got goose bumps and tears and my heart grew a little bigger when they harmonized the words. It was the song that tore me apart on the way home from the Jazz Fest with Noah. It was the one from my dream that night. It was the song that made me realize Noah would never be what I needed him to be. It was as if this song was written for Jake and I. Just when I thought it couldn't get any sweeter, I wiped a few streaming tears as Jason and Colbie swooned about how long it takes to build a special kind of love and how they'd wait for each other.

Jake added this song without me knowing anything about it. Heart. Swelling.

Jake climbed into bed with me, all warm and still a bit wet. We wiggled our way into our favorite best-friend-nap position — him on his back with his right arm under me, me on my left side and my head on his shoulder and my right leg draped over both of his. It was so comfortable with him, I didn't have to worry about anything. No expectations of each other, no disappointments. His iPod played *Lucky* softly from his dock on the table next to his bed.

"I like the new song." I looked up at him from his chest and motioned with my head toward the music.

He took a slow deep breath and squeezed me into his side. I reached around and squeezed him back. He kissed me on the top of my head and then I closed my eyes and drifted off into the most restful night's sleep I had in a long while. The safety I felt when I was by his side was the main reason I could rest as deeply as I did that night.

Fifty-One

Jake's voice was my favorite sound to wake up to. It made me smile before my eyes even opened. It was my favorite way to wake up. It felt like home.

"I wanted to wait until Friday to surprise you, but I can't wait. You're not going to believe this!" He tried to whisper, but I could hear excitement in his words.

"What? They cancelled school for the semester?" My voice was groggy and my eyes still shut.

"Ha! No. Alternate Tragedy is at Mitchell's Friday night...and guess who scored two tickets?"

My eyes sprung open, I picked myself up and lunged at him. I threw my arms around his neck and he chuckled and hugged me back. "Oh. My. Lord! You are definitely my favorite person on the planet!" A little of my hug was for the tickets. Most of my hug was because the calm that ran through my heart when he touched me took my breath away. Jake was my protector, my confidant, my guidance. There was nothing I couldn't tell this man, the man that held my heart and my soul together as though the destruction of those two things would stop the rotation of his world. He listened and hugged and spoke at all the right times.

Something clicked in my heart when he saw me standing in his bathroom doorway. A wave that felt like a new beginning came over us. I knew he felt it, too. There was no denying this connection anymore. This man would stand between me and a bullet, he was willing to hold my hand while my heart was breaking, and he'd offer to clean up the pieces, no matter how messy it got. He was a true man and truly the most beautiful soul on the planet. And he loved me. Me.

He pulled the tickets from the drawer of his nightstand and handed them to me. His eyes were filled with pure unadulterated selflessness. Sure, he enjoyed the band, but Alternate Tragedy was my favorite band of all time. He'd watched me suck in every lyric and feel the pain behind every word they sang. Music touched my soul in a way that most people didn't understand. But Jake did. He understood me in a way no one else did.

Alternate Tragedy used to play all around town. They did classic alternative covers, songs by Nirvana, Jane's Addiction, Henry Rollins, Pearl Jam, and Red Hot Chili Peppers. They were local until some alumni who owned a record label heard them play Homecoming weekend last year. He had them signed in no time, and they'd been writing original songs and on the road promoting their new album, Fallen. Stacy and Becki drove to Chicago over the summer to see them live. They would be so pissed when they found out I saw the band without them. They wouldn't be back from break until Saturday.

"They're back." I stared at the tickets in my hand and ran my fingers across the raised print. The vibration of their deep, soulful angst was almost palpable in my palm. I was in awe that they would come back to campus after making it big.

"Should be a good time. I'm thinking they're looking for some small venues to play to catch their breath before they head overseas. Apparently, they are huge in London."

"And they got their start here, in Knoxville. That's so freaking cool."

"So, what did Noah say when you told him you weren't riding back with him?" He leaned forward and kissed my forehead.

I pushed my face into his bare chest and he put his arms around me. He kissed me softly again on the top of my head. I stayed silent and winced.

"You *did* tell him, didn't you?"

Silence from moi.

"Gracie! What's he going to think when he goes to get you at your house on Friday?"

"I'm assuming he will call to arrange times before the end of the week and I will just tell him then. He will be far, far away and can get as mad as he wants. I won't have to deal with it."

"You haven't talked to him since...that night? Does he know about this?" He drew an imaginary circle in the air around us.

"Yeah, but only because he jammed the question down my throat so many times I had to give him something so he'd back off. I told him we got closer and were kind of seeing each other. I also said anything more than that was none of his business."

"I'm sure that went over like a fart in church."

"Yeah, it wasn't pretty." I giggled when I realized what he had just said. "A fart in church? Where do you come up with this stuff?"

I fell back to sleep in Jake's arms with a smile on my face. He loved me.

That afternoon we spent lying on the lawn at Circle Park, which was usually teeming with people studying or playing a quick game of football between classes, but today it was just us and a couple passersby every now and then. There was something so different about being on campus when there was nothing academic hanging over my head. It felt so amazing to just waste the day away talking and laughing about anything and everything. There was so much Jake and I knew about each other, but there was still so much to know, and it was days like this we didn't get enough of during the semester. We truly had nowhere to be. Our time was ours... for a couple more days. We laid in our usual capital letter T formation with my head on his stomach. I pictured this being my future...a future that didn't include Noah. It was a nice thought.

"So, who was your first?" It was at that moment I realized I had only ever seen Jake with Jessica. I never pictured him with anyone else. I wondered who came before Jessica. I had no idea how many girlfriends he had prior to her. There had been no reason for me to know that part of his past. Now I was curious to piece the past I didn't know together with the Jake I knew at that very moment.

"First kiss? Or first sex?"

"Both."

"Well, nosey, my first kiss was Sarah Lane. She fell off the monkey bars, and when I helped her up, she kissed me. I was too stunned to kiss back." He pulled the brim of his baseball cap down over his eyes and laid his head back down on his clasped hands. I changed positions and used his bent arm as a pillow and snuggled in close. He smelled amazing.

"That's the Jake I know, helping a girl stand on her own two feet." He peeked down at me from under his brim and smiled a sexy grin. My stomach turned inside out from that look.

"And my 'first first' was Amanda Trostle. We were sixteen and we both lied about where we were sleeping after Prom. We did it in a tent by a creek behind the school. I know, I know, I was always so romantic."

"In the woods. By a creek? You wouldn't have gotten in *my* panties if you took me camping. That completely disappoints me, Jake."

"Well, I can tell you Amanda wasn't disappointed, not the way she—"

I smacked him hard on the stomach. He folded in half trying to protect himself all the while laughing until he snorted.

Jake knew Noah was my first. That was no secret. We didn't have actual secrets, just things we'd never asked each other. There were things I would never tell him unless he asked, but much of what I didn't want him to know was way too graphic for him to ask. He didn't need those visuals. Just like I didn't need to know the nitty gritty about he and Amanda in their passion tent. Ew.

We snuggled in the hot sun for hours, napping off and on, until his growling stomach beneath my head roused me enough to realize how hungry I was.

"Where do you want to eat?" He sat up and stretched.

"It doesn't matter. I'm game for anything. Oh, wait, not Chinese. Ever since that night last year when you and Becki and I made that horrible wine and vodka fruit punch concoction, I can't eat Chinese because I know what it looks like half digested. That was so nasty."

"Nasty for who? In case you don't remember, I am pretty sure I held your hair out of the toilet that night."

"Oh, right. I've been meaning to apologize...and thank you for that." I giggled and stood up. I grabbed the folded blanket from him and kissed him on the cheek.

"I need a shower. You starving or can we clean up a little first?" He took my hand in his and we started walking.

"Good idea. I'd like a shower before we head out."

We slowly walked hand in hand back to the apartment and Jake jumped in the shower. I headed in as soon as he left the bathroom. Seeing him in a towel gave me instant butterflies. He took care of his body and it showed. That light trail of hair that led from his belly button down behind the towel held my attention a little longer than it should have.

"Like what you see, do you?"

"Jake! Really?" I smacked him in the belly and hustled into the bathroom.

293

It wasn't until I had finished and opened the curtain that I realized in my ADD over his happy trail, I totally forgot to bring any clothes into the bathroom with me. *Dammit.* All I had was a towel. He'd seen me naked, but I didn't think we were at the point yet where walking around naked in front of each other was completely comfortable.

I peeked out the door and heard him clanging around in the kitchen, so I wrapped the towel around me and quickly shot to the bedroom. I was bending over my bag searching for my other bra when I heard a noise behind me. *Shit.* I slowly stood and turned around and there he was in all his shirtless glory, leaning against the door jamb, seemingly enjoying the voyeur position he had.

I tightened the towel, obviously flustered when he was suddenly right in front of me. He reached out and put his hands on my hips. Everything in my body clenched. We were both almost naked and he was touching me. It was a feeling that threw my mind right back to the morning we made love in that very room. On that very bed.

Without a second thought, I reached out for his chest with both hands. His skin was still warm from his shower, but he shivered a little when my fingers grazed the light smattering of hair on his chest that still held a few water droplets. I looked up at him just as he was leaning in. He took me by surprise when our lips met and he kissed me so gently, my body quaked with shivers. He pulled my hips forward and wrapped his arms around me as our kiss became deeper and more passionate. Our lips devoured each other, and the room spun. Images of us writhing naked in the bed right behind me flashed through my mind. But I wasn't sure that was where this was going. I didn't want him to know that a part of me was hoping he would lay me down and kiss me all over. I wanted him to show me what *he* wanted not what he thought *I* wanted.

We pulled back from the heated kiss like it was a perfectly choreographed dance and we both knew each and every step. When our bodies parted a bit so we could focus on each other's faces, my towel fell to the floor. Instinctively I panicked and tried to catch it in my hands as it slid down my body, but I wasn't quick enough.

"Let it go. I want to look at you." Jake took my upper arms in his strong hands and moved me further away from him. For a couple of seconds, he drank in every inch of my body. Earlier I assumed I would have been crawling out of my skin in that situation, but I wasn't. I had never felt so comfortable naked in front of Noah, and we had been sleeping together for a year and a half. I watched Jake's eyes take in every nuance of my body, the small mole right next to my belly button, the faded pale triangles of last year's bikini over my now swollen breasts, the few freckles on my sun-kissed chest. He ended his tour of my body by gazing into my eyes and lightly gripping my chin with his thumb and forefinger. He lifted my face and smiled.

"God, you're beautiful."

I could see from the bump under his towel that his mind was headed the same place mine had been for the last five minutes. We wanted each other so badly.

Without another word, he bent down and grabbed me by the back of my thighs and lifted me off the ground. As he did, his towel fell and joined mine on the floor. I gasped a bit when he started to walk while holding tight to my legs. I wrapped my whole self around him. He gently pressed me against the bedroom wall and the chill made my back arch, which pushed everything below my waist into his lower stomach. We were both panting. Our kisses were sloppy and his unshaven face scratched across the skin of my neck and chest as he tasted every inch of me he could reach.

Breathy words left my lips, but I wasn't even cognizant of what I said as he worshipped my body. He made a quick move and pressed me harder against the wall and slowly loosened his grip on my thighs. My heated body slowly slid down his. My hands were in his hair as my sighs and light moans told him not to stop.

He pressed against the opening between my legs. He shuddered and moaned when he felt how wet I was. In one firm but gentle thrust, he was inside me and moving his hips in a way that hit all the right spots. Not having to worry about roommates or interruptions made this moment even hotter. I let go with a loud groan and clenched my hands around the chocolate curls at the back of his head.

His hips worked magic. He was slow but intent on pleasing me, and boy, was he pleasing me. I couldn't hold it any longer. The first wave of orgasm made my toes curl and my legs tighten around his hips. I felt him swell as he rocked into me. The intensity built until neither of us could hold it anymore, and we simultaneously erupted in waves of beautiful ecstasy. The sweat beaded between us and I could feel his heartbeat reaching out through his chest to find mine. We collapsed to the floor in a tangle.

He brushed the hair off my sweaty forehead and away from my eyes. He reached for my chin and delivered numerous precious kisses to my gaping mouth as I tried to catch my breath.

"And here I thought, when you said you were starving, you were talking about food." I giggled.

He laughed out loud and hugged me like he never wanted to let go. I melted into him.

"I love you, Gracie Jordan."

Fifty–Two

"*She* would be someone I would pick for you." I pointed my chin in the direction of a thin brunette that had just walked into Café Best.

"Her? Really? I think she's a little too high maintenance for me. See her shoes? Those are richy-bitchy shoes." He winked and took another bite of his club sandwich.

"Richy…bitchy? Are you kidding me? Who are you and where is my rough and tumble Jake?"

"Sorry," he said through a mouthful, "that's what Jessica calls them." He licked his thumb and then dug into his fries. Which was good because I was trying desperately to wipe the jealous grimace off my face with my napkin. What the hell was going on? As soon as the first syllable of her name came out of his mouth, a jolt of I don't know what hit my chest. That had never happened before. I was stunned.

"He's your dream date." I looked up and Jake nodded his head in the direction of the middle-aged guy fumbling through the coffee stirrers and strangely measuring each one against the other. He was dressed in a long trench coat and his greasy hair was stuffed under a Rasta-colored beanie. When he turned around, his unkempt beard sprayed out in all directions and he had an eye patch, not a real one, one of those kid birthday party ones with the cartoon skull and cross bones on it. He grunted and mumbled all the way to an available seat on the other side of the room.

"Oh, no, no, no. Captain Jack is a little out of my league. Look at the duct tape on his shoes. He's a little too high maintenance…you know, having to add bling to his kicks and all."

Jake laughed so loud "Captain Jack" looked over and rolled his eyes, but then continued with his stirrer measuring at his table.

"Do you really think there is one special person out there for everyone, Jake?"

"Yeah, I do, Gracie. I think the whole soul mate thing is real."

"Really?" I looked down and picked up the couple chips that had fallen off my plate onto the dirty table, making a small pile of them on a napkin by the edge of the table so I didn't accidentally eat them.

"You reorganizing your side of chips, Captain Gracie?" He motioned with his finger between the pirate and my little pile of discarded chips.

"Shut up, dork!" I giggled as he smiled, took a sip of iced tea through his straw, and reached for my hand across the table.

"You deserve so much more than what Noah is capable of giving. He's not your soul mate, Gracie." He squeezed my hand.

"Jake, I know he's not. I need to end it, but I am scared to death to be alone."

"Baby girl, I'm not going anywhere."

I looked into those picture perfect blue eyes against his sun-kissed face and my eyes started to burn with unshed tears.

"Have you talked to Jessica since she left?" I needed to change the subject, I was so sick of crying.

"Actually, yeah, we're on really good terms, just friends."

I had heard that before. Just friends. Jake and I claimed that title for quite some time. It was funny to look back at your life and wish you could have skipped the bad parts and just lived through the good ones. I can see it now, there I am holding a pizza in Murphy's when Noah walks in, *Hey, I'm a real dickhead so you will want to stay far away from me. But my roommate, Jake, you two would make the perfect couple. Ya know, like that sappy soul mate kind of thing.*

"I suppose it's healthy to stay on good terms with an ex. I never have." I giggled nervously and wondered what that said about me.

"Jessica just calls to run stuff by me. You know, get my opinion."

"Hmm, I know another girl who did that, and she ended up in your bed...and against your wall." I blushed.

An irresistible grin spread across Jake's face, and we held each other's gaze for longer than we usually do...at least in public. There was no doubt in my mind we were both replaying the scene we created in his bedroom. I blushed again and he smiled.

"So, just friends. You gonna take naps with her?"

"No. I only nap with the best. I'm not a nap slut." He rolled his eyes in jest as if he were offended that I would insinuate he was "easy."

He was so damn adorable.

"Back to the soul mate thing. What do you think that really means? How do you know someone is your soul mate and not just someone you can tolerate for a whole bunch of years?"

"Let's play Buckshot, but I'm changing it up a little. I will give you a word and you describe that word."

"Okay..." I hesitated because I wasn't sure if he was changing the subject or if this had something to do with my question.

"Boyfriend."

"I think of smiles, holding hands, sunshine..."

"Okay, good. Now your word is relationship."

"Two hearts intertwined."

"Hmm, we're getting somewhere. Love."

At first, I had no words and all I could picture was us—Jake and I—but then it hit me both literally and figuratively. "Two people walking in the same direction."

"There you go." He smiled a smile that took my breath away. "Smiles, holding hands, sunshine, two hearts intertwined, two people walking in the same direction…what's the word for that description, Gracie?"

"Soul mates."

There was a silent moment between us that was so loud I winced. I was falling. I was falling fast.

"It's clear to me that under no circumstances was Noah ever my soul mate. But how do I tell him it's really over? Oh God, Jake."

Jake peeked around to see my face. When he saw my tears, his face quickly sobered. "You've ended it with him before, Gracie. You've got tons of practice."

"Yeah, but those were heat of the moment break ups…anything is easy to say when you are ready to throw someone in front of a bus. This is going to have to be an actual conversation about it really being over. That scares the shit out of me."

"Are you afraid he will physically hurt you?"

I held my breath. I didn't know the answer to that question. Was I? Noah had been the dictionary photo for "seething" many times, but hit me? My mind raced back to the fear I felt when Noah swerved to pull the car over on our way to the jazz festival. I remember holding my breath and closing my eyes worried there was a strong hand coming my way.

"Gracie, the fact that you even have to think about it, tells me I need to be there. If he *ever* laid a hand on you…" Jake's fists clenched on top of the table and a look crossed his face that was so serious it made me sit up and lean back a little in my chair.

"Jake, you can't be there."

"The hell I can't!" Now, he was loud. And if I wasn't mistaken, tears were welling up in his eyes, but I had moved far enough away that I couldn't really tell.

"I would be so afraid he would take his anger out on you. And none of this is your fault! I would feel terrible if something happened to you. I would never forgive myself."

He leaned in and his face softened. A single tear rolled down his cheek and he whispered, "So, you understand why I can't let you do this alone."

I thought back to the four sentences I had just spoken.

Be still my heart.

"Thank you, Jake."

"Besides, I can't wait to see you flex the muscles you didn't even know you had."

"Huh?"

"The ones you've been hiding in here." He gently poked me in the chest.

"In my boobs?"

"No, Gracie." He rolled his eyes and giggled. "The ones in your heart. The ones that are strong enough to help you stand on your own two feet."

I smiled and he smiled back as we left *Mitchell's*. The sun beat down on us as though it was blessing our progress on the subject of Noah. Jake giggled and shook his head, "In your boobs?"

I let out a huge laugh and he grabbed my hand and squeezed. There wasn't a time since we met that this man couldn't make me smile. I squeezed back thanking him again silently.

Smiles, holding hands, sunshine

Fifty-Three

The next day was a blur of love making, laughing, and napping. We didn't leave the apartment all day and only left the bed to shower a couple times. We didn't get dressed until the sun was going down and our stomachs were growling. My heart had never felt so full. The feelings I was allowing into my soul were a new level of intensity. As much as I thought I loved Noah throughout our relationship, I didn't know love could feel like this. Nothing about what I was feeling for Jake scared me or made me feel weak. It was as if over the last six months, our souls had combined and built a safe place for my heart. I didn't ever want to let go of that feeling.

"Let's get out of here and feed your growling belly." I couldn't believe that Jake, who ate like he had a tapeworm, had gone until dark without food, especially after exerting himself as many times as he had. I lost count after six. I got goose bumps each time I thought about all the ways he loved me that day.

We sat out on the deck at *Mitchell's* in the warm night's breeze and had a couple beers before our giant plate of chili cheese fries was delivered to our table. There were so many awesome places to eat in Knoxville, but we rarely craved anything but the laid-back atmosphere of *Mitchell's*.

"I'm so excited we'll be here tomorrow night hangin' with Alternate Tragedy!" I could barely contain my excitement. A squeal slipped passed my lips when I thought of lead singer, Calon, singing "Porch" to a bar filled with Pearl Jam fans. Calon was beautiful and his voice was unbelievable. He could sing his grocery list and have panties dropping all around town.

"Easy there, tiger, I know what you're thinking."

"You do not." Who was I kidding, he knew I had a thing for lead singers.

"Ohhhh, Calon, sing to me my rock star God..." Seeing Jake exaggerate that comment and act like a star-gazing girl made me laugh uncontrollably. My eyes teared up but this time from sheer hysterics.

"I love when you laugh. Do you realize how long you went without that beautiful curve on your face?"

"No, I guess it's all a blur. I'd just like to forget it all and move on." I drank the last swig of beer from my bottle and added it to the half dozen empties in the middle of the table.

"Well, I am beyond thrilled to see your face happy." He grabbed my hands across the table. "My heart is happy when I'm with you, Jake."

"Ditto."

We drank and talked for another hour or so before we headed back to the apartment. We were giddy and a little tipsy as we walked and swayed the whole way home.

We brushed our teeth, dropped our clothes at the edge of the bed, and climbed under the covers. The bed felt more comfortable than it ever had before. I lay in Jake's arms as he stroked my hair with one hand and lightly tickled my back with the other.

"Did Noah ever hurt you, physically?" His question left his lips before I had time to prepare myself for the slap it made when it hit my heart.

"No, Jake."

"I've seen him angry before, I know the damage he can do."

"There were a couple times I worried something physical was coming but he never laid a hand on me."

"Jake. Can I ask you something? And you don't have to answer if you don't want to."

"You can ask me anything, angel. We have no secrets." He squeezed my cheeks and made my lips pucker then pressed his lips to mine and made an obnoxious kissing noise against them. I giggled. Everything about him made me feel good. He flopped onto his back and I wrapped myself around him from the side.

"You mentioned a couple times that you know more about Noah than I do."

He nodded and continued trailing his fingers up and down my arm.

"What kind of stuff do you know?"

"Gracie, that part of your life is soon over, for good. You should just let those things die along with your relationship with Noah. Don't create new things to poison your memories of him."

"I just can't fathom how he could have been such a hog freshman year but then came back as a sophomore having made the switch to a decent guy."

"That's why the rest of us were so perplexed at what you could have done to him to straighten him out."

"But was it just his partying, fighting and sleeping around that you're talking about?"

"Gracie, this really isn't a good —"

"Jake, please. I want to know the whole picture. Maybe it will give me a boost when I tell him we are really done this time."

"He didn't respect girls at all. He wanted one thing from them and that was it. He'd decide he wanted to try something he heard or read somewhere and then he was obsessed until he found someone who would do it."

"I found pictures one time of him and Ivy. They looked like freeze frames of porn but they were clothed."

"I remember that night. Poor Ivy. I walked her home and she cried the whole way. He humiliated her. What you probably couldn't tell in the picture was that the room was filled with people. Some of his buddies dared him and came with their phones to get proof. There's something about him that is intimidating enough that girls let him go too far."

"No kidding."

Jake was quiet. I knew he was trying to process my comment. "I guess the biggest thing was, after he would do all these things he would brag about them to anyone who would listen. He would point the girls out in the dining hall or on campus and go into explicit detail of how he—well, you get the idea. His lack of respect for them made me sick."

I thought about my private life with Noah and all the things I did that I would never want anyone to know. All the things that made me feel dirty now. It never dawned on me that Noah could be telling people the things we did behind closed doors.

"Jake—"

"Don't ask me, Gracie. Please don't ask me."

"I want to know, Jake. What did he tell you about me?"

Jake pushed himself up onto his elbow and looked down at me. "Gracie, he never told me anything about you. He knew I thought he was a pig, and I never would have stood and listened to details of something that should have stayed between the two of you."

"So you never heard anything."

Jake threw his head back on his pillow and sucked in a deep breath. We had no secrets. He knew if I pushed it, he would have to tell me. "I overheard him bragging to other people. Things about you. But, Gracie—"

"Jake. Please."

"Gracie, I can't stand the things I know he did to you or asked you to do. I will tell you because you asked. No secrets. But you need to be sure you really want to know."

I rolled over with my back to Jake and closed my eyes. I would give anything to be able to take all that back. I was blinded by him. I longed to be who he wanted me to be. I was too intimidated to say *no* and he knew it. But there was nothing Jake could tell me that I didn't already know. I was obviously there for all of it. So, there would be no surprises. The only thing I'd have to deal with is coming to terms that Jake knew what I had done. Even though those things weren't depraved or grotesque, they still pushed the limits, my limits. And the girl who let Noah get away with that wasn't the girl I wanted to be. Jake knew I wasn't that girl. Jake was my safe place. It was okay to do this with him.

"I need you to tell me, Jake." I rolled over and took his face in my hands. "I'm sure, Jake. I need to know what you know. Please."

He pulled me in for a huge hug and then pulled back and looked me in the eyes, "Gracie, after I tell you, I am blocking these things out of my mind. It kills me to think of how much of what he bragged about happened as a result of his intimidation. Had I known those things he bragged about doing with you were a result of that intimidation, I would have killed him with my bare hands. I will tell you but then I am locking those things up in a vault." He tapped himself on the head. "And, you need to know, I don't see those things when I look at you. I never will."

My breath caught on Jake's words. He never ceased to amaze me. At that moment, I fell a little deeper.

"Before you tell me—"

"Anything, Gracie."

"Just hold me tight. Please."

He held me like he'd never let me go. "You sure you want to do this, Gracie?"

I nodded into his chest.

Jake's voice was soft and gentle as he spoke of things that weren't either. "I heard Noah bragging to some guys at one of our parties about what he said he asked you to try in the shower at Sigma Chi."

"He didn't ask." My body started to quake.

"Gracie, we don't have to do this. I don't see how this is *helping* you?" His hands were in my hair as he held me against him. His touch lulled me into a quiescent state and my body stilled.

"Jake, I can't stand thinking there are things that I don't know you know about me. Does that make sense? I just need you to do this for me. I'll be okay as long as you're holding me when you tell me."

"I got you, Gracie." I scooted up and tucked my head into his neck. He placed his hand on the back of my neck and rubbed my jawline with his thumb. "I won't let go."

Those four words made my heart trip over itself.

Please, don't ever let go, Jake.

"There are only three other things I overheard. We're going to do this like a Band-Aid." I nodded and he took a deep cleansing breath. I squeezed my eyes closed and prepared myself for a final rip of demoralization. "He also bragged about the toys he got for you to try, the public places you did it and the videos you made."

It took me a couple seconds to work through that list, even though it was a short one. My brain slammed into the last item on that list and I immediately felt sick. I sat straight up and tried to speak but nothing came out. I put one hand on my chest and the other across my mouth in preparation for completely losing it.

Jake, who by then was sitting straight up as well, held my face in his hands and tried his best to calm me down. "Gracie. Baby. Listen, no secrets, right? It's okay that I know these things. You know I would never judge you or think less of you for the things he convinced you to do."

I slid my hand from my mouth to my forehead and my biggest nightmare tumbled from my lips. "*We* didn't make any videos. If there are videos of us having sex, they were not consensual."

As if my heart could handle more pain, a fleeting comment from drive-thru Hank came to mind.

"Oh, God. Jake." I ran to the bathroom and heaved. Jake was next to me in seconds, on his knees, holding my hair back with one hand and rubbing my back with the other. In a daze, I stood and rinsed my mouth then dabbed a bit of toothpaste from my finger onto my tongue. We stood in silence for a second then walked back to bed and climbed in. Jake's eyes didn't leave me.

I cleared my throat. "Right before Christmas break I stopped by the house but I couldn't find Noah. I texted him and he said he was in a brothers meeting and to just wait in his room. I was looking through a magazine when Hank barreled into the room holding a DVD in a plain white sleeve. He chuckled and raised his eyebrow and said, "Gracie, this is hot." Just then Noah walked in and snagged the DVD from Hank and tucked it in a drawer. When I asked him what it was he brushed it off as some bootleg Henry Rollins concert video that Hank was letting him borrow. I didn't think twice about it."

I saw Jake's jaw clench and I knew why. It was bad enough Noah was making movies of our sex life without me knowing but apparently he was sharing them with the brothers at Sigma Chi. That's when another strange comment came to the forefront of my brain.

"And just before spring break, I passed Brad on campus. He was walking with two pledges and he winked and said, "Two thumbs up, Gracie." The pledges laughed and elbowed each other as they passed. I didn't know what to think so I just chalked it up to some inside joke that I wasn't privy to. Jake, *I* was the inside joke."

Jake wrapped his arms around me and I soaked his shoulder with mascara and tears. I knew Noah could be a sick son of a bitch. Some of the things he admitted to getting off on were more than borderline kinky. But how could he cross that line with *me*? Me. I wasn't just some girl from the dining hall. Not that any of his other conquests deserved what he did. No one deserved that but we were different. Or so I thought.

After what seemed like hours, I wiped my face and looked up at Jake. "Take it back, please. Please take your words back." I wasn't expecting to find out something Noah did to me without my knowledge or consent. I felt so violated and raw.

I collapsed onto his chest again and heaved as I let out all the pain of what this meant. I felt dirty. I didn't know how my life could ever be the same. I forced myself to sleep as a means to escape Noah...who had now chased me into Jake's bed.

Fifty-Four

Trying to digest what I had just uncovered was like trying to swallow feathers. The harder I tried, the harder my body wretched to reject it. It was revolting. It stung my soul. I slipped into sleep to escape the pain and fear of a ghost from the past.

"You awake?" Jake's voice was tired and barely a whisper.

"Yeah, I don't think I slept at all." I rolled over and nuzzled into his chest. His arms pulled me into him.

"You slept. You may not feel like you did, but I watched you sleep all night."

"You didn't sleep?"

"Couldn't."

"Jake, how do I come to terms with my most private moments becoming public entertainment? I don't know how to begin to own what he did to me. How do I do this?"

"We do it together. Tell me how your brain is processing it."

"It's as if my life is a book, and by revealing this secret, we just wrote a chapter that doesn't match the tone of the rest of the book. It's out of place. Now I have to try to make that chapter fit.

You're telling me this heinous part of my story, and I have to figure out where it belongs because it will now affect every part of my life. There are videos of me. Who knows how many! It makes me sick that he could do this to me."

The salty water filled my lungs as my body fought to keep it out. Its taste was foreign. It was something that was not supposed to be inside me. I fought to expel it with heaving gasps, but it wouldn't go. It filled me with its burning poison. What I had just swallowed threatened to steal my life.

I didn't know when the tears would stop, but Jake and I lay in bed most of Friday and I cried for hours. There was a time I prided myself on my innocence. I enjoyed being known as the goody-two-shoes. I knew I would one day grow up and feel comfortable making my own decisions about mature things. It went against everything I had been taught when I made the decision to give up my virginity, but I was over eighteen and I was ready to start making my own decisions. And of course, I thought my private life was mine, just mine. But apparently my privacy had been stolen right out from under my nose. How could he live with himself all this time knowing what he'd done?

Jake held me for hours as I cried and tried to make excuses for Noah.

"Maybe he made it up. Maybe he was lying when he bragged about the videos."

"Gracie, I wish I could tell you that's what it was, but you got confirmation from Hank and Brad."

Silence.

Sleep.

"Do you think Hank and Brad are the only ones who have seen it?" I was talking but was between sleep and consciousness. I didn't even know if Jake heard me.

"Baby girl, unfortunately, I don't think that's the kind of thing that stays quiet in the Sigma Chi house." His entire body was taut. His muscles strained against the flesh covering them. Jake was trying to hold his anger in, but I was sure if Noah walked through the door at that moment, Jake would kill him.

Silence.

Sleep.

I rolled over, yawning as I stretched. The face that calmed all my storms smiled down at me. The sun was going down. We hadn't eaten or left the bed all day except to use the bathroom and grab more tissues. It certainly wasn't looking like the picture perfect long weekend we'd had in mind. We had plans to go to *Mitchell's*. We had tickets for Alternate Tragedy. I couldn't let Noah steal one more thing from me. I needed to get out of the apartment. We needed to get out, breathe some fresh air, and do something that made us both smile.

"I want to go out tonight." I rubbed the last tears from my eyes.

"To *Mitchell's*? Are you sure you're up to it?" If I hadn't said anything, Jake would never have mentioned the tickets I'm sure he spent a fortune on.

"We have to go. Jake, I don't want this to cripple me. I don't want him to steal my joy any longer. I couldn't bear it if you felt you needed to sacrifice your college life to pull me out of the muck when I fall apart again."

"Gracie, when will you get it? You are stuck with me. I love you unconditionally, whether we are laughing or crying, happy or hurting, lovers or just friends. I am here for you forever. You can't shake me."

That made me smile, and after not doing anything but cry for hours, I welcomed the change in shape on my face.

I really didn't want to leave Jake's room. I didn't want to go outside, or dance, or listen to music, or have fun. I wanted to sink into his bed and stay there forever. I knew there was more sadness that would have to make its way out of me. I knew I'd be dealing with the feeling of vulnerability that the people I passed on campus may very well have seen me naked. I'd probably hadn't heard the last of the comments from Sigma Chi brothers. But I chose to put myself second. I wanted to give this night to Jake. He was so sweet to make these plans for us, knowing how much I loved a good night with Calon. I needed to put all this pain aside and make this a great night for both of us. I needed to do this for him as much as I needed to do it for me. I wanted to love him with the love he showed me, by putting him first. I knew he would have stayed in bed with me until next Christmas if I needed him to, but I didn't want him to always be the one sucking it up for me. It was time for me to show him I would do anything for him. Because I would.

We walked down the sidewalk staircase and into the basement entrance of *Mitchell's*. The familiar smell brought a rush of memories of Alternate Tragedy flooding through my brain. Upstairs was café and food. The basement was reserved for live bands and dancing. We had been coming to Mitchell's since my first night at U of T. It was an eighteen and over kind of place. Eighteen to get in, twenty-one to drink. We had been drinking at Mitchell's since we were nineteen, but I didn't think anyone really cared as long as no one was causing any trouble. The bouncers took fights very seriously. Numerous Sigma Chi brothers were banned.

I heard the crackle of the mic just as we took our seats at the bar. I turned and saw Calon then heard the drums and the rest was a whirlwind of Smashing Pumpkins, Candlebox, Everclear, and every other band Jake and I loved. I didn't want them to play any of their new stuff. I so loved the covers they did. I just wanted to sing songs I knew, not strain to learn new ones. I wanted *my* Alternate Tragedy, not the one the whole hemisphere was getting to know.

"They sound great." Jake handed me another beer and kissed me on the cheek. He squeezed my knee under the bar and his eyes asked if I was all right. I smiled and gave him a thumbs up. I was trying my hardest not to think about our revelation from late last night. I was still telling myself it couldn't be possible. But right now wasn't the time to think about it.

"Jake, thank you for just being there for me last night and today." I leaned over and put my head on his shoulder. My love for Jake had grown exponentially since I pulled into the parking lot on Tuesday. We were so connected. I was falling for him. Maybe I had already fallen for him, but was just now giving myself the freedom to feel it.

"Any time." He winked and spun his stool around so he was in front of me and we were both facing the stage. Calon was straining to sing the painful words of Pearl Jam's "Deep." The song was about three people who had let themselves sink so deep they couldn't touch the bottom. I now heard this song on a much different level than I ever did.

Jake fell back into me. He translated the words as deeply as I had. My stomach flipped. I was overwhelmed by the thought of opening myself up to all of the painful emotions I was feeling. But maybe that's just what would heal me. But not right then. I needed to explore all the emotions in a safe place, just me and Jake. Not in the basement at Mitchell's. I pushed the wretched visuals deeper and gulped half my beer. *Not tonight, Gracie. Not tonight.* A single tear slid down my cheek.

I leaned forward and put my lips to Jake's ear. "Through all of this, you have helped me start to remember who I once was. It's like you're helping me put the pieces back together even if some of those pieces are hideous."

He turned his stool around so we were face to face. "And I will always say the hard things when no one else will. I will always want what is best for you. I am so proud of you. You don't know it, but you are so strong, Gracie."

It was at that moment that I could see our future. There would never be another day in my life that I would question my love for Jake. I had to go through Hell to know how beautiful Heaven was. And I would do it all again if it meant I would end up in Jake's arms. I felt dizzy. My realizations over the past two days weren't small ones. They were life changing. Some threatened to suck the life out of me and one promised to breathe it back in.

Two hearts intertwined.

My thoughts were interrupted by Calon's voice speaking, not singing. I tried to follow what he was saying, but I hadn't caught the first part. Jake leaned forward and smiled. The crowd went crazy and Jake mouthed, "New song." I stood up and leaned forward to tell him I was going to use their new song as a bathroom break, non-customary sounds of acoustic instruments lulled me back against Jake's legs. It was a slow song. I had never heard Alternate Tragedy sing anything that didn't leave their voices hoarse and my ears ringing. The tune held me spellbound.

Jake gently took my hand and led me to the only empty space in front of the stage. It was the no-frills, make-shift dance floor at *Mitchell's*. I held the back of his head in my hands and we rubbed the tips of our noses together.

"I hope you enjoy our new song about finding a perfect love. This one's called, Fallen."

> *"She spins into the darkness, she slides down the wall.*
> *She didn't see it coming, she wasn't prepared to fall.*
> *There was film on her mirror, fog on the glass*
> *Her body torn wide open, by secrets of her past.*
> *Down, down, down*
> *Where there is no bottom*
> *Down, down, down*
> *Where the suffering begins*
> *Down, down, down*
> *She didn't know she'd fallen*
> *Now she's searching for her wings*
> *Her heart was frozen in time, her mind was gagged and bound*
> *She cried a million tears, but barely made a sound*
> *But now someone lay beside her, he was the music to her soul*
> *He held her 'til the demons passed, and he kissed away the cold*

Down, down, down
Where there is no bottom
Down, down, down
Where the suffering begins
Down, down, down
She didn't know she'd fallen
She's still searching for her wings
The bad memories fade, and her scars begin to heal
New life breathed into her soul, Her heart was his to steal
He came unexpectedly, the savior
of her heart
He held her close and warmed her soul and watched her life restart.
Down, down, down
He caught her at the bottom
Down, down, down
Where the healing begins
Down, down, down
True love is where she'd fallen
Where she finally found her wings!"

Calon had just told our story in an ethereal melody only he could deliver. The band left the stage for a break and the crowd dispersed, but Jake and I stayed on the dance floor stunned by the providence of the song.

All those months of feeling guilty that I couldn't reciprocate three simple words came barreling back through my mind. It was at that moment I knew without a doubt what my next words would be.

"I love you, Jake Rockwell."

He sucked in a deep breath, tears came to his eyes. He wrapped me in his signature hug and lifted my feet off the ground. The brilliant smile that grew across his face was well worth waiting until I could say "I love you" without a doubt in my heart.

"Well, look what we have here. It's the Jake and Gracie show." There was no mistaking that sinister voice I was all too familiar with.

Noah was back. He was drunk and his fists were clenched.

Fifty-Five

"Noah, take it easy." Jake positioned himself in front of me and slowly took a few steps back to put some space between us and him.

"Take it easy? You were my roommate, man, and now you're fucking my girlfriend!"

"Noah! I am not your girlfriend!" I tried to step in between the two of them, but Jake's arm shot out to hold me at a safe distance.

"Looks like you're a little bit of everyone's girlfriend the way you're whoring around these days!"

"That's enough!" Jake's voice was cacophonous.

"Look here, asshole…" Noah staggered into Jake's personal space like he was going to throttle him. Jake didn't budge. I wanted so badly to run and hide because I had seen this rage in Noah once before and it ended with fists being thrown. But I would never leave Jake's side.

"Noah, we can act like adults. No one here wants to see a fight." A crowd started to form around us.

I squeezed my eyes closed and held on for dear life. I couldn't make my feet move from the spot they were in, and if Noah hit Jake, I knew I was going down, too.

"Are you kidding me? Jake, you're not that stupid. Now, walk away. Gracie is coming home with me. We need to discuss where she was when I got to her house to pick her up this morning."

Oh shit. With everything that was exposed over the previous twenty-four hours, I completely forgot to text Noah that we weren't coming back to school together.

"Noah, she is not going anywhere with you. Especially not when you are this drunk and this angry."

"The hell she's not!" And with that, he grabbed Jake by the shoulders and flung his body just enough to could get to me.

"You are coming with me!" He grabbed my wrist and twisted so hard I was sure he would break it before we got to the door.

"*Noah!* Stop! Don't do this! Please don't do this!" Where the hell were all the bouncers? Why was no one doing anything? I frantically looked around, and when I saw the bright yellow BOUNCER shirt as Noah dragged me closer to the exit, I yelled for help. But he was blatantly ignoring the melee. I turned to see where Jake was and if he was close enough to reach, but I couldn't see anyone I knew in the crowd of faces.

We got to the bottom of the staircase and the bouncer turned around. It was drive-thru Hank. Noah nodded and handed him a wad of cash. "Thanks, bro. I owe you one."

Hank had just turned his back so Noah could drag me up the stairs and out of *Mitchell's*...and back to Sigma Chi like a caveman with his cavewoman. My wrist was throbbing and I was falling over my feet by the time we got to the sidewalk. I assured Jake that Noah had never hit me, but I was pretty sure that would only be true for another five minutes. He could do a lot of damage with one blow.

"We are going to have a little chat about the rules of the game, Gracie Jordan. This shit won't happen again! You don't just go fucking around behind my back and make me look like an idiot. I showed up at your house this morning and you'd been gone for three days already?"

"Noah..."

"*Shut up*! That's Rule Number One." He turned and scowled at me as he spoke.

I saw Jake coming toward us over Noah's shoulder. The back door. I forgot about the back door at *Mitchell's*. Jake knew which way Noah would head so he took a short cut through the alley to cut us off. I had to keep Noah's eyes on me so he wouldn't see Jake yet.

I tried to yank my arm away to keep him engaged and facing me. "Does this make you feel like a man, Noah? Huh? Dragging me up the sidewalk in the middle of the night? Taking me back to your cave? What the hell is wrong with you? Let me go!"

He twisted my wrist a little further for breaking Rule Number One.

"Ow! God, Noah, you are really hurting me. Let me go!"

Before I knew what happened, I was torn away from Noah's grip and someone pulled me around the side of the research building on the corner, and Jake squared off with Noah.

"I asked you politely to be an adult. She is not going anywhere with you." Jake's stance was bold and unforgiving. "Gracie, you okay?"

I whimpered a yes and gasped for the breath that fear had stolen from me.

I was stunned. I took a split second to see who was holding on to me. It was Pete. Pete who I always assumed was going to get his ass kicked during Hell Week.

"How did you..." I spoke toward him but locked my eyes on the altercation before me.

"Not everything stays a secret at Sigma Chi. I overheard Noah and Hank earlier, I was coming to warn you."

"You really think you can take me, Jake?" Noah stumbled a couple times, trying to keep his balance.

"Gracie! Are you okay?" Jake must not have heard my attempt at an answer.

Pete called out, "She's good, Jake. I got her."

"You're dead, Pete!" Noah didn't even look at him. He wasn't taking his eyes off Jake.

I was breathing so hard I had to lean against the building to steady myself. Sheer terror pumped through me at a rate that was probably not healthy for extended periods of time. I tried to steady my breathing so I didn't pass out.

Jake actually took two steps forward and looked Noah square in the face. "She is not your property, Noah. You have done enough damage. It's time to walk away."

"You don't know anything! All she had to do was spread her legs and she sucked you in. Been there, done that!"

Jake lunged forward and threw his fist square into Noah's jaw. I heard the crack just before Noah went down. Jake shook his hand and looked over at me. I knew he needed to lay eyes on me to believe I was really okay. But he should never have looked away.

"*Jake!*" I screamed as soon as I saw Noah lean forward to get up. It was too late.

Noah was up and grabbed the front of Jake's shirt. I heard buttons hit the cement. He pulled him in so close, I was sure Jake could see the flecks of gold in Noah's eyes. I used to try to memorize their intricate striations, but Noah wouldn't let me stare into his eyes for too long. He said it made him uncomfortable. Now, I knew why. He was afraid I would see who he really was. I was terrified for Jake, but Pete was holding me back. He wouldn't let me go.

Noah swayed, trying to keep his balance as he mumbled something to Jake in almost a growl. I couldn't hear what he said, but when he let go of Jake's shirt with his right hand and cocked his arm back slowly, I knew he had just threatened to kill him.

"*Noah! Stop!*"

He held his arm back, but his eyes lifted to mine. I held his gaze even though it made me shudder.

"Noah, stop," I whimpered. "Please. If you ever loved me, please stop." He let go of Jake with a push that made Jake stumble backwards. I made sure Jake was okay before I looked back at Noah. Jake straightened his torn shirt and winked at me letting me know he was okay, and it was time to end it. Noah rubbed his jaw, thrust his other hand deep in his pocket and lifted his gaze from the ground to me. The gold of his eyes smoldered.

"Right now, Gracie, I want to beat the shit out of him for taking you from me."

"You lost me, Noah. Jake didn't take anything from you."

"Lost you? You're mine, Gracie. Mine." He poked himself in the chest with his forefinger for effect.

I was too far away to feel the strength I knew Jake summoned in me. I shook Pete loose and quickly bolted over to him. I stood behind him, putting Jake in harm's way again, but I needed to catch my breath if I was going to do this the right way.

"Noah, you have hurt her enough. It's time to say goodbye." Jake reached back and took my shaking hand in his. He was steady. He was ready for whatever was coming his way.

"Fuck you, Jake! She's sloppy seconds, now. She gave me so much of herself there's nothing left for you."

My heart frosted over and my stomach lurched when I heard his description of me. The warmth coming from Jake's body protected me from the chill of Noah's insults.

"She's all used up, dude. I took it all."

Before I knew what happened, Jake let go of my hand, took two long strides and caught Noah's jaw in another mean right hook. Noah stumbled backwards, tripped on a lifted sidewalk square and landed on his ass with a drunken thud.

This time, Noah didn't get up. I wasn't sure if he could. He was conscious, but stunned.

"Dammit!" he rubbed his jaw again and thumbed away the blood that was spilling from his bottom lip. "If it's over, she's got to be a big girl and tell me herself. And she's never been strong enough to do that."

My heart stopped beating and my lungs stopped breathing. The level of anger and passion on the sidewalk was overwhelming and now I was supposed to put the icing on the cake and literally kick Noah to the curb. No pressure.

"Noah…" I don't know what Jake was going to say, but Noah interrupted him and stood up.

"You're going down and she's coming with me unless I hear her dirty little mouth say she's choosing you over me."

Jake didn't turn to see if I was still standing with him. He didn't need to. He could feel me. I knew he would want me to stay behind him, but if this shit was ever going to end, I needed to stop hiding from Noah.

I took a step so I was standing shoulder to shoulder with Jake. He took my hand and squeezed. I could feel his knuckles were swollen so I didn't squeeze back. I needed to finish what Noah started the night he blocked the back door of Murphy's so I couldn't leave. That night I naively gave him permission to make the decisions for me and ever since then he had me like a puppet on a string. He pushed me away and I would go. He pulled me back in and I would come. Well, not anymore. He had sliced me raw way too many times to count, and it was time to stop the bleeding once and for all.

I started to walk toward Noah, but Jake wouldn't let go of the grip he had on me. I squeezed his hand very gently and he turned his face toward mine. "Together, baby girl. I'm not leaving your side."

So, it was from Jake's side and through the strength he pumped into me just by holding me tight that I, Gracie Jordan, stood up for myself and took Noah Foster down for the very last time.

"There is nothing in me that wants to be with you, Noah. You have done nothing but make my life hell since the first time you broke my heart."

Noah sat forward and put his elbow on his bent knee. He grimaced and rubbed his forehead like he was trying to make sense of what I was saying.

"You cheated. You lied. You laughed when you knew you hurt me. But as soon as I stood up for myself and walked away you would crawl back and convince me that you just couldn't live without me. You had my mind so warped it was scary. I gave you a piece of myself that I can never give anyone else. I think I held on to you for so long because I was afraid to let go of that piece. I thought being with you would keep me whole. But you stole so much from me."

By this time, both his elbows were on his knees and his head was resting in his hands. I couldn't see his face. I thought it would be easier if he wasn't looking at me, but I needed him to look me in the eyes as I told him everything that was pouring from my heart.

"Look at me." He tilted his head up and his eyes locked on mine. "You knew what kind of love I needed. And when you realized you couldn't love me that way, you should have been man enough to just let me go, not lead me on to think that one day you would magically become who you once pretended to be.

"I needed you to be gentle and kind. But, the things you did to me were wrong. You hurt me emotionally and physically and did things to me that were degrading and wrong. Some of which you did not have my consent to do."

His eyes widened and bounced back and forth between Jake and me. He knew exactly what I was referring to. It was true. Jake's thumb rubbed my hand, and I knew he was proud of me for letting that out.

"I needed you to be honest and fair but instead, emotionally, you shredded me. You had no intention of changing. Mentally, you drove me into the ground. But you can't touch me now. This time I get to decide. We are over for the last time, Noah."

He didn't move, but when he spoke his voice was strained like he was holding back more emotions he'd never set free. "Gracie, I told you why I push you away. I explained to you why I do the things I do."

"Yeah, you did. And in that same conversation I asked you to never to give up on me—"

"I never gave up on you. Gracie, please don't do this." It was like he forgot Jake was even there.

I shook my head, refusing to let any pity flow from my heart toward him. "Stop it, Noah. Just listen. You said if you ever gave up on anyone, you'd give up on yourself. Well, it's time to give up."

"But, Gracie, that talk we had. I opened up to you and laid my heart out—"

"All of it was lies! You can't fool me anymore, Noah. That was all part of your manipulation. Would you listen to yourself? You are so sick you've started to believe your own lies. You actually think you can change. Well, I am one step ahead of you, asshole, because I know you'll never change. The grace and trust are gone." I pointed to the empty finger his ring used to adorn.

"So, now you're in love. With Jake?" He said it so sarcastically it made me want to claw his eyes out.

"Jake gives my heart something you're incapable of. Unconditional love. I have never felt anything close to what I feel for him. He loves me in a way you never did, with gentleness, respect and consideration. I choose happiness and true love, Noah. I choose Jake."

"Gracie—"

"It's over, Noah."

I turned around and looked into my favorite set of blue eyes. "Thank you, Jake, for saving me."

"You did this, Gracie. You saved yourself, and I am so proud of you. I love you." He took my face in his hands and kissed me so gently I shivered.

"I love you, too. Forever." I kissed him again.

Against my lips he whispered, "Forever."

When we turned around, hand-in-hand, Noah was already a block away. He was finally walking away for the last time.

The sky was clear that night as we walked toward the apartment. I looked up toward Heaven and was sure I could see every star in the galaxy. Some of them winked at me.

I laid my head on Jake's shoulder and whispered, "Two people walking in the same direction."

I expelled the lethal breath and cleared my lungs of their salty contents. I watched as the tsunami that hit me receded so far into the murky depths I could no longer see it. But I knew the struggle to stay afloat wasn't over, there would be residual aftershocks to survive. Small waves crashed around my feet, but I was standing. And filling the cracks of my broken heart was a love I knew was strong enough to pull me to shore every time. My soul mate. My Jake.

Acknowledgements

First and foremost, Ken, I thank you for saving me time and time again and for loving me with every ounce of your being. Thank you for giving me the courage to bring Gracie and Noah to life and for being my real life Jake. I have loved you for more than half of my life and I'll love you all the rest of my days. You truly are my hero!

Matthew and Emily, you two have been so tolerant of my "can I just read you something" requests. And I have never doubted that I have your full attention. Thank you. Your excitement about my writing thrills me to no end. And Izaiah, you have put up with more repeats of "two minutes, buddy" than any little kid should. Thank you for always giving Mommy two more minutes.

Thanks and applause goes out to my family for supporting me and entertaining my imagination for all these years. Mom, Dad, Tif, thank you for being my cheerleaders all along. And, Daddy, the "Kemper" is for you so the name lives on since you and Mom couldn't seem to make boys.

And my family-in-law, Grandpa, Bev, Gram, Gordon, Dottie, Kristin, for the last seven years you've never gone a visit without asking about my writing. You kept me going because how would I answer your questions if I quit?

My BFFs (and first editors), Michele and Sally, you girls helped me to shape this story as you became part of mine. You named characters and told me when Gracie was pissing you off. Thank you for never getting sick of my requests to read just one more chapter. And thank you for loving me even on the days you thought I may be a little crazy...okay a lot crazy. You've been with me through it all. Should there ever be a book tour, you're my entourage, so get ready to spring for some Jimmy Choos!

Without a doubt, this story would never have made it out of me without the assistance of my confidant, Shirley Henry Lyons. Thank you for your patience, your gentle spirit and your love for what you do.

I couldn't have gotten to this point of my career without someone believing in Gracie's story as much as I do. The amazing Amy Lichtenhan is not only my editor, she is someone who has shown my manuscript the kind of attention that proves her devotion to this book. Thank you for putting up with my zillions of emails, especially when the subject line said, "HELP!" Because of you, I am living my dream. Thank you!

And thank you to Todd, Lauren and Jeni...you know why.

Last, but certainly not least, I thank you, Eddie Vedder. The very first paragraph of IN TOO DEEP came to me while listening to DEEP on a particularly difficult day; the day I realized I was in too deep. I listened to your voice bring the emotion in the lyrics to life, cried and this book was born. Your stunning performances leave me breathless because of the raw emotion your soul brings to the stage. Those performances have taught me never to hold back truly feeling life. The many tears I have shed during this process would never have sprung free without the courage your lyrics have given me. And damn that feels good. So good. Thank you, friend, for being who you are and sharing every ounce of yourself with your fans.

Emotional abuse is like brain washing in that it systematically wears away at the victim's self-confidence, sense of self-worth, trust in their own perceptions, and self-concept. Whether it is done by constant berating and belittling, by intimidation, or under the guise of "guidance," "teaching," or "advice," the results are similar. Eventually, the recipient of the abuse loses all sense of self and remnants of personal value. Emotional abuse cuts to the very core of a person, creating scars that may be far deeper and more lasting than physical ones (Engel, 1992, p. 10).

If you feel you are in an abusive relationship and need help, you are not alone. Please reach out to a professional in your area, at your school, your church or workplace.

There are also a wide variety of resources and hotlines available to you.

National Teen Dating Abuse Hotline — 1-866-331-9474

…and, of course, if you are in immediate danger, **call 9-1-1**

LoveIsRespect.org — A National Teen Dating and Abuse Helpline 1-866-331-9474 TTY 1-866-331-8453 or chat online on their website

~~~~

LoveIsNotAbuse.com — An Organization Committed to Stopping Teen Dating Abuse

You can also find them on Facebook and Twitter — @Love_isnotabuse

LoveIsLouder.com — A movement started by The JED Foundation, MTV and Brittany Snow that spreads the message that love and support are louder than any internal or external voices that bring us down.

You can find them on Facebook and Twitter — @LoveIsLouder